Dynamic Psychology in Modernist British Fiction

Other publications by the same author

J.D. BERESFORD

LATE-VICTORIAN AND EDWARDIAN BRITISH NOVELISTS, First Series, Vol. 153, Dictionary of Literary Biography (*Ed. and Intro.*)

LATE-VICTORIAN AND EDWARDIAN BRITISH NOVELISTS, Second Series, Vol. 197, Dictionary of Literary Biography (*Ed. and Intro.*)

BRITISH NOVELISTS BETWEEN THE WARS, Vol. 191, Dictionary of Literary Biography (*Ed. and Intro.*)

Dynamic Psychology in Modernist British Fiction

George M. Johnson

First published 2006 by
PALGRAVE MACMILLAN
Houndmills, Basingstoke, Hampshire RG21 6XS and
175 Fifth Avenue, New York, N.Y. 10010
Companies and representatives throughout the world

PALGRAVE MACMILLAN is the global academic imprint of the Palgrave Macmillan division of St. Martin's Press, LLC and of Palgrave Macmillan Ltd. Macmillan® is a registered trademark in the United States, United Kingdom and other countries. Palgrave is a registered trademark in the European Union and other countries.

ISBN-13: 978-1-4039-4228-9 hardback
ISBN-10: 1-4039-4228-5 hardback

This book is printed on paper suitable for recycling and made from fully managed and sustained forest sources.

A catalogue record for this book is available from the British Library.

Library of Congress Cataloging-in-Publication Data
Johnson, George M. (George Malcolm), 1961–
    Dynamic psychology in modernist British fiction / by George M. Johnson
        p. cm.
    Includes bibliographical references and index.
    ISBN 1-4039-4228-5
    1. English fiction—20th century—History and criticism. 2. Psychological fiction, English—History and criticism. 3. Modernism (Literature)—Great Britain. 4. Psychology in literature. I. Title.
    PR888.P75J64 2005
    823'.08309091—dc22   2005049205

10   9   8   7   6   5   4   3   2   1
15   14 13 12 11 10 09 08 07 06

Printed and bound in Great Britain by
Antony Rowe Ltd, Chippenham and Eastbourne

The difference between Pastism and Futurism is the difference between statics and dynamics.

– May Sinclair, *The Tree of Heaven* 242

Contents

List of Illustrations

Preface

There you get the first 'int of this new Aquarian Age, and from the moment we entered it – not so long ago, forty years or so – this idea of the Subconsciousness 'as showed itself as the key-word of the day. It's everywhere already. Even the scientific men 'as got it. Bergson began with 'is intuition, and professors like Frood of Vienna and Young of Zurich caught on like lightning. William James too, and a 'undred others. Why it's got down into our poietry and novels...
            – Algernon Blackwood, *The Promise of Air*, 1918, 220

In *The Promise of Air*, Algernon Blackwood captures the excitement gener-ated by discoveries about the subconscious mental realm in the early twentieth century. A new age was dawning, one in which the subconscious would be made conscious, a new sympathy with one's fellow beings would emerge, and the underlying unity of all things would be revealed. It was this sense of promise, of potential for transformation that could make Algernon Black-wood claim, in spite of, or perhaps because of the ravages of war that humanity's spiritual consciousness was evolving, and that could also prompt a writer with very different aims, Virginia Woolf, to claim that in 1910 or thereabouts human character changed ("Character" 421). *Dynamic Psychology in Modernist British Fiction* explores those discoveries and how they "got down into" fiction of widely varying types, that is, how they altered the way some novelists perceived and constructed characters and fictional worlds.

Blackwood's novel also playfully alludes to the distortions that can occur in the translation of discourse from one sphere to another, in this case the popularization of psychological theories. Blackwood's protagonist is a traveler in "tabloid knowledge", a representative for the "What's-in-the-Air-To-day" publishing company, who has absorbed "the Spirit of the Age" on the fly, so to speak (*Promise* 61). *Dynamic Psychology* also interrogates distortions that have occurred, not only through popularization and assimilation in fiction, but through literary historians and critics' telescoping of dynamic psychology's impact on Modernist British Fiction. This book restores the (possibly not quite) "undred others" besides Bergson, "Frood", "Young" and James who contributed to dynamic psychological discourse, some of whose work has been marginalized because no longer considered within the realm of contemporary psychology. Perhaps not coincidentally, Blackwood dates the beginning of the Aquarian Age at 1881 (*Promise* 210), just around the time that the Society For Psychical Research came into being. Psychical research plays an important role in *Dynamic Psychology*, partly because its impact on fiction has been undervalued. Psychical research kept metaphysical questions within the realm of turn-of-the-century psychology, legitimated the study of psychical extensions of personality, including telepathy, clairvoyance and automatic writing, and captivated writers with strange case studies intimating the "astonishing potentialities yet undeveloped in the great mystery of man" (Beresford, *What* 31).

The path taken that has resulted in this book is the proverbial long and winding one, but there have been many encounters and discoveries along the way, which I hope I have conveyed with something of Blackwood's enthusiasm. The journey probably began when I became dangerously fascinated by two disciplines simultaneously, and completed a double Honours degree in English and Psychology. At that time psychical research did not receive so much as a whisper in either discipline, even in, oddly enough, an entire psychology course devoted to Freud. When I started to write this book as a dissertation in the late 1980s, the study of psychical research in literature was considered nothing less than eccentric, and the focus on obscure, non-canonical novelists just slightly less so. Nevertheless, an encouraging (and perhaps slightly indulgent) Ph.D. committee enabled me to complete the project. Since that time the field has filled in, as they say, as attitudes have changed towards historicizing Freud, reviving non-canonical novelists, and even interrogating psychical research and the occult. A number of detours delayed my entering that field, but typically they provided new vantage points. For instance, in editing three volumes of the *Dictionary of Literary Biography* on *Late-Victorian and Edwardian Novelists* (Vols 153 and 197) and *British Novelists Between the Wars* (Vol. 191), I gained perspective on just how extensively dynamic psychological discourse, and particularly psychical discourse permeated non-canonical British fiction. So-called minor fiction truly proved to be "the Baedeker of the soul", as George Dangerfield put it. For a composite picture of the impact of dynamic discourse that goes beyond the scope of the present work, I would recommend perusing those volumes. The present work has benefited from the contributions in them, and yet, I believe, still covers an untrammeled patch in the history of literature and psychology. Throughout this project I have, like my Edwardian and Georgian subjects, attempted to keep an open mind about psychical phenomena, while acknowledging inevitable biases.

For their perspectives and comments offered on my work, I would like to thank John Ferns and John Roy, my original dissertation committee members, and above all my thesis supervisor Andrew Brink, who not only greatly extended my understanding of dynamic psychological processes but also extended his friendship to me in so many ways. For several grants and a sabbatical, spent in England, that enabled me to revise this book I am grateful to the University College of the Cariboo, now Thompson Rivers University. For a General Research Grant I would like to thank the Social

Sciences and Humanities Research Council of Canada. The chapter on J.D. Beresford has been enriched through the generosity of both Jon Wynne-Tyson and Elisabeth Beresford, who shared with me their memories of "J.D." as well as the materials of his in their possession. For their help with translations I am thankful to Maria Nebesny and especially to Roland Katzer and Kathy March. I want to thank my parents as well for their patience and understanding over the years of this project's evolution, particularly my father, George J. Johnson, a long-time supporter of and contributor to my academic projects.

In addition I wish to acknowledge the assistance of staff members in the special collections departments of the following libraries: the Berg Collection, New York Public Library; Library of Congress; the Van Pelt Library, University of Pennsylvania; British Library; University of Sussex Library; J. Rylands University of Manchester; Trinity College, Cambridge Library; and the Inter-library Loans Departments at McMaster University and Thompson Rivers University. For their advice and patience I would like to thank Paula Kennedy and Helen Craine at Palgrave Macmillan as well.

Photographs are reproduced by kind permission of the following: Elisabeth Beresford, for the photograph of J.D. Beresford; the National Portrait Gallery for Elliott and Fry photographs of James Sully, Henry Sidgwick, David Eder, Virginia Woolf and Leslie Stephen, and for portraits of D.H. Lawrence, Frederic Myers and Arnold Bennett; Paterson Marsh/Sigmund Freud copyrights for the photograph of Freud and Jones. Houghton Library, Harvard University for the photograph of William James; Duke University Press for the photograph of an engraving of William McDougall and the university of Pennsylvania for the photograph of May Sinclair. For permission to reproduce Vanessa Bell's "Dancing Couple" (1914) on the cover I would like to thank Henrietta Garnett. I have not been able to trace copyright holders for the following, and would be grateful for any information on them: Photographs of Henri Bergson by Gerschel, Paris; of Carl Jung and Pierre Janet [from Henri Ellenberger, *The Discovery of the Unconscious. The History and Evolution of Dynamic Psychiatry*. New York: Basic Books, 1970]; a photograph of "The Psycho-analysis Apparatus" [from William Brown, "Is Love a Disease?", *The Strand* (January 1912): 96–103].

Earlier versions of several sections of this book have appeared as follows: " 'The Spirit of the Age': Virginia Woolf's Response to Second Wave Psychology", *Twentieth Century Literature* 40.2 (Fall 1994): 139–164; "May Sinclair: The Evolution of a Psychological Novelist", in *Literature and Psychoanalysis*. ed. Frederico Pereira. Lisbon, Portugal: Instituto Superior de Psicologia Aplicada, 1998. I am grateful to these publications for permission to reproduce material.

I dedicate this book with much gratitude to my wife, Nina, who like a medium has helped this project materialize in so many unseen ways, and to Sophia, who is just becoming dynamic in the most fundamental sense.

1 William James in 1903, the year *Varieties of Religious Experience* was published. Photo by Notmann. Reprinted by permission of the Houghton Library, Harvard University. Pf ms Am 1092

Photo. Gerschel, Paris.

2 Henri Bergson in 1914

3   William McDougall, Reproduced from a bronze plaque by Angus McDougall

4 Pierre Janet

5 Frederic W.H. Myers, by William Clarke Wontner. National Portrait Gallery, London

Photo]   [Elliott & Fry.

6   Henry Sidgwick

For testing the mental condition of lovers, and other emotional patients.

1.—Each word appears through the aperture of the screen A, and the subject or "patient" speaks the associated word into the "voice-key" B, which is in electrical connection, through the relay F, with the chronoscope, or clock, E, in the adjoining room (see Fig. below).

7 (a) The Psycho-analysis apparatus, 1912. Perhaps the first concrete representation of psychoanalytic method in England. (b) The other end of the apparatus in an adjoining room

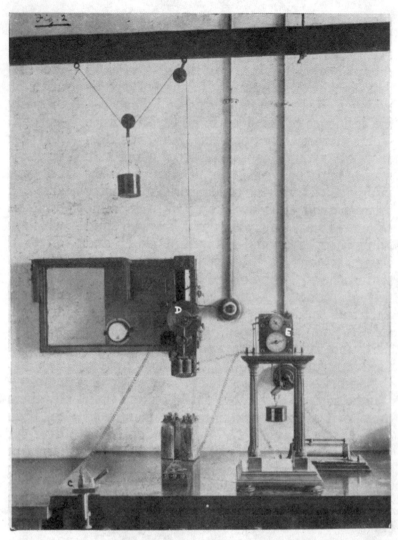

2.—Closure of the electric key C exposes a word through the aperture of the screen A of Fig. 1, by means of the electrically-worked revolving spindle D. It also starts the hands of the chronoscope E moving. When the subject responds into the voice-key, the electric circuit is broken and the hands stop. The position of the hands gives the association-time in thousandths of a second.

7 (Continued)

8 Sigmund Freud with Ernest Jones, in the Kobenzl, Vienna, about 1919. Reproduced by permission of Sigmund Freud copyrights Paterson Marsh Ltd

[Photo: Elliott and Fry Ltd.

9 M. David Eder

10   Carl Jung

11   May Sinclair. Reprinted by permission of the University of Pennsylvania

12   Arnold Bennett. Copyright reserved: collection National Portrait Gallery, London

13 D.H. Lawrence. National Portrait Gallery, London

14   J.D. Beresford. Reprinted by permission of Elisabeth Beresford

Photo]   [Elliott & Fry.

15   James Sully

16   Sir Leslie Stephen and Virginia Woolf by G.C. Beresford. National Portrait Gallery, London

Introduction

A tale of telepathic healing gone astray, May Sinclair's "The Flaw in the Crystal" (1912) dramatically interrogates the boundaries between self and other:

> In the process of getting at Harding to heal him [Agatha] had had to destroy, not only the barriers of flesh and blood, but those innermost walls of personality that divide and protect, mercifully, one spirit from another. With the first thinning of the walls Harding's insanity had leaked through to her, with the first breach it had broken in. ("Flaw" 176)

Sinclair's preoccupation is of course not unique. The English novel at least since the eighteenth century has both reflected and contributed to changes in societal conceptions of self and its relation to the other. The novel is well suited to these roles because it traditionally has described in vivid, compelling language individual protagonists who move through space and time and whose sense of self is challenged and developed through encounters with others along the way. The novel also is capacious and adaptable enough to assimilate insights from other discourses that have something to say about selfhood, notably philosophy and psychology.

At the turn of the twentieth century, however, a particularly close, symbiotic relationship developed between the novel and a cluster of discourses pertaining to selfhood that were labelled the "new psychology", or, more accurately, dynamic psychology. A number of novelists, including Sinclair, rapidly absorbed but also interrogated these new constructions of selfhood, and generated eclectic, multi-layered approaches to characterization – distinctive blends of the spiritual, the psychical, and the psychological. Sinclair's "Flaw", for example, constructs the self of her protagonist, Agatha Verrall, out of the resonances between the spiritual concept of purity, the psychical ramifications of telepathy, and the psychological implications of sexual repression and psychosis.

1

I.1 Dynamic psychology

What were the conditions that brought about this symbiosis? In order to broach this question, it is necessary to touch on the origins and definition of dynamic psychology. Dynamic psychology emerged from the second of two dominant waves of nineteenth-century psychological discourse. These waves ebbed and flowed during the century, and admittedly overlapped, both paradoxically gathering strength as a result. The first drew on developments in associationist philosophy, biology, and physiology, tended to be positivistic in nature, and typically viewed man from a mechanistic and materialist perspective.[1] Reality about man's will and consciousness could be determined by examination of physical matter. Spiritual or metaphysical questions lay outside the province of this psychology. An earlier generation of writers than those under study here, such as Charlotte Bronte and George Eliot, took advantage of this new knowledge, as critics Sally Shuttleworth, Gillian Beer and others have shown. Charlotte Bronte drew on the vocabulary and assumptions of the "sciences" of phrenology and mesmerism, while Eliot assimilated social Darwinian thought.

The second wave gathered momentum from the philosophical traditions of idealism and romanticism, and their inquiries into consciousness and the unconscious respectively; however, the distinctive features of this psychology did not emerge until the late 1880s when its explanatory model of mental functioning reached a state of crisis on at least one frontier. The study of hysteria and hypnosis revealed anomalies in that model, and, as philosopher of science Thomas Kuhn claims, awareness of anomaly touches off the major discovery which necessitates a paradigm shift (52–53). The prevailing explanation of hysteria, famously propounded by Jean Charcot, as a physiological condition occurring only in individuals tainted by heredity, could no longer adequately account for the facts. Hysteria, it was discovered by Pierre Janet and others, was psychosomatic and could be treated by bringing buried conflicted ideas to consciousness. Furthermore, the belief that hypnosis was a pathological condition found only in hysterics was successfully challenged by the Nancy school, and the widespread application and success of hypnosis as a therapeutic technique gradually brought it into a more orthodox position in medical psychology. The phenomena observed while patients were under hypnosis, including the emergence of secondary or multiple personalities, led researchers such as Janet and Frederic Myers to investigate unconscious processes more precisely. They began to theorize about the dynamics of the mind, that is, the elements exerting psychic energy on mental processes.

I.2 Definition

The changes in attitude towards mental functioning precipitated by the study of hypnosis and hysteria are at the core of dynamic psychology, or more accurately dynamic psychologies, since there were a number of them. Dynamic psychology can be characterized first, then, by its use of the extraordinary, typically the abnormal, to make claims about normal mental functioning. Second, dynamic psychology developed models of mental energy or psychic reality, as distinct from material, external reality.[2] Third, in these models dynamic psychologies tended to map the mind, that is, to give psychic forces locality and structure, and some depicted the struggles or conflicts between forces or elements. Fourth, a few of these psychologies developed psychological approaches to healing, and tended to focus on the psychosomatic origins of illness rather than the organic. Later dynamic psychologies included analysis of interpersonal relations, of the relations between inner conflict and social conflict. Since dynamic psychology tended to make more detailed accounts of man's inner realities, it proved on the whole to be a greater contributor to culture and literature than the materialistic strain.

I.3 Aims

This book is devoted to exploring the interplay between dynamic psychology and a particular form of cultural activity, British prose fiction, and it develops a number of related arguments in order to do so. First, it argues that dynamic psychology is a valid, appropriate and useful construct that makes possible a more accurate and inclusive view of the history of psychological discourse than has prevailed. The Society for Psychical Research (SPR), typically marginalized, emerges as the principal shaping force on British attitudes towards dynamic psychology. Psychoanalysis finds a more precise historical context as a later, albeit significant, contributor to dynamic discourse. Second, the book proposes that the distortions in histories of psychology have been magnified in literary studies. Histories of Modernism have in the past ignored pre-Freudian dynamic psychologies and exaggerated Freudian impact. *Dynamic Psychology* redresses this problem by making available the key debates in dynamic psychology in proportion to their impact on fiction writers. Third, I argue that the traditional focus on the major modernists' discovery of the "dark places of psychology", as Woolf put it ("Modern Fiction" 215–216), and their expression of its features through experiments in form, has overshadowed pre-modernist writers' appropriation of dynamic discourse. The Edwardians and non-modernist Georgians' engagement prompted innovations in the subject matter of the novel, notably in approaches to selfhood, memory and time. Reading these novelists in the context of dynamic psychology will bring a greater appreciation of their accomplishments and help to restore them from their neglected status. Fourth, examining both pre-modernist and modernist novelists from the perspective of dynamic psychology, broader than that of psychoanalysis, reveals continuities between these novelists. Most significantly, they held in common the project of extending the boundaries of realism. Not only did they attend to unconscious and subliminal motivation, but they incorporated into a plausible construct of realism phenomena formerly considered as belonging to the realm of Gothic fantasy, including apparitions, clairvoyance, psychic possession, and trance or mystical states. I want to elaborate on the first of these arguments here before considering the methodology and parameters of the study.

It may seem something of a stretch to gather under the umbrella of dynamic psychology the respectably mainstream discipline of academic psychology, psychoanalysis (always controversial but arguably a powerful twentieth-century influence on any number of fields), and psychical research, often considered a pseudo-science at best. In so doing, I do not mean to deny the distinctive features of each or the qualitative differences between them. However, these three fields of inquiry only seem impossibly disparate in their current twenty-first century contexts. At the turn of the twentieth century the disciplines of knowledge were not nearly as well defined as they are in our society of specialization. Formal psychology in particular was still in an amorphous state, not fully separate from various philosophical concerns. The *Encyclopedia Britannica* first devoted a separate article to psychology in the ninth edition, published in 1886. Though psychology had been defined as the "science of mind or mental life" at least since this date, psychologists had not been able to decide what constituted mind (or, for that matter, science, as applied to this field). By the time the eleventh edition of the *Encyclopedia Britannica* had been published, in 1911, prominent psychologist James Ward was led to conclude that "psychology cannot be defined by reference to a special subject matter" as the concrete sciences can; consequently, he resorted to a definition based on the standpoint from which psychology views experience:

> The standpoint of psychology is individualistic; by whatever methods, from whatever sources its facts are ascertained, they must – to have a psychological import – be regarded as having place in, or as being part of, *some one's consciousness or experience....* Psychology then is the science of individual experience. ("Psychology" 548)

This definition would not have been universally accepted since it side-stepped the important issue of the constitution of mind; it is revealing, however, because it acknowledges the diversity of methods and sources upon which psychology drew.

Psychical research fits well within this paradigm, since although its sources were often occult and esoteric, it applied scientific method to phenomena not normally perceivable by the five senses but considered as extensions of consciousness. Even psychical research's main goal, of determining whether personality survived bodily death, could be considered within the realm of individual experience. Among the psychological, psychical, and what might be called spiritualist phenomena studied are included hypnosis, hysteria, hallucinations, crisis apparitions, and thought transference. Unlike occult-ists, psychical researchers did not communicate with supernatural beings such as demons for the purpose of worship (Surette 24), nor were they spiritualists in possessing an unwavering faith in their ability to communicate through mediums with deceased humans. Rather, they actually exposed a great deal of occultist and spiritualist chicanery. That is not to say, however, that the psychical researchers' own beliefs did not occasionally occlude their scientific objectivity, or that the boundaries did not occasionally blur between these fields.

In fact, psychical research played several key roles in developing and disseminating dynamic psychology, and in so doing very nearly became part of the psychological orthodoxy, as historians Alan Gauld (338) and John Cerullo (99) have argued. Psychical research was mainly promulgated by the SPR, formed in 1882. The nucleus of the SPR's original membership hailed from Cambridge University, and their membership consistently included eminent psychologists, philosophers, and scientists. Although their findings typically generated controversy, from the 1880s to the 1920s the organization was a highly respected body. Most importantly, a prominent member, Frederic Myers, articulated in the 1890s the first comprehensive British dynamic psychology, centred on his conception of the subliminal self. William James, a founder of modern psychology, acknowledged Myers's contribution in 1901:

> For half a century now, psychologists have fully admitted the existence of a subliminal mental region, under the name either of unconscious cerebration or of the involuntary life; but they have never definitely taken up the question of the extent of this region, never sought explicitly to map it out. Myers definitely attacks this problem, which, after him, it will be impossible to ignore. ("Frederic Myers" 218)

Myers's genius was to assimilate the evidence for extensions of mental powers, including telepathy, clairvoyance, and possession, into a wide-ranging psychological system, thereby legitimizing the study of these "supernormal" phenomena. Myers engaged with contemporary debates about the substan-tiality and unity of selfhood and suggested the composite, "polypsychic" nature of selfhood. Through Myers's and other key Society members' par-ticipation in the first four International Congresses of Experimental Psychology (1889–1900), they kept debates about the spiritual dimension of personality at the forefront of the discipline of psychology. The Society's important role of introducing psychoanalytic discourse into England has long been acknowledged, but its shaping of the perceived significance of this material has not. Psychoanalysis was assessed according to the degree that it provided evidence for the existence of an afterlife, and this is the context that psychoanalysis continued to be perceived in for many years in Britain, and not just by psychical researchers.

Since the Society attracted not only prominent academics to its ranks, but also the leaders of British Society, including politicians, aristocrats, artists, and writers, it proved effective in spreading and popularizing dynamic discourse in the culture at large. A considerable number of writers perceived the significance of dynamic psychology through the lens of psychical research. Several writers became directly involved in the SPR, and many more drew on the case material and findings of dynamic psychology that the Society presented in its *Journal* and *Proceedings*. The Society introduced new language, including subliminal and telepathy, in theorizing about the mind, and it altered the meaning of other words, a clear indication of its profound impact. Prior to the advent of the Society, "psychical" denoted "of or pertaining to the mind; mental, as distinct from physical" (*Oxford English Dictionary*). In the Society's first major treatise, *Phantasms of the Living* (1886), Myers, Gurney, and Podmore apologized for giving "psychical" the specific meaning of "a group of subjects that lie on or outside the boundaries of recognised science" (Gurney 5). This meaning, however, gained currency, and in fact both meanings coexisted and intermingled, just as the figures of psychologist and psychical researcher were often melded in the popular imagination well into the 1930s, as Agatha Christie's fiction strikingly illustrates.[3]

Most importantly, the SPR helped to keep debates over psychical, spiritual, and mystical dimensions of humanity at the forefront of British culture, literary and otherwise. The fundamental premise of *Dynamic Psychology* is that this more inclusive, complex, and speculative approach to the human psyche or self provided writers with richer material for portraying characters in relation to the world around them than a materialistic approach to human behaviour could do, which might be reductive of possibilities. For instance, the SPR stimulated a debate about telepathy, and this debate encouraged writers to explore a diverse array of its imaginative implications in fiction, from mind control in Du Maurier's *Trilby* to Mrs Dalloway's uncanny sensitivity to Septimus Smith in Woolf's novel. Psychical research provided the discourses and, through the controversies surrounding it, the stimulus to challenge the dominant positivist, materialist culture. It thus needs to be seen as a significant and largely overlooked force on modernism.

The cultural climate that psychical research helped to establish was arguably one of considerable open-mindedness, spiritual questing, and eclecticism, and into it Freudian psychoanalysis was received, interpreted, and in some cases transformed. Since debate about psychoanalysis only began to emerge in England between 1908 and 1914, psychoanalysis represents a later manifestation of dynamic psychology. It was more scientifically orthodox in many ways than psychical research, and certainly better aligned with the dominant materialist culture. The main objection raised to the Freudian system was not so much to its subject matter, but to the absolute and universal claims that it was perceived to make about psychic conflicts, especially involving sexuality. In contrast to the expansionist, inclusive tradition of British psychology, psychoanalysis appeared reductionist. For these and other reasons, orthodox Freudian discourse never gained wide acceptance in Britain, though elements of it were assimilated into various branches of psychology. Nevertheless, histories of psychoanalysis in Britain have frequently mythologized psychoanalysis by treating it in isolation or "sanitizing" it (Wallace, "Science" 598), and by suggesting that it completely superseded all other dynamic psychologies (for example, Jones, *Sigmund Freud*). The prevalence of these accounts has meant that other, earlier influential dynamic psychologies, such as those put forward by Pierre Janet, and in England William McDougall, have been overshadowed.

I.4 Methodology

In interrogating various mythologies about the history of psychology and modernism, *Dynamic Psychology* participates in rupturing traditional notions about the history of ideas, particularly its assumption of an inevitable upward progression from ignorance to current enlightenment, by suggesting that valuable information has been lost in this movement. In addition, I have demonstrated that attitudes towards ideas, and the emotions that they arouse, are often as important as the ideas themselves, especially when they enter literary discourse. The book recognizes the limitations of traditional studies of influence and the complexity of interaction between and within domains of discourse. Ideas, images, and tropes from one discourse may be appropriated by another along two related continua – superficial to serious, or conscious through to unconscious. For example, even novelists with an extensive knowledge of dynamic psychology will employ clinical terms, such as hysteria or obsession, casually for the purposes of quick characterization. I have not completely dispensed with the concept of influence, however, but have used it as a starting point because in some cases writers themselves have acknowledged direct influence; in other cases they have denied influence. I have examined both types of statements critically and have marshalled evidence from other sources either to support or to refute these statements. Where there are several distinct possibilities of direct influence, I have suggested the most promising, without making an absolute judgement. Since I consider individuals, as well as institutions, as nexi of ideas and tropes, I have examined the nature and extent of the personal relations between the novelist subjects of this study and psychical researchers, psychologists, and philosophers knowledgeable about dynamic psychology.

Although this study focusses on dynamic psychological discourse in fiction, it recognizes that the psychological is by no means the master discourse from which language and insights are drawn. Psychological discourse just as frequently incorporated rhetoric and insights from the literary discourses of the past, such as Shakespeare's, as well as those of contemporaries. Frederic Myers's neo-Romantic approach to the psyche, for instance, bears the impress of his favourite writer, William Wordsworth, as well as conversations and correspondence on dream states with his contemporary Robert Louis Stevenson. I have also tried to avoid a hierarchical model of popularization which suggests that ideas are increasingly diluted as they are popularized.

The revisionist histories that I offer draw on Foucault's conception of archaeology, in the sense that they attempt to examine discourses at a particular period in time without allowing subsequent shifts in values or terminology to disturb or distort meanings and impact contemporary to that time. Historian of Psychology Katherine Arens has shown that failure to adopt an archaeological approach has been the main weakness in modern histories of psychology (Arens 34). Thus, current definitions and disciplinary divisions have not been imposed on this earlier period.

This approach has profoundly influenced choices made, most significantly about the concept of dynamic psychology. In earlier histories of psychology and modernism the term "new psychology" has prevailed. Although it had contemporary currency, its use perpetuated confusion, particularly surrounding the status of psychoanalysis. The initial followers of Freud, in their enthusiasm, claimed "new psychology" for Freudian psychoanalysis exclusively. For example, in the first book of Freud's to be translated into English, *Selected Papers on Hysteria and Other Psychoneuroses* (1909), A.A. Brill claimed that "Freud's views are not only new and revolutionary, being based on an entirely new psychology, but unless one is thoroughly familiar with their development one is apt to misunderstand them."[4] Freud himself only rarely used the phrase, usually in the context of his contributions *to* the new psychology.[5] Nevertheless, Freud's propagandists triumphed and the phrase became exclusively identified with psychoanalysis. By the 1920s A.G. Tansley, who had been analyzed by Freud, referred to psychoanalysis in his title *The New Psychology and Its Relation to Life* (1920); Charles F. Haanel in *The New Psychology* (1924) employed the phrase in a popularized, pseudo-mystical way to refer to psychoanalysis's recognition of the new transformative powers of thought. Traditional literary historians, such as H.V. Routh, William Frierson, and Leon Edel, uncritically accepted the narrow equation of new psychology with psychoanalysis. In actual fact, the term "new psychology" was applied prior to psychoanalysis in so many contexts as to render it problematic if not meaningless, except as illustration of the fluidity of the discipline and psychoanalysis's erasure of rivals.

As early as 1879, in an essay entitled "The New Psychology" in the *Fortnightly*, the change away from older associationist psychology and metaphysics towards laboratory experimentation, and in particular the contributions of biology, were represented as the new psychology (as qtd in Oppenheim 237). Twenty years later, psychical researcher Frank Podmore wrote, "the vocabulary of the new psychology owed much to Myers; amongst his best-known coinages were *telepathy*, *subliminal*, and *supernormal*".[6] At the turn of the century, E.W. Scripture in *The New Psychology* addressed the problem:

> During the last few years a wide interest has been aroused in the growth of a science of mental life which employs methods hitherto peculiar to the physical sciences. The interest has been followed by misconceptions of the most varied character. Some have supposed the new science to concern itself with experiments on thought-transference and clairvoyance; others have regarded it as a presumptuous sub-department of the physiology of the senses and the brain; and still others have treated it as merely a materialistic philosophy in one of its aberrations.

> Amid such confusion it is no wonder that people ask: "What *is* the new psychology? Is it brain-physiology, or spiritualism, or a new kind of metaphysics?" And the chemist, geologist, or physicist is also inclined to ask: "Is it a science at all?". (ix)

Scripture tried to reserve the term new psychology to describe "a purely mental science founded on careful experiment and exact measurement" (14), but a few years later Annie Besant applied it in a less "scientific" way in her published lectures, *Theosophy and the New Psychology* (1904), and it continued to be attached to various psychologies, including behaviourism (Woodworth, *Contemporary* 13).

The term "dynamic psychiatry", used by Henri Ellenberger in his profoundly influential history, *The Discovery of the Unconscious*, has more coherence than "new psychology". However, dynamic psychiatry was not contemporary to the time, only being coined in the 1940s. Also, the discourses of dynamic psychology did not fall solely within the field of psychiatry, in that they did not only pertain to mental disorders. In England particularly, the field of psychiatry, or mental science as it was then called, stagnated from the 1880s to the First World War and did not make a significant contribution to dynamic theories of the mind. The term I have finally adopted, "dynamic psychology", however, has the most integrity since it was actually used during the period in question: William James developed a dynamogenic psychology in 1896, William McDougall explored a "dynamic" view of mind in 1908, and Robert Woodworth employed the exact term "dynamic psychology" as early as 1916. Woodworth used it in order to move beyond the definition of psychology as the descriptive science of consciousness. Dynamic psychology referred to the complete processes of mental activity and development (*Dynamic* 36).[7]

Other means by which this study attempts to be archeaological include my decision to use the earliest translations of various thinkers, including Bergson, Freud, and Jung, even when these have been shown to contain inaccuracies, in order to obtain a clearer picture of what the British public potentially read of these psychologists. In acknowledgement that disciplinary boundaries were not as strictly drawn during the period as they now are, I have shown how a wide range of subject areas contributed to the burgeoning discipline of psychology and particularly the debates on selfhood. This effort to provide a synthesis of the self psychology of the time parallels the typical Edwardian strategy of synthesizing, of attempting to reconcile opposites, that historian Jonathan Rose has identified (3). Thus, the technique employed attempts to fit the subject matter and *mentalité* of the early twentieth century. Furthermore, the established literary canon for this period has not been taken for granted. Instead, excavation has unearthed writers who were among the first to assimilate dynamic psychological ideas intelligently, but who have been excluded from the canon, in some cases for extra-literary reasons. All of these techniques are designed to disturb and disrupt the accepted tenets of psychological and literary history.

I.5   Parameters

Given dynamic psychology's importance in early twentieth-century British literature, it is surprising how few studies have been undertaken. Most focus on psychoanalysis or on a specific influence on an individual writer. The first significant study was Reinald Hoops's 1934 published dissertation, *Der Einfluss der Psychoanalyse auf die Englische Literatur*. Hoops's essay retains value because he queried writers directly about their use of psychology; however, his work suffers from several limitations. Since Hoops attempts to describe the impact of psychoanalysis on all genres of literature and on at least thirty writers, his treatment is necessarily superficial. Similar to other literary critics, he isolates psychoanalysis from other expressions of dynamic psychology and draws too rigid a delineation between psychoanalytic novels and novels of psychological analysis (Hoops 30).

Frederick Hoffman's *Freudianism and the Literary Mind* (1945, rev. edn 1957) represents a considerable advance over Hoops's. His analyses of psychological impact are more carefully articulated and profound than Hoops's, and he shows himself to be more aware of the intricacies of influence. However, he examines only Freudian influence, rather uncritically, and is more oriented towards American than British modernism, and exclusively high modernism at that.

Two more recent studies move beyond psychoanalytic influence. Keith May's *Out of the Maelstrom: Psychology and the Novel in the Twentieth Century* (1977) identifies analogies between psychology and literature in order "to clarify contemporary views of human nature and human possibilities" and, as he admits, covers a vast time period (ix). Judith Ryan's *The Vanishing Subject: Early Psychology and Literary Modernism* (1991) traces the symbiosis between empiricist psychology and modernist literature, concentrating on continental European developments in both.

There have been a number of illuminating histories of psychical research, including Alan Gauld's *The Founders of Psychical Research* (1968), John Cerullo's *The Secularization of the Soul* (1982), and Janet Oppenheim's *The Other World* (1985). Several of these set psychical research into traditions of mental healing, notably Adam Crabtree's *From Mesmer to Freud* (1993) and Alison Winter's *Mesmerized* (1998), but their concern is not with literary appropriation of these discourses. Several contemporary cultural studies have enlisted psychical research in support of various fascinating projects. Pamela Thurschwell's *Literature, Technology and Magical Thinking, 1880–1920* (2001) links psychical research's exploration of paranormal communication with emerging "teletechnologies" (including the telegraph and telephone), and with psychoanalysis' articulation of intimacy. She works from the assumption (not made in this study) that telepathy and other forms of paranormal communication are false, referring to them as magical thinking, and reads their expression in Du Maurier, Wilde, and Henry James as fantasies betraying anxiety. Helen Sword's *Ghostwriting Modernism* (2002) treats psychical research as tangential to low cultural popular spiritualism, and emphasizes the latter's links with the modernist literary aesthetics of Joyce, Eliot, Yeats, and H.D. Roger Luckhurst's *The Invention of Telepathy* (2002) historicizes Myers's concept of telepathy and considers its diverse cultural implications, particularly for neo-gothic fiction. In focussing exclusively on this concept, however, Luckhurst neglects to situate Myers's work within the context of emerging dynamic psychologies. Although Luckhurst uses the term "dynamic psychology", he never defines it. In fact, none of these studies centres on or considers the claims for legitimacy of the psychological paradigm developed by psychical research, assesses it within the broader framework of dynamic psychology, or evaluates its cultural impact, particularly on prose fiction, alongside other dynamic psychologies.

In order to accomplish this task without spreading the analysis too thinly by treating too broad a time period or too many writers, several contours have been established. Although this project unavoidably traces the influx of the most significant European psychological discourse into Britain, the study of the reception and transformation of these discourses is confined to Britain and British literary figures. The book covers the impact of dynamic psychological thinking primarily on the novel from the late 1890s up to the mid-1920s, though the main focus is on the Edwardian and war years. Following the war, dynamic psychological discourses infiltrate all areas of British society; consequently, teasing out individual writers' encounters with particular ideas or tropes becomes increasingly complex.

The mid-1920s also seems an appropriate time to draw the analysis to a close since, in 1924 and 1925, Freud's *Collected Works* were published, leading to even more widespread dissemination of his thought in England. As well, in 1926 J.D. Beresford, one of the subjects of the present work, astutely proclaimed the decline of a certain category of psychoanalytic influence on the novel.

Several criteria were developed in order to select those writers who would best illuminate the progression of interactions between writers and dynamic psychology. The main concerns were to discover those novelists who earliest encountered dynamic psychology within the period delineated, became most knowledgeable about it, and contributed to its discourses not only in fictional works but also in critical writing, autobiographies, letters, and other primary source material. An attempt was made to choose writers who worked on several levels, from those who were popular, but whose work merits attention, to the most critically acclaimed. The rationale for this manoeuvre was that popular novelists would be better guides than canonized ones, not only to the impact of discourses, but also to the way those discourses are (mis)interpreted. Cultural currents run closer to the surface in their books than in more strikingly original works; moreover, those writers were sought out who had been neglected, perhaps even *because* of their avid interest in the latest psychology. I became particularly interested in novelists whose early assimilation of dynamic psychology brought into relief several popular misconceptions about the advent of modernism, for instance that it represented a complete break from the past. In general, writers who best revealed distortions in literary history were considered most desirable.

May Sinclair, J.D. Beresford, and Virginia Woolf best fit these criteria, both individually and collectively, and none of them have been analysed in the light of a construct of dynamic psychology inclusive of psychical research. Sinclair's assimilation of dynamic psychology can be detected in her first novel, *Audrey Craven* (1897), and Sinclair's encounters with its discourses underwent vicissitudes throughout her career, as she made the transition from Edwardian to modernist novelist. She had written her most compelling work by 1924, after which her energies petered out. J.D. Beresford, relegated to obscurity as a non-experimental Georgian, deployed dynamic psychology in support of extending realism, both through exploration of psychical phenomena and in "clinical dissections". Nonetheless, in 1928 he penned a stream of consciousness novel *manqué*, fascinating for its conscious articulation of challenges in making dynamic psychological discourse acceptable for fiction readers.

At first glance, Woolf does not appear to fulfil the criteria listed. Now considered a pillar of modernism, she criticized the Edwardians for their neglect of the dark places of psychology, and helped foster the myth that the moderns forged a completely new aesthetic. Most importantly, her response to dynamic psychology is highly problematic. She claimed in 1931, for instance, that she knew of Freud "only in the way of ordinary conversation" (Hoops 147), but these conversations were held with adherents of psychical research and pioneers of psychoanalysis. An examination of the milieu in which she was raised, and her Cambridge and Bloomsbury connections, suggests that she was far more aware than she ever admitted of the psychological and philosophical discourses from the time of her father's generation on. A study of her earliest novels provides further evidence that she worked from some similar psychological assumptions as the Edwardians, and that these continued to challenge and modify her conception of characterization in her modernist experiments.

All three novelists received hostile reviews not based on the quality of their work, but on its psychological subject matter and approach to characterization. They challenged and expanded readers' expectations of what the acceptable parameters of the novel were, or readers' horizon of expectations, in theorist Hans Jauss's terms. Sinclair and Beresford's work in particular was considered too clinical or unpleasant (especially so because of Sinclair's gender), and this may have contributed to their critical neglect. Furthermore, all three contributed to debates about dynamic psychology, or at least its impact on fiction, in their non-fiction work. Perhaps the most striking example of dynamic psychologists' reciprocal engagement with the novelists is that both Sinclair and Beresford's novels were used as therapy for patients in clinics, thus comprising the first known use of bibliotherapy in a formal clinical setting.[8]

Though Sinclair's, Beresford's, and Woolf's success varied in assimilating dynamic psychology into their own imaginative visions, overall dynamic psychology facilitated their exploration of new fictional waters. These novelists believed they were plunging deeper into reality than had their forebears. Reading them through dynamic psychology brings into relief geographical formations in those waters, providing fresh perspectives on occluded features of their texts.

Sinclair's, Beresford's, and Woolf's appropriation of common dynamic psychological ideas suggests that this discourse affected writers with quite different aesthetic principles and cut across period divisions. As a particularly vivid illustration of this, I have drawn on two additional novelists with widely varying aims, Arnold Bennett and D.H. Lawrence, leading up to my discussion of Beresford, as a means of contextualizing his assimilation of dynamic psychology in realism. Dismissed as a "materialist culprit" by Virginia Woolf, Arnold Bennett nevertheless appropriated elements of dynamic psychology as a means of exploring ghosts that act upon the mind in *The Ghost* (1907) and in evoking an out-of-body experience in *The Glimpse* (1909). Although much has been written about D.H. Lawrence's mythologizing of later dynamic psychologies, notably Freud's and Jung's,[9] there has not been much probing of his appropriation of earlier ones, particularly Frederic

Myers's, despite projects devoted to exploring Lawrence's occult sources, such as P.T. Whelan's *D.H. Lawrence: Myth and Metaphysic in The Rainbow and Women in Love* (1988). A number of other novelists might have been treated in depth in this project, since they too engaged with dynamic psychological discourses, but had to be excluded either because of space limitations, as in the case of Algernon Blackwood, or for one of the following reasons: dynamic psychology had already been thoroughly discussed in their work, as with Henry James and James Joyce; dynamic psychology influenced only one main aspect of the writing, as in Dorothy Richardson's engagement with stream of consciousness technique; the use of dynamic psychology was superficial, as in H.G. Wells's work, or primarily satirical, as in Aldous Huxley's fiction. Nonetheless, I have taken the liberty in drawing on some of them in Chapters 1 and 2 for succinct, striking examples of engagement with a particular dynamic concept.

In summary, Chapter 1 surveys the philosophical and psychological discourses that contributed most forcefully to dynamic psychology. Chapter 2 identifies the strongest currents of medical, psychiatric, and psychical thought to shape dynamic psychology. Both Chapters 1 and 2 point out similarities and differences between these discourses and later dynamic psychologies, notably psychoanalysis. However, the main aim is to identify key debates and concepts, and to suggest potential impact on writers. In both chapters I have focussed on conceptions of selfhood, comprising the following elements: consciousness and the unconscious, including memory, time, sexuality, and spirituality. Chapter 2 emphasizes the conditions and techniques found to be most revealing of selfhood, including hysteria, hypnosis, genius, nervous illness, and psychotherapy. Chapter 3 interrogates myths about the reception of psychoanalysis in England and suggests that British academics and health professionals drew eclectically on Freudian and Jungian thinking in constructing their own versions of dynamic psychology. It highlights developments with potential appeal to fiction writers. As a whole, these three chapters provide extensive evidence that there was a substantial body of dynamic psychological knowledge of both British and foreign origin available to fiction writers in the first two decades of the twentieth century. Chapter 4 demonstrates the complexity of May Sinclair's engagement with dynamic psychology, initially to introduce innovations in characterization and theme and then to forge stylistic innovations. Chapter 5 ruptures the mythology surrounding the break between Edwardian and Georgian realism by demonstrating the continuities in engagement with psychological discourse from Edwardian Arnold Bennett, through diverse Georgian realists D.H. Lawrence and J.D. Beresford. Perhaps more speculative than earlier chapters, Chapter 6 shows that psychological discourses were very much a part of the milieu in which Virginia Woolf lived and worked. She, in particular, interrogated and challenged these ideas and constructs from her earliest work through to her modernist experiments. Chapter 7 advocates reading dynamic psychology in and through other types of modern fiction, from the satires of Huxley and Macaulay to the mysteries of Agatha Christie, as well as other genres such as drama and poetry. It reaffirms dynamic psychology's critical role in providing the impetus to challenge the dominant materialist culture of early twentieth-century Britain.

1
Philosophy and Psychology

Several strong and opposing philosophical traditions, as well as a number of non-dynamic psychological systems, shaped the emergence of dynamic psychological discourse, and provided perspectives and insights taken up and in some cases formalized by dynamic psychologists. My intention is not to detail these traditions and systems, but, drawing on philosophers' and psychologists' own work as well as that of historians who have contextualized them most accurately, to sketch briefly their contributions to the following discourses: on consciousness; on what lies beneath the threshold of consciousness, whether figured as a subconscious, subliminal, or unconscious; and on selfhood, including the debates on time, memory, and will. The main focus will be on selfhood, and particularly on the thinkers whose discourse functioned as the most richly associative nexi of ideas for writers.

1.1 Consciousness and idealism

Probably the philosophy most influential in shaping the discourse on consciousness in the nineteenth century was idealism. It also had perhaps the greatest impact on early twentieth-century novelists, including May Sinclair and J.D. Beresford. The roots of idealism lie in several German philosophers. Immanuel Kant had founded a new idealism in the late eighteenth century with his proofs that if any knowledge were possible, then logic had priority and most validity, and with his identification of logic with the cognitive consciousness. However, his idealism was empirical, analytic and not, strictly speaking, metaphysical. Nevertheless, his conception was promptly converted by Hegel into a metaphysical form, which posited that being depended "on a knowing mind that transcends and envelops both the physical and psychical orders" (Perry 148). Primarily in this Hegelian form, Idealism was revived in Britain in the 1870s by a school comprising T.H. Green, F.H. Bradley, and J. McTaggart, among others. Green, perhaps the foremost British exponent, conceived of the world as a single, unalterable, all-inclusive system of thought-relations (Sidgwick 21). This presupposed a relating, unifying consciousness, or Divine eternal spirit. Each individual's consciousness had the potential to realize in a limited way something of the Divine consciousness. Thus, Green claimed, "the unifying principle of the world is indeed in us; it is our self" (Green, *Works* 145). For Green, self-realization assumed great importance and was the true good. The goal of individuals should be to help one another attain self-realization, and society and its institutions should also foster this. Green held up as ideals duty and even self-sacrifice as means of attaining common good. He emphasized good works and social reform over debates about theological dogma.

The significance of the discourse on Idealism in England, for both psychology and the culture in general, cannot be underestimated. During its revival from the 1870s to about 1910, Idealism effectively countered the dominant psychological tradition in philosophy of empiricism, associationism, and positivism. On the one hand, its recognition that there were problems requiring attention which lay outside the field of positivistic science kept the horizon of psychology broader than it might otherwise have been. Idealism also had the effect of keeping metaphysical questions closely linked with psychological ones, and it sustained the plausibility of religious belief for many. One of the most prominent British psychologists of this period, James Ward (1843–1925), favoured idealism over empiricism and associationism, partly for religious reasons (Hearnshaw, *Short* 136). This approach caused him to stress the importance of an active unitary self in psychological analysis. He also asserted the necessity of keeping the biological sciences separate from psychology, but was quite willing to include metaphysical speculation within its realm. On the other hand, the Idealists' concentration on consciousness narrowed the focus of psychology by diverting attention from neo-Romantic conceptions of the unconscious, and this is true of Ward's psychology as well.

For fiction writers, Idealist discourse typically shaped their thinking in a number of ways. Idealism provided impetus for the intense concern with spirit and unseen realities demonstrated in the fiction under consideration here. Idealism suggested that a finite consciousness could be interpenetrated by the infinite or Divine or Absolute consciousness at times. This concept helps to account for the high value Sinclair, Lawrence, Beresford, and Woolf placed on moments of being or illumination, since these provided glimpses into absolute spiritual reality. Expansion of consciousness helped an individual realize his highest self, through which he might perceive and even realize the Absolute in himself. Idealism bolstered these writers' subjective certainty that individuals could know one another's minds and attain intimacy – occasionally even through experiences beyond those traceable by the five senses.

Of the writers in this study, May Sinclair probably assimilated idealism most thoroughly. Her first significant article assessed "The Ethical and

Religious Import of Idealism", and she remained an idealist throughout her life. In her article she emphasized Green's ideals of self-realization and self-sacrifice. Each individual has the right "to the best and highest that life can offer him. We regard the individual as under a positive obligation to develop to his utmost all the powers and latent capabilities of his nature" (Sinclair, "Ethical" 702). Moral progress, she continued, requires self-sacrifice: "Only in following self-less and universal ends can [an individual] realize his own" ("Ethical" 702).

Furthermore, Idealism significantly conditioned several Edwardian writers' view of dynamic psychology and especially psychoanalysis. May Sinclair, in particular, attempted to align and integrate what she referred to as "the purified spirit of psychoanalysis" – by which she meant the concepts of the will-to-live, the unconscious, and sublimation – with Idealism, in *A Defence of Idealism* (11).

In spite of that belated defence, idealism did not withstand attack from several sides. Sinclair herself made pertinent psychological criticisms when she claimed that objective idealism failed to take into account unconscious thinking, sleep, and forgetting, and that it did not know what to make of "the great energies of instinct and love" (*Defence* 137). More systematic criticisms came from the philosophers; thus, part of the importance of idealism must be in the reactions it provoked in turn.

1.2   The Unconscious and Romantic philosophy

Without a doubt Romantic philosophy had the greatest impact on shaping nineteenth-century discourse on the unconscious. Similarly to idealism, Romantic philosophy entertained metaphysical questions, for instance in postulating the existence of underlying spiritual laws, and this coloured the debate on the unconscious. In its less religiously motivated German form, which developed between 1790 and 1830, Romantic philosophy focussed on the relations between man and nature, stressing the existence of polarities in conflict both in the natural world and within the psyche. This dynamism forms the fundamental source for dynamic psychology. Both German and English Romantic writers like J.P.F. Richter, Wordsworth, and Coleridge explored the importance of unconscious sources of thought through intro-spection, but the philosopher-psychologist J.F. Herbart (1776–1841) was the first to study systematically the relations of unconscious and conscious processes from a dynamic perspective. His contributions to the discourse on the unconscious were among the most influential prior to Freud's among writers, notably May Sinclair and Lawrence, but even Arnold Bennett, disinclined to read psychology and metaphysics, imbibed Herbart through a secondary source (*Journals* I 284; cf. Chapters 4 and 5). Herbart also had considerable impact on Freud himself, and resemblances between Herbart's and Freud's discourses have on a number of occasions caused literary critics mistakenly to assume writers have assimilated Freudian discourse when it is actually Herbartian. Herbart's ideas were presented as contributions to general and educational psychology in his *Textbook of Psychology* (1816) and *Psychology as Science* (1824).

Similarly to Freud, Herbart developed a topographical model of mind, which posited that it had three layers. The top layer consisted of representations available to consciousness, which was described as narrow. The lower two levels occupied a much larger area and were divided between those representations which were partially inhibited or obscure and those which were completely so (Sand 470). Herbart termed the dividing line between the top level and the two lower levels of representation the threshold of consciousness. Since only a limited number of representations could enter consciousness at once, ideas were often what he referred to as "repressed" or "inhibited". As ideas were repressed below the threshold of consciousness, they were not destroyed, but moved from a state of reality to a state of tendency (Boring 244). Not only did Herbart introduce the idea of repression, but he stressed that repressions ranged in duration from a single moment to years. Novelists, such as May Sinclair and Virginia Woolf, who illustrate the brief "repressions" of their characters have more likely assimilated (whether consciously or not) a conception originating with Herbart's than Freud's conception. Despite the inevitable clash of ideas striving to enter consciousness, Herbart believed that the mind required unity (Sand 471), an idea which aligned well with idealism. What he termed "resistance" was encountered when two ideas were mutually and actively opposed (Sand 471). However, when ideas were compatible with one another, they were assimilated into what Herbart referred to as the "apperceptive mass" (Sand 472). As several of these masses were integrated, the ego gradually formed (Sand 472). The imagery that Herbart used to illustrate his concepts was nearly as important to the discourse on the dynamics of mind as the concepts themselves. Rosemary Sand points out that Herbart had borrowed from earlier philosophers the imagery of light and darkness and rising and falling to describe the relation between consciousness and unconsciousness; however, he added imagery of movement and of space in order to render vividly his ideas about consciousness. He also introduced the image of a web connecting trains of thought to describe the organization of apperceptive masses (Sand 473). All of these metaphors resurface in the works of the British novelists under consideration.

Of more immediate consequence, Herbart's ideas were so powerfully inscribed and resonant that a Herbartian school came into being. Through one of Herbart's followers, Adolf Lindner, Freud may have become acquainted with Herbartian ideas (Sand 465). Several of Lindner's elaborations on Herbartian ideas deserve mention. He compared consciousness "with a closed room with limited dimensions and the representations with people who go in and out of it" (as qtd in Sand 475), a metaphor that reappears in

May Sinclair's earliest work (*Audrey Craven* 54; *Helpmate* 153). Lindner discussed the possibility that the ego could split, leading to the impairment of an individual's moral functioning (Sand 477). Finally, he posited the existence of a destructive drive that had to be "transformed" or sublimated (though he did not use this word) "into the more noble cultural and artistic drive by which, instead of destroying, he produces new creations..." (as qtd in Sand 478).

The high esteem for Herbart in turn-of-the-century Britain is suggested by the 1902 and subsequent *Encyclopaedia Britannica* entries on Herbart, in which James Ward ranked him second in importance only to Hegel out of all post-Kantian philosophers (Ward, "Herbart" 477). In Britain, philosopher Sir William Hamilton as well as psychologist G.F. Stout disseminated and developed some Herbartian concepts. Most notably, Stout elaborated on the idea of Beneke, a follower of Herbart's, that "psychical energy" was the element that flowed between mental representations (as qtd in Sand 474) and claimed that at all levels the mind was active.

A number of other nineteenth-century Romantic philosophers mapped the unconscious, but space limitations permit only the briefest mention of their contributions. In *Psyche* (1846), Carl Gustav Carus argued that the unconscious had several layers and emphasized psychic dynamism: "conscious feelings, when becoming unconscious, undergo continuous modification and maturation" (Ellenberger 207–208). Eduard von Hartmann's *Philosophy of the Unconscious* (trans. 1884) extensively analysed the unconscious and, according to historian L.L. Whyte, "it proves that when Freud was twelve years of age, twenty-six aspects of unconscious mental activity in man had already been considered in detail in a famous work" (Whyte 164). In the 1880s there was a revival of Arthur Schopenhauer's (1788–1860) ideas about the will as consisting of unconscious driving forces, the fundamental irrationality of mankind, the importance of the sexual instinct, and repression as the origin of mental illness (Ellenberger 208). Among the similarities to Freud's ideas, Schopenhauer's concept of the will as opposed to the intellect, bears striking resemblance to Freud's "id" and "ego" respectively. Schopenhauer's student, Frederich Nietzsche, had an even greater impact than his mentor on dynamic psychology. He viewed the mind as a system of drives; he also introduced the terms "id" to designate impersonal elements in the psyche subject to natural law (Whyte 175), and inhibition to describe what would, in Freud's system, be termed "repression". Nietzsche developed the concept of sublimation of sexual and aggressive drives, also made use of by Freud. However, unlike Freud, Nietzsche eventually stressed the will for power over other drives (Ellenberger 274). Not only did Freud, Jung, and Adler draw on Nietzsche, as Ellenberger notes (276), but in some early twentieth-century fiction, such as that of D.H. Lawrence's, it is almost impossible to distinguish the assimilation of Nietzsche, along with Schopenhauer, from those psychologists who borrowed from them (Schneider 29–57).

1.3   Dynamic psychologies of self

This section will first trace the most significant contributions by Victorian philosophers and psychologists to the more inclusive discourse on selfhood or personality. It will then focus on three transitional figures who most firmly established the debates on selfhood interrogated by the novelists under study: William James, Henri Bergson, and William McDougall.[1]

1.3.1   Victorian polymaths

Victorian polymath George Henry Lewes (1817–1878) "was perhaps the first British psychologist to employ the term personality in approximately its modern sense", according to Hearnshaw (*Short* 50). As a novelist and journalist, he represents a striking example of a literary figure who contributed significantly to psychology. Though an empiricist, he did not view the mind as composed of separate, static elements, but instead believed that body, brain, and mind only had significance in relation to one another (Hearnshaw, *Short* 49). This holistic, dynamic perspective he referred to as organicist, and it took account of both psychological product and underlying processes.

Eventually Lewes placed primary emphasis on experience. Impressions and experiences combined and recombined according to laws of grouping which Lewes formulated, and evolved into an "Inner Life", the basis of personality (*Short* 50). Significantly, he was the first to describe consciousness as a stream, claiming in 1860 that "there is a general stream of sensation which constitutes [an individual's] feeling of existence – the Consciousness of himself as a sensitive being" (Lewes 66). Many streams in fact combine to make up consciousness:

> Consciousness, in the general sense, is the sum total of all our sensibilities, the confluence of many streams of sensation. Consciousness, in the particular sense, is only another term for Sensibility: we have as many different forms of consciousness as we have different kinds of sensation. While some of these confluent streams are so slight that they are no more appreciable than are the stars at noonday, others are so equable and constant, that they attract no attention unless their currents are disturbed. (Lewes 68–69)

Lewes also stressed the role of the symbolic in thinking, as did Freud later (with an admittedly different emphasis on psychic conflict and libido). Finally, Lewes recognized that unconscious regions "play by far the greater part in mental life", and he located "motors" which determine motivation within these regions (Hearnshaw, *Short* 52).

Another literary figure, Samuel Butler (1835–1902), in his opposition to Darwinian evolution, contributed significantly to the discourse on selfhood, particularly regarding the role of memory. Although an evolutionist, Butler could not accept that "chance variations could explain continuous development", but held instead that heredity was a form of memory (Hearnshaw, *Short* 53). Following Lamarck, he postulated that "acquired characters could be transmitted to, or were remembered by", as he preferred to put it, "subsequent generations" (Hearnshaw, *Short* 54). Both habits and instincts, then, were memories which had been forgotten or become unconscious. Thus, the unconscious assumed a tremendous role in Butler's system, as in later dynamic psychologies. Unlike the Freudian unconscious, however, Butler's comprised a vast storehouse of "knowledges and aptitudes that serve [an individual] better than anything he can learn or cultivate on his own account" during his lifetime (Sinclair, *Defence* 6). These "race memories" are closer to Jung's collective unconscious (Jung, "Psychological Foundations" 85). Butler's idea that an underlying directive life force determined which memories survived bears striking resemblance to the later-developed Jungian libido.

Although Butler made a less significant contribution to psychology than Lewes, his writing was interrogated much more closely by the next generation of writers, including G.B. Shaw, H.G. Wells, Rebecca West, Dorothy Richardson, May Sinclair, J.D. Beresford, and Bloomsbury members E.M. Forster, Virginia Woolf, and Lytton Strachey. They found particularly attractive his novel *The Way of All Flesh* (1903), which illustrates his theory of the necessity of listening to inner impulses over the voices of others in order to achieve individuality, an act of genius. Shaw and Forster, virtually Butler's disciples, adopted his attitude of probing beneath surfaces to reveal hidden psychological truth. Forster especially drew on Butler's discourse on inherited instinctual wisdom in creating the figures of Mrs Wilcox and Mrs Moore of *Howards End* (1910) and *A Passage to India* (1924) respectively (L.E. Holt 816–817). However, it was May Sinclair who took Butler's psychology most seriously, devoting a pivotal chapter to it in her *A Defence of Idealism* (1917). Though she accepted his theory of heredity, she rejected his view, following from the theory, that personality amounted to no more than a cluster of buried memories. Butler's stance did not allow for the immortality of the soul; instead, Sinclair posited that memory and the organism are dependent on personal identity (37–38). Nevertheless, Sinclair's criticism comes several decades after his theories were put forward. While most late nineteenth-century psychologists would not have subscribed to Butler's extreme position on the principles of inheritance, many held that personal identity depended on memory.

1.3.2   William James: The psychology of everyday life

1.3.2.1   *Stream and selfhood*

William James's contribution to the discourse on selfhood was much wider-ranging than Butler's, and it gradually evolved into one of the most comprehensive and influential dynamic psychologies. James's prominence as a philosopher and a psychologist has long been recognized, but neglect or misunderstanding of his dedicated exploration of psychical research has distorted his contribution. James Kantor, for instance, claims that "Jamesian psychology is a magnificent failure: magnificent because James intended to naturalize mental states, a failure because he in no sense divested himself of the assumption that psychology is concerned with spiritistic processes" (147). However, this divestment was never James's intention. Even in the *Principles of Psychology* (1890), his most positivistic work, he claims that his positivism "is anything but ultimate" ("Preface"; I 182). Following the *Principles*, James realized even more fully the folly of ignoring data arising from the flux of experience, regardless of whether or not it transcended scientific positivism and lent support to spiritist theories. For this reason, he joined the SPR shortly after its inception, serving as Vice-President from 1890 to 1910 and as President in 1894–1895, founded the American branch in 1884, and investigated the medium Mrs Piper throughout the 1890s. His interest in exceptional mental states, including trances and automatic writing, led to his becoming an expert on the subconscious and to propose, in 1896, a dynamic model of the psyche. These pursuits informed his groundbreaking study of the psychology of religion, *Varieties of Religious Experience* (1902). James's expansionist view of human psychology aligns more closely with his friend Frederic Myers's, and later Jung's, approach, than with Freud's reductionist model. James's psychology has been a failure only in the sense that it has not sustained the recognition that it once had, a fate it shares with the other expansionist theories.

James's impact on the literary consciousness of the period was no less profound. Except for his idea of the stream of consciousness, this impact has been similarly undervalued. James was an American, but three of his texts, *Principles of Psychology*, *Varieties of Religious Experience*, and *A Pluralistic Universe* had a particularly strong influence in Britain. Their contribution to the psychology of selfhood will be emphasized, and comparisons made between his major ideas, those of Freud's and other prominent psychologists' in order to bring into relief his impact on early twentieth-century culture.

Modestly intended as a textbook, *Principles of Psychology* (1890) was immediately recognized, as Frederic Myers put it, as "perhaps the completest treatment of the subject, from the purely scientific side, which any single work in our language contains" (Myers, "Principles" 111). It became a nexus of current discourse on the psychology of the self. In the "Preface" to the monumental 1400-page work, James defines psychology as the science of finite individual minds which has as its data thoughts and experiences (I vi). Although James tends to have a materialistic bias, his work increases understanding of the complexity of selfhood and its relation to bodily processes.

Despite its length, there are certain deliberate restrictions, most notably in his rejection of the concept of an unconscious. He argues that the distinction between the unconscious and the conscious being of a mental state "is the sovereign means for believing what one likes in psychology" (I 163). Instead, James asserts that the entire thought (even of a complex object) is the minimum entity with which psychology can deal (I 177). Though he also rejects the spiritist soul theory, he does propose that the soul is possibly "a medium upon which . . . the manifold brain-processes *combine their effects*" (I 181), and he confesses that this conception "seems to me the line of least logical resistance" (I 181). However, the only thing we can know immediately is the state of consciousness; thus James confines himself to studying it.

James deals with the essential nature of consciousness in his famous chapter "Stream of Thought". He begins by characterizing thought, which is part of personal consciousness, always changing, sensibly continuous, selective, and impulsive (I 526). According to James, the Lockean view that ideas are associated or linked in the mind does not correspond to reality:

> Consciousness, then, does not appear to itself chopped up in bits. Such words as "chain" or "train" do not describe it fitly as it presents itself in the first instance. It is nothing jointed; it flows. A "river" or a "stream" are the metaphors by which it is most naturally described. In talking of it hereafter, let us call it the stream of thought, of consciousness, or of subjective life. (I 237)

James's view represents a fuller analysis of consciousness because it analyses the transitive parts of thought. Previous theories ignored these "fringes" because they were "in-flight" and therefore anonymous, and instead concentrated on the resting places or substantive elements of thought (I 246). Conversely, James stresses the dynamic nature of thought:

> When we think, we are to a great extent caught up in the sweep of our states of consciousness, vividly aware of images or words present until displaced by others, but also continuously aware, although less vividly and on the fringes of the words and images, of a felt direction of thought movement in thinking. (as qtd in Myers, *W.J.* 256)

Although James did not originate the idea of a stream of consciousness, as Robert Humphrey, J. Isaacs, and others have claimed,[2] James's conception of a dynamic, fluid consciousness permeated early modern culture (as Humphrey and others have detailed).

This conception had several important implications for his concept of the self. James at least partially replaces the traditional notion that there is a single, unified self with the idea that there are several selves – material, social, spiritual, and the Ego – and he also reduces the substantiality of each. For example, he claims that "a man has as many social selves as there are individuals who recognize him and carry an image of him in their mind"

(I 294). More significantly, the spiritual self, defined as the most inner or subjective being taken concretely, is only "a certain portion of the stream abstracted from the rest...." (I 296). Furthermore, James demonstrates his materialistic bias when he states that this self is really a feeling of bodily activities whose exact nature is by most men overlooked (I 302). Rather than a mental Arch-Ego or soul, the present, "judging" thought provides what unity there is in personal identity since it is "the representative of the entire past stream" (I 340). This present thought appropriates to itself

> the hook from which the chain of past selves dangles, planted firmly in the Present, which alone passes for real, and thus keep[s] the chain from being a purely ideal thing. Anon the hook itself will drop into the past with all it carries, and then be treated as an object and appropriated by a new thought in the new present which will serve as living hook in turn. (I 340–341)

Findings from psychical research and pathology further suggest that the self lacks substantial boundaries and could be disjunctive (I 350, 373–400). Thus, though James strives to demonstrate continuity in the stream of consciousness, he effectively removes confidence in the unity of selfhood.

James's investigation of consciousness and its impact on selfhood colours his approach to the other forces shaping selfhood with which he deals, most importantly habit, time, memory, instinct, and emotion. James accords great importance to habit, referring to it as "the enormous fly-wheel of society" (I 121). This causes him to elevate the importance of childhood and also to sound very deterministic: "It [habit] dooms us all to fight out the battle of life upon the lines of our nurture or our early choice" (I 121). Philosophically, however, James was an indeterminist, believing in the necessity of purposive striving to overcome habit (G. Myers, *W.J.* 392). Habit affects our field of consciousness in that it diminishes the conscious attention with which our acts are performed (I 114).

Next to James's "stream of consciousness", his conception of time had most impact on subsequent discourses, including fiction, though, as he acknowledges, it was not wholly original (I 609). As Gerald Myers observes, for James, consciousness and time were intimately connected because if time is not continuous, then neither is consciousness (*W.J.* 150). Nevertheless, James neglects the flowing nature of time in his preoccupation with its fine-grained structure (G. Myers, *W.J.* 153). He focusses on the enduring present, alternately referred to as duration, or specious time (G. Myers, *W.J.* 144), and claims that time is directly sensed or felt. The present endures, for a maximum of about twelve seconds, and this amount of time just elapsed, along with "a vaguely vanishing backward and forward fringe", constitutes the specious present (I 613). Gerald Myers comments that

> The idea of the specious present helps clarify "the present moment" and the past–present–future distinction within the now. It suggests how an immediately past event can be said to be presently remembered when it would be odd to say it is remembered; or how an event coming to be is in a way both future and present. (*W.J.* 160)

Though James thus broadens and deepens the present moment through analysis of its elements, he also claims that our immediate experience of time is synthetic, and in this sense it is analogous to the perception of space (I 610). In keeping with his pluralism, James postulates the existence of a multiplicity of times rather than one Real time, and in this characteristic, time resembles space as well. However, Myers asserts that James did not deny objective time altogether (*W.J.* 156). Finally, James's apparent denial that times and spaces are connected with larger unities reinforces the implication made earlier about the self that there is no enveloping ego or soul to organize experience (G. Myers, *W.J.* 154).

Memory also acts as a significant force on selfhood, for two reasons. At least from one viewpoint there are many past selves (I 335), and false memories have the power to distort the consciousness of the "me", since that is constructed through the appropriation of the past by the present Thought (I 373). James evokes the relation of the stream to memory in the following: "The stream of thought flows on; but most of its segments fall into the bottomless abyss of oblivion" (I 640). Memory serves to retrieve states of mind from oblivion, presuming these originally endured long enough in consciousness to make an imprint. Memory is complex because psychic fringes of images and thoughts of the object remembered must be assimilated in the mind. In order to feel the object substantively,

> we must reproduce the thought as it was uttered, with every word fringed and the whole sentence bathed in that original halo of obscure relations, which, like an horizon, then spread about its meaning. (I 275–276)

In his section on association, James comments on the importance of childhood memory, although he does not elaborate on its developmental aspect (I 576).

James is clearer on the role of instincts in the self's development. He argues that "most instincts are implanted for the sake of giving rise to habits..." and then they naturally fade away (II 402). He also posits many diverse instincts in humans.

For James, instinct and emotion are closely linked since "every object that excites an instinct excites an emotion as well", the difference between the two being that "the emotional reaction usually terminates in the subject's own body, whilst the instinctive reaction is apt to go farther and enter into practical relations with the exciting object" (II 442). James's theory of emotion was actually the most revolutionary notion in *Principles*, and it generated a great deal of commentary. He argues that "emotion follows upon the bodily expression in the coarser emotions at least" (II 449). Though materialistic, James's conception aligns with dynamic psychology because it focusses on the *activity* of emotion. It also, as James himself notes, "makes us realize more deeply than ever how much our mental life is knit up with our corporeal frame" (II 467). James's physiological emphasis did not, as Gerald Myers observes, lead him to conclude that a person's inner life is unimportant (*W.J.* 228).

In fact, James increasingly attended to the nature of inner life after his masterpiece, *Principles*. In "The Hidden Self", published the same year as *Principles*, James argues for the urgent necessity of bringing together psychical research and abnormal psychology in "a comparative study of trances and subconscious states".[3] He outlined the contributions of psychical research in *The Will to Believe* (1897), consisting of popular, accessible essays on philosophy, that was reviewed by Virginia Woolf's father Leslie Stephen (Annan 250).

In his 1896 Lowell lectures, James attempted to summarize the relations between abnormal and exceptional states. While these lectures have only recently been published, they are important because they show that, by this time, James had developed a dynamic or, as he referred to it, "dynamogenic" psychology of the subconscious, a point neglected by traditional Jamesian scholars (Taylor, *W.J.* 10). According to Eugene Taylor, James defined dynamogenic as

> the movement of psychic energy – in pathology when energy is locked up and expresses itself through symptoms of depression, hallucinations, or explosive emotion; and in health when we go beyond our normal limits and tap those vital reserves of energy and power that each of us always holds in abeyance. (Taylor, *W.J.* 10)

In taking into account the dynamics of both illness and health, James owes much to Frederic Myers's twin concepts of subliminal and supraliminal.

James's dynamic view of the psyche informs his next major work, *The Varieties of Religious Experience* (1902), important for several reasons. It represents the first major integration of dynamic psychology with religion, defined as feelings and conduct associated with religious states, rather than dogma or theories. As William McDougall claims, prior to James's book, "psychology had been regarded as the natural enemy of religion" (McDougall, "In Memory" 93), but *Varieties* changed all that. Although James looks to the abnormal for better understanding of normality (James, *Varieties* 22), he avoids the reductiveness of previous medical approaches to religious behaviour:

> To the medical mind these ecstasies signify nothing but suggested and imitated hypnoid states, on an intellectual basis of superstition, and a corporeal one of degeneration and hysteria. Undoubtedly these pathological

conditions have existed in many and possibly in all cases, but that fact tells us nothing about the value for knowledge of the consciousness they induce. To pass a spiritual judgement upon these states, we must not content ourselves with superficial medical talk, but inquire into their fruits for life. (*Varieties* 413)

Partly because of this pragmatic emphasis, *Varieties* became immensely popular, and thus brought dynamic psychological discourse to the attention of a wide audience.

However, most significantly for present purposes, James explores further the fringes of consciousness, and their effect on personality and religion. James argues that the development of religious consciousness is affected by personality type and temperament, significantly by whether one has a healthy-minded or morbid-minded way of viewing life (*Varieties* 162–163). Furthermore, conversion experience is seen as the unification of a divided self. In order to understand this phenomenon, James examines the characteristics of the field of consciousness. Consciousness may expand or contract and has a margin: "Our whole past store of memories floats beyond this margin, ready at a touch to come in..." (*Varieties* 232). Taking Frederic Myers's subliminal concept as a basis, James claims that the subliminal region lies beyond the margin, and it is "the larger part of each of us, for it is the abode of everything that is latent and the reservoir of everything that passes unrecorded or unobserved" (*Varieties* 483). Though James believes that "it is the source of our dreams, and apparently they may return to it..." (*Varieties* 483), he is too pragmatic to argue that it is simply a source of strength. He notes that

That region contains every kind of matter: "seraph and snake" abide there side by side. To come from thence is no infallible credential. What comes must be sifted and tested, and run the gauntlet of confrontation with the total context of experience, just like what comes from the outer world of sense. (*Varieties* 426–427)

Instantaneous conversion, like automatism, is "an explosion, into the fields of ordinary consciousness, of ideas elaborated outside of those fields in subliminal regions of the mind" by people who "are in possession of a large region in which mental work can go on subliminally" (*Varieties* 235, 237). Similarly, mystical states spring from the subliminal or transmarginal region (*Varieties* 426). Though much of *Varieties* deals with the extremes of religious experience, James extends his hypothesis to ordinary people. In general, what James refers to as the "more" with which individuals come into contact in religious experience is partly the subconscious continuation of conscious life. He is less definite about what this more is on the spiritual side, but he posits the "overbelief" that a power larger than ourselves impinges on the subconscious (*Varieties* 515). He thus brought dynamic psychology, and in particular Myers's concept of subliminal, into a central position in his psychology and demonstrated the explanatory power subliminal.

In certain respects – notably in its exploration of the subliminal and multiple personality – *Varieties* can be seen as the third volume of *Principles*; however, it also represents a departure since he acknowledges more fully the limitations of positivism and of reason itself. His observation about the reality beyond the five senses is indicative of his stance:

> It is as if there were in the human consciousness a sense of reality, a feeling of objective presence, a perception of what we may call "something there," more deep and more general than any of the special and particular "senses" by which current psychology supposes existent realities to be originally revealed. (*Varieties* 58)

Since positivism proves inadequate to measure extraordinary phenomena, James opts for a piecemeal or pluralistic view, that the universe is multi-faceted and no one system of ideas is true. James asks,

> And why, after all, may not the world be so complex as to consist of many interpenetrating spheres of reality, which we can thus approach in alternation by using different conceptions and assuming different attitudes.... On this view religion and science, each verified in its own way from hour to hour and from life to life, would be co-eternal. (*Varieties* 122)

James thus provides a convincing depiction of both science's and religion's province, if not a reconciliation between the two. James demonstrates clearly psychology's relevance to larger questions, traditionally the domain of metaphysics. Dynamic psychology in particular could make sense of the seemingly disparate material of religious experience, often previously shrouded in mystery. Thus *Varieties* became an important work of dynamic psychology.

James elaborated on his pluralistic view of reality in *A Pluralistic Universe*, based on his 1908 Hibbert lectures at Oxford. In denying that the world is fundamentally one enormous, indivisible whole, pluralism directly opposed the idealistic monism then prevalent at Oxford, but the doctrine had several psychological implications as well.

James realized that the position he took in *Principles* that states of conscious-ness could not compound themselves did not correspond to the reality of the continuity and simultaneity of mental states. In order to acknowledge this reality, he had to either posit some spiritual agent that compounded mental states or admit the limitations of logic and the irrationality of life (*Pluralistic* 95–97). James opts for the latter and finds support in Henri Bergson's critique of intellectualism. The rationalist and the intellectualist know the world by concepts, but these abstractions

> quite fail to connect us with the inner life of the flux, or with the real causes that govern its direction. Instead of being interpreters of reality, concepts negate the inwardness of reality altogether. (*Pluralistic* 110)

Following Bergson, James turns to the world of sensation to discover features of the perpetual flux (James, *Pluralistic* 111). He examines closely the "passing moment", the minimal fact of sensation, and discovers that "inside of the minimal pulses of experience, is realised that very inner complexity which the transcendentalists say only the absolute can genuinely possess" (*Pluralistic* 128).

He enlists two philosophical methods in this examination. Pragmatism, which he first outlined in 1898, evaluated "ideas in terms of their dynamic significance – their consequences for concrete experience and practice" (Morris 26). The distinctiveness of ideas can be tested by their effect on the stream of experience, their potential for changing current realities, rather than on their relation to prior knowledge or eternal principles. Radical Empiricism, developed in 1904, focussed attention on the conjunctive and disjunctive relations between things, rather than on the things themselves or the terms or concepts by which they are expressed (Bird 66). The theory thus acknowledged the flux, and muddled, partial nature of experience. Concrete pulses of experience "run into one another continuously and seem to interpenetrate. What in them is relation and what is matter related is hard to discern" until the process of conceptualization takes over and creates order (*Pluralism* 127).

James's philosophy essentially examined reality in a more intimate way than had been done and shifted emphasis from object and concept to relations and the flux of experience. Although James's philosophical approaches were eventually eclipsed in philosophy by logical positivism, and in psychology by trends as diverse as behaviourism and individual psychology, many acknowledged a profound debt to James, including Bertrand Russell and Carl Jung. As the emergence of pragmatic societies suggests, James's philosophy also became very popular among more general audiences, though his arguments were often misinterpreted (Morris 5).

1.3.2.2   *The widening stream*

The significance of James's discourse on selfhood can be brought into relief by comparing his innovations with Freud's, especially since some concepts attributed to Freud had already been suggested by James. In the interests of brevity, I have summarized only essential differences, similarities, and debt.

The most fundamental difference in James's and Freud's thinking is that, whereas Freud believed that the key to psychic conflict lay in dream analysis, which led to his theories of sexuality, James distrusted any single overarching system. Freud's system emphasizes universals, is reductive, and reaches into the past of an individual's mental life, while James's theories tend to be partial, expansionist, and forward-looking in their emphasis on the necessity of purposive striving to develop selfhood.

Both psychologies view instinct as the basis of selfhood. Throughout most of his career, Freud maintained a dual instinct model, though these instincts changed from hunger and love in his early work, to sexuality, and then eros and thanatos in his later writing. James, however, posited a wide variety of instincts in man; many of these, including a child's instinct to suckle, as well as sexual passion, ripen at a certain age, initiate habits, and then fade away (*Principles* I 398, 403). Whereas Freud stressed that instincts are in conflict with reason and socio–cultural reality, James argued that instincts underpin our capacity to adapt to environmental challenges (Browning 165). The consequences of this difference are profound, for example in their contrasting perspectives on creativity. Where Freud depicted the artist as a neurotic who channelled his daydreams and fantasies into a socially acceptable end result, James saw the aesthetic instinct as natural, and the artist or writer as sensitive and highly sympathetic (Barzun 237). James also suggested a number of dynamic mechanisms of mind that Freud developed and systematized, including psychic conflict, inhibition of brain-energy and the function of a presiding arbiter, the latter two analogous to Freud's conception of resistance, repression, and the censor or super-ego.

Jung's assimilation of James's discourses is more direct, profound, and, therefore, easier to document than James's impact on Freud. In 1936 Jung acknowledged the significance of

> William James, whose psychological vision and pragmatic philosophy have on more than one occasion been my guides. It was his far-reaching mind which made me realize that the horizons of human psychology widen into the immeasurable. (Taylor, "James and Jung" 166)

Perhaps most importantly, James's thought guided Jung's when in 1911 he redefined libido to include not only sexual but also spiritual energy. Jung cited James's pragmatic rule that a theory should act as a "program for more work", as justification for expanding libido (as qtd in Taylor, "James and Jung" 163). James thus helped Jung to move back on to the line of thinking he had been developing before encountering Freud.

As well, Jung's psychological types elaborated on James's distinction in *Pragmatism* between tender- and tough-minded characters (Taylor, "James and Jung" 164). Jung's idea of a collective unconscious was shaped by his reading of James's early interpretation of Myers's concept of subliminal thresholds that extended from the bestial to the transcendent. James's formulation of the characteristics of consciousness, including the notion of "fields" and psychic fringes, and the action of memory impinging on the margin of consciousness, had great impact on Jung's view of the relation between the consciousness and the unconscious.

James's broad-minded vision, derived from his studies in psychical research, that abnormal phenomena could represent contact with a wider sphere of knowledge, also had an effect on Jung. Jung cited James's description of Mary Reynolds's double personality, in which her second personality was actually wiser and superior to her "normal" self (Taylor, "James and Jung" 158), and he continued to be interested in psychical research throughout his career. Perhaps most importantly, Jung adopted James's attitude that science consisted of a plurality of principles based on individual visions, analogous to religions (Taylor, "James and Jung" 165).

Not only did the wider framework for psychology that James espoused clearly shape both Jung's and Freud's thoughts, but it also had considerable impact on prominent English psychologists, including James Ward (1843–1925), G.F. Stout (1860–1944), both of whom were discussed earlier, and James Sully (1843–1923), the last-mentioned a probable influence on Virginia Woolf (cf. Chapter 6).

However, James's own writing functioned as a particularly strong nexus of ideas and tropes to the culture and, in particular, the literature of early modernism. Associations made from his discourses are often so subtle that their effect is not always as clearly recognizable as the presence of Freud's more dramatic, contentious discourse. Furthermore, as touched on, his thinking was absorbed by so many others that Jamesian ideas may well have been assimilated from secondary sources. In *Principles*, James explored human nature in a more complex way than had hitherto been done. "Normality" was not cleanly demarcated from aberration and abnormalities, but rather integrated with them. Less concerned with concepts, James placed more emphasis on genuine experience than most earlier psychologies. His practical appeal was strengthened by his vivid writing style. James's general view of the world as artistic creation was guaranteed to appeal to the artist. Similarly, his assertion that the mind functioned like an artist made artistic endeavour appear natural and fundamental (Barzun 71). Like the artist, the mind responded spontaneously and unpredictably to experience and shaped a vision out of that experience. It selected some details and rejected others in order to do so. James stressed that the mind was not composed of ideas corresponding with objects, but that it was characterized by relations, and relations were far more important in the work of art than the individual elements of composition.

Not only did James image the mind as artistic, but he offered many specific insights about human psychology that writers found invaluable. James highlighted aspects of consciousness that had been undervalued, such as its fluidity and dynamism. Subsequently, novelists attempting to construct a more intimate inner reality than had been done were faced with the challenge of imitating that fluidity. James pointed out how intensely personal each stream was, perhaps prompting writers to interrogate the effectiveness of omniscient narration and the veracity of readily identifiable character types. James's exploration of the anonymous, "in-flight" fringes of consciousness provoked writers to capture these in language. Algernon Blackwood's *The Promise of Air* (1918) is perhaps the most striking example of an attempt to render the transitive fringes using an extended trope of bird-in-flight, and Blackwood directly acknowledges James in the process (220). James's argument that a normal person possessed several selves intrigued novelists like May Sinclair. In her first novel, *Audrey Craven*, Sinclair depicts her rather bland protagonist adopting different selves depending on current influences (141).

James's intensive exploration of the enduring moment in time corresponded with writers' emphasis on the expanded moment. Three of the novelists under scrutiny convey these moments, Sinclair and Beresford terming them "mystical moments", and Woolf referring to them as "moments of being". James's suggestion of each moment's importance in evoking personality possibly contributed to making writers much more self-conscious about each descriptive detail included in a story, although direct causal links prove elusive.

James brought the role of memory and habit to the fore, as did several other psychologists, and these aspects of psychic functioning became powerful forces in early modernism. Even the tropes James used to describe memory, for instance, resurface in the fiction of the period. James speaks of words "fringed" in memory, sentences "bathed in that original halo of obscure relations" (I 266), and of how the memory of unusual impressions result in the "haunting of consciousness" (I 648), all metaphors frequently employed by several writers, including Algernon Blackwood, Sinclair, and Woolf, in whose work memory plays such an important role. In a more formal way in her *Defence of Idealism*, Sinclair considered very carefully the arguments of James, as well as Bergson and McDougall, that personal identity depends on memory (46). Sinclair and Beresford probe very closely the implications of habitual behaviour as a force almost as significant as heredity. Throughout Sinclair's fiction she portrays characters destroyed by the powerful force of habit, whether it is a habit of sensualism, as in *Mr. and Mrs. Nevill Tyson* (1898, 242) (where she first directly cited *Principles of Psychology*), or more frequently the habit of repressing feelings, as in *Two Sides of a Question* (1901, 82), *The Three Sisters* (1914), *Mary Olivier* (1919), and *Harriet Frean* (1922). In Beresford's first novel, *Jacob Stahl*, the protagonist's mother's habit of procrastination initiates the crisis leading to the protagonist's lameness.

James's legitimating of psychical research contributed to its inclusion in a wider conception of the realistic novel. As early as the 1880s, William's brother Henry identified as his fictional project "the great extension, great beyond all others, of experience and of consciousness" (as cited in Banta 57). Algernon Blackwood similarly claimed that his "fundamental interest" was in "the extension... of human faculty" (qtd in Penzoldt 229).

James's pluralism and pragmatism reinforced writers' awareness of the partial nature of experience and truth. Sinclair's *Audrey Craven*, for instance, privileges pragmatist Flaxman Reed's worldview. Of all males influencing Audrey, Reed might have helped her mature because "he did not want to overwhelm her with dogmas – mere matter for the intellect – he would prefer her to accept some truths provisionally and see how they worked out. He wanted her to see that it was a question of will" (137).

Pragmatism reinforced the romantic emphasis on process, without necessarily asserting the irrationality of the world; instead it highlighted human effort. Don S. Browning comments that James's normative image of the good life comprised "the strenuous mood" (13), the self's active engagement with life. He adds that "James believed life must be lived in alternating rhythms of ethical action and relaxation, strenuous moral effort and mystical contemplation" (36). Sinclair frequently examines characters leading the strenuous life, with varying degrees of success. In *The Helpmate* (1907), the perceptive Dr Gardner possesses "a strenuous soul" (225), and advocates a perpetual striving after ideals, but he also has a dreamy, mystical side (62). Sinclair's 1908 novella, *The Judgement of Eve*, in contrast, portrays a protagonist's unsuccessful reaching after the strenuous life after she rapidly bears six children, causing her soul to pass "beyond strenuousness to the peace of dullness" (58).

James's pluralism corresponded well with the techniques of the more experimental Modernist writers, including Virginia Woolf. If only a portion of reality could be known, which might or might not be a totality in itself, then first-person narration, the *bildungsroman*, stream of consciousness, open-endedness, and even fragmentation could more closely represent reality than traditional narration.

James's struggle between introspection and scientific objectivity aligned with the modernist tension between entering a character's stream of consciousness and maintaining a distance, as Joyce's *Portrait of the Artist as a Young Man* strikingly illustrates. Joyce gets closer to Stephen's subjective experience using an imitative prose structure, and yet ironically has Stephen espouse an image of the supreme artist remaining "invisible, refined out of existence, indifferent, paring his fingernails" (215).

Overall, James provided writers with a much wider conception of human psychology than had previously appeared, as well as a deeper understanding of, and language to articulate, the dynamics of inner reality.

1.4 Henri Bergson: The metaphysics of selfhood

The metaphysical psychology of Henri Bergson (1859–1941) also captivated the imagination of English psychologists and culture in general just prior to

First World War. In the cascade of enthusiastic accounts which followed the translations of his most important works, *Time and Free Will* in 1910 and *Matter and Memory*, *Creative Evolution*, and *Laughter* in 1911, Bergson was alternately hailed as the revolutionary harbinger of "the new philosophy" (Baillee 2; Le Roy 3) or "the new psychology".[4]

Though these claims exaggerate, Bergson's neo-Romantic vision was refreshing and either had a direct impact on or shared several characteristics of the discourse on dynamic British psychology then developing. He showed the limitations of idealism, realism, and associationist psychology because of their dependence on abstract concepts, which distort concrete reality. Like James's philosophy, Bergson's was less a system than a method which recognized the need to account for the empirical facts of psychology, but also insisted that psychology must transcend empiricism to address metaphysical issues. James's and Bergson's mutual, active interest in psychical research reflects this expansionist view. Both rejected psychic atomism and described psychic process as a dynamic continuum (Rao 4). They also reaffirmed common-sense views (Kitchin 6; Stephen 11; Rao 13), for example, of the "essentially utilitarian character of our mental functions" (Rao 5).

Karin Stephen (Virginia Woolf's sister-in-law), in *The Misuse of Mind. A Study of Bergson's Attack on Intellectualism* (1922), observed that Bergson's pragmatic and yet intuitive approach to knowledge became immensely popular in England because of a general distrust of systems and logical constructions there (Stephen 10). However, he also appealed because of his poetic writing style, in which he applied metaphor to make metaphysical problems vivid. Though he often lamented the limitations of language, his philosophical discourse proved a rich source for writers in particular, since he articulated an aesthetic by continually comparing his fine analysis of inner states with the aims of the literary artist. A sketch of Bergson's topics bearing on selfhood – time, space, consciousness, memory, creative evolution, psychopathology, psychical research, and aesthetics – will make clearer his contribution to dynamic psychological discourse as well as his appeal to writers.

In *Time and Free Will*, Bergson attempts to refute determinism by demonstrating determinists' confusion about the characteristics of time and its relation to space. Essentially, Bergson argues that time is real, but only as conceived by memory, not by physics (Kolakowski 2). This idea of time, or "*durée*", builds on William James's and James Ward's conception of duration, the direct sensation that time is enduring for a maximum of about twelve seconds immediately after it has passed. Duration thus involves a little of the past, present, and future, all imperceptibly shading into one another. Whereas James and Ward's conception implies that duration exists in space, that it has extensity, Bergson argues that pure *durée* lacks quantity. If measured, it becomes spatial, rather than pure time. *Durée* is, therefore, not tied to matter, existing completely in the spiritual realm. Associationist psychologists err because they conceive of psychic states as successive and external to one another, linked as in a chain. Pure *durée* is, rather, qualitative and indivisible, as is felt in dream states (*Time* 101, 126). Bergson concludes that there are two kinds of time, distinguished by two forms of multiplicity: quantifiable, homogenous time, given spatial characteristics; and qualitative, heterogenous time which could only be symbolically represented in space (Kitchin 51).

Bergson's vision of time conditions his approach to consciousness and the self. In general, consciousness is web-like (Kitchin 68) because of its interpenetrating strands, but it is also completely mutable and fluid (Cunningham 97–98). The two kinds of time correspond with two aspects of our consciousness, one which is

> clear and precise, but impersonal; the other confused, ever changing, and inexpressible, because language cannot get hold of it without arresting its mobility, or fit it into its commonplace forms without making it into public property. (*Time* 129)

Furthermore, these two forms of consciousness are functions of two selves: a superficial or social self, imaged as sharply cut crystals (*Intro* 9–10), which

> comes in contact with the external world at its surface; our successive sensations, although dissolving into one another, retain something of the mutual externality which belongs to their objective causes...(*Time* 125);

and a

> deep-seated self which ponders and decides, which heats and blazes up,[ ] a self whose states and changes permeate one another and undergo a deep alteration as soon as we separate them from one another in order to set them out in space. (*Time* 125)

Virginia Woolf, for one, seems to have drawn on this conception of two forms of consciousness and two selves, which are really continuous with one another, beginning with her character Hewet's recognition of two layers of existence in *The Voyage Out* (*Voyage* 278) and continuing through to Mrs Dalloway's self-conscious construction of a "dart-like", "diamond" social self (*Mrs. Dalloway* 32). Bergson's model is analogous in some respects to distinctions made by other dynamic psychologists, including Frederic Myers's between subliminal and supernormal and Freud's between conscious, preconscious, and unconscious. However, in opposition to Freud's views, Bergson's identification of these two selves (corresponding to two times) is the foundation on which he builds his argument for free will. Whereas determinism argues that, given identical conditions, an event can be repeated, Bergson argues that this cannot happen because the centre of consciousness, in the deep-seated self, consists of pure *durée*. If successive moments of its experience could be isolated, it would be seen that they each contain the entire past, and that, therefore, each one is different (Kolakowski 20). The self is thus continually absorbing more past and can never return to a former state. Each act or experience is, then, free, since it cannot be predetermined by past acts or experiences.

Bergson consequently stresses memory's importance in consciousness, even claiming that consciousness means memory (as qtd in Kolakowski 25). In *Matter and Memory* (1913), Bergson shows that memory has two main functions. Its primary one is "to evoke all those past perceptions which are analogous to the present perception" (299). In so doing, memory lends a subjective character to perception (*Matter* 80). Memory also contracts those numerous past moments of duration into a single intuition. Each one of these intuitions of memory is unique, suggesting that memory is not merely a brain function (*Matter* 315). Bergson supports this argument using abnormal cases of impaired memory. States of dementia and aphasia show that the brain acts only as the transmitter of memory, not the repository of memory itself. In these states the transmitters and selection devices become damaged, but the amounts and types of memories lost indicate that memory as the sum of past experience is not destroyed (Kolakowski 47). Bergson thus uses the example of memory to demonstrate the existence of spirit, independent of matter.

Bergson's most widely read and influential work, *Creative Evolution* (1911), likens these qualities of consciousness to the characteristics of the universe. The dynamic energy of consciousness is a product of what Bergson terms the *élan vital*, which one commentator, Kolakowski, has summarized as

> the original energy that, by infinite bifurcations and wrestling with the resistance of matter, produces higher and higher variations of both instinct and intelligence. Something of this original impulse is preserved in all species and all individual organisms, all of them working unconsciously in its service. (57)

As in consciousness, in life there is continuity of change, preservation of the past in the present and real duration. Both consciousness and life, or evolution, are creative in the sense that both continually give birth to new forms, which are incommensurable with their antecedents and, therefore, cannot be predicted (Kolakowski 56).

Bergson's view of life as the struggle of spirit to overcome the limitations of matter made him very open to the aims of psychical research and affirmative of its findings. In his Presidential Address to the London Society for Psychical Research in 1913, he argued that the facts about psychical phenomena ought to be determined, since these resemble scientific facts, in that they can be repeated and are subject to laws (Rao 162–163). Psychical research had excelled in investigating the fringes of perception, which enter into consciousness in exceptional cases or predisposed subjects (Rao 165).

Bergson's metaphysical psychology engaged literary figures for a number of reasons. His conception of life as unpredictably changing resembles an artistic creation more closely than a machine's operation (Kolakowski 58). Consciousness is creative since it is constantly generating totally new experience. Because experience goes beyond reason, Bergson elevated intuition as a means of knowing reality, over intellectualizing. Language generally prevents knowledge of reality and contributes to intellectual distortion since it obscures and limits experience by artificially defining it, and so separating it into elements. Bergson thus offered writers a challenge of capturing feelings in a perpetual state of becoming, without letting language cover over, or make impersonal, the delicate and fugitive impressions of individual consciousness (*Time* 131). Artists, however, through their intuitive capacity could restore to feelings and ideas "their original and living individuality" (*Time* 164). Furthermore, Bergson suggested that artists were more capable of attaining freedom than many others because their creative acts sometimes sprang from and expressed their whole personalities (*Time* 172). Not only did Bergson acknowledge that art originated in the deepest levels of consciousness, but he asserted that art is a powerful force because it makes us open to suggestion, and is thus comparable to the act of hypnosis (*Time* 14).

Bergson also offered numerous specific insights about the psyche that were potentially adaptable to fiction. Bergson placed more emphasis than other psychologies on the role of memory, particularly in contracting similar past moments into a present intuition. He made it clear that consciousness, as well as life, was in a continual process of flux. The self was similarly fluid and its evolution irrational (Cunningham 113). If, as Bergson claimed, the whole personality can be found in each moment of consciousness (*Time* 165), then each psychological detail of a narrative had to reflect that personality in order to approach reality. May Sinclair, J.D. Beresford, and possibly even Virginia Woolf found in Bergson confirmation of a number of their conceptions, including those about consciousness, memory, and the idealistic belief in a wider, unseen reality independent of matter. Both Sinclair and Beresford have characters reading Bergson's *Évolution Créatrice*, Sinclair as a means of showing a character attempting to sublimate her passion (*The Three Sisters*, 1914, 347) and Beresford as an exceptionally profound text in his child genius' education in *The Hampdenshire Wonder* (1911, 236). As well, Sinclair presents an aspiring writer as the living embodiment of Bergson's *élan vital* in her novel *Tasker Jevons* (1916). Overall, Bergson's work drew attention to the need for a finer portrayal in fiction of the dynamic processes of consciousness and the psychic fringes of consciousness. His inclusive view of human psychology accorded a place for the spirit in a world dominated by determinism and Darwinian evolutionism.

1.5 William McDougall: The Social Psyche "here and now"

A more systematic thinker than Bergson, William McDougall (1871–1938) developed the first comprehensive dynamic psychology in Britain. Compared to James and Bergson, his wide-ranging work has more completely and unjustly been displaced by Freudianism. His hormic, or instinctually-based purposive psychology, created independently of psycho-analysis, receives no mention in histories of psychodynamic thought or the "new psychology", although McDougall's introduction of it in *Social Psychology* (1908) was equally as ground-breaking as Freudian doctrine. It rivalled, if not surpassed, Freudian theory in influence on the direction British psychology took for several decades, as psychologist Sir Cyril Burt recognized:

> To McDougall both British psychologists and British psychology owe a vast debt which has never been fully recognized.... In other countries, when psychology changed from a branch of philosophy to an experimental science, it adopted the general materialistic basis that had become so popular among scientists toward the close of the nineteenth century. The fact that this did not happen in Britain is due primarily to McDougall. He was the first experimental psychologist which this country produced. Yet, unlike many who followed him, he never became *purely* an experimentalist. Indeed, he was forever emphasizing the limitations of the mechanistic approach. (as qtd in Van Over 26)

The breadth of McDougall's psychology resembles that of his principle influences, William James, Lloyd Morgan, and G.F. Stout (McDougall "Autobiography" 200). McDougall began by studying psychophysics, quickly became disillusioned with its limitations, pioneered the study of the social environment's impact on the self, and proposed a theory of animism which postulated a goal-directed soul. Most importantly in the present context, he kept questions of spirituality and immortality within the realm of psychology through his life-long dedication to psychical research, which he elevated to a new level of sophistication. McDougall played a crucial role in disseminating dynamic psychological discourse, since he published many accessible books on various aspects of current psychology filtered through his critical viewpoint. These include *Psychology, The Study of Behaviour* (1912), *An Outline of Psychology* (1923), *The Energies of Men. A Study of the Fundamentals of Dynamic Psychology* (1932), and *Psycho-analysis and Social Psychology* (1936). This discussion will focus on a few of his most important innovations.

In *An Introduction to Social Psychology* (1908), McDougall bases his "dynamic, functional, voluntaristic view of mind" (16) on the relation of instincts to mental processes. Whereas earlier moral philosophers up to Henry Sidgwick had assumed that man normally acts reasonably, McDougall postulates that the evolutionary process determined mankind's impulses (*Introduction* 10). The problem of psychology is, then, to determine how man came to act morally, and the answer is through "the moulding influence of the social environment" (*Introduction* 16). In his view, primary instincts include flight, repulsion, curiosity, pugnacity, self-abasement, and self-assertion. Each of them conditions a specific, primary emotion (*Introduction* 47). As these emotions conflict, then interact, and are modified by the social environment, they become organized into more complex sentiments. The sexual instinct, innately connected with the parental instinct, is not directly linked with an emotion, and "its specific character remains submerged and unconscious" (*Introduction* 82). The self-regarding sentiment forms the basis of the self, which develops through interplay with the social environment. Thus McDougall's system places new emphasis on social factors.

McDougall's general introduction to *Psychology, The Study of Behaviour* (1912) deserves mention since it provides an outline, from a typical British perspective, of the "fruitful field" of abnormal psychology and because it was enormously popular, selling close to 100,000 copies (Autobiography 210). McDougall credits the French school with having made the study of hysteria and allied conditions scientific (*Psychology* 196). The field owes more to Pierre Janet than to anyone else for his conception of a synthetic energy that, unless defective, keeps the stream of mental activity unified. Freud, cited for the first time by McDougall, has "further enriched" the study of pathological states of mind (*Psychology* 201) by "bringing morbid psychology into fruitful relations both with normal psychology and with the study of mental states and processes that are abnormal without being morbid" (*Psychology* 211). McDougall identifies repression as Freud's most novel idea. However, he interprets Freud in his language and through his concern about society's role in the development of morality, claiming that

> the fundamental fact from which the [Freudian] theory starts out is that our organized conative tendencies are apt to come into conflict with one another, producing what we called moral struggles. (*Psychology* 202)

In a typically British response to Freud, he observes that Freud's "hypotheses are by no means generally accepted" (*Psychology* 202), and he criticizes those "most enthusiastic exponents" of Freudianism who "have gone too far in asserting that every dream is determined by the subconscious working of a repressed tendency..." (*Psychology* 205).

Most strikingly, however, McDougall makes the typical link between abnormal psychology and psychical research:

The study of abnormal psychology has thus become a field in which it is sought to find empirical evidence for two of the most ancient and widely held beliefs of the human race; namely, the belief in the survival of human personalities after bodily death, and the belief in the communion of human with divine mind. (*Psychology* 224)

He then goes on to explain how the "well-known Society for Psychical Research" has provided empirical support for each of these beliefs (*Psychology* 222). As an active member of the Society from 1901, McDougall fully sympathized with their aims, but he maintained a tough-minded scientific attitude towards their findings (Autobiography 219). He was just as interested in Myers's conception of the supernormal, which revealed positive, transcendent subconscious operations, as he was in the morbid. Furthermore, in *Body and Mind* (1911), he had argued that "...animism is the only solution of the psycho-physical problem compatible with a belief in any continuance of the personality after death..." (as qtd in Van Over 17). His version of animism centred on the soul, "a concept more or less summed up in the phrase 'unity of consciousness'" (as qtd in Van Over 18). Unlike earlier pan-psychists such as Fechner, however, he rejected the concept of a universal consciousness.

Thus, for McDougall, as for several other prominent British psychologists, psychical research was integral to psychology, since it provided evidence to address the psychological aspects of larger metaphysical issues. As historian of psychical research Janet Oppenheim remarks, deceased psychical researchers like Edmund Gurney and Frederick Myers "would have delighted in the knowledge that one of the creators of social psychology was building upon foundations furnished by the SPR" (Oppenheim 264).

Though McDougall – independently of Freud – had emphasized the role of instincts, conflict, and subconscious activity in mental life, and had early on appreciated Freud's contribution to knowledge about both mental disease and normality (*Psychology* 210), he became increasingly critical of Freudian doctrine. He could not accept the Freudians' insistence on the universality of the Oedipus complex (Autobiography 194–195), the existence of distinct entities like "the unconscious" and "the libido", the latter of which he refused to accept as the single source of instinctive energy, or what he regarded as "the fundamental doctrine of Freud's social psychology, that all social relations are sexual" (*Psycho-analysis* 29). He also became annoyed at the public's uncritical absorption of sensational doctrines, including Freudism: "What the public likes is to be told straight-forwardly that it has an Unconscious, source of all mysteries and all solutions; or a terrible Oedipal Complex, source of all disorders" (Autobiography 222). McDougall's animism and his defence of indeterminism were directly opposed to Freud's mechanistic, deterministic model of the mind.

Nevertheless, since he recognized the value in Freud's work (*Psycho-analysis* 17), he attempted to open a dialogue with the Freudians but was unsuccessful. To make matters worse, McDougall did not receive proper acknowledgement from the Freudians, even though Freud's forays into social psychology in the 1920s moved his system closer to McDougall's.

Despite the neglect, in his *Psycho-analysis and Social Psychology* (1936), McDougall welcomed Freud's modifications (105) to the conception of selfhood, including revoking the topographical aspect of the unconscious and adopting the super-ego, ego, and id because they did not imply such a wide gulf between conscious and unconscious activities as his earlier model had (*Psycho-analysis* 59–62). Also, McDougall viewed as progression Freud's recognition of non-libidinous instincts, notably aggression and death, to which he transferred some of the functions of the self-preservation and sexual instincts, and thus abandoned the dogma of the "all-efficient" libido. Most importantly, McDougall accurately observed that Freud's revised schema of mental structure bore a striking resemblance to the four successive stages of conduct outlined by McDougall in 1908:

> Freud's four "realms, regions or provinces into which we divide the mental apparatus of the individual", namely, the *id*, the ego, the super-ego and the ego-ideal (of which the second develops out of the first, and the third out of the second, and the fourth within the third) correspond to the four levels of function of my scheme: namely, (1) the purely instinctual level; (2) the level of control of the instinctive impulses which comes with increased range of foresight and the growth of self-consciousness and the concrete sentiments; (3) the level of self-conscious control and restraint of impulse that comes with the growth of the sentiment of self-regard or self-respect; (4) the topmost level which is achieved by the formation of the moral sentiments and an ideal of self shaped by the moral tradition. Freud's "ego" is, in short, what in my *Social Psychology* is called character; while his super-ego (with its ego-ideal contained within it) corresponds to what in my book was called "moral character".
> (*Psycho-analysis* 104)

Yet McDougall was still not completely satisfied, since Freud neglected other important instincts, notably fear and the tender impulse (the root of altruistic behaviour), and the role of sentiments, including respect and admiration, "which, at these higher levels of mental life, are the all-important dynamic factors" (*Psycho-analysis* 107).

McDougall also criticized other schools of psychoanalysis. He found Adler's system "ill-balanced" (Autobiography 222), but in typically British fashion favoured Jung. He recognized the importance of Jung's archetypal modes of thinking and distinction between introversion and extroversion, though he was sceptical about Jung's attempt to establish personality types on this basis (*Psycho-analysis* 109–110). He also came to doubt Jung's therapeutic procedure after undergoing an analysis with him (Autobiography 211).

Thus McDougall's work well illustrates the British propensity to extract what was sound and could be replicated from psychoanalytic doctrine, rather than to reject the new theories out of hand. More significantly, his 1908 *Introduction to Social Psychology* contained the essential elements of a dynamic psychology of selfhood, available to most British readers before psychoanalysis. If not as rich as its psychoanalytic competitor in its treatment of unconscious activities, conflict, and dreams (as McDougall admits in *Psycho-analysis* 103), in certain respects it accounted for phenomena, like social activity, which Freudian theory originally overlooked and eventually incorporated.

McDougall's impact, both on the discipline of psychology and on literary artists of the period, is not less significant. Hearnshaw claims that, above all, British psychology was largely shaped by McDougall's *An Introduction to Social Psychology*, reprinted twenty-four times between 1908 and 1938. McDougall's postulation of

> a number of primary instinctive drives, developed, organized and canalized into "sentiments", integrated into character and a directing self – such was what C.K. Ogden in his *A.B.C. of Psychology* (1929) would have described as the nucleus of accredited opinion. (Hearnshaw, *Short* 212)

Since McDougall's views were so widely disseminated and accepted, it is difficult to demonstrate the impact of specific discourse on writers, but many of them would have found appealing his willingness to admit the limitations of materialism, his discerning attitude towards new psychological theories and his acceptance of psychical research as a legitimate avenue of inquiry. In common with prominent psychical researcher, F.W.H. Myers, McDougall was thoroughly immersed in, and drew upon, the English literary tradition. Both men idolized Wordsworth, whose *Prelude* epitomized introspective psychology in poetry (Van Over 11–12). That Romantic element in turn helped shape McDougall's view of man's essential irrationality and his belief in the positive activity of the unconscious, both of which would also have appealed to fiction writers. May Sinclair, probably the most widely read in psychology of any Edwardian novelist, refers to McDougall "as a classic authority – and on the whole, the clearest, simplest, and most convincing authority – on the behaviour of the psyche here and now" (*Defence* 84). She drew on his work extensively and supported his revitalization of the concept of a soul, but opposed his version of animism.

Though McDougall was hailed as a leading psychologist at his death, his increased involvement in psychical research in later life, in particular his advocacy of it as a university study, and his unpopular Lamarckian "conviction that he had experimentally proved that acquired characteristics can be inherited", all contributed to his neglect by historians of psychodynamic theory (Shepard 202). Also, though McDougall was as controversial a figure as Freud, he, like the other important British psychologists discussed, did not gather around him a band of adherents to disseminate his doctrine as did Freud.[5]

1.6   Pre-Freudian dynamic psychologies

Thus, by 1913, when *The Interpretation of Dreams* appeared, Freud's first book published in England, discourses contributing to dynamic psychology had proliferated. An energetic debate on the dynamics of selfhood was available to fiction writers to interrogate and assimilate into their work. From philosophy, idealism contributed a construction of the self as active, unitary, and spiritual, that is, able to glimpse absolute spiritual reality in moments of expanded consciousness; romantic philosophy complemented this view in some ways by articulating the dynamics of unconsciousness, notably in Herbart's conceptions of a threshold and repressions. In psychology, Butler, James, and Bergson emphasized the importance, to varying degrees, of memory in shaping selfhood. Both James and Bergson closely analysed the dynamics of consciousness, down to the finest perception, termed "duration" or *durée*, and recognized the existence of numerous selves in normal life. James and McDougall examined the activity of a variety of instincts, James claiming that instincts increased and decreased in intensity as needed, and McDougall showing how instincts condition emotions, which are modified by the social environment. Neither ignored the sexual instinct; Havelock Ellis exhaustively catalogued its varied manifestations without moralistic prejudice. All of the main discourses on selfhood acknowledged the flux of experience and continued to consider the soul or spirit as an important dimension of selfhood. Most engaged with psychical research as legitimate means of revealing that dimension. In fact, several discourses entertained psychical research as a potential means for uncovering the fundamental question of psychology, whether man's personality survives bodily death? These discourses invariably expressed a distrust of overarching systems of thought, and instead embraced an eclectic garnering of insights. Dynamic psychologists tended to adopt a discerning attitude towards Freud's ideas, integrating those that fit with the available evidence.

Since psychological discourse received an enormous impetus from abnormal or medical psychology and psychical research, as has already been intimated, these fields require closer examination.

2
Medicine, Mental Science, and Psychical Research

Since the histories of medical psychology, mental science, and psychical research have become subjects of vast and controversial discourses, this chapter attempts only to highlight key developments within each field which had the most profound implications for dynamic psychology and which most engaged fiction writers. The rise of debates on psychosomatic illness and pathological states of mind transformed the discourse on selfhood in several essential ways. The conception of a single, unified self was increasingly called into question, and the boundaries between normal selfhood and abnormality became blurred. Mental science emphasized that abnormal conditions could arise in the so-called normal life. This focus contributed to inculcating widespread cultural anxiety about mental instability or nervous illness. In order to understand and heal these conditions, mental scientists developed new therapies, including hypnosis and psychotherapeutics in general. Not only pathological conditions and therapies but also those treating these conditions with the new therapies, the psychotherapists, were scrutinized in fiction. Writers initially portrayed them as having considerable powers of insight and healing, and certainly more than the older type of medical doctor whose approach was based on scientific materialism. The new doctors were typically referred to as doctors of the soul or psychic doctors, and might even be granted supernormal capabilities. Their relations with patients were of considerable interest, and only later when abuse-of-power stories emerged in the media was there scepticism and satire directed at these figures. This chapter begins by focussing on hysteria and hypnosis before highlighting the impact of Pierre Janet, yet another underrated figure whose discourses on medical psychology were frequently assimilated by fiction writers.

2.1 Medicine: Hysteria and hypnosis

Interrelated developments in the study of hysteria and hypnosis are the key contributions of medical psychology to dynamic psychology. The phenomenon of hysteria challenged fundamental assumptions about the nature of disease, eventually forcing medical professionals to shift from focussing exclusively on somatic aspects of illness to paying closer attention to the patient's psyche (characteristic of dynamic psychology). Diagnosis of hysteria also led to the further development of hypnosis, which became the primary tool for analysing non-conscious layers of the mind and led to more precise mapping out of these regions. Sigmund Freud was only one of many lured away from the study of neurology by the rising interest in these "abnormal" mental conditions. In Britain, the controversy over hysteria and hypnosis clearly reveals the shift in paradigms that was taking place, as well as, once again, the crucial role of the SPR.

In general, nineteenth-century medicine, with its pragmatic focus on description and diagnosis, was less engaged with philosophical discourse and more engaged with scientific materialism than the burgeoning discipline of psychology. The revolutionary germ theory of disease, which led to the discovery of cures for several infectious diseases such as typhoid, gave impetus to the materialistic bias (Drinka 62). Not until discourses about subconscious activity began to gain acceptance did medicine make a significant contribution to dynamic psychology. Hearnshaw claims that

> as long as mind was identified with consciousness, as it was by Descartes and his successors, the 'alien' forces responsible for mental breakdown could not be located within the mind itself; they had to be regarded either as material or as supernatural. (*Short* 150)

The story of the gradual acceptance of hypnosis and hysteria into medical orthodoxy is crucial to an understanding of that shift in perspective.

Mesmerism, the eighteenth-century forerunner of hypnotism, posited that a fluid called "animal magnetism" coursed through the body: its flow was disturbed in illness. Franz Mesmer, the French originator of the theory, believed that by putting patients into a trance and then precipitating a crisis in them, he could transfer into them his own healthy animal magnetism (Drinka 127–128). Although magnetism became immensely popular, it remained on the margins of science and eventually was banned in France (Drinka 131). Renewed interest in mesmerism did not occur until the late 1840s in the United States. While in a trance state, one Andrew Jackson Davis dictated revelations about the world of spirits (Ellenberger 83). Other incidents of paranormal communications were reported, engendering the Spiritist movement. Spiritism quickly spread into Europe, where its manifestations were eventually examined more systematically by the SPR, among others.

In the wake of this popularity, mesmerism, renamed "hypnosis" by an Englishman, James Braid (Drinka 133), came under scrutiny by the French medical community in particular. In the 1870s the world-famous neurologist

Jean Martin Charcot rediscovered hypnosis and applied it to his work on hysteria. Before outlining his view of the former, it will be helpful to consider briefly the history of the latter.

From ancient times until just prior to Charcot, hysteria had been considered a woman's disease related to the uterus and had latterly been thought to be the result of erotic cravings or frustrations. Briquet initiated the systematic study of hysteria in 1859 and found that hysteria did not have a sexual root, but that both hereditary and environmental influences contributed to its onset (Ellenberger 142). Charcot generally expanded on Briquet's ideas, but he realized that very often there was a sexual component to hysteria. He divided hysterical symptoms into two categories, the seizure and the stigmata, and he held impressive demonstrations using patients to show the various stages of the seizure. Aside from his detailed descriptions of hysteria, Charcot made two main contributions to the field. He located the cause of the illness, not in the uterus, but in a weak central nervous system. More importantly, based on investigations made in 1884 and 1885, he argued that a psychic trauma or shock, like the psychological effects of a railway accident, a death or rape, could precipitate the disorder (Drinka 100). Charcot's psychic trauma theory proved the most compelling for fiction writers, and from the 1880s on it was not uncommon to reveal a psychic shock at the root of a character's conflict or abnormal behaviour. May Sinclair's early fiction typically employs the psychic shock, most notably in *The Divine Fire* and *The Helpmate*.

Although Charcot initiated the shift towards a psychological model, he ultimately held that a hereditary taint and a weak nervous system, predisposed one to hysteria and to domination through hypnosis (Ellenberger 749; Drinka 101). Despite Charcot's dramatic demonstrations and powerful following, though, his position did not go unchallenged. In 1860, an obscure doctor named Liébeault had begun to hypnotize French peasant patients. He attracted the attention of Hippolyte Bernheim at the University of Nancy, who proposed that "hypnosis was not a pathological condition found only in hysterics, but it was the effect of suggestion" (Ellenberger 89). The Nancy school, as Bernheim's eclectic group came to be called, found that suggestions made to patients in a waking state were more effective than hypnosis. By the time of Charcot's death in 1893, their theory, supported by the successful results of suggestibility on thousands of patients, had thrown Charcot's ideas into disrepute. The Nancy school's triumph was crucial to dynamic psychology's development in two respects. Their conception of suggestion formed the basis of a "psychotherapeutics", which took into account psychological factors. Also, their realization that susceptibility to hypnosis did not depend on the condition of one's nerves (but was nearly universal) initiated the trend towards collapsing the gulf between abnormal and normal, a trend which prominent dynamic psychologists like Freud continued.

Nevertheless, Charcot had done much to bring hypnosis into scientific orthodoxy. He left his impress on dynamic psychologists like Pierre Janet, Frederic Myers, and Sigmund Freud, who made pilgrimages to Charcot's Saltpetriere lecture hall. His fame and clash with the Nancy school served to bring the discourses on hysteria and hypnosis to the attention of a larger audience than medical practitioners, notably fiction writers in both Europe and England. In particular, writers quickly explored and in some cases exploited in fiction the imaginative possibilities and consequences of one character using suggestion to influence another. The most popular and powerful evocation of hypnotism's misuse in English fiction was George Du Maurier's *Trilby* (1894). In it Svengali uses hypnotism to control Trilby, and transform her inept singing into that of a virtuoso's, through which he can manipulate her audience of thousands. Subsequent to the novel's huge success, hypnotists claimed in both Europe and America to demonstrate that inept singers could be thus transformed (P. Alexander 32–33). The hysteric became a stock figure in late nineteenth-century English fiction and was treated most directly and strikingly by the New Women novelists. They tended to interrogate the socio-political dimension of hysteria, to view it as a failed rebellion against social constraints on women, but some New Women novels like Sarah Grand's *The Heavenly Twins* (1893) questioned that construction as well (Heilmann 124). Early modernist novels tended more subtly to embed elements of discourses on hysteria and hypnosis into psychological narratives. Woolf's Rachel Hewet in *The Voyage Out* possesses hysterical symptoms, as do Sinclair's Miss Quincey in "Superseded" (1901) and Beresford's Helen Binstead in *Housemates* (1917).

2.2   Pierre Janet's dynamic psychology

Pierre Janet (1859–1947) began as a philosopher with psychological lean-ings, trained in medicine in order to pursue research in psychopathology, and later held appointments in experimental psychology. He represents yet another significant contributor to the discourse on selfhood who was eclipsed by Freud. Yet his work was frequently interrogated and assimilated by his fiction-writing contemporaries. His ideas on the subconscious, a term that he coined, multiple personality, the mechanism of dissociation, fixed ideas, and psychasthenia, along with his case studies illustrating these conditions and his method of treatment called psychological synthesis, became rich sources for novelists.

Before joining Charcot, Janet had established his reputation with hypnotic experiments on a girl called Leonie, beginning in 1885. Leonie could be hypnotized at a distance and would exactly carry out Janet's suggestions (Ellenberger 338). This case of multiple personality, or in Janet's term, successive existences, attracted such interest in England that a delegation of psychical researchers, including Frederic Myers, his brother, Dr A.T. Myers, and Henry Sidgwick, visited Janet at Le Havre. Leonie's case along with several others, analysed in *L'Automatisme Psychologique* (1889), provided the evidence for several of Janet's ground-breaking theories.

Janet contended that, as a result of psychological weakness, the "field of consciousness" of hysterical patients was narrowed. Parts of the personality, designated subconscious fixed ideas, were split off or dissociated from the rest and existed autonomously, and this discovery became his most influential. He also found that hypnosis could elicit two types of manifestations: a subject's role playing to please the hypnotist, and the appearance of an unknown personality or personalities possibly linked to childhood disturbance (Ellenberger 358). His conceptualization of psychic force and weakness underpinned the first full-fledged dynamic psychology (Ellenberger 361).

However, not until Janet joined Charcot's Salpetriere staff in 1890, and completed a medical degree, did he develop further his "psychological analysis". His method consisted of searching out pathogenic subconscious fixed ideas in his hysterical patients using hypnosis, automatic writing, or distraction. Unlike Bernheim, he did not believe that getting patients to forget original painful incidents cured them. Bringing these ideas to consciousness was not sufficient either because they would only become conscious obsessions. Instead, he attempted to reconstruct the illness's development and then to remove fixed ideas by dissociating them from their source. With one patient, Justine, he discovered that dissolving one main fixed idea was ineffective because other fixed ideas developed, which he named "secondary". He classified them as: derivative, resulting from associations to the main one; stratified, an unrelated idea resulting from an earlier period in the patient's past; and accidental, which were "new and provoked by any incident in daily life" (Ellenberger 368). Sometimes Janet transferred the affect associated with these fixed ideas to himself, and also attempted to re-educate his patients. He thus attended closely to the rapport between therapist and patient, first encouraging it and then gradually restricting it (Ellenberger 374). This "psychological synthesis", as he referred to the process, comprised one of the first talking cures, and marked the inception of a radical shift in perspective towards therapy.

Janet extended his theories about subconscious fixed ideas and dissociation to other ailments, including severe sleeplessness, but his main interest shifted to "neurasthenia", which he renamed "psychasthenia", since "neurasthenia" implied an unsubstantiated neurophysiological theory (Ellenberger 375). "Psychasthenia" incorporated both phobias and obsessions, and it differed from hysteria mainly in that fixed ideas were conscious rather than subconscious. Work on these neuroses led him to elaborate on his dynamic theory of psychic energy in terms of force and tension. Force, the capacity to mobilize psychic energy to perform psychological acts, and tension, the capacity to utilize energy at various levels of synthesis, should operate together to create an equilibrium. If they oscillate severely, pathology results (Ellenberger 378). This economic model of the psyche is too complex to do justice to here, but it is important to note that Janet constructed a system of therapy based on it which was flexible enough to deal with virtually any neurotic illness or patient (Ellenberger 386).

Throughout his adult life, Janet was fascinated by psychical research, having performed successful experiments with telepathy and suggestion at a distance, early in his career (Ellenberger 348). He kept an open mind about Myers's hypothesis that subliminal energies could be positive, claiming that he would like to see clinical evidence (Janet, *Psychological Healing* 258–259). For many years he was an active corresponding member of the British Society for Psychical Research and, like many psychical researchers, he hoped to reconcile science with religion through researching abnormal psychology.

The issue of Janet's influence is particularly complex. The publication of Janet's original cases preceded Freud's by several years, and Janet was generally regarded as a potential founder of a great school of psychopathology before Freud was known at all (Ellenberger 407). His discourse on subconscious fixed ideas and dissociation of personality had great impact on Myers's, William James's, Henri Bergson's, William McDougall's, Bernard Hart's, and Carl Jung's thinking about personality. The influence on both James and Bergson was reciprocal. Janet was particularly indebted to James's concept of psychic energy.[1] McDougall's focus in personality development on tendencies in conflict bears some resemblance to Janet's (Ellenberger 405). Jung's distinction between introversion and extroversion is based on Janet's classification of two main neuroses, hysteria and psychasthenia (Ellenberger 377). Jung's conception of "complex" was originally the equivalent of Janet's subconscious fixed idea (Ellenberger 406). In general, Janet, whose term "subconscious" gained widespread currency, is seen as the founder of modern psychiatry (Ellenberger 331; Drinka 346).[2]

Despite this tremendous impact, however, Janet's theories were almost totally obliterated by Freudian doctrine. On a number of occasions, aware of being unjustly treated, Janet argued that the Freudians had appropriated his theories. Freud, he maintained,

> changed first of all the terms I was using; what I had called psychological analysis he called psychoanalysis; what I had called psychological system, in order to designate that totality of facts of consciousness and movement, whether of members or of viscera, whose association constitutes the traumatic memory, he called complex; he considered a repression what I considered a restriction of consciousness; what I referred to as a psychological dissociation, or as a moral fumigation, he baptized with the name of catharsis. But above all he transformed a clinical observation and a therapeutic treatment with a definite and limited field of use into an enormous system of medical philosophy. (Janet, *Principles* 41)

Undoubtedly Janet's allegations contain some truth, which is, perhaps, part of the reason he was so virulently attacked by the Freudians, notably Ernest Jones in Britain (Ellenberger 408); however, this attack does not explain why Janet failed to propagate his terminology as successfully as the Freudians. Unlike Freud, Janet formed no school of disciples, but remained fiercely independent (Ellenberger 408). Also, he did not theorize as powerfully as Freud, nor was his system as comprehensive, a point Janet himself alludes to in the above quotation. Furthermore, in keeping with the bias of his day towards hereditary factors, he tended to locate the root source of neurosis in abnormal physiological make-up, which caused him to neglect the role of fantasy in mental illness.

Nevertheless, Janet's account of the psyche and its potential malfunctions quickly caught the fancy of imaginative writers. As Ellenberger has discovered, Janet himself holds the distinction of being probably the first European psychologist to be fictionalized, in Marcel Prevost's *The Autumn of a Woman* (1893; cf. Ellenberger 766–767). Though Janet was by no means the only researcher into multiple personality, his work inspired some of the many novels and plays on that topic which appeared in the 1880s and 1890s. In Britain, Janet's discourse provided an important source for the *fin de siècle* novel of morbid psychological analysis or pathological novel. Concepts such as dissociation and idée fixe, sometimes used judiciously and sometimes not, permeated these works. George Gissing, George Moore, and H.G. Wells wrote fiction touched by these discourses, as did a host of less well-known novelists, including Lucas Malet, W.L. George, and Hubert Wales.

May Sinclair was probably the first English writer to portray a therapist based on Pierre Janet, and his thinking permeated her work. In her 1901 novella "Superseded", Dr Bastion Cautley employs Janet's technique of "psychological synthesis" on an hysteric spinster teacher, not realizing that she develops a fixed idea of love for him ("Superseded" 289). Sinclair subsequently portrays a number of characters who have dissociated painful memories or feelings, with disastrous consequences. In *The Three Sisters* (1914), she has a doctor reading Janet's *L'État mentale des Hystériques* (*Sisters* 179). In *A Defence of Idealism* (1917), Sinclair made explicit the immense importance Janet's concept of dissociation had to her way of thinking. In describing the mystic sensibility, Sinclair claims:

> M. Janet's account of the matter in his *État mentale des Hystériques*, leaves us in no doubt as to what is happening here. He shows that the root of the neuroses and psychoses, of all mental maladies in fact, lies in dissociation: the break between one idea, or group of ideas and its normal context and logical connections; the cutting off of one psychic state, or group of states, from the stream of consciousness itself. This isolated and abandoned tract is the home of all the obsessions, the fixed

ideas, the morbid "complexes" unearthed by the psychoanalysts, the day-dreams and phantasies of neurotic and insane persons; it is the home of lapsed instincts and memories, of things forgotten because of their dreadfulness or simply because of their uselessness; it is our ancestral and racial territory, the place of our forgotten and yet undying past, of what has been conscious once, and is no longer conscious. (290–291)

In her unpublished essay "The Way of Sublimation", she similarly privileges a concept of Janet's as the overarching approach to psychological healing, under which is subsumed Freud's psychoanalysis: "psychoanalysis is only a means to an ultimate psycho-synthesis" (21).

2.3   Medical psychology in Britain

Since continental European medical practitioners like Janet often led developments in nineteenth-century medical psychology, their advances provide a necessary backdrop against which to view British idiosyncrasies. The British medical profession lagged behind its European counterpart until the 1890s because it deliberately rejected psychological approaches to mental disorder and thus a dynamic conception of selfhood. Several reasons have been proposed for this. According to Michael J. Clark, the British tended to believe that bodily disorders caused mental disorders, which restricted psychic autonomy and increased suggestibility. Hughlings Jackson (1835–1911), the most prominent nineteenth-century neurologist, asserted that it was necessary to be "brutally materialistic" in studying nervous disease (Hearnshaw, *Short* 71). Not only was psychotherapy considered futile, then, but "morbid introspection" might also exacerbate the problem (Clark 288–290). Doctors believed that their moral duty was to take charge of patients whose unsound minds rendered them irresponsible. The psychoneuroses, and in particular hysteria, were viewed as signs of moral depravity and morbid egoism. Thus, the doctor provided a moral example by which the patient could be re-educated (Clark 298). The laws about institutionalization entrenched this physiological and moral approach to insanity. Until 1915, individuals were prohibited from voluntarily admitting themselves to public lunatic asylums. According to Hearnshaw,

> An individual was either mad, in which case he was certified and compulsorily shut up, or sane, when nothing need or could be done about him. No half-way stages were officially recognized, and the early treatment of incipient breakdown was thus actively discouraged. (Hearnshaw, *Short* 145)

The strength of these impediments to dynamic approaches is important to note when the question of literary assimilation of medical discourse arises.

Those Edwardian and Georgian novelists, including May Sinclair and J.D. Beresford, who divorced psychic difficulties from morality in their characterization and who portrayed doctors as being concerned with their patients' psyches were far in advance of their time. Virginia Woolf, on the other hand, provided a damning critique of the old style moral approach to mental health, through Dr Holmes's and Sir William Bradshaw's attitudes towards Septimus Smith in *Mrs. Dalloway*, for example.

However, Clark overstates his claim that psychological approaches were consistently rejected; he bases it almost exclusively on evidence from the medical orthodoxy. He minimizes British pioneering achievements and does not pay enough attention to what he himself refers to as "the impeccably orthodox Society for Psychical Research" (Clark 282). Though few in number, the pioneers had a great effect on subsequent development.

Admittedly, hysteria was not studied much in England until about 1880.[3] British surgeon George Tate's early nineteenth-century postulation that hysteria resulted from defective menstruation held sway until then. Hypnosis fared slightly better during the nineteenth century and flourished in the final decades. James Braid (1795–1860), a Manchester physician, did not merely rename mesmerism but proposed the new theory that trances originated within the mind (Drinka 133). His views on hypnosis were not immediately accepted; however, by 1872, D. Hack Tuke (1827–1895), an influential specialist in mental disease, was praising Braid and encouraging the use of hypnotism, at the very least because it often controlled undesirable effects of mind on the body. More importantly, he advocated psychological approaches in the treatment of mental illness, and coined the term "psycho-therapeutics" in an attempt to make these approaches more acceptable to orthodox medicine (Ellenberger 765; Clark 281). In the 1870s, several other medical men began to practise hypnosis, notably Milne Bramwell, C. Lloyd Tuckey, and T.W. Mitchell (Oppenheim 248). These pioneers became SPR members after 1882. Essentially, the Society carried on the distinctively British approach to abnormal psychology initiated by Braid. In an 1896 article, "On the Evolution of Hypnotic Theory", for example, Bramwell, the biographer of Braid, makes clear that Myers's theory of hypnosis directly descends from Braid's (564–565). The Society not only promoted research into both hypnosis and hysteria, but became the main vehicle for disseminating information about the latest continental developments in medical psychology, as will be discussed later in the Section 2.5, Psychical research.

2.4 Mental science in Britain

The relatively new field of psychiatry, or "mental science" as it was then termed, was constrained by the same biases as orthodox medicine, but was in an even worse position in the late nineteenth century, since little research was being carried out in mental institutions. However, early in the twentieth century a new generation of mental scientists or alienists began to engage with eclectic continental discourses on abnormal psychology, including those of Janet and Freud.

One of the first, and most important, of these was Bernard Hart (1879–1966). Trained as a mental scientist, his wide scope led him to become the first Psychologist at University College and the National Hospitals (Jones, *Free* 99). His eclectic approach to Freudian doctrine and competing theories typifies the response of British mental scientists. Several of his articles introduced the latest dynamic theories to his alienist colleagues at the turn of the century, including one on Freud's theory of hysteria, important because it included a 281-item bibliography of "most of the works of Freud and his followers".[4] Although this article summarized even Freud's most controversial views on sexuality, it was really Hart's very popular *The Psychology of Insanity* (1912, reprinted twenty times in the next forty years) which most significantly shaped attitudes towards Freud in Britain. In its Preface, Hart carefully stated his position on Freud, whom he acknowledged was a genius:

> Although, however, I cannot easily express the extent to which I am indebted to him, I am by no means prepared to embrace the whole of the vast body of doctrines which Freud and his followers have now laid down. Much of this is in my opinion unproven, and erected upon an unsubstantial foundation. On the other hand, many of Freud's fundamental principles are becoming more and more widely accepted, and the evidence in their favour is rapidly increasing. (*Psychology* vi–vii)

Hart thus concentrated on Freudian conceptions that could be substantiated, including repression, projection, identification, and the role of fantasy in shaping the self. He also accepted Freud's claims that the lunatic's mental processes did not differ greatly from the normal (*Psychology* 40), that psychological determinism must be adopted (*Psychology* 58), that conflict was fundamental in precipitating insanity, and that conflicts were rooted in primary instincts. The book did not "deliberately omit[ ] any consideration of the sex instincts", as Hearnshaw claims (*Short* 167). Hart gives several examples of sex complexes (*Psychology* 103, 118) and even allows that the sexual instinct frequently lies behind conflict and mental disintegration, but he cannot concur with Freud that it is the sole source, based on the accumulated evidence (*Psychology* 166–167). According to Hart, the "herd instinct", a concept proposed by physician Wilfrid Trotter, can be another source when in conflict with primitive instincts (*Psychology* 168). In addition, Hart drew on Jung's idea of the complex and Janet's concept of dissociation. Jamesian discourse enters through Hart's repeated use of the stream of consciousness metaphor (*Psychology* 40, 45, 61, 98), as well as in his description of James's Rev. Ansel Bourne case of double personality (*Psychology* 48). *The Psychology of Insanity* set a trend among the mental science profession in its partial critical acceptance of Freud's doctrines and in its eclecticism. Increasingly, other alienists like Emmanuel Miller, Hugh Crichton-Miller (founder of the Tavistock), and Millais Culpin adopted similar attitudes to psychoanalysis, and orthodox Freudianism consequently never gained a large following in the first quarter of the twentieth century in English psychiatry. Nevertheless, Hart's work was also exceptional in that it garnered high praise, both from Freud, who claimed that Hart's paper on the unconscious was "the best on the damned topic of the unconscious I had read in the last years",[5] and from Freud's followers Ernest Jones and Edward Glover. The latter claimed that Hart did much in England "to introduce psychoanalysis to intelligent readers and the psychiatric faculty at large" (Glover 535). As will be seen in Chapter 3, the British public, as well as fiction writers, also seems to have adopted attitudes similar to the psychological and psychiatric professions, though they did not always interrogate Freudian theory with as sound reasoning.

In England a strong materialistic bias and entrenched professional attitudes slowed down developments in the selfhood debate, but by the 1880s a distinctly British discourse was evolving largely through contributions made by Braid, Hack Tuke, and the psychical researchers. In the following decades, British fiction writers assimilated a number of key ideas from medical psychology and mental science. They explored Charcot's theory of the psychic shock, which could precipitate a range of disorders, notably hysteria. The manifestations provided a rich source of conflicts within and between characters. Charcot's and Janet's case studies, among others, engaged writers like Sinclair. The challenge became to move beyond the stereotypes. Both the healing and the destructive implications of hypnosis were probed. Janet's concepts of subconscious, multiple personality, dissociation, fixed ideas, and psychasthenia had a particularly significant impact on fiction writers.

2.5 Psychical research

> Our method has revealed to us a hidden world within us, and ... this hidden world within us has revealed to us an invisible world without.
> (Frederic Myers, *Human* II 299)

Although links have been suggested between psychical research and the disciplines of philosophy, psychology, and medicine, it is now necessary to evaluate the full impact on dynamic psychology of the discourses generated by the SPR[6] as an entity. In brief, the SPR provided the British with the most complex and comprehensive native discourse on human psychology that they had ever possessed, prior to the development of McDougall's system. Since the SPR transgressed traditional professional boundaries, that discourse was assimilated by many individuals in diverse fields, including fiction writing. In forging a dynamic psychology, the SPR not only introduced Freudian discourse into England, but also introduced and provided a forum for the discussion of continental developments in dynamic psychology. By positing that insight could be gained into the supernormal and even the afterlife through psychological examination of the extraordinary, the SPR shaped the perceived significance and interpretation of findings. Although the SPR very nearly became part of mainstream psychology, its original contributions to dynamic psychology eventually conflicted with, and helped create resistance to, complete acceptance of Freudian theory. Paradoxically, however, psychical research was ultimately eclipsed by Freudian discourse, for a number of reasons to be considered.

In his history of British psychology, L.S. Hearnshaw claims that, "The links between psychical research and academic psychology in Great Britain have been few" (*Short* 241), and the relation between abnormal psychology and psychical research problematical (*Short* 157). However, the relation is only problematic if one plays down the SPR's vital role in shaping the burgeoning discipline of psychology. Links between the two were forged shortly after the establishment of the SPR in 1882, when Frederic Myers and Edmund Gurney were among the first (along with SPR members Milne Bramwell and C. Lloyd Tuckey) to rediscover and publish on hypnosis in England. The Society moved into a central position in the discipline of psychology through its involvement with the first four International Congresses of Physiological (later Experimental) Psychology. During the first, at Paris in 1889, Frederic Myers and William James discussed parapsychological phenomena alongside the pioneer experimental psychologists Theodule Ribot, Francis Galton, Hippolyte Bernheim, and Pierre Janet. At the second Congress in London in 1892, psychical researchers Henry Sidgwick and Frederic Myers served as President and Secretary respectively and, according to them, the majority of participants were sympathetic to the SPR (Oppenheim 245). Nobel-prize winning (1913) French physiologist Charles Richet claimed that

> To Myers the success of the International Congresses of Experimental Psychology at Paris [1889], London [1892], Munich [1896] and again at Paris last year [1900] was largely due. He compelled the adherents of the classical psychology and philosophy to pay attention to the new problems which he presented to them. (*Journal of SPR*, April 1901, 56)[7]

By 1896 the Society could boast that its members included the following eminent psychologists: Professors James, Ramsay, Beaunis, Bernheim, Bowditch, Stanley Hall, Ribot, Liegeois, Lombroso, Richet, and Stout; as well as the following Doctors: Max Dessoir, Fere, Liebault, Schrenck-Notzing, von Hartmann, and Janet. In the twentieth century, the Society added to its ranks Freud, Jung, Morton Prince, Cyril Adcock, Michael Balint, Sir Cyril

Burt, William Brown (SPR Council 1923–1940), J.C. Flugel, William McDougall (SPR Pres. 1920–1921), T.W. Mitchell (Pres. 1922), Ira Progoff, Joan Riviere, David Stafford-Clark, and R.H. Thouless (Pres. 1942), to mention only those most prominent in their fields.

However, lists which identify major involvement and interest do not explain how or what psychical research contributed to psychology, in spite of the latter's materialistic trend, and we need to glance at psychical research's origins in order to begin to answer these questions. Psychical Research was a direct response to the anti-scientific Spiritualist movement, popular in Britain from about 1852. When the SPR was formed in 1882 it determined to adopt rigorous scientific methods in studying psychic phenomena. Although the Society's original mandate covered spiritualism and physical manifestations, it gradually focussed more on non-material mental phenomena, largely because of the influence of a group from Cambridge University, led by well-respected philosopher Henry Sidgwick.

Two prominent members of this group, Edmund Gurney (1847–1888) and Frederic W.H. Myers, did more than anyone else to expand the territory of psychology to encompass evidence about psychic phenomena generated by the Society. In 1885 they wrote of their "hope to lay the corner-stone of a valid experimental psychology",[8] and in their major work, *Phantasms of the Living* (1886), they began the attempt. It amassed and categorized 702 cases, mainly of crisis apparitions, in order to prove the existence of telepathy, coined by Myers to describe communication from mind to mind by an agency other than the five senses (Gauld 162). Gurney died prematurely by chloroform overdose in 1888, but Myers continued to integrate the evidence for extensions of mental powers into a wide-ranging psychological system and yet one that admitted the limits of current understanding. He focussed initially on automatic writing, arguing that it suggests mental activity can be at least partially independent of the brain.

His study of this and other automatisms led to his developing a theory of the "subliminal self", the single most popular and influential contribution made by the SPR to British psychology. Myers proposed that

> the stream of consciousness in which we habitually live is not the only consciousness which exists in connection with our organism. Our habitual or empirical consciousness may consist of a mere selection from a multitude of thoughts and sensations, of which some at least are equally conscious with those that we empirically know. I accord no primacy to my ordinary waking self, except that among my potential selves this one has shown itself the fittest to meet the needs of common life. ("Subliminal" 301)

Below the threshold of ordinary, empirical consciousness, which he named the "supraliminal", was psychical action that he called "subliminal". The spectrum of consciousness in the subliminal extended from automatic physiological processes no longer required as part of memory in order to survive to psychic impressions "which the supraliminal consciousness is incapable of receiving in any direct fashion", such as telepathic and clairvoyant messages ("Subliminal" 306). Dreams, considered indicators of "intensified power", clearly demonstrated the simultaneous involvement of more than one level of subliminal consciousness. The subliminal consisted of "an aggregate of potential personalities, with imperfectly known capacities of perception and action, but none of them identical with the assumed individuality beneath them..." ("Subliminal" 308). These potential personalities or subliminal selves consisted of continuous chains of memory each with a distinctive character. Myers preferred "subliminal" to secondary self, which implied that only one other self could exist ("Subliminal" 305–306). Also, although the subliminal self could be diseased, it was not necessarily inferior to the supraliminal self, which the word "secondary" implies. On the contrary, Myers believed that messages from the subliminal self could indicate expansion and evolution of the personality, as found in the visions of genius ("Subliminal" 317). As well, Myers viewed the supraliminal as a spectrum bounded by organic functions and the highest efforts of reason ("Subliminal" 328). However, this spectrum was discontinuous, marked by gaps and interruptions in perceptions. By positing many different strata of consciousness both below and above a threshold point, Myers offered a more complex and balanced view of the psyche than had hitherto been proposed; it is worthwhile to examine some of the discourses shaping it, as well as to compare competing explanations.

Most strikingly, Myers's theory draws on James's conception of consciousness as stream. Myers inadvertently made the self seem even less substantial than James had by emphasizing the multiplicity of selves, each one potentially transcendent at any given moment. Myers also extended consideration of the potential capacities of personality. Unlike James, he claimed that what he called individuality supplied an underlying unity to personality, but this received scant notice. Similar to James in *Principles*, Myers's theory rejected the existence of an unconscious as misleading and unprovable.

In this and in several other ways, Myers's theory differed from Freud's economic theory of the psyche. Freud claimed that forces like resistance blocked access to consciousness from the unconscious, a repository of elements deliberately rejected. However, Myers, using an iceberg analogy hypothesized that

> Where the floating iceberg meets the sea there is no internal line of stratification. The proportion of submergence is determined by nothing in the iceberg's essential structure, but solely by the relation between the specific gravities of water in different states. Even so the water-line

between the empirical and the subjacent consciousness in man may be determined by no break of continuity in the processes which take place within him, but merely by the relation which his transcendental self bears to the material world in which it is immersed. (Myers, "Principles" 122)

What was above the threshold of awareness in a normal person depended on how well suited it was to meet the exigencies of everyday life.

Significantly, Myers's theory was the first to propose that secondary or subliminal consciousness need not be pathological, but is a normal and fundamental part of every individual. In this respect, he differed from Janet and Freud, believing that, in the pragmatic interests of developing cures, pathologists had neglected the psyche's positive potential, as demonstrated in genius.

In order to avoid charges of mysticism, Myers carefully based his theory on "actual phenomena observed and interpreted" ("Subliminal" 307), notably hypnotism and hysteria; his theory has implications for both. Myers did not view hypnosis as a disease nor as the sole consequence of suggestion, but argued that

hypnotism is not a morbid state; it is the manifestation of a group of perfectly normal but habitually subjacent powers, whose beneficent operation we see in cures by therapeutic suggestions; whose neutral operation we see in ordinary hypnotic experiment; and whose diseased operation we see in the vast variety of self-suggestive maladies. ("Subliminal" 309)

The phenomenon of hypnosis revealed several types of powers. Pain could be inhibited under hypnosis, its "great dissociative triumph" ("Subliminal" 329). Second, organic processes could be both produced and controlled, an associative or synthetic triumph. Third, intellectual or moral progress, such as the cure of kleptomania, could be achieved. These manifestations suggested, not only that consciousness encompassed more than formerly surmised, but that there was great potential for increased control over thought processes (what Myers referred to as patients' "self-suggestive power", "Subliminal" 352).

Myers's claim that hysteria represented dysfunction or disease of the mind's hypnotic stratum was equally ingenious since it explained why certain hypnotic and hysterical phenomena resembled one another. It also helped explain the recent finding that hysterics often proved difficult to hypnotize. In a review praising Myers's conception, Bramwell asked,

May not the difficulty of inducing hypnosis in the hysterical – of making one's suggestions find a resting-place in them – be due to the fact that the hypnotic substratum of their personality is already occupied by irrational self-suggestions which their waking will cannot control? ("Hypnotic Theory" 545)

Myers explored further the implications of his subliminal theory for understanding hysteria and its relation to genius in 1897. Building on Janet's conception, Myers claimed that "all hysterical symptoms... are equivalent to *idées fixes*; and a hysterical access is the explosion of an *idée fixe*" ("Hysteria" 55). However, departing from Janet, Myers argued that an *idée fixe* could be either positive or negative. Similarly, acquisitions as well as losses could occur in hysteria, a point supported by the phenomena of hyperaesthesia. If the acquisitions, or uprush from the subliminal self, over-powered the losses and resulted in some achievement, then hysteria became genius ("Hysteria" 56–58). Myers cited, among other examples, Robert Louis Stevenson's dreams, in which "the content of the [nocturnal] uprush was congruous with the train of voluntary thought" ("Hysteria" 57).

Myers's stance is important for several reasons. It precedes Freud's statements about the links between neuroses and genius. His stress on the psychological aspects of hysteria shows that this approach was not completely rejected, nor was mental illness always viewed as defect by the British. Finally, in statements like: the student of human personality "will justly argue that if we can trace a road by which man has gone downhill, we may be tracing a road by which man can also climb up. Processes of disinte-gration are lessons in integration" ("Hysteria" 51), Myers expresses a view of the human psyche similar to the one Jung would articulate in Britain a decade or so later. Though Myers's theories should not be seen as proto-typical of Jung's, they do help explain Jung's widespread acceptance since Myers had prepared the way.

For the rest of his life, Myers investigated the abnormal with the intent of illuminating normal potential and addressing the question of whether human personality survived death. His researches culminated in his masterpiece, *Human Personality and Its Survival of Bodily Death*, published posthumously in 1903. Myers self-consciously referred to the book as a "provisional systematisation" (vii), a synthesis of the latest findings in both psychical research and dynamic psychology. It focussed on what Myers termed "supernormal" phenomena, those which transcend ordinary experience but obey natural laws. The work's foundation was the "doctrine of telepathy", established to Myers's satisfaction as a "law of the spiritual or *metetherial* world" (8). Myers fleshed out earlier arguments on many other topics as well, including the composite, or as he termed it, "multiplex", "polypsychic" nature of personality (*Human* 34), dreams, genius, and apparitions, and he substantiated his claims by devoting over half of the 1360-page book to an exhaustive classification of cases. A discussion of dreams figured prominently as the starting point for examination of disintegrations of personality. Myers extended his theory about the relation between hysteria and genius to cover "moral genius", the "genius of sanctity", or that possession "by some altruistic idea which lies at the root of so many altruistic lives", especially religious ones (*Human* 56).

Human Personality received a great deal of critical notice, much of it positive, though not all. Professor of Metaphysics and SPR member G.F. Stout (Gauld 338), for example, argued that Myers's hypothesis of the subliminal self was "baseless, futile, and incoherent" (as qtd in Oppenheim 262). The subliminal implausibly acted as a "tutelary genius or a guardian angel", and its manifestations could be otherwise explained (as qtd in Gauld 294). As Alan Gauld claims, Stout misconstrued the subliminal since it is anything but a separate, unified entity and because it could just as easily fall prey to disease as the "empirical" self (295). William McDougall also felt that Myers had stretched the subliminal concept in order to support the hypothesis of survival. In other respects, though, McDougall praised the book, claiming that posterity would "accord to Myers a place in the history of the intellectual development of mankind" (McDougall, "Critical" 526). One of the most favourable reviews came from William James, who found the work "a masterpiece of coordination and unification" and claimed that Myers "shows indeed a genius not unlike that of Charles Darwin for discovering shadings and transitions, and grading down discontinuities in his argument" ("Review" 235).

Myers offered the English a distinctive, if controversial, dynamic psychology that attempted to address "the all-important problem of the existence, the powers, the destiny of the human soul" (*Human* 1). His impact on psychologists was considerable. William James summarized it in claiming "that Frederic Myers will always be remembered in psychology as the pioneer who staked out a vast tract of mental wilderness and planted the flag of genuine science upon it" ("Frederic Myers" 225). James owed much to Myers, particularly to his conception in 1886 of subliminal, which according to James is "the most important step forward that has occurred in psychology since I have been a student of that science" (*Varieties* 233). Myers's exploration of supernormal phenomena, most of which according to James are "rooted in reality" (*Pluralistic* 142), inspired James's examination of religious belief in *Varieties of Religious Experience* and his adoption of a pluralistic view of reality (*Pluralistic* 140). William McDougall similarly drew on Myers to refute the mechanist materialist model of mind, for example in *Body and Mind* (1911). Several of McDougall's students, including Sir Cyril Burt and J.C. Flugel, tested the implications of Myers's psychical theories alongside their rather diverse pursuits in psychology. Burt, a leading expert on child development and statistics, investigated telepathy and mediums throughout his life (Shepard 189). William Brown (1881–1952), an expert on mental measurement and creator of the first experimental psychology laboratory at Oxford, owed much to Myers's work. A long-time SPR member, Brown in *Psychology and Psychotherapy* (1922), for example, considered the implications of psychical research for psychotherapy. In 1932, Brown reviewed the evidence collected by the Society over the past fifty years and declared that it was "Sufficient to make survival [of the soul after death] scientifically extremely probable" (Shepard 182). As well, the SPR's medical section, formed in 1912, specifically tested and published on therapeutic applications of Myers's subliminal. These psychologists and physicians included Lloyd Tuckey, Milne Bramwell, V.J. Wooley, Constance Long (a translator of Jung), T.W. Mitchell, and William McDougall.

Other psychologists like James Ward and James Sully, not directly affiliated with psychical research, also felt its impact since they were forced to explain the phenomena that Myers had, with varying degrees of success, raised to the level of scientific status. At the very least his work served to keep a discourse on the larger ontological and metaphysical issues within the realm of psychology in Britain, even if through debate and controversy.

Despite Myers's impact, his model of the psyche was gradually supplanted by those of the newer dynamic theories, notably Freud's, though the reasons for this are not immediately apparent. Of all the psychical researchers, Myers was most influential in introducing Freudian discourse to a British audience. In the *Proceedings* of the SPR for June 1893, he made the first reference in English to Breuer's and Freud's preliminary account of hysteria, claiming that their perspective on the relation between hypnosis and hysteria fully supported his own ("Mechanism" 14). On subsequent occasions, Myers similarly derived support from Freudian case studies, which he interpreted in the language and structure of his subliminal theory (*Human* 50–56). He seems to have ignored any differences between his theory and Freud's, which in any case did not become significant until after Myers's death in 1901; certainly he could not have foreseen that Freud's view would eclipse his own.

Both Freud and Jung reciprocated the interest, and for their part took psychical research seriously, publishing several papers on the subject. Though Freud's attitude towards the phenomena remained cautious, even ambivalent (Ellenberger 534), he was delighted to be offered an SPR membership in 1911 and equated it with increasing English interest in psychoanalysis in a letter to Ernest Jones: "Do you think it is a sign of rising interest in psycho-analysis in your dear old England, that I have been invited to become a corresponding member of the London Society for Psychical Research? The names on their list are all excellent" (Letters to Jones, 26 February 1911, 4). Most extraordinarily, in 1921 he wrote to Hereward Carrington that "If I had my life to live over again I should devote myself to psychical research rather than psycho-analysis", though he later denied the claim (Jones, *Freud* III 419).

Despite Freud's ambivalent interest in psychical research, he and especially his followers made increasing efforts to dissociate psychoanalysis from it, and psychoanalytic discourse eventually eclipsed psychical research. Several explanations for psychoanalysis's triumph have been put forth. John Cerullo claims that the Freudian paradigm offered a more functional view of the self than the protean Myersian view, in that it provided clear under-standing of the way individuals were to deploy themselves in the modern world; this approach appealed more "to a mass society organized for functional efficiency" (168–169). However, this claim is only partially true, since Freudianism had its main impact on intellectual elites in Britain and was never embraced by the masses. More accurately, Freud's theory thrived not only because it arose from clinical observation, but because its motive force was directed towards developing diagnosis and therapeutic technique, a more functional aim than Myers's. Myers was not interested in treatment of psychic dysfunction since his goal was to reveal how occasionally diseased manifestations of the subliminal could reveal supernormal potential.

Furthermore, as has been the case with all unsuccessful rivals of Freudian theory discussed thus far, Myers did not attempt to attract a coherent group of followers in order to propagate his view of the psyche, and in fact hoped that his work would be "speedily" superseded (*Human* vii). The SPR as a whole never really manifested much concern about the differences between Freudian theory and Myers's conceptions, probably because it did not perceive the Freudian view as a threat to the beliefs that it was attempting to place on scientific footing.[9] In 1912, Freud contributed "A Note on the Unconscious in Psycho-analysis" to the *Proceedings* of the SPR. He argued that the concept of an unconscious better accounted for the observed psychical phenomena than theories which assumed consciousness could be split up, because consciousness of which one was not aware was an abuse of the word "conscious". Even after this alternate view appeared in the main SPR publication, the Society mounted no defence of Myers's subliminal self (Freud, "A Note" 315). Chance also appears to have played a role in the paradigm shift to Freudian dynamic psychology. The most prominent late nineteenth-century psychical researchers Henry Sidgwick and Myers died prematurely in 1900 and 1901 respectively. Myers had been the only researcher to attempt a synthesis of disparate phenomena, and his theoretical framework remained essentially unchallenged within psychical research until the 1920s (Cerullo 103).

Most importantly, I would argue that Myersian psychical research was in some respects more radical and subversive than psychoanalysis. Myers provided a challenge to the dominant materialist culture, whereas psycho-analysis tended to align with it, especially since Freud carefully avoided metaphysical questions, at least in his early work.[10] In the "Preface" to *Human Personality*, Myers wrote that he expected his subject to evoke "not only legitimate criticism of many kinds, but also much of that disgust and resentment which novelty and heterodoxy naturally excite" (viii). Myers had to overcome prejudice against extending scientific method into the traditional preserves of philosophy and metaphysics, prejudice which he called "scientific superstition" (*Human* 1). Psychical research had been attacked on these grounds since its inception, as Brian Inglis has documented. Carl Jung succinctly summarized that opposition, claiming that the psychical researchers possessed

> the immortal merit of having thrown the whole of their authority on to the side of non-material facts, regardless of public disapproval. They faced academic prejudices, and did not shrink from the cheap derision of their contemporaries; even at a time when the intellect of the educated classes was spellbound by the new dogma of materialism, they drew public attention to phenomena of an irrational nature, contrary to accepted convictions. (Jung, "Psychological Foundations" 76)

From another angle, Myersian psychology appeared subversive of traditional religious dogma, and Myers had to deal with criticism of it on these grounds as well (*Human* II 296–297). Furthermore, not only was the existence of the phenomena Myers drew upon frequently contested, but often these phenomena evoked repugnance and were associated with occult pursuits, charlatanism, superstition, and degeneration. William James felt strongly that

> the *great* obstacle to the reception of a *Weltanschauung* like Myers's is that the superior phenomena which it believes in are so enveloped and smothered in the mass of their degenerative congeners and accompaniments that they beget a collective impression of disgust, and that only the strongest of mental stomachs can pick them over and seek the gold amongst the rubbish. ("Frederic Myers" 238)

Myers's disinterest in developing techniques for transforming this degenerative material, as well as his various heterodoxies, may have ultimately caused his paradigm to lose ground to Freud's. After all, Freud's system focussed on individuals' adaptation to their social circumstances through sublimating base instinctual desires.

Nevertheless, the challenges Myers presented to various orthodoxies paradoxically held an appeal for creative writers who engaged with Myers's discourse and that of psychical research in general on a number of levels. In its attempt to grapple with the relations of body, mind, and spirit, to probe the ultimate questions of man's destiny, psychical research answered a deep-seated need in those for whom Darwinism and scientific materialism presented a bleak prospect and yet who could no longer accept the tenets of traditional religious dogma. From its inception, the SPR attracted the attention, and often the active participation, of many notable literary figures, including Tennyson, Ruskin, Lewis Carroll, Mark Twain, J.A. Symonds, Arthur Conan Doyle, Oscar Wilde, and W.B. Yeats. In the twentieth century, a diverse array of writers interrogated psychical research, including Grant Allen, J.M. Barrie, R.H. Benson, Algernon Blackwood, Marjorie Bowen, Goldsworthy Lowes Dickinson, E.M. Forster, Roger Fry, Radclyffe Hall, Aldous Huxley, Henry James, Rudyard Kipling, Lytton and James Strachey, Rebecca West, and the main subjects of this study: May Sinclair, Arnold Bennett, D.H. Lawrence, J.D. Beresford, and Virginia Woolf.

Literary historians and critics have tended to ignore or obscure the impact of psychical research on fiction, Julia Briggs, for example, claiming that psychical research "did not enjoy popularity as a literary theme" (*Night Visitors* 63). For literary historian Jonathon Rose, stories by Forster and Saki clearly demonstrate that "the psychical researcher was a plodding figure of fun" (5). It is true that many writers felt some degree of scepticism or ambivalence towards psychical research, or at least were reluctant to acknowledge its impact on them; this is not surprising, given its controversial nature, frequent confusion between it, spiritualism and occultism, and the scorn contemporary literary critics heaped on imaginative treatment of psychical research. Some writers may have satirized psychical research (or more likely credulous attitudes towards it), but they engaged with it nonetheless and were just as likely to satirize dogmatic materialist viewpoints within the same stories.

A number of writers found greater merit in Myers's dynamic psychology than in either Freud's or Jung's. Aldous Huxley, despite initial scepticism, reflected that:

> His [Myers] account of the unconscious is superior to Freud's in at least one respect; it is more comprehensive and truer to the data of experience. It is also, it seems to me, superior to Jung's account in being more richly documented with concrete facts and less encumbered with those psycho-anthropologico-pseudo-genetic speculations which becloud the writings of the sage of Zurich. Jung is like those classical German scholars of whom Porson once said that "they dive deeper and come up muddier than any others." Myers dives no less deeply into that impersonal spiritual world which transcends and interpenetrates our bodies, our conscious minds and our personal unconscious – dives no less deeply but comes up with a minimum of mud on him.

> How strange and unfortunate it is that this amazingly rich, profound and disturbing book [*Human Personality*] should have been neglected in favour of descriptions of human nature less complete and of explanations less adequate to the given facts! (Huxley, "Foreword" 7–8)

Huxley viewed Myers's psychology as wider-ranging and more balanced than other systems, and this attitude was typical:

> F.W.H. Myers ... was not a doctor and so had no vested interest in sickness. As a classical scholar, a minor poet, a conscientious observer and a platonic philosopher, he was free to pay more attention to the positive aspects of the subliminal self than to its negative and destructive aspects. (Huxley, "Foreword" 7)

May Sinclair similarly saw no reason why the unconscious "should overflow with things hideous and repulsive any more than with beautiful and attractive things" (*Defence* 6), effectively aligning herself with Myers's view. Myers did not conceive of the subliminal as being an entity, circumscribed, or reductive; instead he emphasized its potential and extensions of capacity. "The business of the psychologist", he wrote, is

> to look out for extensions of capacity – to recognize evolution. And these morbid visions take on a new importance if they are regarded as indications of a power of visualization, of combination, of invention, existing in subliminal strata of our being, and accidentally revealed by the volcanic upheaval of fever. ("Subliminal" 315)

All psychic events could potentially figure in a stream of consciousness. The number of these streams and possible personalities was apparently limitless.

Novelists such as Sinclair, Beresford, Blackwood, and D.H. Lawrence grasped the significance of this for conveying the multidimensional nature of character and coming closer to capturing inner reality in fiction. As Huxley mentioned, Myers was a poet, and he imaginatively applied images and analogies from the sciences, such as the spectrum of light and the analogy of iceberg meeting sea to describe the range and variability, respectively, of subliminal material; this strategy would also have held an appeal for writers. D.H. Lawrence, for example, drew on Myers's description of how certain states can form in the subliminal (*Human* II 85) in outlining his new approach to character. He adopted Myers's term "allotropic", denoting modifications on a single underlying element along with his metaphor of carbon becoming diamond, as will be discussed in Chapter 5.

For Myers, genius was a manifestation of extended capacity, of the carbon becoming diamond, not a product of psychic conflict or neurosis, and this view also attracted writers. Myers wrote that the genius "is for us the best type of the normal man, in so far as he effects a successful cooperation of an unusually large number of elements of his personality – reaching a stage of integration slightly in advance of our own" (Myers 74), though the genius is prey to the "degeneration and insanities" emanating from subliminal uprushes (*Human* I 56). Sinclair, for one, draws directly on this advanced integration model of genius, and its link with hysteria, in both *The Divine Fire* and *The Creators*.

Furthermore, writers found much material in Myers's analysis of the dynamics of supernormal powers, also emanating from the subliminal, including telepathy, clairvoyance, psychic possession, and automatic writing. He argued that these powers are integral to natural experience, perhaps giving an indication of higher evolutionary development, but not above or beyond nature as the word "supernatural" implies (*Human* I xxii). Since Myers did not treat these phenomena as aberrations, but as normal and worthwhile subjects of scientific investigation, they gained a more serious status. In turn, writers considered them more seriously, treating them not as gothic fantasy but as extensions of psychological realism. A number of fiction writers, from Rudyard Kipling to Aldous Huxley, including those under study here, entertained the probability of man's supernormal powers, particularly telepathy. In her treatise on idealism, for example, May Sinclair could claim after sifting the evidence that "whatever spiritualism may be, telepathy is a fact" (*Defence* 351).

Myers frequently drew support for his theories from individual case studies, and writers found these fascinating, some even adapting the form for fiction. J.D. Beresford most directly articulates this fascination in his 1946 novel, *The Prisoner*, when his protagonist reads Myers's *Human Personality*: "It was less, perhaps, Myers's general philosophical argument than those remarkable cases in the Appendix that haunted Paul's imagination" (168). Perhaps most famously, Henry James drew on SPR case studies for "The Turn of the Screw", although he disparaged the modern antiseptic psychical ghost story (Banta; H. James *Art* 169). Some writers, such as Wilde in "The Canterville Ghost", Arthur Conan Doyle in "The Parasite", Algernon Blackwood in *The Centaur*, and J.D. Beresford in "The Night of Creation", adopted the dialectical structure of typical SPR case studies, in which tension exists between a sceptic and a believer. A number of SPR cases present testimony from multiple witnesses, and these do not always align. Most SPR case studies remain in the voices of witnesses, rather than being filtered through an authority, as Freud's case studies are, and thus SPR cases would appear more closely to anticipate modernist multiple-voiced narratives. Henry James in "The Turn of the Screw", G.K. Chesterton in "The Miracle of Moon Crescent", and May Sinclair in "The Flaw in the Crystal" are among those who exploit discrepancies between perspectives on apparent psychic phenomena.

Many of Myers's cases involved apparitions, and several writers appear to have assimilated the conclusions Myers drew from them. Contrary to preconceived notions, phantoms tend not to perpetrate evil, but as they become more distinct "rise also into love and joy" (*Human* II 78). Corresponding treatments of phantoms were entertained by Algernon Blackwood, who actually investigated SPR cases (Ashley 35), in "The

Woman's Ghost Story", Oscar Wilde in "The Canterville Ghost", and Virginia Woolf in "A Haunted House".

Perhaps most importantly, psychical research shaped writers' attitudes towards later dynamic psychologies, since they tended to evaluate the new developments in terms of the light shed on metaphysical questions, particularly whether human personality survived death. Since psychoanalysis, for example, did not address such matters it was typically perceived as materialist, reductive, and limited in scope. Although Sinclair recognized psychoanalysis's potential, she argued that psychoanalytic theories "do not seem to me to take due account of the extreme multiplicity and variety of human interests" ("Way of Sublimation" 111). J.D. Beresford recalled that he rejected Freudian theory for a number of reasons, including that psycho-analysis "gave no support to the theory of the survival of consciousness after the earthly partnership was dissolved" (*What* 37). Thus, although psychoanalysis eventually eclipsed psychical research, ironically psychical research had, somewhat indirectly, a detrimental effect on Freud's reception in Britain, a point Ernest Jones fully realized (*Freud* III 421).

Psychical research thus provided a breadth of inquiry into the dynamics of mind, legitimizing a "borderland" of phenomena (Scott-James 237), where perception shades off into indistinctness and insubstantiality. It developed new terms and conceptions, including subliminal, supraliminal, supernormal, and telepathy, in order to probe that borderland. This expansionist investi-gation greatly appealed to writers attempting to interrogate the boundaries of identity and convey their conviction of the non-material dimension of reality within a plausible construct of realism.

3

"A Piece of Psycho-analysis": The British Response to Later Dynamic Psychology

> Regarded in a broad way, the Freudian body of doctrine which I have already ventured to describe as essentially an embryology of the mind gives one the impression of being mainly descriptive and systematic rather than dynamic, if one may with due caution use such words.
>
> – Wilfrid Trotter, *Instincts of the Herd in Peace and War* 1916, 89

3.1 Introduction

In 1909 Sigmund Freud wrote to Ernest Jones, a native of Britain, that

> I consider it is a piece of psycho-analysis you are performing on your countrymen...you are not to say too much or at too early a moment, but the resistance cannot be avoided, it must come sooner or later and it is best to provoke it slowly and designedly. (22 February 1909, Freud, Letters to Jones)

This chapter interrogates several myths surrounding that "analysis" by considering the British reception of Freudian discourse in a wider context than is typical in histories of psychoanalysis. Freud's ideas need to be viewed alongside other dynamic psychologies and their reception gauged in the light of the general British attitude towards psychology, in order to clarify Freud's impact.

The first myth suggests that orthodox Freudianism was unfairly rejected out of hand because of psychological resistance to its theories and that, after a long struggle, it emerged as the dominant force among British dynamic psychologies, from which it was clearly demarcated. Freud's biographer Ernest Jones claimed about early opposition to psychoanalysis that

In those days Freud and his followers were regarded not only as sexual perverts but as either obsessional or paranoic psychopaths as well, and the combination was felt to be a real danger to the community. Freud's theories were interpreted as direct incitements to surrendering all restraint, to reverting to a state of primitive license and savagery. No less than civilization itself was at stake. As happens in such circumstances, the panic aroused led in itself to the loss of that very restraint the opponents believed they were defending. All ideas of good manners, of tolerance and even a sense of decency – let alone any thought of objective discussion or investigation – simply went by the board. (*Freud* II 121–122)

In actuality, many prominent British social scientists and intellectuals were initially attracted to and seriously considered Freud's views. However, their eclectic approach and judicious weighing of evidence prompted them not to accept Freud's hypotheses as a completed doctrine. Instead they typically incorporated "a piece of psycho-analysis" but remained eclectics, though many were attracted by Jung's expansionist view of human psychology, which was more in keeping with the British tradition of Myers, William James, and James Ward. Ernest Jones was primarily responsible for the "sanitization" of psychoanalysis, that is the concerted attempt to distance it from other discourses, notably psychical research and the occult, perceived as less reputable than it.[1] Jones accomplished this through creating exclusionist professional associations and by distorting historical accounts to erase psychoanalysis's interconnections with psychical research and other dynamic psychologies.

Another related myth, created largely by Ernest Jones and perpetuated by orthodox Freudians, claims that Jones was the most important if not the only significant representative of psychoanalysis during its formative stages in England. Although Jones was the most tenacious doctrinaire Freudian Britain ever produced, a colleague of his, M.D. Eder, was more influential in setting the British tone towards later dynamic psychologies in Britain. Certainly Eder was far more important than Jones in disseminating later dynamic psychological ideas among literary figures. Numerous other individuals contributed significantly to the acceptance of dynamic psychology in Britain. Jones typically diminishes their roles as he exaggerates his own.

A third myth, woven by Freudian literary critics like Lionel Trilling and Frederick Beharriell, states that doctrinaire Freudianism was the most subtle and compelling psychology to writers. Beharriell, citing Trilling, claims that there is

no other psychology [than Freudian] subtle enough to compare with the mass of unorganized insights accumulated through the centuries by literature; no other psychology sophisticated enough to impress the twentieth century writer. (124–125)

Although this claim may hold for European or American writers, in Britain literary figures drew on nearly every major dynamic psychology, including Freud's, even more eclectically and idiosyncratically than their counterparts in the helping professions, as will become apparent in Chapters 4 through 6. If any trend dominated, it would be writers' greater attraction to Jungian discourse than to psychoanalysis.

Following a more detailed analysis of the first two of these myths, a chronology of selected publications and events will clarify when later dynamic psychological discourses, particularly those focussing on concepts of selfhood, began to circulate in England. Emphasis will be placed on response to key concepts rather than on summaries of them. I then want to suggest some reasons for the popularity of later dynamic psychologies among the general public and in literary circles.

Several striking features of British dynamic psychology emerged in the early twentieth century, which conditioned how psychoanalysis was received. Systems of thought were viewed with distrust, and eclecticism prevailed; thus it was Freud's claims about the universality of psychic conflicts which disturbed British psychologists, not the described conflicts themselves. Many psychologists appear to have accepted that dreams could represent wish fulfilment, but hardly any were willing to agree that *all* dreams had this function. A similar attitude was held about Freud's claims that sexuality invariably played a role in the etiology of the psychoneuroses and that conflict aroused by the sexual instinct was the primary motivator of behaviour. The expansionist view of human psychology, which included consideration of the spiritual aspect of man, continued to be influential.

The SPR remained the single most significant vehicle for the dissemination of dynamic psychological discourses, at least until the end of the war. Even recent histories of Freud's reception in Britain have tended to minimize and distort the Society's roles, however. Dean Rapp acknowledges that psychical researchers, spiritualists, and occultists published 28 articles and reviews on psychoanalysis in their own journals between 1910 and 1919 ("Early" 241), but does not distinguish between these groups and limits the analysis of their impact to one paragraph at the end of his article on Freud's reception. He does not acknowledge the dynamic psychology developed principally by Myers prior to Freud's ("Early" 242). R.D. Hinshelwood reduces the role of the SPR to Myers's "very superficial reading of Freud", particularly his theory of hysteria (137). He does mention that several psychoanalysts and writers came to psychoanalysis through psychical research, but he does not consider the ramifications of this (137, 142–143). These are considerable. Writers involved with the SPR typically had an interest in the issue of whether personality survived death, and this interest coloured their interpretation of dynamic findings. Many early reviewers of psychoanalytic books had previously had some involvement with psychical research. This explains why, for example, psychoanalysts were sometimes referred to in the press as "soul-doctors" or "psychic doctors", terms that have puzzled historians such as Dean Rapp ("Early" 236).

Dynamic psychology was integrally connected with the socialist movement in Britain as well. Social scientists and writers alike quickly recognized the educative potential of these newest psychologies and used them as a vehicle for social change. Most importantly, British intellectuals tended to focus on the literary, imaginative qualities of dynamic psychologies, and this concentration helps account for the considerable engagement with these discourses by literary figures or well-educated individuals with literary sympathies.

The prevalence of several of these characteristics in British psychology helps explain why Carl Jung's psychological analysis came to be viewed as more acceptable than the Freudian paradigm. Jung drew eclectically on the evidence from many cultures to make his points, as well as on various psychologies, including Janet's, James's and, in the English tradition, Francis Galton's and Myers's. Early reviewers, for example, praised Jung's use of word association tests, a technique pioneered by Francis Galton (Ellenberger 691). Jung's overall strategy of synthesis is completely consonant with the typical Edwardian approach to knowledge. In common with many British psychologists, he never accepted Freud's assertion about the universal role of sexuality in the origin of neuroses, or his idea about sexual symbolism and the Oedipus complex (Ellenberger 727). Similarly to psychical researchers, Jung attacked the materialist hypothesis and was open to the careful investigation of unknown psychic phenomena. His view of the unconscious as a creative force and a potential source of strength aligned better with Myers's and James's concept of the subliminal and supraliminal than Freud's portrait of the unconscious as a seething mass of instincts striving for release. Jung's position was also more attractive to writers since it did not imply that the artist was a neurotic, but rather that he had access to privileged, intuitive information. Jung's claim that religious experience was a valid part of personality (Progoff 22) that "must receive positive consideration" in psychotherapy also fit in well with Myers's and James's visions (*Collected Papers* 223–224).

Thus, it is not surprising that, as Jones claims, "Jung's conversion was hailed in the *British Medical Journal* as 'a return to a saner view of life' than Freud's", as early as January 1914 (Jones, *Freud* II 151). Freud, too, was well aware of the strength of Jung's position in England from as early as 1913 (Letter to Jones, 22 November 1913). By 1922, he admitted that Jones's claim was correct "that psycho-analysis was better known in England by Jung's work than by my own..." (Letter to Jones, 4 June 1922).[2] According to Dean Rapp, this was also partly because the British Jungians championed Jung's theories in the popular press. Rapp claims that "between 1916 and 1919, Jung or his followers received fourteen favourable reviews and articles, but only one mixed and one unfavourable review" (Rapp, "Early" 232).

Several of these characteristics of British psychology in the first two decades of the twentieth century are reflected in the first British institutions employing dynamic psychology: the "Medical Society for the Study of Suggestive Therapeutics", later called the "Psycho-Medical Society", formed in 1907 (Wright, Obituary 204); the Medico-Psychological Clinic, formed in 1913; and the Tavistock Clinic, established in 1920. All three developed eclectic approaches to psychological healing, and incorporated Freudian ideas. The Psycho-Medical Society gave Ernest Jones his first public forum to introduce psychoanalysis, and in 1913 it gave Jung his first opportunity to explain his differences from Freud, which led to their rift. The Medico-Psychological Clinic was probably the first institution in England to recognize formally the therapeutic value of literature, and involved writers in its activities, notably May Sinclair, as will be described in Chapter 4. The first two of the abovementioned institutions were largely supported by members of the SPR.[3] Both the Medico-Psychological and the Tavistock clinics had socialist impulses, accommodating lower income patients with nominal fees (Boll 317; Dicks, *Tavistock* 1).

Not until the post-war period did British psychological institutions become more exclusive, elitist, and doctrinally rigid. These comprised: the British Psychoanalytic Society, founded in 1919; the Institute of Psycho-analysis (Brome, *Jones* 138); and the London Psychoanalytic Clinic, the latter two formed in 1924 (Jones, *Free* 258). Ernest Jones (1879–1958) was the driving force behind all three and thus had an important hand in making their nature different from earlier institutions.[4] The forerunner of the British Psychoanalytic Society was the London Psycho Analytic Society, formed in 1913 by Jones and David Eder. As Vincent Brome points out, Jones attempted to handpick the membership (Brome 105). When the Society became too eclectic for him, and wanted to discuss Jung's innovations, he dissolved it, just after First World War (*Free* 239–240). He immediately reconstituted it, according to him, "with an improved membership" (*Free* 240) but, as Paul Roazen points out, "the British Society in the early 1920s was substantially non-medical and somewhat amateurish" (Roazen 345). Jones had merely excluded eclectics, including David Eder and Constance Long.[5] Jones followed a similar course when he initiated the London Psychoanalytic Clinic.

As an historian of the British Psychoanalytic movement, Jones also attempted to exert control. In several articles, his memoir, *Free Associations*, and his biography of Freud, he sanitized psychoanalysis, suppressing the value of precedents to Freudian discourse or outright denigrating them. Like most twentieth-century psychologists, Jones was first introduced to Freud's work through the discourses of earlier dynamic psychologists. Jones admitted to reading Frederic Myers's *Human Personality* in 1903 ("Reminiscent Notes" 9), along with the works of William James and Milne Bramwell. He and his brother-in-law, Wilfrid Trotter,

> were especially interested in what is now called medical psychology, to which the French had contributed by far the major part.... The cases of multiple personality, and the beautiful experimental work carried out on patients in a state of deep hypnosis, seemed to furnish convincing proof that the mind was not coextensive with consciousness, and that complicated mental processes could be going on without the subject being in the least aware of them. The conception of an unconscious mind was therefore perfectly familiar to us, though we knew nothing about what it contained. (*Free* 158)[6]

Either Jones did not read Myers's work carefully or, more likely, he withholds information here, since Myers certainly offered a view of what the subliminal contained (although Myers did not believe in an unconscious as such). Jones continued to play down the interconnections between psychoanalysis and psychical research in particular. Although he does treat Freud's fascination with telepathy and other psychical phenomena in his biography of Freud, he titles the chapter "Occultism", thus occluding psychical research's contribution to dynamic psychology. As well, he ascribes Freud's interest, along with Jung's and Ferenczi's, to excessive "credulity" (III 402, 410, 411). He also describes his repeated (and unsuccessful) attempts at damage control, to persuade Freud not to accept psychical phenomena like telepathy, since it encouraged English opponents of psychoanalysis to affirm psychoanalysis as a "branch of occultism" (III 422). It would appear that Jones saw it as his duty to sanitize psychoanalysis. Jones denigrated psychical research in other publications as well. In an obituary of psychologist, psychoanalyst, and psychical researcher J.C. Flugel, Jones criticises his "penchant for unconventionality": "Worse than all that he studied the black art of hypnotism and conducted séances under the auspices of the Society for Psychical Research, of which he was already a member" (Jones, Obit. of Flugel 193).

Furthermore, Jones mythologized psychoanalytic history by exaggerating his own importance and playing down or suppressing the contributions of others, especially if they deviated from doctrinaire Freudianism. Typically he suggested that eclectics failed to make progress in the field because of personal resistance, or they slipped into conventionality, or blindly accepted Jung's or Adler's ideas. Two brief examples must suffice. Jones exaggerated his role at the Seventeenth Congress of Medicine (as well as recording its date as August 1914, when it was actually August 1913; *Free* 241). He asserted that

> in the first week of August, there was a duel between Janet and myself at the International Congress of Medicine, which put an end to his pretensions of having founded psychoanalysis and then seeing it spoiled by Freud. (*Freud* II 99)

Jones was in reality one of nine respondents to Janet, five of whom supported Freud, and his intervention, unlike others, was not reported in the detailed *Times* account (Ellenberger 818–819). Second, Jones claims that after speaking at the Psycho-Medical Society in 1913, Dr T.W. Mitchell and Dr Douglas Bryan "were evidently impressed and before long could be counted as recruits" (*Free* 229); however, Dr Mitchell could hardly be considered a recruit since he had reviewed psychoanalysis favourably three years earlier and throughout his career drew eclectically on Freudian ideas (Wright Obituary 205, 203).

Nevertheless, Jones's most significant suppression involved David Eder. A close examination of the original records reveals that David Eder better represented the eclectic British response, and proved far more influential than Jones in setting the tone towards later dynamic psychology among both medical professionals and literary figures. In the Foreword to Eder's memoirs, Freud praised Eder highly for his "rare combination of absolute love of truth and undaunted courage, together with toleration and a great capacity for love", qualities which led him to become "the first, and for a time the only doctor to practise the new therapy in England" (*Memoirs* 9). Freud's assertion so distressed Jones that he wrote to Anna Freud (since by the time Eder's book was published Freud had died) that

> I was indubitably the first person in this country (and so far as I know in the whole English-speaking world) to assimilate your father's work and to practise psycho-analysis. In the conditions of forty years ago it was a considerable feat and I suppose my reputation rests largely on it. (as qtd in Brome, *Ernest Jones* 211)

However, Jones's biographer, Vincent Brome, claims that Jones followed Janet's method of therapy involving hypnosis during these years (*Ernest Jones* 43–45). Furthermore, Jones quickly lost all respectability and chance of furthering his career when he was accused three times of molesting children (Brome 39). By early 1908, he felt forced to leave England to start afresh in Canada. Jones resided outside Britain (although he made several visits to it) from March 1908 to August of 1913, when, as we shall see, psychoanalysis took root in England (*Free* 197, 199, 228). Another of Jones's claims as the original pioneer of British psychoanalysis was that he published six papers on psychoanalysis between 1907 and 1909, a "couple" in "English periodicals" (*Free* 229). This claim can largely be discounted since all six of these papers were published in highly specialized American periodicals (cf. Hart, "Freud's Conception" 362). By his own admission, he did not speak to a British audience until a January 1913 Psycho-Medical Society meeting (*Free* 229), well after several others, including David Eder, had presented psychoanalytic papers both at this Society and to other British Institutions.

David Eder (1881–1936), on the other hand, had established a medical practice in London in 1905. He had been interested in psychology as a young medical student, and described himself "as a diligent student of Ward's enlightening article on Psychology in the *Encyclopaedia Britannica*" (*Memoirs* 14, 43). In 1904, he met Jones and, like him, first employed suggestion and hypnosis in his medical practice (Glover, "Eder" 90). Eder claimed that he "first came across Freud's work in 1905", but that he had some resistance to the ideas (Eder, "Present Position" 1214). By 1908, however, he had published *The Endowment of Motherhood*, aimed at a popular audience. In it he referred to Freud as "one of our leading neurologists" and supported Freud's theory of sexuality, but did not commit himself to it absolutely until more evidence could be gathered (*Endowment* 6, 15). Although Edward Glover incorrectly dates the beginning of Eder's interest in psychoanalysis as 1909, he does claim that Eder

> read everything about psycho-analysis he could lay his hands on and soon began trying out what he had gathered of psycho-analytic technique on patients who came to him in the course of his ordinary work in Charlotte Street. (Glover, "Eder" 90)

In the summer of 1911, Eder gave the first clinical lecture in Britain on Freudian psychoanalysis at the British Medical Association's annual meeting (Glover, "Eder" 89). Printed the same year in the *British Medical Journal*, it was the first – not one of the first, as Jones claims ("Obituary of Eder" 144) – psychoanalytic case study published in England. Beginning in 1912, he contributed numerous articles on psychoanalysis and other dynamic psychologies to both the medical and the popular press (Glover, "Eder" 95); thus, he was certainly more influential in disseminating Freudian discourse in these early years than Jones.

Several other accomplishments and characteristics of Eder's suggest his greater significance than Jones in shaping attitudes towards dynamic psychology. A socialist, Eder quickly realized that psychoanalysis could substantiate the argument for liberating society's oppressive sex morality (*Endowment* 5–6). Eder's socialism prompted him to oppose the Mental Deficiency Act of 1912, and to advocate educational reforms (Roberts 81, 77). Glover claims that in 1907 he initiated and ran the first school clinic in London ("Eder" 95); Eder's involvement in this and similar projects provided him with material for the earliest papers to be given in Britain on child psychology based on psychoanalysis (Roberts 77). He was the first person in Britain to recognize psychoanalysis's and dynamic psychology's potential for social and educational change, a potential emphasized by most other intellectuals and literati who later became interested in psychoanalysis.

Eder's involvement in the Fabian movement, as well as his position from 1907 to 1915 on the editorial staff of the left-wing cultural and political weekly *The New Age*, brought him into contact with some of the leading literary figures of the day, including Bernard Shaw, H.G. Wells, and, later on, D.H. Lawrence, whom Eder and his sister-in-law, psychoanalyst Barbara Low, met in June 1914. Eder also introduced Jones to this circle (Brome, *Jones* 37). Jones, however, maintained the doctrinaire Freudian view that creativity was a neurosis and consequently never established a rapport with writers. Although Jones apparently gave psychological advice to Frieda Lawrence on one occasion (*Free* 251–252), his general attitude is represented by his claim about D.H. Lawrence's "obvious lack of balance" (*Free* 251) and his description of James Joyce as a highly pathological case (as cited in Roazen 353). In contrast, Eder befriended many literary figures, including Lawrence (*Memoirs* 25–26, 119), J.D. Beresford, Dorothy Richardson, Rebecca West (*Memoirs* 131), and the poet, Isaac Rosenberg (*Memoirs* 24). They typically spoke highly of him. According to Frieda Lawrence, D.H. Lawrence was very fond of Eder, who became his physician and with whom he discussed psychoanalysis (*Memoirs* 123). Rebecca West similarly felt very "warmly" about him and claimed that "he was such a strange mixture of charm and solid sense – an ideal combination I never saw elsewhere" (*Memoirs* 131). Dorothy Richardson called him "one of the kindliest human beings I have ever known" (as qtd in *Memoirs* 16) and remembered that his expression "carried conviction, not necessarily in regard to the ideology he represented, but as to the value he set upon humanity" (as qtd in *Memoirs* 16).

Finally, Eder typified the eclectic British response to dynamic psychology. Originally he had practised a form of psychotherapy based on Janet's, and then visited Freud and underwent a brief analysis with Victor Tausk (Glover, "Eder" 98). Around 1913, just as Jung parted ways with Freud, Eder became attracted to what he perceived as Jung's wider and more optimistic perspective. In the early 1920s, he moved closer to the Freudian position again, and underwent an analysis with Ferenczi (Glover, "Eder" 100). Throughout this period he remained a more independent thinker than Jones. Thus, through Eder's role as dynamic psychology's first publicist and popularizer, interests in socialism, numerous literary contacts, and eclecticism, all facilitated by his solid, trustworthy, and courageous personality, Eder did more than any other individual to gain early acceptance in diverse circles of dynamic psychology.

A selective chronological survey of the development of and response to psychoanalysis along with other dynamic psychologies in Britain will clarify the eclectics' contributions and demonstrate when these discourses achieved circulation. I have emphasized the literary qualities of these texts in order to suggest their potential appeal for fiction writers.

3.2 Pre-First World War

As was detailed in Chapter 2, British contributions and response to dynamic psychology began as early as the late 1880s, primarily through figures, like Frederic Myers, who were associated with psychical research. The first British reference to Freud, Myers's June 1893 summary of Freud and Breuer's preliminary account of hysteria, "The Mechanism of Hysteria", represents a good example. Not only did Myers find support for his own conception of hysteria ("Mechanism" 14), but he noted Freud and Breuer's finding that certain hysterical symptoms were "*symbolical*" reproductions of an original shock" and that "a momentary accident" during the shock could "determine the character of years of malady" ("Mechanism" 12). In the second British reference to Freud and Breuer's work, in 1894, Dr J. Michell Clarke similarly summarized their psychic shock theory and noted their claim that these disturbing moments often occurred in childhood ("Hysteria" 126); thus by 1894 another potential source, besides Charcot and Janet, for the psychological shock theory had been brought to the attention of the British. Clarke also wrote an extensive review of *Studien über Hysterie* (1895), published in *Brain* (XIX, 1896).[7] This piece was the first to distinguish Freud's views on the origin of hysteria in violent emotional disturbances from Janet's emphasis on fixed ideas or innate psychical weakness ("Review" 404, 410). Clarke noted Freud's insistence that "the sexual factor is by far the most potent and most pathologically fruitful in the production of hysterical phenomena" ("Review" 410). Finally, Clarke compared Breuer's and Freud's therapeutic method to religious confession ("Review" 407), and he noted their claim that success hinged on patients' confidence in their doctors ("Review" 412).

F.W.H. Myers again referred to Breuer's and Freud's work in an April 1897 *Journal of the SPR* report (50–59). Havelock Ellis made the fifth reference to Freud in "Hysteria in Relation to the Sexual Emotions", published in the American Journal, *The Alienist and Neurologist*, in 1898 (XIX 599–615), and reprinted in *The Evolution of Modesty* (1899), Volume I of *Studies in the Psychology of Sex*. Ellis emphasized Freud's claim about the sexual etiology of hysteria, but misinterpreted Freud by claiming that he took the sexual impulse as the sole root of behaviour, a point with which Ellis took issue (Brome, *Ellis* 123). Ellis continued to cite Freud in subsequent volumes of his popular *Studies in the Psychology of Sex*, as did Myers in his magnum opus *Human Personality* (1903). Myers, for example, summarized Freud's Lucy R. and Anna O. cases and noted that Fraulein O. referred to her therapy as "The Talking Cure" (51–55).

In 1908, Wilfrid Trotter and Ernest Jones attended the first International Psychoanalytical Congress, held at Salzburg (Jones, *Free* 167–168). In that same year, and in 1909, Trotter published articles drawing on the dynamic psychology of William James and others to analyse the herd instinct, which he argued was biologically based; later he elaborated on the theory in *Instincts of the Herd in Peace and War* (1916), to be discussed in chronological sequence.

M. David Eder's *The Endowment of Motherhood* (1908) also tried to establish a biological basis, in this case for socialism. Eder argued that society should be organized in conformity with instincts. In support, he cited Freud's claim that "all the disastrous effect of civilisation can be essentially reduced to the harmful repression of the sexual life among civilised races (or classes) owing to the prevalent 'civilised' sex-morality" (*Endowment* 6). Eder also drew on the idea of bisexuality, widespread in later dynamic psychologies, to argue that the sexes should be treated equally (*Endowment* 10). Motherhood, he argued, should be a paid occupation, in order to encourage early unions and

> to avoid the voluntary suppression of sexual desires at an age when such desires are strong and to inhibit the various forms of sexual perversion in so far as the latter are not due to inherited traits, but are merely the expression of quelled instincts finding expression in unusual channels. (*Endowment* 12)

In support of his plan, Eder cited Freud's, Janet's, and Muthmann's findings that all neuroses originated in childhood or adolescent sexual disturbance (*Endowment* 14). This remarkably modern document shows how implications of which Freud may not have approved were drawn from his theory and how, as a result, his ideas were very early linked with fairly radical socialism in England. The booklet was reprinted from Eder's articles on endowment published in *The New Age* in 1907 (Roberts 78), testimony to the popularity of Eder's proposal. Since this journal was the main organ of humanitarian intellectualism, Eder's ideas would also have reached leading intellectuals (Roberts 78). According to J.B. Hobman, Eder's phrase "endowment of motherhood" passed into the currency of all parties; the conservative reformer in H.G. Wells's *New Machiavelli*, for instance, holds it as an ideal (Eder, *Memoirs* 13). Eder's book would thus have done a great deal to popularize Freud's name, if not his theories about sexuality.

As we have seen in Chapter 1, William McDougall also proposed an instinct-based theory in 1908 in *Introduction to Social Psychology*. Furthermore, in the following year, the psychologist William Brown proposed that psychology was the science of the *un*conscious rather than of consciousness, as was traditional ("Epistemological Difficulties").

The year 1909 was also an important year for psychoanalysis, though more so in the United States than in Britain. Not only did Freud and Jung lecture at Clark University in Massachusetts, but the first English translation of Freud, his *Selected Papers on Hysteria and Other Psychoneuroses*, was published in New York, as was the first translation of Jung's books, *The Psychology of Dementia Praecox*. Freud's work reinforced that the "accidental moment" conditioned the onset of hysteria (*Selected* 1), and that understanding it was crucial to the therapist (*Selected* 51). More significantly, Freud provided the cue that his subject matter was the stuff of fiction:

> even I myself am struck by the fact that the histories of the diseases which I write read like novels and, as it were, dispense with the serious features of the scientific character. Yet I must console myself with the fact that the nature of my subject is apparently more responsible for this issue than my predilection. (*Selected* 55)

However, Freud's predilection was apparently for literary language to describe his technique. He claimed that

> The grouping of similar reminiscences in a multiplicity of linear stratifications, as represented in a bundle of documents, in a package, etc., I have designated as the formation of a theme. (*Selected* 105–106)

Further on in his narrative, he compared the revelation of a new "theme" just before the close of an analytic hour to the way fiction appears in installments in a newspaper (*Selected* 114). Symptoms were often manifestly determined (*Selected* 110), just as symbols were in literature. Thus, in his concentration on the moment, his manipulation of it for dramatic purposes, and in his use of the developmental case study, literary metaphor and style, Freud virtually extended an invitation to writers to make use of his material. Furthermore, Freud repeatedly used the "stream of thought" metaphor made popular by James (*Selected* 94). Finally, he corrected the popular view that all neuroses had a sexual etiology, by underlining that repression played a key role (*Selected* 184).

As Ernest Jones duly acknowledged, Jung's *The Psychology of Dementia Praecox* (1909) "made history in psychiatry … and extended many of Freud's ideas into the realm of the psychoses proper" (*Freud* II 34). What Jones neglected to mention was that Jung's ideas owed as much to his thesis supervisor, Eugene Bleuler, to Janet, and to Theodore Flournoy, as to Freud (Ellenberger 692–693). Jung introduced the idea of emotional complexes, the existence of which were experimentally supported by word association tests. Complexes of various types, including those surrounding ambition, money, and sexual needs had been discovered in numerous patients, but he concentrated on a sixty-year-old woman's complexes (*Psychology* 99–146). Jung concentrated on the symbols his patient created to image her suffering (*Psychology* 144), and he drew numerous analogies between her and the poet, including the following:

> our patient has created a long-drawn-out and elaborately woven tissue of fancies, comparable on the one hand to an epic poem and on the other

to the romances and fantasy productions of somnambulists. In our patient, as with the poet, the web of fantasy is woven in the waking state... (*Psychology* 145)

As with Freud's case studies, Jung's had great potential appeal for literary figures such as May Sinclair. Many English readers of Jung's work would have found reassurance in Jung's eclecticism (for which he was apologetic *Psychology* 3), including his disagreement with Freud about sexuality's universal role in the psyche (*Psychology* 4). However, the book had a limited circulation (*Psychology* xi).

The next major work of dynamic psychology, Freud's *Three Contributions to the Sexual Theory*, did not suffer the fate of Jung's book. Its translation in 1910 marks the beginning of a fairly wide analysis of, and response to, Freudian discourse in British medical, psychiatric, and psychological journals. As Ellenberger has shown, by 1905 the European zeitgeist was of extreme interest in sexual problems (502). In England, Havelock Ellis's *Studies in the Psychology of Sex* (1899–1910) very definitely paved the way for Freud's acceptance. Contrary to A.A. Brill's pronouncement that before Freud "sex had been treated as an isolated phenomenon, or as (more or less) an abnormality" ("Introduction" 15), Ellis had previously treated sexuality as a part of normal life, a stance he considered to be his most original contribution (Delavenay 318). In the *Three Contributions*, Freud outlined his theory of infantile sexuality. He described the various erogenous zones, developmental phases, and concept of ambivalence (*Three Contributions* 587–589, 597, 598). Tunnel imagery made vivid sexual development:

The normality of the sexual life is guaranteed only by the exact concurrence of the two streams directed to the sexual object and sexual aim. It is like the piercing of a tunnel from opposite sides. (*Three Contributions* 604)

This tunnel image stands out because, perhaps coincidentally, both J.D. Beresford, in *God's Counterpoint* (1918), and Virginia Woolf, in *The Voyage Out* (1915), later use tunnel complexes or dreams to image sexual conflict. Writers also engaged with Freud's conceptualization of sublimation. Sublimation, by which sexual motive powers are deflected from sexual aims to new aims,

forms one of the sources of artistic creativity, and, depending on whether such sublimation is complete or incomplete, the analysis of the character of highly gifted, especially of artistically gifted persons, will show every kind of proportionate blending between productive ability, perversion and neurosis. (*Three Contributions* 625, 584)

For instance, sublimation became a key concept in May Sinclair's thinking, and one she explored in several of her novels. She wrote that the "theory of sublimation is the one thing of interest and value that Professor Freud and Professor Jung have contributed to Psychology" (*Defence* 7), although she preferred Jung's development of it.

Along with other followers of Freud, Edward Glover claimed that "Freud's discovery of infantile sexuality was a profound shock to everyone who came to hear of it . . ." ("Eder" 91). As Ellenberger notes, a myth has grown up that Freud's *Three Contributions* provoked widespread outrage and abuse;[8] however, in England, Freud's *Contributions* actually garnered some praise. A positive review in the *British Medical Journal* (3 June 1911) concluded that

> Certainly no one can read these essays without an inward acknowl-edgement of the author's acumen, courage and endless patience in the pursuit of truth; nor, having read them, fail to realize more clearly the need for fuller knowledge and more careful guidance of the gradual unfolding of the sexual life. (as cited in Ronald Clark 234)

In the same year, 1910, that Freud's essays on sexuality were translated, the work of British psychiatrist Bernard Hart stands out, both for its quantity and for its quality. Hart assessed Freudian psychoanalysis in three articles, two of which were published in England. The first, "The Conception of the Subconscious", was published in America, but deserves mention because Freud considered it "the best on the damned topic of the unconscious" (Letter from Sigmund Freud to Ernest Jones 10 March 1910). A second, "The Psychology of Freud", had been presented before the British Psychological Society at Oxford in May 1910. It thus has the distinction of being the first British public lecture summarizing Freud's ideas. However, the third, "Freud's Conception of Hysteria", offered the most detailed account of psychoanalysis to be published in England by that time. Hart referred to all of Freud's major developments, including his dream, sex, and psychic shock theories, as well as Jung's concept of the "complex". The article was undoubtedly an important resource since it contained a bibliography of 281 psychoanalytic references, forty-one of them published in English. Hart's concluding remarks characterize the British response:

> Freud's psychology has now reached a stage of development which calls imperatively for complete investigation and appraisement of its value. The whole subject must be submitted to searching and impartial criticism, the basic facts must be confirmed, and the justification of the deductions built upon them accurately estimated. Should it be found that the structure satisfies the requirements of science, then Freud's achievement must be reckoned among the most considerable in the history of human knowledge. ("Freud's Conception" 358)

Hart followed up these articles with *The Psychology of Insanity* in 1912. This work, already summarized in Chapter 2, was far more important as a popular but discriminating introduction to Freud's and other dynamic psychological discourse than was Jones's *Collected Papers* (1912), the only other book, aside from Freud's own, published in England on dynamic psychology by 1912. All of Hart's contributions, it should be noted, were made while Jones remained in exile, and for them alone Hart deserves a more prominent position than Jones accords him; however, Hart's independent thinking probably accounted for Jones's minimization of his role.

In 1910, Dr T.W. Mitchell likely reached a more varied audience than Hart's when he summarized several psychotherapy methods in the *Proceedings of the Society for Psychical Research*. A committed psychical researcher, Mitchell served as President of SPR in 1922, the year he published *Medical Psychology and Psychical Research*. He later chaired the Medical Section of the British Psychological Society, becoming its first *Journal* editor (Wright 204). Although Jones mentions his high regard for Mitchell (*Free* 229), he does not acknowledge his significant contribution to psychoanalysis in England, probably because of Mitchell's eclecticism and his leaning towards Jung, whose work Mitchell translated. Mitchell's 1910 article was not "mainly devoted to psychoanalysis" as Freud's biographer Ronald Clark claims (373), but considered the Freudian method along with several others, including Morton Prince's, Boris Sidis's, and Milne Bramwell's ("Some Recent" 673–678).

In the years 1911 and 1912, dynamic psychologies continued to make inroads in Britain. Ellis (*The World of Dreams*, 1911) and McDougall (*Psychology, The Study of Behaviour*, 1912) published their approaches to dynamic psychology, while at the same time acknowledging Freud's work. T.W. Mitchell published two more papers referring to psychoanalytic findings, one of which included a case study ("Some Types" and "A Study"). David Eder gave the first clinical lecture on psychoanalysis in England, to the British Medical Association ("A Case" 1911), and the first of several psychoanalytically oriented papers to the Psycho-Medical Society ("Freud's Theory" 1912).

Perhaps most significantly, in 1912 Freud's name and ideas first appeared in large circulation general interest periodicals, with William Brown's "Is Love a Disease", published in January in *The Strand Magazine*, probably being the first. Given Brown's interest in psychical research (cf. Chapter 2), it is not surprising that he draws on its discourses or that his view was eclectic. In explaining sexual love, Brown refers to Schopenhauer, Janet's concepts of fixed ideas and the subconscious, and Myers's view of the subconscious's telepathic capacity (without mentioning the latter two researchers by name). He also peppered his discussion with literary examples. His attitude towards "psycho-analysis" as a therapy was positive; psycho-analysis was employed "with remarkable success upon certain forms of mental disease" (102). Interestingly, he equates psychoanalysis with Jung's word association experiments, describing how delayed responses indicated an unconscious emotional conflict at the nervous disorder's root. The article was illustrated with photographs of a large timing machine dubbed the "Psycho-Analysis Apparatus", thus providing the first, if somewhat misleading, concrete representation of psychoanalytic method (102). It is tempting to speculate that this image formed one source of the electric psychical apparatus parodied by Virginia Woolf in "Kew Gardens" (86). Following close on Brown's article was A.E. Randall's review of Louis Calvert's *An Actor's Hamlet* in *The New Age* (15 February 1912) in which he summarized the Oedipus complex and Jones's analysis of *Hamlet* (Whelan 16). From 1912 to 1915, as Dean Rapp has discovered, "fifteen general interest magazines published sixteen articles containing information about psychoanalysis, along with seventeen reviews of psychoanalytic books". Half of these were favourable, one-quarter mixed, and only one-quarter unfavourable (Rapp, "Early" 221–222).

In December of 1912, Jones's *Collected Papers on Psychoanalysis* was published, the most comprehensive study of Freud's work to date. In the Preface, Jones attempts to place Freud in historical context by comparing his idea of libido, or "sexual hunger" (*Collected* 22), to both Schopenhauer's and Nietzsche's *Wille Zur Macht*, Bergson's *Élan Vital*, and Shaw's "life force" (*Collected* x). Jones then condenses Freud's varied researches into seven fundamental principles (*Collected* 13–22), in the manner of an acolyte. Jones also tends to exaggerate Freud's claims, as did other early adherents like Brill. Freud's suggestion of the importance of early childhood becomes in Jones's words "the general law that nothing happening to a child after the age of five can cause a psychoneurosis" (*Collected* 132). In the Preface, Jones stresses that "Freud's views had met with considerable opposition" (*Collected* ix), but Jones's own work was well received in Britain. A review in the prestigious journal *Nature* claimed that "his [Jones's] book is extremely readable and good, chiefly by reason of its wealth of concrete examples."[9] *The Times* quite properly considered Jones's book along with other dynamic psychological books on hypnotism and psychotherapy by psychical researchers C. Lloyd Tuckey and Milne Bramwell. The reviewer disagreed with Jones that psychoanalysis, which was difficult and costly, would replace hypnotism.[10]

The year 1913 was a pivotal year in the reception of psychoanalysis in England. The first English translation of Freud's magnum opus, *The Interpretation of Dreams*, appeared in that year. Despite the fact that Freud devoted nearly a quarter of the work to his predecessors, the translator, A.A. Brill, made the large claim in the Preface that "it was Freud who divested the dream of its mystery, and solved its riddles" (*The Interpretation* xii).[11] The work did offer the most detailed theoretical formulation of the structure of the unconscious to date, based on imaginative analysis of dreams and common symbols found in them. Freud introduced the Oedipus complex and suggested its universality:

> Perhaps we are all destined to direct our first sexual impulses towards our mothers, and our first hatred and violent wishes towards our fathers, our dreams convince us of it. (*The Interpretation* 223)

He outlined several dream processes, including condensation, displacement, censorship, and manifest and latent dream content (*The Interpretation* 274, 287, 372, 260). Further into the work, he elaborated on the mechanism of repression (*The Interpretation* 474–476). As in *Selected Papers* and *Three Contributions*, the "stream of thought" metaphor appeared repeatedly (*The Interpretation* 414, 418, 450, 470) and Freud drew numerous analogies between the dream and literature. In one of these he claims that

> just as every neurotic symptom, just as the dream itself, is capable of re-interpretation, and even requires it to be perfectly intelligible, so every genuine poetical creation must have proceeded from more than one motive, more than one impulse in the mind of the poet, and must admit of more than one interpretation. (*The Interpretation* 225)

Freud stressed the verbal nature of the dream:

> The whole range of word-play is thus put at the service of the dream activity. The part played by words in the formation of dreams ought not to surprise us. A word being a point of junction for a number of conceptions, so to speak, a predestined ambiguity, and neuroses (obsessions, phobias) take advantage of the conveniences which words offer for the purposes of condensation and disguise quite as readily as the dream. (*The Interpretation* 315)

In the conclusion, he stated that the dream was valuable more for knowledge of the past than the future (*The Interpretation* 493). As we shall see, contemporary writers frequently employed dreams in order to reveal the past. In addition, they increasingly exploited the dream's subject matter and its literary qualities, and some modernists, including Sinclair and Woolf, transformed the dream processes identified by Freud into literary technique.

The early reviews of *The Interpretation of Dreams* indicate a generally, though not entirely, favourable British response. In 1913 the unnamed *Athenaeum* reviewer wrote:

> His conclusions are sometimes far-fetched, and fit the premises incompletely, whilst an atmosphere of sex pervades many parts of the book

and renders it very unpleasant reading. The results he reaches are hardly commensurate with the labour expended, and reveal a seamy side of life in Vienna which might well have been left alone. (as cited in Kiell 196)

The typical main point of contention, however, was the distinctively British one that Freud's sweeping and even absolute claims were not well enough supported by evidence. As *The Nation* reviewer put it, the psychologist must object to "the building of a huge structure upon a very slim and unstable foundation".[12]

Furthermore, William Brown wrote a number of pieces highly praising Freud's new dream theory, including a popularized version in *The Strand*, entitled "Dreams: The Latest Views of Science". Brown called Freud's theory "exceptionally original, as well as being highly ingenious and interesting" (83), but he argued that a number of dreams could not be explained "without the assumption of telepathic communication between the mind of the dreamer and some other outside mind" (88). He referred to the numerous examples in the SPR Proceedings as well as "F.W.H. Myers's well-known book" and concluded that "many, if not all of them, make the view of telepathic communication between minds during sleep unavoidable" (88). He also praised "Freud's Theory of Dreams" in *Lancet* articles (19 and 26 April 1913) and in "A Case of Extensive Amnesia of Remote Date cured by Psycho-analysis and Hypnosis" in the *British Medical Journal* (8 November 1913). In 1914, the year he became University of London Reader in Psychology, Brown published two more articles on psychoanalysis. The first, entitled "What is Psychoanalysis?", appeared in *Nature*. Brown called Freud's theory "perhaps the most important and startling scientific theory of modern times" (643). The second, published in the *British Journal of Psychology*, attempted to align Freud's work with fellow psychologist and SPR member William McDougall's. Despite these very early efforts to disseminate Freudian discourse, his continuing interest in psychoanalysis, and his eventual prominence[13] as President of the British Psychological Society, Brown is completely ignored in Jones's historical accounts.

Another psychical researcher, the American Hereward Carrington, gave a similarly positive review of *The Interpretation of Dreams* in the *New York Times Review of Books* (1 June, Part 6, p. 328). Norman Kiell finds it "far-fetched" that the Director of the American Psychical Institute and a prolific writer on psychical research would have been given the review, but, as we have seen, this decision makes perfect sense. Carrington's only reservation about Freud's work was to note that Freud's followers' "idea that all dreams are in reality of sexual origin, taking the word 'sexual' in its broadest sense" had not been generally accepted (as cited in Kiell 202).

Yet one more pioneer neglected by Jones, who first published on Freud in 1913, was David Forsyth. Jones does admit that Forsyth practised psychoanalysis and published several papers on it before First World War (*Free* 228, 229), but he claims Forsyth's engagement was limited because of "personal jealousy" of him (*Free* 239). Jones might well have been the jealous one, since a few years earlier Forsyth had won out over Jones for a Charing Cross Hospital post, when Jones desperately needed a job (*Free* 132). Forsyth's obituary claimed that "it must have needed great courage, twenty-five years ago, for a physician in a teaching hospital publicly to declare himself favourable to Freud's doctrines." In 1919 Forsyth was the first foreigner to be analysed by Freud after the war, and was described by Freud as "the first dove after the deluge" (Freud, "Dreams" 103, 107). Like Brown, Forsyth continued to publish extensively on psychoanalysis from an eclectic standpoint.[14] In 1924 he also became a founding member of the Institute of Psychoanalysis.

However, to return to the chronology, the main psychoanalytic event of 1913 was the Seventeenth International Congress of Medicine, held in London in August. In his history of British Psychology, L.S. Hearnshaw claimed that, in Britain, psychoanalysis did not receive any conspicuous publicity like the 1909 Clark conference in the USA; hence psychoanalysis percolated into the ken of British Psychology (*Short* 165). I would argue that the Medical Congress came closest to playing that role in England, and it thus marks a crucial turning point. The stage was set on 5 August at a meeting of the Psycho-Medical Society, whose President was T.W. Mitchell, and honourary Secretary, another eclectic pioneer disparaged by Jones, Douglas Bryan, translator of works by Karl Abraham and Theodor Reik (*Free* 229). At the meeting, Jung read "Psycho-analysis", in which he announced his new method of "psychological analysis" (*Collected Papers* 206). Jung criticized Freud's method of dream interpretation by pointing out the arbitrariness of viewing some elements in a dream as symbolic and others as concrete in order to arrive at an interpretation of the contents as sexual (Ellenberger 698). Similar to Havelock Ellis, Jung stressed the many-sidedness of the meaning of dreams, including the prospective aspect (*Collected Papers* 220).

The Congress of Medicine opened two days later. During one session, Pierre Janet criticized Freud on several counts, including for having appropriated several of his own ideas; in response Jung defended psychoanalysis from his own perspective rather than Freud's. Not only were the Proceedings published, but of more immediate and popular impact, the sessions were summarized in *The Times*. One report claimed that

> Professor Janet, one of the greatest psychologists living, made a very damaging attack on Dr. Freud's school of thought, in a discourse abounding in acute criticism and as full of wit and literary finish as any novel by Bourget or Anatole France. (Saturday 9 August 1913: 3)

Another compared Janet's and Freud's positions in more detail and stated that

> the originality of the doctrine of Dr. Freud lies in the fact that instead of stating that a sexual basis is found in some neuroses, it asserts that it is found in all. (*The Times* 9 August 1913: 3)

This reviewer pointed out that Jung's paper proved that he differed from Freud, notably about "the sexual basis of all neuroses; [Jung] found this standpoint too narrow. He believed that the true cause occurs later in life" (*The Times* 9 August 1913: 3).

Thus in the popular press, Freud is identified with an absolute and extreme position, which came under attack, while Jung's view is considered less narrow. Through reports of the Congress, then, psychoanalysis, as well as Jung's variants on it, achieved recognition, though not always the most positive in nature. The aforementioned review concluded with a Dr J.J. Walsh's remark that "psycho-analysis had a large vogue at present owing to the sex element being introduced, that being to the front in people's minds at the present" (9 August 1913: 3).

David Eder contributed to that popularity by writing the first newspaper column devoted to psychoanalysis, in the Manchester *Daily Dispatch* in 1913. In it, titled "Doctors and Dreams", he positively reviewed *The Interpretation of Dreams* and also announced the Congress.[15] Later in the year he presented a more detailed account of Freud's psychoanalysis in relation to Jung's and Adler's developments (Eder "Present Position"). Eder explained why Freud discarded the "shock" theory of neurosis, and he summarized Freud's theories of sexual development, the Oedipus Complex, resistance, and sublimation. He was careful to point out that Jung's and Adler's opposition to Freud's sexual theory was "not the result of mere prejudice" ("Present Position" 1214). Jung found the theory "too narrow" and argued that the essence of neurosis was the failure to adapt to life. Eder also mentioned Adler's ideas that the desire for power was the more general condition of which the sexual disturbance was a particular function, and that neurotics strove to compensate for feelings of inferiority arising from early illness ("Present Position" 1215). Eder concluded by stating that none of the theories had reached finality ("Present Position" 1215). Probably in response to growing interest displayed in psychoanalysis, Eder and Jones founded the London Psycho-Analytical Society in the late autumn of 1913, with nine original members (Brome 105).

The year 1914 opened with several articles exploring various aspects of Freud's ideas on dreams. William Brown's in the *British Journal of Psychology* was immediately followed by the psychologist T.H. Pear's lengthy "Analysis of Some Personal Dreams with Reference to Freud's Theory of Dream Interpretation". Pear claimed that he had been analysing his own dreams for one and a half years ("Analysis" 288), and followed Freud's method in dissecting them. H. Wildon Carr, a mentor of May Sinclair's, examined "The Philosophical Aspects of Freud's Theory of Dream Interpretation" in *Mind* (July 1914). Carr proposed that wish indulgence needed to be distinguished from wish fulfilment and concluded that Freud's doctrine of psychic reality was "profoundly suggestive" but needed to be restated ("Philosophical Aspects" 333). V.J. Woolley, a member of the SPR's medical section, applied Freud's theory to phenomena of psychical research in "Some Auto-Suggested Visions as illustrating Dream-Formation" (1914).

Freud's popularization of his dream theory, entitled *On Dreams*, also appeared in 1914. Translated by David Eder, this concise and clearly written book did more than any other of this early period to make Freud's dream theory accessible to the British public. In this work, Freud again notes the unusual wording of dream thoughts and claims that they are "expressed symbolically by allegories and metaphors like the figurative language of the poets" (*On Dreams* 54). Although the book mentions that "most of the dreams of adults are traced by analysis to erotic desires" (*On Dreams* 100) and cites several sexual symbols, including agricultural and building symbols, passages on more explicit sexual symbols were deleted from the translation "in deference to English opinion" (*On Dreams* 104).

Another English translation of Freud's work appeared in 1914, *The Psychopathology of Everyday Life*, which proved quite popular. This work argued that forgetting and other slips did not occur arbitrarily but followed lawful and rational paths (*Psychopathology* 4). It went further than any previous book of Freud's in collapsing the distinctions between normality and abnormality. For instance, Freud made the important point that even in healthy persons "resistances are found against the memory of disagreeable impressions and the idea of painful thoughts" (*Psychopathology* 152). Because of its original premise, the book attempted to account for many so-called superstitions. Freud even went so far as to state about religion that

> I believe that a large portion of the mythological conception of the world which reaches far into most modern religions *is nothing but psychology projected into the outer world*. (*Psychopathology* 309)

Interestingly, however, in light of his membership in the SPR, Freud stopped short of repudiating all supernatural phenomena (*Psychopathology* 311).

The Psychopathology overflowed with vivid and varied examples guaranteed to appeal to the imaginative, and perhaps for this reason above any others was widely reviewed.[16] In *The New English Weekly*, Leonard Woolf asserted that Freud "writes with great subtlety of mind, a broad and sweeping imagination more characteristic of the poet than the scientist or medical practitioner", but he also acknowledged that there was a "substantial amount of truth" of great value in Freud's main thesis (*Psychopathology* 36, 37).

Constance Long, in the SPR *Proceedings*, and H. Ellis, in *The Journal of Mental Science*, likewise commended it. Most probably the publication of *The Psychopathology of Everyday Life* in the spring prompted the Symposium on "The Role of Repression in Forgetting", published in the *British Journal of Psychology* in several parts in September, 1914.

The Jungian position continued to have a hearing in Britain in 1914. Constance Long published "Psychoanalysis" in *The Practitioner* (July). She was an early member of Eder and Jones's London Psychoanalytic Society but since, according to Jones, she "soon became an ardent follower of Jung", her subsequent role in disseminating dynamic psychology was ignored by him (*Free* 239). She was one of the first Medico-Psychological Clinic supporters (Boll, "M.S. and the Medico-Psychological" 312), belonged to the SPR Medical group under T.W. Mitchell, contributed to SPR publications, and, most importantly, translated Jung's *Collected Papers* into English. Jung himself returned to London in the summer of 1914 to give several papers, including "The Importance of the Unconscious in Psychopathology", before the British Medical Association. According to Jones, Jung's visit was a great success (Brome, *Jones* 107).

In *Free Associations*, Ernest Jones claims that "concerning England there is little to say [about psychoanalysis] in the pre-war time" (228). It should be clear by now that Jones was particularly "free" with the facts on this point. By the early months of the war, there was a fertile, eclectic discourse on dynamic psychologies, including psychoanalysis, among British medical professionals and academics from various fields, and literati. At least nine well-respected British periodicals had published mostly favourable reports of Freud's and Jung's ideas alone, as had at least four more popular presses, including *The Strand* and *The Times*. Several public lectures and case studies had been presented in Britain. More emphasis had been placed on Freud's theory of the neuroses and dreams than on his sexual theories, but almost all of his theories to date had been mentioned. Amendments and elaborations to Freud's dream theory had been proposed. The British objected not so much to the content of his ideas, but to Freud's claim of having proof, which appeared absolute, as well as his insistence on the universality of the phenomena he described, particularly about sexuality in dreams and psychoneurosis.

3.3   Inter-War years

Much has been made by Ronald Clark and others of the war's impact on fuelling negative opinion about German variants of dynamic psychology (Clark 374–376; Hoops 23–25; Brome, *Jones* 109). Although war did arouse a few such emotional attacks on psychoanalysis in particular, it was also vigorously defended. Jones neglects to mention in any of his accounts the fact that, in 1915, W.H.B. Stoddart gave "The Morrison Lectures" at The Royal College of

Physicians in Edinburgh on "The New Psychiatry". According to Stoddart's obituary, these made history (Rickman 286). He pointed out in the strongest terms possible the danger of a prejudice against psychoanalysis that was motivated by nationalist sentiment and went on to outline Freud's theories of the unconscious, sexuality, and dreams (Rickman 286).

More typical was qualified acceptance of Freud's theories, as found in Wilfrid Trotter's *Instincts of the Herd in Peace and War* (1916). Trotter praised Freud's "remarkable" dream theory and his central conception of mental conflict (74, 79), but criticized "a certain harshness in his grasp of facts and even a certain narrowness in his outlook" (76), along with his "enumeration of absolute rules" and "superb" confidence in his hypotheses.[17] Most striking for a study of reception is Trotter's "impression" that the Freudian doctrine is "mainly descriptive and systematic rather than dynamic" (89). Trotter's main contribution was to emphasize the irrationality of crowd behaviour, but his book entered the realm of mythology when it characterized Germany as a "perfected aggressive herd", its model the wolf, and England as a "socialized" herd, modelled on bee behaviour; this propagandistic dimension may partly account for its enormous popular appeal, though it was also read and discussed in literary circles, including Bloomsbury, as will be seen.[18] Although Jones highly praises his friend Trotter's understanding of human nature and his wide knowledge of English literature (*Free* 102), he curiously avoids any assessment of Trotter's impact.

Even more importantly, psychoanalysis actually made great progress in gaining acceptance during the war. Large numbers of war casualties began to appear whose disorders could not be attributed to physical or organic sources. Psychoanalysis offered a more comprehensive explanation than other dynamic psychologies of the mental processes behind these disorders. As W.H.R. Rivers put it,

> The great merit of Freud is that he has provided us with a theory of the mechanism by which this experience, not readily and directly accessible to consciousness, produces its effects, while he and his followers have devised clinical methods by which these hidden factors in the causation of disease may be brought to light. ("Freud's" 914)

While on the staff at the famous Craiglockhart Hospital near Edinburgh, Rivers wrote six papers, both theoretical and practical, utilizing Freudian findings. Jones gives the impression in his biography of Freud that Rivers was only brought into the psychoanalytic movement in 1919 as President of the British Psycho-analytic Society because of his distinguished reputation as an anthropologist (*Freud* III 12). However, in reality Rivers was familiar with Freud's and Jung's work before First World War and developed a parallel theory of instincts and consecutive layers of mind (Slobodin 54). Despite disagreeing with psychoanalytic theory on several scores, including its claim of the universality of sexual symbolism in dreams, he continued to draw on it eclectically in the post-war period, writing "in the area where psychology, psychiatry, sociology and ethnology converge" (Slobodin 74). Typical of the British response, he also began to apply psychoanalysis to his socialist political views (Slobodin 69–79). Like Eder, he had extensive literary and intellectual connections with, for example: H.G. Wells, G.B. Shaw, and Bertrand Russell, as early as before the war; the war poets, including Siegfried Sassoon and Robert Graves, during the conflagration; and Arnold Bennett afterwards (Slobodin 68, 70–71). Rivers contributed to Graves's theory of poetics (Slobodin 70), for instance; he also became an intimate friend of Bennett's, and advised him on his stammering (Slobodin 78). Rivers, too, thus deserves more prominence in the history of British psychoanalysis than Jones gives him.

During these war years, Rivers also developed techniques of psychotherapy based on the Freudian, as did other psychologists, including C.S. Myers, William McDougall, T. Pear, and William Brown (Hearnshaw 245), all of whom had published supportive essays on Freud before the war. In the war years a psychodynamic theory of shell shock was developed as well. Whereas in *Free Associations* Jones leads his reader to believe that he himself advanced such a theory, since he does not mention any other British contributors (242), in actuality David Eder's observations and theory were far more influential in Britain. He first described his theory in a 1916 *Lancet* article ("An Address") and then published the first British book on the subject, *War Shock: The Psycho-Neuroses in War Psychology and Treatment* (1917).[19] According to Glover,

> This notable contribution [*War Shock*] did much to advance the cause of clinical psychology. Up to that time a variety of functional disturbances under war conditions had for lack of psychological insight been pigeon-holed under the classification of organic diseases. Eder's book did much to rescue them from therapeutic oblivion. Moreover, by substituting the title "war shock" for "shell shock," he succeeded in broadening enormously the current aetiological conception of the whole group of war neuroses. ("Eder" 99)

The book also proves that Eder had not become devoted exclusively to Jung's ideas, but maintained a selective approach to Freud's theories, since Eder found that in

> some cases sex, in the form of the typical Oedipus myth, is very clearly brought out, while in other cases it was highly probable that adequate psycho-analysis would have laid bare a sexual complex which again would have shown to be itself symbolic of the individual's maladaptation. (Eder, *War Shock* 12)

Nevertheless, the war neuroses clarified to many that the Freudian sexual theory of the aetiology of neurosis was not all-encompassing. This may have been one reason why Jung's ideas, based on a more general conception of the libido as psychic energy, became so popular in Britain during these years. Another reason may have been that Jung's view of humankind affirmed the importance of man's higher qualities and his potential for adaptation and regeneration, when it appeared as though these aspects of humanity had been all but shattered by war atrocities. In 1915 Jung published nine lectures, originally given in New York in 1912, as *The Theory of Psychoanalysis*. He laid bare his differences with Freud about the libido, developmental stages, and the Oedipus conflict (Ellenberger 697–698). Repeatedly he stressed the importance of psychological moments, each with a special history of its own (*Theory* 62, 73, 81, 82). More important to the British public was his *Collected Papers on Analytic Psychology* (1916), since it reprinted most of the papers he had given in England. The content of the opening chapters on "The Psychology and Pathology of So-called Occult Phenomena", somnambulic personalities, and automatisms would have seemed natural and appealed to Britishers introduced to dynamic psychology through the SPR's work. In T.W. Mitchell's SPR review of the book, he stressed that Freud and Jung differed most in their treatment of the symbol, for which Jung found a positive and prophetic value ("Review" 193). Whereas Freud emphasizes man's infantile, primitive cravings, and claims that these are fulfilled in the wishes of dreams, Jung views the dream as "an attempt at the solution of an unsolved problem" ("Review" 194). Mitchell concluded that, in Jung's paradigm,

> The symbol of the dream may play a part in the moral education of the individual similar to that which the religious symbol has played in the history of civilization. ("Review" 195)

The English translation of Jung's *Psychology of the Unconscious* appeared in the same year. This work drew extensively on the literatures and mythologies of the distant past in order to shed light on problems of the individual in the modern world. In it Jung introduced his conception of the collective unconscious, that aspect of the unconscious "which not only binds the individuals among themselves to the race, but also unites them backwards with the peoples of the past and their psychology" (*Psychology of the Unconscious* 199). David Eder emphasized the poetic, imaginative qualities of Jung's writing, as well as Jung's undogmatic attitude in his review for *The New Age* ("Psychological Perspective" 284–285). Eder's concluding remarks allude to the potential of Jung's work to counter the bleak vision of humanity which the war prompted:

> Jung's great work points out to us, indeed, the dying gods; his great understanding of the human psyche would help to find new ways of life,

to replace the dying with the nascent faith, to make the transition less painful and less destructive; harmless it cannot be: witness the great war. ("Psychological Perspective" 285)

May Sinclair also reviewed what she referred to as Jung's "great and terrible book", *The Psychology of the Unconscious*, in *The Medical Press and Circular*. Similarly to T.W. Mitchell, she highlighted the educative possibilities arising from Jung's work. She also took the opportunity to develop her idealistically motivated argument about the importance of sublimation in arriving at an ultimate "psycho-synthesis" (119).[20] As well, Jung's dream theories were developed in Maurice Nicoll's *Dream Psychology* (1917). Nicoll was yet another early member of the London Psychoanalytic Society who became more attracted to the Jungian perspective than the Freudian (Jones *Free* 239).

Freudian ideas not linked with the treatment of psychoneuroses in the war effort also continued to be made available to the British. In 1916, Brill's translation of Freud's *Wit and Its Relation to the Unconscious* was published. Freud explained the basic operation of wit using Jamesian language: "in wit formation a stream of thought is dropped for a moment and suddenly emerges from the unconscious as a witticism" (*Wit* 266). The merit of wit was that it enabled one to rebel against authority and "afford[ed] us the means of surmounting restrictions and of opening up otherwise inaccessible pleasure sources" (*Wit* 147). These statements on its value would have appealed to Lytton Strachey's generation, which was by this time fully engaged in using wit to rebel against its Victorian forbears. In addition, Freud offered another potential reason for valuing memory in fiction. He claimed that

> considering the close connection between recognition and remembering, the assumption is no longer daring that there exists also a pleasure in remembering, ie. that the act of remembering in itself is accompanied by a feeling of pleasure of a similar origin. (*Wit* 180)

The following year, 1917, several articles appeared on various aspects of Freudian discourse, including J.C. Flugel's contribution to the *British Journal of Psychology*, "Freudian Mechanisms as Factors in Moral Development". The second symposium to be published in the *British Journal of Psychology* on "Why is the 'Unconscious' unconscious?" (with contributions by Jones, Rivers, and Nicoll) stands out in the list of publications on dynamic psychological topics in the final years of the war.

Finally, during the war years, Adler's ideas received some exposure. His ideas about organ inferiority and compensation had been summarized as early as 1913 by David Eder in "The Present Position of Psychoanalysis" (1213–1215), but in 1918 the first British edition of Adler's own outline of his theory appeared (*The Neurotic Constitution*). Like McDougall's system, Adler's psychology stressed the dynamics of interpersonal relationships.

3.4 Post-War years

In *Free Associations*, Jones claims that "there seemed to be a psychological moment in every country when interest in the newness of psycho-analysis became acute" (230). Jones located this English moment "to be within the first five years after the end of the war" (*Free* 230). If we extend his observation to other later dynamic psychologies, including Jung's and Adler's, we can agree with him. Publications on all three psychologies, and events in which their ideas were discussed, proliferated to such a degree that only the most striking can be mentioned here.

In 1919, the year that Jones reconstituted the Psychoanalytic Society in Britain along narrower doctrinal lines, Carl Jung lectured to the SPR on his belief that spirits were projections of the psyche ("Psychological"). Jung returned to England in 1920 to give a seminar and lectures at the University of London (Wehr 218), and it is thus no wonder that Jones wrote to Freud that Jung's theories were better known in England than Freud's (Letter to Jones, 4 June 1922).

J.C. Flugel (1884–1955), a University of London psychologist and SPR member, came to the fore of British psychoanalysis in 1921 with his *The Psychoanalytic Study of the Family*. The book applied Freudian and Jungian tenets to family life, focussing particularly on emotions and conflicts, including incest. It helped popularize the concept of the Oedipus conflict in Britain (Zusne 135). Interestingly, Flugel's study was published by the International Psychoanalytic Press, which was taken over by Leonard and Virginia Woolf's Hogarth Press; Leonard is known to have read and commented favourably on it, as will be discussed in Chapter 6.

Early in 1921 as well, a debate on the dangers and merits of psychoanalysis ran concurrently with one on "The Future of the Novel" in the pages of the *Pall Mall Gazette*. Drs Arthur Lynch and Bernard Hollander attacked "the present craze for psychoanalysis", most justifiably for its exaggerated claims (6 January 1921). However, Flugel just as strongly defended psychoanalysis and warned against "wild" analysis (7 January 1921). One cannot help but feel that this debate influenced the discussion on "The Future of the Novel", since the question of sex in the novel was raised (7 January 1921). Both May Sinclair and J.D. Beresford participated in the literary discussion.

A similar, although much more lengthy, debate on psychoanalysis appeared from June to October 1925 in *The Nation and Athenaeum*, of which Leonard Woolf was literary editor (Abel 15). This debate followed the Woolf's Hogarth press publication of the first two volumes of Freud's *Collected Papers* (1924), translated by James and Alix Strachey. By this time the ideas of dynamic psychology, and psychoanalysis in particular, had permeated the Bloomsbury circle. Not only did Leonard Woolf consider himself a Freudian, and Alix and James Strachey take up careers in psycho-analysis, but the following people associated with the circle also became psychoanalysts: Adrian and Karin Stephen (Virginia Woolf's brother and sister-in-law), John Rickman, and Lionel Penrose. By the mid-1920s, psycho-analysis was both a craze and a curse, as J.D. Beresford asserted in his proclamation of the decline of psychoanalytic influence on the novel ("*Le Déclin*").

Although a full analysis of the attraction to, and in some instances notoriety of, later dynamic psychologies on a popular level is beyond this book's scope, some contributing elements must be mentioned since these also have a bearing on writers' responses to dynamic psychology. The following comments most strikingly apply to psychoanalysis, but they hold for other dynamic psychologies, including Adler's, Jung's, and Janet's, as well. Several motives for the attraction reflect the less noble characteristics of human nature. Since this group of ideas and therapies deals with the deepest emotional level of human beings, where they are most vulnerable, these ideas were continually exploited. Vincent Brome offers one vivid example:

> Charlatans took full advantage of the widespread publicity and every kind of exploitation for commercial purposes was brazenly explored. The bogus English Psycho-Analytical Publishing Co. put an Advertisement in *The Evening Standard* which read 'Would you like to make L 1000 a year as a psycho-analyst...Take eight postal lessons from us at four guineas a course.' (*Jones* 109)

In addition, because these ideas encroach on traditionally taboo territory, they were bound to feed a certain morbid curiosity about pathology and voyeuristic impulse towards sexuality. In many condensed summaries of the theories in the press, only the most sensational ideas and terms were mentioned. Descriptive terms deteriorated into jargon, such as *idée fixe*, collective unconscious, and Oedipus complex, which could be easily tagged and remembered. In 1930, William McDougall articulated the most negative results of psychology's popularization:

> In many ways the popular interest in psychology is a disturbing and distorting influence, especially in that it gives an undue prominence and prestige to views that are extreme, ill-balanced, fantastic and bizarre, if only they contain some modicum of truth and are put forward with persuasive skill. In America, especially, the general public, including not merely the seekers after personal benefits but also the more cultivated public, is keenly interested in the extravagances of the Freudian school, in the equally ill-balanced system of Adler with its gross exaggeration of one factor of our constitution to the neglect of all else, and in the still

more ill-balanced, extravagant, and bizarre dogmas of the behaviorist school.... On the other hand, it ignores the labours of those who try to maintain and, by patient research, to develop a sane, all-round, well-balanced system of psychology that founds itself on general biology and takes account of facts revealed by all relevant lines of research, by biology, by physiology, by anthropology, by the study of animal behavior, by the medical and social sciences, by "psychic research". For the general public such psychology is too difficult, too labourious, too lacking in sensational claims, in promises of immediate solutions of practical problems, too humdrum, too tame, too full of unverified hypotheses and confessions of ignorance. What the public likes is to be told straightforwardly and dogmatically that it has an Unconscious, source of all mysteries and all solutions; or a terrible Oedipus complex, source of all disorders; or an Inferiority Complex, source of all achievement; or a few Conditioned Reflexes that explain all human activity.... And whatever the dogma, it must be one that promises immediate profits in health, or pocketbook, or domestic harmony and relief from personal responsibility. (McDougall Autobiography 222)

However, not only the extravagances of dynamic psychology, especially as reported in the media, fostered interest. Though some dynamic psychological ideas had been introduced in the nineteenth century and before, it was only when reformulated in the early twentieth century that they received widespread attention. This suggests that, in some sense, their timing was right, that these ideas met some emotional and psychological needs of the period in Britain. As has been well documented, certain traditions and practices were increasingly perceived as oppressive and inadequate around the turn of the century. Religious belief no longer sustained, child-rearing practices seemed authoritarian, and the negligible status of women in a patriarchal society was seen increasingly as unjust. Dynamic psychologies appear to have offered liberation from some of these oppressions, and so it was no coincidence that psychoanalysis, for example, was taken up by early twentieth-century socialists in Britain.

Instead of attempting to suppress "undesirable" human instincts and to isolate those perceived as "abnormal", dynamic psychology acknowledged not only the fundamental importance of instincts, but also the harm in repressing them. It showed that normal and abnormal behaviour occurred on a continuum. For these reasons, dynamic psychologies were employed in arguments for free expression of instinctual impulses, as in free love, and for equality between the sexes. The therapies of these psychologies typically advocated confession of one's conflicts, not to a punitive father-figure, but to an understanding ear. Jung, for instance, wrote that "the psychoanalytic physician knows his own shortcomings too well, and therefore cannot believe that he can be father and leader. His highest ambition must only

consist in educating his patients to become independent personalities..."
(*Theory of Psychoanalysis* 105). In psychoanalytic technique, the patient's
associations were "free", in the sense that they were freely given, but also
freely responded to, without moralistic judgement.

Although generally more discriminating about the ideas of dynamic
psychology, writers too occasionally applied them in their work, not always
for the best motives or with the best results. In the post-war period when
dynamic psychologies became fashionable, some less scrupulous writers
exploited that popularity; hence the denigrating biography and lurid
"case-history" novel thrived. As J.D. Beresford has pointed out, the deliberate
and arbitrary use of these ideas "produces an effect on the [intelligent]
reader that may be variously irritating, unconvincing, and negligible, but is
rarely, if ever, psychologically valuable" ("Psychoanalysis" 430). However,
even serious writers like Beresford himself occasionally let their enthusiasm
for the new theories override their better aesthetic judgement. The question
of why writers of a higher calibre so frequently made use of these discourses
is a complicated one, and largely depends on each individual writer, but
a few brief generalizations can be made. Dynamic psychological discourses
tend to be dramatic, in the sense that they depict the dynamics of the mind,
by showing how elements, which can be likened to characters, are in active
conflict with one another. Dynamic psychology provides insights into
human existence, including aspects formerly considered taboo, from birth
to death and, in some cases, beyond. It thus envelops a wide range of behaviour and phenomena. Many of the theoretical entities that it explores
cannot be seen, such as the unconscious; thus an air of suspense surrounds
them, which attracted writers. Dynamic psychology rewrites the definition
of various aspects of behaviour: most notable is the extension of the
meaning of sexuality in psychoanalytic theory (Miller, *Freud* 81). Dynamic
psychology thus contributes to rearranging as well as enlarging the subject
matter of literature. The therapies of these psychologies also absolutely rely
on language for their success. An incoherent story is a sign of unhealthiness
and, as Jones makes explicit, the patient must translate and revise his story
in order to make the transition to healthiness:

> The symptoms constitute a veiled language in which hidden thoughts
> and desires find the only means allowed them of coming to expression.
> We will have to get the patient to translate his symptoms into more
> direct language, and thus to understand and appreciate the origin of
> them. (*Collected* 189)

Furthermore, as Steven Marcus, Patrick Mahoney, and others have convinc-
ingly argued, Freud's literary style (Mahoney x) and his modernist approach
(Marcus 58) contributed to his appeal. This claim might be extended to
Janet and to some of Jung's cases as well. All three were faced with the same

challenge of articulating psychic reality, as was the creative writer tuned in to this reality (Mahoney 7). Writers met this challenge by developing experimental techniques which were either analogous to, or directly derived from, therapeutic techniques. The most striking of these were the various types of stream of consciousness employed by the modernists. Whereas Freud would have been more attractive as a writer than Jung, whose prose could become cloudy and convoluted, both Jung and Myers had greater appeal on two other counts. While Freud continued to view the artist as a neurotic fleeing from reality, they portrayed the artist as having special access to the supernormal, or visionary, archetypal world. Both fully incorporated mankind's spiritual nature in their systems and thus took a step towards satisfying the widespread need felt in Britain of replacing traditional religious dogma with some other acknowledgement of spirituality. Thus, dynamic psychology both reshaped the subject matter available to artists and suggested possibilities of style and structure because of the literary qualities of much of its work. In the following chapters, more specific results of writers' attraction to dynamic psychology will be analysed in some detail.

In summary, we have seen that the later dynamic psychologies, particularly psychoanalysis, were reported on from 1893 onwards. Their discourses proliferated in England from 1908 to the First World War. By this period, Freud's theories of hysteria, sexuality and repression, sublimation, and dreams had been introduced and discussed in Britain. Jung's ideas about emotional complexes and the psychological basis of dementia praecox, as well as his divergence with Freud over the significance of sexuality, the universality of the Oedipus complex, and symbolism, had been brought to the attention of the British. Adler's theories about power and inferiority had also been mentioned. In these years, Ernest Jones, the self-proclaimed leading British pioneer of psychoanalysis, lived mainly in exile in Canada and thus had little impact in Britain. It was, rather, David Eder, William Brown, Bernard Hart, David Forsyth, and others who first brought psychoanalysis to the British and who set the tone of eclecticism towards it. Ernest Jones did not single-handedly perform a psychoanalysis on the English, since dissemination of Freudian ideas continued to be a collective effort after he returned to Britain. During the war, psychoanalysis flourished, mainly because psychoanalytic therapy could be adapted for the treatment of war-shocked soldiers. Nevertheless, in these years Jung's ideas also achieved greater recognition. In the post-war period, dynamic psychological discourse circulated widely in Britain through the popular press. At this time Jones's deliberate attempt to keep psychoanalysis from being assimilated into other medical and social science fields began to succeed. He reformed the London Psychoanalytic Society, removing those whose ideas extended beyond orthodox Freudian ones, set up a clinic which used Freudian therapy exclusively, and arranged through James Strachey to have Freud's *Collected Papers* published.

Several writers gained information about psychoanalysis directly from David Eder and, during the war years, from W.H.R. Rivers. The eclectic response of these pioneering doctors to the latest dynamic psychologies was reflected in the attitudes of writers, who characteristically appropriated whatever psychological discourse helped them to construct a denser version of reality that included aspects undetectable by the five senses.

4
May Sinclair: The Evolution of a Psychological Novelist

> I consider that the attitude of the modern novelist towards sex
> relations is more enlightened and more sane than that of those
> Victorian novelists who ignored this fundamental aspect of human
> nature. I don't deny that his work is sometimes "unpleasant"; but it
> need not be.
>
> – Sinclair, "Unpleasant Fiction", *Bookman* (London), April, 1925: 6

Though interest in May Sinclair has revived within the last ten years (J. Miller; Pykett; Raitt), she remains the most undeservedly underrated novelist of the five under discussion in this book, and, indeed, of all Edwardians who made the transition into modernism. She once held a very different reputation, however. As her career peaked in the early 1920s, she was recognized as the best and most widely known female novelist (Boll, *M.S.: Novelist* 16). One critic, John Farrar, confidently asserted that Sinclair is "the greatest psychological analyst in fiction" (as qtd in Boll, *M.S.: Novelist* 16). Unfortunately, the amount of favourable criticism she received declined in proportion to her health in the later 1920s. She died in relative obscurity in 1946, having suffered for sixteen years from Parkinson's disease which forced her to cease writing in 1931 at age sixty-eight. For most of the rest of the century, literary histories, such as Walter Allen's and William York Tindall's, at best accorded her brief mention, and at worst were dismissive and inaccurate.[1]

Sinclair was first and foremost a psychological novelist, and it is as a great, if not the "greatest psychological analyst in fiction", of the transitional period that I want to reconsider her, though revisionist efforts have been made on other grounds as well.[2] Not only was Sinclair in many instances the first to assimilate dynamic psychology into English fiction, but her knowledge of, and commitment to, these discourses extended well beyond that of her contemporaries. This was owing to her voracious intellect and courageous determination to synthesize the latest findings in order to express in fiction hitherto hidden realities, regardless of unpleasantness. A reassessment is necessary since partial views of her engagement with dynamic psychology have led to distortions in interpretation. One of the first studies to place her appropriately among her contemporaries, Dorothy Brewster and Angus Burrell's *Dead Reckonings* (1924), inaccurately discusses Sinclair as a Freudian (201–202). Sinclair's first biographer, Theophilus Boll, corrects this by revealing Sinclair's greater sympathy for Jungian psychology (*M.S.: Novelist*, 256–257), but he elsewhere errs in claiming that "she had shown her inborn genius for psychoanalytic incursion from her very first novel" *Audrey Craven* (1897) ("M.S. Collection" 2). Sinclair's most recent biographers, Hrisey Zegger (58) and Suzanne Raitt, inaccurately assume that Sinclair anticipated psychoanalytic concepts in her 1908–1913 " 'spooky' stories" (Raitt 134), though Raitt does identify "Sinclair's vivid sense of the links between the supernatural and psychoanalytic worlds" (135) without developing the context for this. Actually, in these stories Sinclair drew on pre-Freudian dynamic psychologies, including Frederic Myers's. This chapter will first touch on Sinclair's motivation for incorporating these psychologies before tracing her exposure to and interrogation of them, beginning with Herbart through to Pierre Janet, psychical research, Freud, and Jung. Reading her most significant novels and stories in this broader context will clarify some occluded features of them and reveal dynamic psychology as a fundamental, if not *the* fundamental, source of her initial innovations in characterization and theme, and subsequent innovations in style.

Attraction to, and the use made of, ideas is frequently motivated by psychological need, and this would seem to apply to Sinclair, who believed herself "complicated".[3] Sinclair's earliest efforts to educate herself seem to have been in part attempts to escape from the unhappiness of family conflicts and the pain of loss. Sinclair was the youngest of six children and the only girl raised in a strict religious household. Her mother appears to have been proud and over-controlling while her father, an alcoholic, was unreliable and tyrannical (Boll, *M.S.: Novelist* 27). He went bankrupt when May was seven. Her parents may have separated (Raitt 23), but at any rate the family's attempts to stave off poverty precipitated frequent moves (Steell 513). Sinclair's pursuit of knowledge was fuelled by her rebellion against her mother's attempt to restrain her from venturing beyond religious orthodoxy and from developing herself intellectually, not considered appropriate for a woman. The instability of her family life was compounded by the losses she experienced, effectually of her father at seven[4] and permanently through his death when Sinclair was eighteen. As well, four of her brothers died prematurely by the time May published her first novel at age thirty-four,[5] and her mother, with whom Sinclair lived, died when Sinclair was thirty-eight. Since Sinclair could not depend on the constancy of human relations, she withdrew into the relatively safe world of ideas. Neither Sinclair's early reading nor her creative activity was simply an escape, however. Her reading in evolutionary theory was in part an attempt to come to grips with her perceived tainted heredity, and her philosophical reading in part a consolation for loss, as was her later attraction to mysticism and psychical research. Sinclair's fiction writing enabled her to manage conflict and to reconstruct damaged or severed relations within the structured format of the novel or short story.

Nevertheless, Sinclair's attempts at creative adaptation did not always prove effective, and she suffered several breakdowns and periods of depression (Letters from Gwendolyn "Zack" Keats, Letters, 12 July 1899; to Katherine Tynan, 1 January 1902; Boll, *M.S.: Novelist* 8). Sinclair's attempts to understand these depressions in turn help explain her fascination in fiction with mental states, especially "morbid" ones, and her broad sympathy with sufferers of mental distress. Her own suffering, in combination with her commitment to idealism, also made her determined to play an educative role through her fiction, to show, for example, women thwarted and made ill by their own misplaced sacrifices.

Sinclair's only formal education occurred in 1881–1882 at Cheltenham Ladies College, where she came under the profound and long-lasting influence of Dorothea Beale, the Headmistress. Beale recognized Sinclair's intellectual capacity and encouraged her to read and write on philosophical idealism and psychology. Beale published Sinclair's essay on "Descartes" in the *Cheltenham Ladies College Magazine* in 1882, the first of several contributions made by Sinclair. After leaving Cheltenham, Sinclair continued to correspond with Beale, who would recommend works, including T.H. Green's *Prolegomena to Ethics* (1873), which greatly influenced Sinclair's thinking (Beale, Letters, December 1886 and January 1887). In fact, Sinclair's first important publication, "The Ethical and Religious Import of Idealism" (1893), explicates T.H. Green's idealism. Sinclair emphasizes the importance of man's self-conscious self (as distinguished from his individuality), which makes him one with the universal subject ("Ethical" 706) and accounts for moral responsibility and self-sacrifice.

Psychologist J.F. Herbart profoundly influenced Dorothea Beale's thinking about psychology, as revealed in an 1891 preface she wrote to Herbart's *The Application of Psychology to the Science of Education*. Translated by a colleague of Beale's from Cheltenham, the work must certainly have been read by Sinclair. Beale argued that to Herbart was owed the realization of "the importance of the subjective in every apperception" and of "the unity of the subject" (Beale viii). Herbart taught her to think of the ego as dynamically interacting with ideas, considered "active powers, the living offspring of the thinker" (Beale vi). She described the process as follows:

> That which we have received into the body of our thought does live in us, helping us to form each new conception – rising unbidden, by the laws of association, suppressing other thoughts which we are striving to evoke, passing below the "threshold of consciousness" into the darkness, where we yet feel that it is, though we cannot always call it up.... (Beale vii)

She called for Herbart's "good foundation" to be built upon by English psychologists and philosophers (Beale xi), a challenge taken up by Sinclair in both her non-fiction and fiction.

Beale actually got Sinclair to review a Herbartian-influenced educational psychology text, Mary Pulling's *The Teacher's Textbook of Practical Psychology* ("Review", *Cheltenham Ladies College Magazine*, Spring 1896). In it Sinclair stresses the role of the Herbartian concept of apperception in fostering moral education ("Review" 72). She also demonstrates her familiarity with unconscious influence, in this case on perception, probably deriving from Herbart ("Review" 73). Sinclair's emphasis on habit in education likely owes something to William James. Sinclair demonstrates her own inclination in suggesting "that psychology leads to metaphysics" ("Review" 74). Finally, Sinclair praises Pulling's "touches of humour" and "epigrammatic terseness and vigour" ("Review" 71), qualities Sinclair herself displays in her early fiction.

In that fiction Sinclair drew on Herbart's understanding of how the "psychic mechanism" of several levels of consciousness, including the unconscious, determined which ideas would enter consciousness. From him she learned about the operations of resistance, repression, and sublimation (though he did not name the latter). He believed that repressions could extend in duration from a single moment to years, and Sinclair developed the imaginative implications of this. In fact, much of what appears to be Freudian in Sinclair's pre-1913 work, beginning with *Audrey Craven* (1897), which Dorothea Beale praised for its seriousness, actually draws on Sinclair's awareness of this Freudian precursor, Herbart.

Although the idealist Beale would not likely have approved, Sinclair also read in first wave psychology and heredity, as revealed in two autobiographical sections of *Mary Olivier* (Boll, *M.S.: Novelist* 244). By 1890 Sinclair had read Spencer's *First Principles* (1862), *Principles of Biology* (1864, 1867), and *Principles of Psychology* (1855), along with Haeckel's *History of Creation* (1876), Maudsley's *Body and Mind* (1870) and *Physiology and Pathology of Mind* (1867), and Ribot's *L'heredité Psychologique* (1873, English Trans., 1875). Initially Sinclair was driven to read by fear about her own heredity, and was "terribly enchanted" by the cases of "Dr. Mitchell's ape-faced idiot; Dr. Browne's girl with the goose-face and goose-neck, billing her shoulders like a bird" (*Mary Olivier* 289); she likely received reassurances about her own potential for sanity from an older mentor, possibly the idealist, Professor Henry Gwatkin, as Mary did from the character Mr Sutcliffe in *Mary Olivier* (293–294).

A direct reference to William James's *Principles of Psychology* (1890) in Sinclair's second novel, *Mr. and Mrs. Nevill Tyson* (1898), confirms her familiarity with that cornerstone.[6] Boll claims that Sinclair shared with Richard Garnett, whom she met in 1899, a respect for Samuel Butler, whose contributions to psychology she commended later in *A Defence of Idealism* (1917). Thus, by the turn of the century, in addition to her expertise in idealistic philosophy, Sinclair had obtained a firm grounding in the most advanced nineteenth-century psychology.

In the twentieth century, her interest in the latest developments in psychology increased dramatically. In 1913 Sinclair put her expertise to practical use as one of twelve founding members of the Medico-Psychological Clinic of London. Conceived by Sinclair's friend, Dr Jessie Margaret Murray, who studied under Pierre Janet, the main objective of the Clinic was to treat "by medical and psychological means" functional nervous diseases and disorders (Boll, "Medico" 314). Typical of the British approach to dynamic psychology, it employed an eclectic array of treatments, including psychological analysis and re-synthesis, physical exercise, electrical therapy, and re-education. Nevertheless, the clinic drew on the foremost practitioners in England. Professor Charles Spearman, the distinguished University of London statistician, directed the psychological branch, and the consulting staff included Professors William McDougall, C.S. Myers, Carveth Read, and Francis Aveling. T.W. Mitchell and James Glover, brother of psychoanalyst Edward, were most prominent among the medical staff. Early associates included Dr Constance E. Long, translator of Jung, and Dr Charles Tuckey, psychical researcher and pioneering hypnotist (Boll, "Medico" 312). Though the Clinic has been almost completely neglected in psychoanalytic histories, it played a significant role, being the first public institution of its kind in Britain and the only centre until the opening of the Tavistock in 1920 to train psychoanalysts and to employ psychoanalytic methods of treatment.[7]

May Sinclair played several crucial roles during the Clinic's ten years of operation, and her involvement led to several important developments in her own life and career. She contributed the largest donation, of £500, to it, making its incorporation possible (Boll, "Medico" 312). Shortly after the Clinic's inauguration, attended by Sinclair, she expressed her enthusiasm for it by dedicating her book, *The Judgement of Eve and Other Stories*, to the Staff. She also helped with the clinic's administration, and wrote several reports and prospectuses soliciting funds for it. In addition, she may have aided Dr Murray and training analyst Julia Turner in translating Freud's work, not readily available to English readers in 1913, with the exception of *The Interpretation of Dreams*.[8] She did claim to have begun studying psychoanalysis in this year (Hoops 41). In addition, several pages of her notes on Freud's *Drei Abhandlungen Zur Sexualtheorie* (1905) survive. In them, important phrases in German are bracketed, suggesting that she made the translation herself (Sinclair, Notes). With her expertise in Greek, she almost certainly coined the word "Orthopsychics" by which the Society's educational branch was known (Boll, "Medico" 316). As evidence of her continuing interest in the clinic, in December, 1920, she was the only founding member to attend a performance of Yeats's play, *The Countess Cathleen*, put on by Orthopsychics Society students (Boll, "Medico" 322). Perhaps the greatest tribute to her involvement, and her skill in depicting human nature, occurred when Orthopsychics Society students read her novel, *The Tree of Heaven* (1917), both as literature and as therapy (Boll, *M.S.: Novelist* 234).

Most importantly, Sinclair's involvement in the Medico-Psychological Clinic drew her to those developing dynamic psychology in Britain. At least six Clinic participants were also SPR members, whose *Journal* and *Proceedings* reported on the Clinic's progress. These contacts likely led to her being elected an SPR member, as she was on 14 May 1914 (Boll, *M.S.: Novelist* 105). Boll plays down Sinclair's interest in the Society (and Raitt follows his lead), perhaps not wanting to associate his subject with an organization no longer considered reputable and unaware of its impressive status in 1914. He erroneously claims that

> she [Sinclair] never contributed to either the *Journal* or the *Proceedings*. She had an artist's interest in the occult story as a creative exercise, and in the mysteriously happening psychic phenomena in life, but had no patience with the assumption that psychic phenomena were matters for scientific exploration according to a scientific methodology. (Boll, *M.S.: Novelist* 105)

In actuality, Sinclair contributed two letters to the *Journal*, one in 1917 and one in 1918. These concern the question of cross-correspondences,[9] and they reveal both that Sinclair took psychical research seriously and that she was adamant about treating the evidence scientifically. Though "particularly impressed by the latest Willett scripts", she argues for the necessity of checking an alternative psychological hypothesis that such cross-correspondences may not be signals from the beyond, but may result from telepathic communication between experimenters who desire that survival will be proved (Letter, *Journal of SPR*, 26 April 1917, 67). Her statement about the power of desire, as suggested in the dream-life, reveals her assimilation of Herbart and Freud:

> Now, psychologically, desire, conscious or "sub-conscious," if it be strong enough, is the most purposeful and designing thing in the universe. Dream-analysis gives us some idea of the extraordinary power the *psyche* has of elaborating and designing its material according to its desire. It even *provides* the material. As the conditions of the dream-life are different, so the results are different. But though we may get nothing like the cross-correspondences, we *do* get elaboration, dramatization, cunning and purposeful design. (Letter, *Journal of SPR*, 26 April 1917, 67)

In a 1917 review of Charles Mercier's "Spiritualism and Sir Oliver Lodge", Sinclair similarly focusses on the need for scientific evidence. Highly critical of Lodge's unscientific attitude in books like *Raymond*, she praises Mercier's logical approach. Nevertheless, Mercier "has left human immortality standing in all its impregnable uncertainty. He has only made shell-holes of the rotten grounds on which believers in it have based their belief" (Sinclair, "Spirits" 61). Sinclair claims that some evidence for telepathy and thought-transference stands up to scrutiny ("Spirits" 61), and she concludes that "our wisest course is to suspend our judgment" (62).

Though Sinclair, in common with many psychical researchers, never was completely convinced by the evidence for the survival of psychic consciousness after death, she remained an enthusiastic follower of developments, hoping for a substantial discovery. She had alluded to psychical research in her first novel, *Audrey Craven* (1897, 134), and she had corresponded and socialized with Frederic Myers's widow Eveleen as early as 1908.[10] She remained a member of the Society at least until 1934, the year Reinald Hoops queried her about it (Hoops 47). However, her fiction bears the best testimony to her absolute fascination with psychic phenomena both for its own sake and as metaphor for projection of inner states.

Sinclair's friendship with a Medico-Psychological Clinic director, Dr Hector Munro, led to her brief participation in a Red Cross volunteer medical unit sent to Belgium in September 1914, following the outbreak of First World War. Dr Munro headed up the thirteen-member corps, while Sinclair acted as secretary, stretcher-bearer, nurse, correspondent, and fund-raiser (Boll, "Medico" 315). Interestingly, she remarks on packing Munro's copy of Freud's *Psychopathology of Everyday Life* while at the front (Sinclair, "From" 310). Although her involvement was terminated abruptly when she was sent back to England after less than three weeks, possibly for acting independently from her orders, the experience proved invaluable to her (Boll, *M.S.: Novelist* 107). She came into direct contact with sufferers of shell-shock and became very aware of how the psychopathology of war exacerbated individual psycho-pathology. She also realized how war could engender a feeling of most intense reality, "a curious excitement" and "steady thrill", viewed somewhat positively because of her idealist belief in the benefits of expanding consciousness (Boll, *M.S.: Novelist* 107; Sinclair, "From" 170–171). Her encounter with war was serialized in the *English Review*, elaborated in *A Journal of Impressions in Belgium* (1915), touched on in the novel *Tasker Jevons* (1916), and fully assimilated in her novels *The Tree of Heaven* and *The Romantic* (1920).

Following her return, Sinclair met, at an Orthopsychics Society meeting, yet another member, Professor H. Wildon Carr, who helped direct her career from practical concerns back to the world of ideas (Boll, *M.S.: Novelist* 109). Honorary Professor of Psychology at King's College, Carr was an idealist who had written on the philosophical implications of Freud's theories in 1914 (Carr "Philosophical"). As President of the highly distinguished Aristotealian Society, he was likely responsible for her election to it, considered by Sinclair to be one of her greatest achievements (Boll, *M.S.: Novelist* 19).

Perhaps more significantly, he encouraged her to continue working on the material eventually published as *A Defence of Idealism* in 1917 (Boll, *M.S.: Novelist* 109). The initial result of her research was published in the *Medical Press* as "Clinical Lecture on Symbolism and Sublimation" (118–122; 142–145).

This essay review of Jung's "great and terrible book" (119), *Psychology of the Unconscious* (1916), is significant because it demonstrates how idealism shaped her rather striking grasp of the strengths and weaknesses of later dynamic psychologies, including Freud's, Jung's, and Adler's; it also reveals her knowledge of contributions made by the older dynamic psychologies and her preference for Jungian psychology, though with some reservations.

The main limitation of psychoanalysis from her idealist's standpoint is that it does not emphasize enough the role of sublimation, viewed as essential to an ultimate psycho-synthesis ("Symbolism I" 119). According to Sinclair, "All religion, all art, all literature, all science are sublimations in various stages of perfection. Civilization is one vast system of sublimations" ("Symbolism I" 119). Sublimation, "the striving of the libido towards manifestation in higher and higher forms", is synonymous with mankind's evolution ("Symbolism I" 119, 120). Sinclair did not deny the "muck" that psychoanalysis brought to light, but she did optimistically emphasize the potential educative role of psychoanalysis. In addition, she was well aware of the political implications of psychoanalysis, as well as its misuse, claiming that

> at the present moment there is a reaction against all hushing up and stamping down. The younger generation is in revolt against even such a comparatively mild form of repression as Victorian Puritanism. And the New Psychology is with it. And the psychoanalysts, Freud and Jung and their followers, have been abused like pickpockets, as if they offered us no alternative but license or repression; as if the indestructible libido must either ramp outrageously in the open or burrow beneath us and undermine our sanity; as if sublimation, the solution that they do offer, were not staring us in the face. ("Symbolism I" 120)

Psychoanalysis also underrates the value of repression. She cites in particular the example of the ascetic, "The guardian and often the source of spiritual tradition" ("Symbolism II" 144). Furthermore, Sinclair criticizes Freud's sexual shock theory of the neuroses as being "too narrow to cover all the facts", and she considers Adler's explanation, of an individual's feeling of insufficiency, as a reaction to it ("Symbolism II" 142).

Although Sinclair portrays Jung as dis-illusionist about the "lofty spiritual powers of the unconscious" ("Symbolism I" 118), ultimately she finds Jung's synthetic, prospective explanation of the neurotic as "the failure to solve the problem of his personality, to 'adapt himself to reality'" ("Symbolism II" 142) to be "eminently satisfactory" ("Symbolism II" 143). As an idealist,

Sinclair concurred with Jung's statement that "only through the mystery of self-sacrifice is it possible to be born again" ("Symbolism II" 143). Not only can one see sublimation operating in his libido theory, but it takes into account "all the higher psychic data overlooked by Freud, and all the 'lower' primitive facts whose significance Adler perhaps underrates" ("Symbolism II" 143–144). Sinclair does upbraid Jung for handling "poetry and metaphysics as if they were nothing but primitive myths", and for treating works like the Upanishads and other highly sublimated writing appallingly literally ("Symbolism II" 145, 143). Nevertheless, overall she admires him: "Professor Jung is on the side of the angels, battling for those delicate hopes and aspirations of humanity he is supposed to have trampled under foot" ("Symbolism II" 145).

Sinclair extracted her "Clinical Lectures" from her 137-page unpublished manuscript "The Way of Sublimation", intended as a sequel to *A Defence of Idealism* (1917), on "psychoanalysis and the problems it raises" (*Defence* 383). Actually broader than this, "The Way of Sublimation" most fully reveals Sinclair's comprehension of the philosophical roots of psychology as well as psychoanalysis's limitations, particularly its need to address psychic phenomena and its potential power. In the Introduction, Sinclair deftly shows how philosophy dominated psychology in the eighteenth and nineteenth centuries despite Herbart's and Lotze's efforts to deal with data rather than rely on priori metaphysical systems ("Way" 2). Only Schopenhauer escaped the tyranny of systems, and his conception of the world as will was strengthened by his follower Von Hartmann, for whom Sinclair reveals a "youthful enthusiasm" ("Way" 3). Her statement that Von Hartmann in *The Philosophy of the Unconscious* is "avenged" because the unconscious has "come into its own" demonstrates her uncommon awareness of the continuity in psychology.

She then treats the issues covered in the clinical essays, once again favouring Jung and emphasizing sublimation as the goal of psychoanalysis. The limitations of psychoanalysis, "a small department of General Psychology" are, first, that its theories "do not . . . take due account of the extreme multiplicity and variety of human interests" ("Way" 111). She shares this perception of psychoanalysis's reductiveness with many of her British contemporaries. Second, psychoanalysts "do not always discriminate between the manifestations of primitive and sublimated libido" ("Way" 114). Third, a considerable class of dreams has escaped Professor Freud's net. Drawing on SPR data, she points out that these include telepathic, labour-saving, and problem-solving dreams ("Way" 126). She also questions whether dreams based on abnormal cases can be generalized from, and correctly declares that "it is Professor Freud's critics, and perhaps his followers who have exaggerated" ("Way" 123). Fourth, and most seriously, "psychoanalysts have not found the full consequences and implications of their theory of sublimation" ("Way" 130). Psychoanalysts insist that libido does not change, but also claim that it must be transformed through sublimation ("Way" 131). If the transformative capacity of libido is accepted, as Sinclair believes it should be, then its sexual component "will be brief, trivial incidents in its stupendous career" ("Way" 132). Sinclair was the first to admit that the sex drive was important (see "Way" 130 and her fiction), but she here implies that it is neither the psyche's prime motivator nor exclusive goal.

Despite these criticisms, psychoanalysis confirmed for the idealist Sinclair "the unity of all psychic processes" ("Way" 133). Psychoanalysis provided a bridge between the unconscious and the conscious and linked "our symbolic dream-consciousness with the consciousness of the race" ("Way" 135). In general, psychoanalysis deserved more attention because

> I believe that certain of its findings bear on Psychology and the ultimate questions of Philosophy with a weight and a significance that are unavoidable, and that if Psychology were to ignore them it would do so at some disadvantage to itself. ("Way" 133)

Finally, Sinclair recognized the aesthetic parallels to psychoanalysis in the latest painting and sculpture which "sets the dynamics of art above its mechanics. It is in revolt against realism in the interests of spiritual energy" ("Way" 95). "The Way of Sublimation" thus demonstrates not only that Sinclair was one of the first English critics to recognize the greater implications of psychoanalysis, but also that she was one of the first to evaluate it judiciously and to place it accurately in its historical and philosophical context.

Sinclair's conscientious estimation of psycho-analysis carries over into *A Defence of Idealism* (1917). In this "light-hearted essay", as she later modestly referred to it (*New Idealism* ix), Sinclair marshals considerable evidence in support of the existence of selfhood, unity of consciousness, and an ultimate spiritual reality. Along the way she criticizes those opposing philosophies bearing on these issues, including Samuel Butler's pan-psychism, Bergson's vitalism, James's pragmatism and pluralism, and Russell's realism (*Defence* viii). For example, she agrees with the "unjustly neglected" Butler on his theory of heredity, but rejects his conclusions about the impossibility of individuality above and beyond ancestral inheritance. (*Defence* 36). Bergson is similarly criticized, in his case for putting Pure Time before the self (*Defence* 69).

In a chapter addressing "Some Ultimate Questions of Psychology", Sinclair takes William McDougall as "the clearest, simplest, and most convincing authority on the behaviour of the psyche here and now" (*Defence* 84) in order to examine what constitutes individuality. The will comes closest to comprising selfhood but does not include states of consciousness like remembering. She rejects both of the alternatives proposed by McDougall to account for the relation between self and body because parallelism, a form of dualism, cannot be supported by the evidence. Instead, she opts for the "fairly demonstrated" fact of psychophysical interaction, which once again justifies "the hypothesis of a self or soul as the unique ground of the unity of consciousness" (*Defence* 125). Chapters on Pragmatism show that this philosophy falters because of "an unconscious craving for the unity [it] spurns" (*Defence* 147) and realism because it reduces consciousness to the role of spectator of existence, which does not square with evidence of its dynamism. In the course of her discussion, her indebtedness to Hegelian thought becomes clear, since spirit emerges as central. The result of raising "either psychic energy or physical energy to their highest pitch", spirit is the highest universal, representing the absolute reality of things (*Defence* 265, 332).

Making a bold departure from the traditional ground of philosophy, Sinclair concludes by examining the new mysticism from a psychological standpoint, in the manner of William James in *Varieties of Religious Experience* (1902). In spite of the psychopathology of the mystic, whose detachment is dissociation, in Janet's schema, and whose "psychic phenomena" can largely be accounted for by suggestion, his goal is still the unitive life (*Defence* 290, 300). The uniformity of experience of this "peculiar kind of genius" confirms the unity of consciousness (*Defence* 319). The "psychic powers", including what Sinclair refers to as the "fact" of telepathy (*Defence* 351) and the dream life, in particular, provide evidence that although individuality is precarious, a single self or consciousness transcends the individual's apparent division (*Defence* 295, 377). Sinclair claims that

> though our selfhood would seem to remain inviolable, our individuality holds its own precariously, at times, and with difficulty against the forces that tend to draw us back to our racial consciousness again. The facts of multiple personality, telepathy and suggestion, the higher as well as the lower forms of dream-consciousness, indicated that our psychic life is not a water-tight compartment, but has porous walls, and is continually threatened with leakage and the flooding in of many streams.
>
> It may be that individuality is only one stage, and that not the highest and the most important stage in the real life-process of the self. (*Defence* 375)

For the facts of psychical phenomena, Sinclair relies heavily on SPR evidence. She demonstrates both a thorough knowledge of psychical research, including Frederic Myers's *Human Personality* (1903), and its close link with psychology. Although inconclusive about personal immortality, psychical researchers "are preparing excellent material for psychologists on this side" (*Defence* 353). In summary, Sinclair points out that different kinds of certainty exist, including that of reason and spiritual instinct (*Defence* 348), since "our perceptions, like our passions, maintain themselves at higher and lower intensities" (*Defence* 379). The highest degree of certainty is reached at those moments when all elements support one another "with such heightening of psychic intensity that we discern Reality here and now" (*Defence* 379). She continues,

> No reasoning allows or accounts for these moments. But lovers and poets and painters and mystics and heroes know them: moments when eternal Beauty is seized traveling through time; moments when things that we have seen all our lives without truly seeing them, the flowers in the garden, the trees in the field, the hawthorn on the hillside, change to us in an instant of time, and show the secret and imperishable life they harbour; moments when the human creature we have known all our life without truly knowing it, reveals its incredible godhead; moments of danger that are moments of pure and perfect happiness, because then the adorable Reality gives itself to our very sight and touch. There is no arguing against certainties like these. (*Defence* 379)

Despite Sinclair's ultimate appeal beyond reason to mystical moments in support of idealism, her book was treated respectfully and admired, especially for its style, by the philosophers who reviewed it, including Bertrand Russell (Boll, *M.S.: Novelist* 258).

In 1918, Sinclair brought her knowledge of psychology to bear on "The Novels of Dorothy Richardson" in what is undoubtedly her most innovative and important contribution to literary criticism. At first glance her approach does not appear to align well with *A Defence of Idealism*. Sinclair opens by criticizing the distinction between realism and idealism, objective and subjective, a distinction Sinclair herself made in defending idealism. However, she realizes that these terms are no longer precise and actually obfuscate the literary issue, since "Reality is thick and deep, too thick and deep and at the same time too fluid to be cut with any convenient carving knife" ("Novels" 4). In this view she agrees with J.D. Beresford, who confessed initial confusion about Dorothy Richardson's novel because he attempted to apply the old terms. Sinclair praises Beresford's "admirable" 1915 Introduction to Richardson's *Pointed Roofs* because he claimed that the novelist must "plunge in" to reality, but she does not concur with him that Richardson was the first to do so. Just as she pointed out precedents of psychoanalytic ideas, here she identifies "a growing tendency to plunge" beginning as early as the 1880s with the Goncourts ("Novels" 4).

Significantly, Sinclair was the first to borrow the term "stream of consciousness", probably from William James, to describe this literary method in which the reader encounters the world through the protagonist's senses. Though Sinclair's essay will be remembered primarily for this influential application, her choice appears rather curious when it is realized that, in *A Defence of Idealism*, she claims that she "abhors William James's way of thinking" (ix);

however, she admired his writing style and his genius (*Defence* x). In support of idealism she also found more unity in pragmatism and pluralism than James had acknowledged (*Defence* 158). More importantly, as Gerald Myers points out, tensions exist between James's philosophy and his psychology, between an idealistic and a non-idealistic theory of mind and self. Myers claims that

> the stream of thought looms in Jamesian psychology as an idealistic framework – an alternative to that of the human body and its constitution – in terms of which the *I* is to be interpreted. When, as in the metaphysics of pure experience, he reconstructed the human body from sensations, feelings and the introspectable stream of consciousness, his view is so idealistic and Berkeleyan that commonsense ideas about the body and the bodily self seemed threatened. (353)

The stream of consciousness metaphor thus fit in well with Sinclair's idealism, and it also appeared valid from the psychological perspective familiar to Sinclair, since it accounted for phenomena like dissociation; furthermore, it accurately characterized the technique Richardson had brought to "punctilious perfection" ("Novels" 5).

As in *Defence of Idealism*, Sinclair was attentive to mysticism in Richardson's work. She was attracted to the moments passing one by one or overlapping, "moments tense with vibration, moments drawn out fine, almost to snapping point" ("Novels" 7). When one of these approaches ecstasy, it cannot be explained, lending it a certain mysticism ("Novels" 9). Richardson's novel also appealed to Sinclair since it deals with the idealistic theme of feminine self-sacrifice, central to Sinclair's own work ("Novels" 9).

Sinclair's commentary on "The Future of the Novel" (*Pall Mall Gazette*, 1921) is also thoroughly informed by her psychological awareness and philosophical idealism. Sinclair acknowledges the difficulty of dealing with more than one consciousness in the stream of consciousness technique. However, she believes the method could be used on a man of action, revealing her idealistic slant:

> If you take the consciousness of a man of action, you will have all his actions in his consciousness – the only place where they immediately and intimately are. The method – whatever else may be said for it – provides a more thorough-going unity than any other, for there is nothing more fundamental than the unity of consciousness. ("Future" 6)

Sinclair argued that the analytic novel, in which one is aware of the author all the time, is no longer viable:

> The modern novelist should not dissect; he should not probe; he should not write about the emotions and thoughts of his characters. The words he uses must be the thoughts – be the emotions. ("Future" 6)

This method of direct presentation, in what she called the "synthetic psychological novel", represented the novel's future.

In 1922, as the Medico-Psychological Clinic closed down, Sinclair's second major philosophical endeavor, *The New Idealism*, was published. Once again her knowledge of psychology served her well. Sinclair's argument for reconstructing idealism hinged on the distinction made between primary and secondary consciousness. Whereas our primary consciousness perceives, feels, wills, and remembers without making a distinction between knowing and the thing known, secondary consciousness is the awareness of awareness, clicking in when reflection, judgement, inference, and reason begin. The realists' failure to make the distinction renders their assumption false, "that in knowing we know that things exist in themselves apart from any knowing" (*New* ix). As an illustration, Sinclair mentions that "primary and secondary consciousness work together in all creative art; but the finished work of art, the creation, becomes the object of primary consciousness" (*New* 293). The division overcame the main objection of realism to the older idealism, that being and being known are not the same (*New* 312). Both primary and secondary consciousness are dependent on an ultimate consciousness, holding Time and Space together, resolving their contradictions, and uniting the perspectives of the finite selves (*New* 314). In dealing with the problem of Space–Time in consciousness, Sinclair felt that she had made an advance over the *Defence*, and the reviewers, again including Bertrand Russell, agreed (Russell 625).

After *The New Idealism*, Sinclair's critical writing veered away from philosophical and psychological analysis and commentary. Her fiction similarly shifted, into the comic and satirical, to which psychological stream of consciousness techniques did not lend themselves, as she had recognized in "The Future of the Novel" (6). However, by this time no other English novelist could surpass the range or depth of her knowledge of matters philosophical and psychological.

In summary, several characteristics of Sinclair's approach to that knowledge stand out. The thoroughness of her grounding in philosophy and dynamic psychology is striking, as is her determination to grapple with major philosophical systems in print. The high value that she placed on philosophical inquiry, even above creative writing, is also extraordinary. One cannot but help admiring her open-mindedness and commitment to new ideas, often in the face of adverse criticism, as well as her recognition of the need to gather the best psychological discoveries together in a psychosynthesis.

Sinclair's commitment to idealism, though not rigid, led her to search out psychological discourses which shed the most light on consciousness, its fringes, and its relation to other levels of awareness. She attempted to prove the unity of consciousness, and the existence of selfhood above and beyond memory and individuality, which is precarious and threatened by the flooding in of streams from the past. Self-awareness was crucial to Sinclair since it revealed the underlying unity of knowledge and brought man's spirit in touch with God, or at least the Absolute, a higher, or world, consciousness. Those dynamic psychologies, including Freud's and especially Jung's, which promoted individual self-awareness were viewed most positively since they had the potential to bring humanity onto a higher plane of existence. From her perspective, psychoanalysis also seemed limited because it did not recognize the transformative potential of sublimation, was reductive, and did not consider mysticism or psychic phenomena as revealing the spiritual plane of existence. Jung and the SPR were more inclusive because they integrated the spiritual into their psychological perspectives. Though she remained unconvinced of the evidence for psychic survival beyond death, she accepted telepathy as a fact.

In adopting the ideas of psychophysical interaction and of interplay between a primary and a secondary consciousness, Sinclair developed her own perspective on mental dynamics. In applying the term "stream of consciousness" to Richardson's novels, she recognized the aesthetics of a dynamic approach. Sinclair herself conveyed the dynamics of the mind vividly in her non-fiction works, as the following passage suggests:

> Imagine then what a diagram would look like that attempted to represent the higher psychic processes of man, the complex play of many motives, determining one of many actions seen to be possible and desirable; the conflict between desire and will; the element of choice – the will darting like a shuttle to and fro among all those infinite threads and weaving them to its own pattern. Add to this the emotions saturating the web with their own colours; and consider that you have not yet allowed for the intellectual fabric, different and distinct from this play of action and emotion and desire, yet hardly distinguishable, so close is the psychic web, so intricate the pattern. (*Defence* 117)

Nevertheless, the tapestry of Sinclair's fiction most clearly reveals how imaginatively and with what consequences she wove strands of dynamic psychological discourse.

4.1   Sinclair's psychological artistry

The philosophical and psychological discourses about which Sinclair became so knowledgeable inform the main preoccupations of her fiction in a variety of ways. From her earliest novels on, several concepts of positivist, materialist psychology, manifested in naturalistic themes, are tempered not only by idealism but also, and more importantly, by her probing of characters' psyches. Typically individuals make sacrifices which may or may not be meaningful, but are generally at least partially motivated by unconscious wishes. As her work develops, Sinclair gives greater scope to the role of unconscious influences on behaviour, while placing hereditary factors further in the background. Characters' reactions and adaptations to their environment and the degree of their spiritual and psychological awareness also become more important in determining their destinies.

Throughout her fiction Sinclair adeptly demonstrates the complexity of human motivation, particularly the difficulty of establishing identity or selfhood. Her characters are shown to have fluid and dynamic selves, which are more often than not in conflict. Over the course of her fiction she becomes more explicit about portraying the disastrous effect of repression, or the dissociation of one part of the self from others, particularly when the conflict involves sexuality. Her characters' sexual natures are revealed with a surprising degree of candidness, considering the period in which she wrote. Sinclair also depicts the dire consequences of the misuse of one's sexuality as a tool of manipulation. Several of her novels explore, with open-mindedness, changing attitudes towards marriage and the role sexuality plays in it. Sinclair dissolves traditional boundaries between normal and abnormal by showing perfectly "sane" individuals afflicted by psychosomatic illness. The terminology of medical and abnormal psychology is often used metaphorically to convey the intensity of emotional states. For example, Sinclair will suggest that characters are "obsessed" by material objects, or are becoming "hysterical". Doctors are not stereotyped or distant figures, but rather are shown to have very human flaws. Some are limited by the prejudices of medical orthodoxy, while others, Sinclair's soul doctors, demonstrate greater understanding of, and sympathy for, the "new" psychological symptoms and unorthodox cures like hypnotism. Several of her works adopt elements of the psychological or psychical case study as a means of intensifying the impression of realism. Sinclair's novels exhibit a particular fascination with the multifarious aspects of creative genius. Rarely is creativity viewed merely as a manifestation of neurosis but more frequently as the fortunate coalescing of heredity, talent, intelligence, and temperament. At their best, the fruits of genius represent the supreme achievement of sublimation, a concept Sinclair explored intensively in her fiction.

Sinclair paid particular attention to feminine psychology. More often than not it is women who make sacrifices in an attempt to "do the perfect thing" and who suffer because of their denial of feelings and ambitions. Her novels are populated by women who have negative attitudes towards childbearing and whose babies miscarry or die of neglect. If women who are brought up traditionally are exposed to new ideas about independence, notably the desirability of having a career, then, typically, they rebel. This preoccupation does not mean, however, that the men in Sinclair's novels are painted as villains. Frequently they are victims of birth or circumstance, just as likely to suffer from the puritanical convictions of their female counterparts as to tyrannize their dependents. The relations between the sexes are never idealized in Sinclair's fiction and are often stormy, rocked, or wrecked by failure in communication. Families are shown to be fragile, with children typically faring poorly. An analysis of the eleven most important novels, as well as two each of the most psychologically informed novellas and short stories in Sinclair's canon will confirm her extraordinary ability to adapt, for dramatic fictional purposes, the discourses of dynamic psychology, especially the findings about unconscious motivation. Through this ability she is able to shed new light on the gamut of emotion and issues that she treats.

4.2   Selfhood and sacrifice: Fiction 1897–1910

Sinclair's first published novel, *Audrey Craven* (1897), is a thoughtful as well as an entertaining study, both of a woman's unenlightened quest for self-revelation and of the complex relations between life and art.[11] The novel merges both first wave and second wave, or dynamic psychology, captured in her comment that "in our modern mythology, Custom, Circumstance and Heredity are the three fates that weave the web of human life" (*A.C.* 10). Though one of her characters suffers from an hereditary taint (*A.C.* 202), Sinclair's treatment of selfhood, the relations between unconscious and conscious behaviour, and illness clearly reveal her dynamic approach.

The protagonist, Audrey, is a woman with a room of her own, thirty years before Virginia Woolf evoked the room as a symbol of feminine independence. Nevertheless, Audrey fails to take advantage of this position, even as a social artist, because her mind, like her room, is furnished with the ideas of others. In one passage rich with irony, Audrey says to her latest admirer, Ted, that

> I'm not in the least conventional, and I don't think I'm weak-minded. And I want my room to express my character, to be a bit of myself. So give me some ideas. You don't mind my asking you, do you? You're the only artist I know. (*A.C.* 54)

Her self is shown to be completely fluid, subject to the invasion of another personality, and her soul prey to transformation, as in metempsychosis. As illustration, Katherine Haviland, sister of Ted, one of those who influences Audrey, notices a "change of key" in her and realizes that

> Audrey was playing a new part. Her mind was swayed by a fresh current of ideas; it had suffered the invasion of a foreign personality. The evidence for this was purely psychological but it all pointed one way.... Audrey was actually undergoing another metempsychosis.... No wonder that she would not announce her engagement. At the best of times her fluent nature shrank from everything that was fixed and irrevocable... (*A.C.* 142)

This dynamic portrayal thus fuses the conception of self as stream, popularized by William James, and Pierre Janet's findings about multiple personality, with a popular metaphysical concept, albeit one that had been used by psychologist James Sully.[12]

Sinclair attends to Audrey's unconscious behaviour in order to reveal another dimension of her personality, "the secret places of her soul, its unconscious hypocrisy, its vanity, its latent capacity for evil" (*A.C.* 196). In a confrontation with a lover, Hardy, who returns from Canada to find that he has been thrown over, Audrey claims that she wishes she were dead, while simultaneously "she was trying to wring the neck off a little china image" plucked from her mantelpiece (*A.C.* 191–192). Hardy then asks whether anything has happened, and Audrey responds, while at the same time "the china image slipped through her fingers and was broken to bits on the hearthstone" (*A.C.* 192), thus betraying her unconscious feeling. This occurrence at once symbolizes her frustration at herself, at the ideal she has sacrificed, as well as her desire to destroy Hardy's old image of her as a fragile figurine, and as betrothed to him.

Sinclair's awareness of the consequences of repressing unconscious impulses is made clear in the following description of Audrey's maiden aunt chaperon:

> If you, being young and vivacious, take a highly nervous old lady and keep her in a state of perpetual repression, shutting her out from all your little confidences, you will find that the curiosity so natural to her age, will be sure to burst out, after such bottling, in alarming effervescence. (*A.C.* 23)

Her use of the term "repression" here must surely derive from her reading of Herbart. Sinclair also frequently shows characters suffering from psychosomatic illness, including morbid sensitivity (*A.C.* 207), nerves (*A.C.* 230, 243), depression, and moral shock (*A.C.* 142), the latter likely based on Janet's and others' psychic shock theory.

Though Sinclair's idealism permeates the novel, she plays off various philosophies against each other by depicting the consequences for various characters of adhering to them. Katherine Haviland's idealism causes her to make many futile sacrifices, including own artistic ambitions for her brother Ted's greater genius (*A.C.* 48). Sinclair's portraits of Langley Wyndam and Flaxman Reed best reveal Sinclair's own aesthetic and moral position. A self-proclaimed uncompromising psychological realist, Langley Wyndam probes "below the surface...below the solid layer of traditional morality – deep down to the primitive passions" in his novels (*A.C.* 158). His belief that "the stuff of nature" constitutes art places him in the naturalist school (*A.C.* 159). He does achieve critical success through his cruel exposé of Audrey as "a mixture of vanity, stupidity and passion" in his "An Idyll of Picadilly", but Katherine Haviland suggests that it fails to probe how the composite of other people that is Audrey holds together, and thus is "terribly superficial"

(*A.C.* 266). Although Wyndam firmly believes that he understands himself, and prides himself on his knowledge of women and his scrupulous conscience, he is lacking in all three areas (*A.C.* 120, 121, 235); he is revealed as morally bankrupt and as egoistic as Audrey (*A.C.* 256).

Another stronger personality to whom Audrey turns is Flaxman Reed, an Anglican priest (*A.C.* 372). Though Reed believes in the provisional acceptance of truths in order to "see how they worked out", thus aligning him with pragmatism, he manages to penetrate further than Wyndam into Audrey's motivation because he takes into account her spiritual dimension (*A.C.* 137). The narrator claims,

> Flaxman Reed would certainly not have called himself a psychological realist; but by reason of his one strength, his habit of constant communion with the unseen, he had solved Langley Wyndam's problem. It would never have occurred to the great psychological novelist, in his search for the real Audrey, to look deeper than the "primitive passions," or to suspect that the secret of personality could lie in so pure a piece of mechanism as the human conscience. (*A.C.* 325)

Flaxman is not idealized, since his "sensitive soul, made morbid by its self-imposed asceticism", recoils from Audrey's confession of sin, and he is unable to help her (*A.C.* 322); however, he was "the one man by whom and for whom she [Audrey] could have grown womanly and good" (*A.C.* 322).

Thus, Sinclair's recognition that individuals are limited and even trapped by the systems they embrace gives her characters depth and complexity. Also, Sinclair's characterization of Wyndam and Reed strongly suggests that, while aware of naturalism's potential for conveying reality, she finds it superficial and instead privileges an approach which integrates the spiritual. Sinclair's study in the failure of self-awareness clearly reveals her engagement with a variety of dynamic psychological discourses.

Sinclair moved towards fulfilling the "promise" of this first novel, praised by no less than George Gissing for its "characterization and construction" (qtd in Boll, *M.S.: Novelist* 56), in her second, *Mr. and Mrs. Nevill Tyson* (1898). In this study of marital incompatibility, Sinclair broadens the scope of her psychological enquiry by investigating in depth the fluid natures of two characters, Nevill and Molly Tyson, and their family dynamics. She introduces what might be called a method of progressive revelation in order to do so. In addition, though idealism provides the underpinning, more attention is paid to sexuality as a motivator, to dreams, to psychological moments, and to psychosomatic illness.

The character of Nevill Tyson best illustrates these new developments. Initially he appears to be the quintessential sub-aristocratic rake. Only after his marriage to Molly and the birth of his child do we get a glimpse of more complex motivation. Nevill

> was insanely jealous of this minute masculine thing that claimed so much of her attention. He began to have a positive dislike to seeing her with the child. There was a strain of morbid sensibility in his nature, and what was beautiful to him in a Botticelli Madonna, properly printed and framed, was not beautiful – to him – in Mrs. Nevill Tyson. He had the sentiment of the thing, as I said, but the thing itself, the flesh and blood of it, was altogether too much for his fastidious nerves. (*Tyson* 78)

At this stage his incongruous squeamishness is a mystery, though the dynamics convey with perspicacity what, from a post-Freudian perspective, would be seen as the oedipal conflict from the father's viewpoint.

Gradually the sources of Nevill's paradoxical nature are revealed, as layer after layer of his past is brought to light. He bitterly resents his repressive Baptist upbringing as a "little city tailor's son" (*Tyson* 119). His revolt against this past spurs his ambition, but his origins also help explain his tendency to dissipation. In a comment evoking Butler's discourse on inheritance, the narrator explains that, at Oxford, Nevill

> had flung himself into dissipation in the spirit of dissent. His passions were the passions of Demos, violent and revolutionary. Tyson the Baptist minister had despised the world, vituperated the flesh, stamped on it and stifled it under his decent broadcloth. If it had any rights he denied them. Therefore in the person of his son they reasserted their claim; and young Tyson paid it honourably and conscientiously to the full. (*Tyson* 120–121)

Nevertheless, Tyson's early environment helps account for his repulsion at the sight of his wife breast-feeding his son, whom he perceives as the product of his sexuality and refers to as "the animal" (*Tyson* 80).

Further revelations occur when Tyson suffers a psychic shock after his wife is badly burned while rescuing him from a fire he caused while in a drunken stupor. During a dream-like state of introspection, Tyson glimpses the truth that his feelings for Molly are solely physical, but he suppresses it, with psychosomatic consequences (*Tyson* 238). Nevill develops a "nervous dread of going into [Molly's] room", and his senses become "morbidly acute" (*Tyson* 241). With Jamesian emphasis on habits, Sinclair suggests that Tyson has ruined any higher capabilities he once had through his habit of sensualism: "Tyson was paying the penalty of having lived the life of the senses; his brain had become their servant, and he was horrified to find that he could not command its finest faculties at pleasure" (*Tyson* 242). One further clue as to the origins of Tyson's character then surfaces. Apparently a premature sexual episode destroyed his "immortal soul" (*Tyson* 263), but this does not excuse his unrealistic attitude towards his wife.

At the time of his death during a military campaign, Tyson writes three contradictory documents capturing his complex nature and revealing his self-deceptions (*Tyson* 290–292). When he receives news of Molly's death he destroys two of them and rushes into the desert, "his heart beating with the brutal, jubilant *lust* of battle" (*Tyson* 296), suggesting that Tyson's lust for Molly's flesh has merely been sublimated. Ironically, he leaves behind the impression of being unified, and his sins, unlike his wife's, are forgiven because of his war heroism (*Tyson* 297).

In contrast to her method of developing Nevill's character, Sinclair draws on the ideal of self-sacrifice to deepen Molly Tyson's character. Molly first makes a "supreme sacrifice", of her motherhood (*Tyson* 233), by weaning her child abruptly on Nevill's demand, causing her to go "into a fit of hysterics" (*Tyson* 82) and the child to deteriorate and die. She next sacrifices her physical beauty by saving Nevill from the fire which disfigures her. Despite the agony, the disaster transforms her:

It seemed as though her beauty being dead, all that was blind and selfish in her passion for Nevill had died with it. She was glad to be delivered from the torment of the senses, to feel that the immortal human soul of her love was free. (*Tyson* 215–216)

Her cleansed soul lifts his up temporarily, and this is framed as a psychological moment of unity:

For one luminous perfect moment he stood face to face with her in the mystic marriage-chamber of the soul; he heard – if it were only for a moment – the unspeakable epithalamium; he saw incomprehensible things. (*Tyson* 224)

However, Molly enters a new life of the spirit alone. She further develops into a perpetual thinker (*Tyson* 229), her thought processes conveyed adroitly: "...so many ideas cropped up to be gathered instantly, and wreathed into the sequence of her thought" (*Tyson* 231). Upon becoming pregnant again, Molly dauntlessly renews hope, only to descend into delirium when she "divines" Nevill's departure for the battlefront. Her response is most compellingly revealed in a dream, in which, among flames, dead child and unborn child are one, and she walks over sand towards a dead man (*Tyson* 283–284). Although overlooked by the attending doctor, who diagnoses brain fever brought on by shock, the dream suggests not only Molly's mingled guilt and fear about her babies, but that she has, in the lexicon of psychical research, attained the supernormal capacity of prevision by prophesying Nevill's death in the desert. In *Mr. and Mrs. Nevill Tyson*, then, Sinclair moves from character type to complex human being by weaving a web of conflicting motivations, and showing the impact of both heredity and psychosexual dynamics on Nevill and idealistic sacrifices on Molly.

Though *Mr. and Mrs. Nevill Tyson* was panned by critics for its unpleasantness, Sinclair continued to probe the so-called unpleasant psychic states and psychopathology in particular in the two novellas that make up *Two Sides of a Question* (1901). The first, "The Cosmopolitan", a tale of a young woman's overcoming repression, is notable mainly for a character's claim that, of all motives, "the last reality was sex" (*Two Sides* 58). The second story, "Superseded", is more significant because it features Sinclair's first dynamic psychologist, focusses on the implications of psychotherapy, and is her most moving study of psychological suffering to date. The patient, an elderly school mistress, Miss Quincey, loses her job to a younger woman, succumbs to hysteria, and develops fantasies for her psychotherapist. When she realizes that the younger woman has superseded her not only in her job but in gaining her therapist's love, Quincey's dream is shattered and she dies, a victim of both a fixed idea and a family history of pathology. Sinclair apparently consulted a medical textbook for accuracy (Boll, *M.S.: Novelist* 177); judging from the description of Miss Quincey's hysteria, the work was likely Pierre Janet's *The Mental State of Hystericals*, published in English in 1901, though available to the French-speaking Sinclair from 1893.

Dr Cautley, the therapist, has gradually become disillusioned with medicine, "finally coming to the conclusion that the soul of things was Neuroses" (*Two Sides* 273). Whereas Miss Quincey voices the materialist attitude to mental disease in her resolve to "suppress" the existence of a psychosomatically induced heart problem "by ignoring it. That she understood was the right treatment for hysteria" (*Two Sides* 323), Dr Cautley implements a very forward-thinking talking cure. On his first visit he has Miss Quincey give him "a complete pathological story of the Moons and Quinceys", her relatives (*Two Sides* 233). Realizing that she suffers from "brain exhaustion", he advises a rest cure, but also "prescribe[s] a course of light literature" (*Two Sides* 244), perhaps the first instance in fiction of bibliotherapy. He also clarifies the dynamics of psychosomatic illness to her, stating "Don't you know...that overstrain of the higher faculties is sometimes followed by astonishing demonstrations on the part of Nature" (*Two Sides* 276). What he fails to realize is that Miss Quincey's astounding demonstrations are directed towards him, causing his psychotherapy to misfire. While this dynamic might seem to strikingly anticipate Freud's concept of transference, Sinclair probably drew on Janet's discussion of the rapport between hypnotist and patient, which he called "somnambulic influence" when it extended beyond the hypnotic session (Ellenberger 374). Janet noted that the patient might constantly think about the hypnotist and might demonstrate intense and varied emotions towards him, either consciously or in dreams. Cautley's attending to Quincey releases suppressed emotion, causing her to fall prey to "the fixed idea" that he loves her (*Two Sides* 289). Pathetically, she succumbs to the "sinful passion for a blouse" in order to attract him (*Two*

Sides 253). Gradually her delusion overtakes her, Sinclair emphasizing that "the dream is the reality" (*Two Sides* 322), a conception consonant with dynamic psychological thinking. Only after Quincey sees Dr Cautley with his young lover is her dream shattered; she dies that night. This story is thus significant because the entire plot hinges on the psychology of an illness, and yet the clinical background does not obtrude.

In *The Divine Fire* (1904), the novel which garnered her widespread recognition, Sinclair continues to explore the nature of identity and self-hood, particularly its multi-faceted, permeable qualities, but most importantly she focusses on the problems of identity particular to a genius. Her conception aligns with Frederic Myers's, as expressed in *Human Personality and Its Survival of Bodily Death* (1903). Myers claims that

> the man of genius is for us the best type of the normal man, in so far as he effects a successful cooperation of an unusually large number of elements of his personality – reaching a stage of integration slightly in advance of our own. (*Human* I 74)

The genius may approach "supernormal" capacity through his "power of appropriating the results of subliminal mentation to subserve the supral-iminal stream of thought", but he is also prey to the "degeneration and insanities" emanating from subliminal uprushes. The border between genius and hysteria consequently blurs: both hold *idées fixes*. Myers broadened his conception of genius beyond the purely intellectual form to include " 'moral genius,' the 'genius of sanctity,' or that 'possession' by some altruistic idea which lies at the root of so many heroic lives" (*Human* I 56).

At the outset, Sinclair makes it quite clear that the protagonist, Savage Keith Rickman, "had not yet found himself" because he is composed of numerous, conflicting personas (*Divine* 29), including businessman, recluse, cockney, genius, and drunk: "In short, it was a very confusing state of affairs, and that made it almost impossible for Mr. Rickman to establish his identity" (*Divine* 31). In the course of the novel, Rickman struggles to achieve integration, viewed by Sinclair as a necessary antecedent to the highest artistic accomplishment. Sinclair focusses on the development of his moral genius, touched off by his contact with a beautiful, morally insightful woman, Lucia Harden. Above him in social class, she represents an unattainable ideal, inspiring him with the "divine fire". Following her father's death, her family library is sold to Rickman's father, who unscrupu-lously profits from the sale. The plot is driven by Rickman's attempts through sacrifices, including starving himself, to restore the library to its rightful owner. Though his creative energy is diverted, Rickman "felt that his genius, conscious of its hour, 'possessed him utterly' " (*Divine* 513). His obsession brings him close to madness, preventing him from continuing to write:

> Now it [his sensation] was of a plunging heart that suddenly reversed engines while his brain shivered with the shock; now of a little white wave that swamped his brain with one pulse of oblivion; now it was a sudden giving way of the floor of consciousness, through which his thoughts dropped downwards, headlong, into the abyss. He had great agony and distress in following their flight. At night, as he lay in bed, watching the feeble, automatic procession of ideas, he noticed that they arrived in an order that was not the order of sanity, that if he took note of the language they clothed themselves in, he found himself listening as it were to the gabble of idiocy or aphasia. At such moment[s] he trembled for his reason. (*Divine* 520)

Sinclair's powerful description assimilates the tropes of psychic shock, perhaps drawing on Charcot or Janet, and of engines reversing, perhaps alluding to a common source of late nineteenth-century psychic shock in train accidents (cf. Chapter 2). Her image of "a sudden giving way of the floor of consciousness" reflects Herbart's metaphor of the threshold between consciousness and subconscious. Most importantly, Sinclair draws on Janet's conception of partial automatism and dissociation, defined by Sinclair in *A Defence of Idealism* as "the break between one idea, or group of ideas, and its normal context and logical connections; the cutting off of one psychic state, or group of states, from the stream of consciousness itself" (290–291). Rickman passively observes the autonomous, subconscious development of part of his personality as it rises into consciousness.

Nevertheless, in passing through this condition he obtains clarity about himself. Through his struggle and his love for Lucia, finally reciprocated, he achieves integration, confirmed by the high achievement of his verse drama, "The Triumph of Life" (*Divine* 560). Thus, suggests Sinclair, moral and spiritual growth and the growth of literary genius are mutually dependent. In attaining his highest self, Rickman realizes his divine fire of inspiration and glimpses the Absolute, an achievement very much consonant with philosophical idealism. Unfortunately, as Hrisey Zegger has noted, the philosophical, allegorical framework occasionally obtrudes (31).

Sinclair's second novel dealing with marital difficulties, *The Helpmate* (1907), breaks fresh ground because it shifts to a male's perspective on sexual repression in marriage and because of its more direct style than *Mr. and Mrs. Nevill Tyson*. A wife's rigidity and fastidiousness cause her to withhold sex; the inspirational moral purity admired in *The Divine Fire* is here taken to an extreme and shown to be destructive. Sinclair maintains sympathy for the husband, Walter Majendie, when he attempts to sublimate his longings by finding pleasure in making money (*Helpmate* 266) and even when in desperation he has an affair with a flower-shop girl. The novel's most striking feature is Sinclair's evocation of emotional antagonism between the couple at an almost Lawrentian level of intensity. On one occasion, after Walter Majendie escorts his wife to church, "the door was shut in Majendie's face, and he turned away, intending to kill, to murder the next hour at his club" (*Helpmate* 52). Meanwhile, inside, Anne manages to "annihilate" her husband (*Helpmate* 53). The novel also contains the first of Sinclair's many portrayals of Jamesian strenuous souls. Dr Gardener, one of the novel's most perceptive characters, immediately grasps Majendie's difficulty, suggesting Sinclair's admiration of James's concept (*Helpmate* 225).

Sinclair had opened the novel with the newly wed couple arguing in bed, and her candid portrayal of a problem marriage exceeded readers' horizon of expectations, attested to by reviewers who castigated its morality. The *London Bookman* reviewer, for example, called it "a morbid, sickly dream of life" (as cited in Robb 229).

The Creators (1910), Sinclair's next major effort,[13] returns to the subject of genius, treating it more comprehensively and with greater realism and insight than in *The Divine Fire*. She follows the development of five strikingly different geniuses and the effects of their gifts on their personal relationships, drawing on conflicting discourses about genius in order to do so. She also articulates more fully and yet subtly the power of unconscious motivation, particularly in influencing choice of marriage partners. For the first time in her fiction, two doctors are used to contrast the medical or psychiatric view of genius as neurosis, quite common in the late nineteenth century through Lombroso, Morel, and Moreau's work (Drinka 52–54), with the neo-Romantic, visionary rhetoric of Myers, who held that the genius had an advanced capacity to integrate and channel spiritual energies, "a kind of exalted but underdeveloped clairvoyance" (*Human* II 282). This conflict underlies the central dilemma addressed in the novel, of whether literary genius is a handicap or a benefit, a taint or a gift, insanity or visionary, especially for a woman.

Early in the novel we are introduced to novelist George Tanquery's perspective on genius:

He denied perversely that genius was two-sexed, or that it was even essentially a virile thing. The fruitful genius was feminine, rather, humble and passive in its attitude to life. It yearned perpetually for the embrace, the momentary embrace of the real. But no more. (*Creators* 15)

The narrator's assumption that bisexuality and virility are a dimension of creativity evokes Nietzchean rhetoric. Although Tanquery is considered one of the two greatest psychological novelists, ironically, like his precursor, Langley Wyndam in *Audrey Craven*, he "can't see inside himself" (*Creators* 183), causing him to marry an undemanding, uneducated woman instead of

Jane Holland, the other great psychological novelist, with whom he has a challenging relationship.

More psychologically aware than Tanquery, Jane experiences moments of heightened illumination, bearing uncanny resemblance to those described by Virginia Woolf over a decade later:

> She could not say how or at what moment the incredible thing happened, but of a sudden the world she looked at became luminous and insubstantial and divinely still. She could not tell whether the stillness of the world had passed into her heart, or her heart into the stillness of the world. (*Creators* 111)

Her genius only becomes divided after she marries Hugh Brodrick, a materialistic, magazine editor, who discourages her literary ambitions. Initially she succumbs to married life's comforts, ceases writing, and then concentrates her passion on her new-born son; however, she becomes fatigued and depressed (*Creators* 327).

Hugh's brother, Dr Henry Brodrick, propounds the mental science view of genius in "diagnosing" Jane. He claims that writing "wrecked her nerves" and equates genius with "a great Neurosis" (*Creators* 360). Henry influences Hugh to regard "genius as a malady, a thing abnormal, disastrous, not of nature" (*Creators* 328).

The main opposition to Henry's medical opinion comes from a third genius, Owen Prospero, a medical doctor who has become a doctor of the soul and poet (*Creators* 183). He allays Jane's fears that she is neurotic (*Creators* 413) and expresses a more sympathetic view of genius that aligns well with Myers's:

> There were cases, he declared, where disease was a higher sort of health. "Take," he said, "a genius with a pronounced neurosis. His body may be a previous poor medium for all ordinary purposes. But he couldn't have a more delicate, more lyrical, more perfectly adjusted instrument for his purposes than the nervous system you [Henry] call diseased. (*Creators* 420)

Owen's vindication of genius is credited by his successful marriage to yet another creator, Laura, a woman who has made deep sacrifices for her art. His view is also born out by Jane's experience of healing while alone in the countryside: "Nature's beneficient intention was to restore her whole to the genius which was also part of Nature's plan" (*Creators* 459). There she has a moment of illumination that, consonant with Myers's view of the genius's supernormal capacity, is framed as an apparitional visitation:

> Walking back to the farm late one evening, the moors veiled from her passion by the half-darkness, her Idea came back to her. It came, not yet

with the vividness of flesh and blood, but like a ghost. It had ghostly hands and feet, and like a ghost it walked the road with her. But through its presence she felt in herself again that nascent ecstasy which foretold, infallibly, the onset of the incredible act and labour of creation. (*Creators* 459)

Nina Lempriere, the fifth creator, confirms Jane's experience that a woman must be independent "to do anything stupendous" (*Creators* 106). She handles her genius, which feels like a second, aggressive sex within, plaguing her (*Creators* 105), by sublimating sexual frustration into great art (*Creators* 451–452). Although Sinclair treats the psychological difficulties associated with genius in all their complexity, and gives fair consideration to the medical view, later elaborated on by Freud, she illustrates that creativity as a natural activity transcends this paradigm, a perspective very much contingent with Myers's, the SPR's, and, later, Jung's.

4.3   Sex and the supernormal: Fiction 1911–1918

Sinclair continued to explore the imaginative implications of psychical research's expansionist dynamic psychology in numerous short stories, a few of which can only be touched on here. "The Intercessor" (July, 1911) represents the first to probe the idea that if certain features of personality, particularly intense feelings, are blocked from expression during a lifetime, they persist in the spirit world, indestructible until satisfied. Sinclair embroiders psychical research discourse on persistence of personality after death, psychic invasion, and suggestion, and does not simply anticipate psychoanalytic concepts, as Raitt and Zegger have claimed (Raitt 134; Zegger 62–63). In the tale, a recluse, Garvin, becomes possessed by a child ghost, consults a psychic doctor, and discovers that the child was his landlady, Mrs Falshaw's; it died owing to her neglect (*Intercessor* 182). When Falshaw bears a second, still-born child, and becomes unhinged, refusing to bury it, Garvin acts as intercessor. He removes the dead baby from its sleeping mother's arms, enabling the spirit child to substitute itself and "recover the love that had been withheld from her" (*Intercessor* 185). Mrs Falshaw's guilt dissipates and she eventually returns to sanity. In suggesting that an apparition can effect a positive intervention, "The Intercessor" reinforces Myers's finding that spirits can express love (*Human* II 78).

"Between the Lines" (December 1911) deserves mention because its comic treatment of similar themes of suggestibility and invasion of personality reveals Sinclair's versatility with psychical discourse. Also, this story is the first of several fictions structured as case studies, and explained at the denouement by its narrator, in this case Simpson; he claims that

just as he [Lumby] had produced his neurasthenia at a hint from Miss Manisty, so at a hint from me [Simpson] he had produced that astounding tale of his. I'm inclined to think, myself, that the whole thing was written in him somewhere and could have been read by those queer people who do read things, you know – between the lines of consciousness, I mean. But it was a sort of uprush from the submerged depths of Fitz's personality; that it could only have appeared under the excitement, the disintegration, if you like, of a supreme terror; that, in the grip of his mortal danger, he gave out something that was not his and yet was in him – perhaps as an ancestral passion, an ancestral memory. (*Tales* 114)

With one deft touch, Sinclair pokes fun at dynamic psychology's unmasking impulse, psychic shock theory, and Butler on ancestral memory.

Although Sinclair's "The Flaw in the Crystal" (*English Review*, 1912) also assimilates aspects of the case study, in this instance of the psychical variety, Sinclair deploys the supernormal quite differently than in "Between the Lines" to show that belief in it can hinder psychological self-awareness. The novella draws unobtrusively on Herbartian rhetoric of thresholds of consciousness and repression, as well as mystical, psychical discourse on moments of inspiration, telepathy, and psychic invasion.

The protagonist spinster, Agatha Verrall, probably named after prominent SPR investigators Arthur, Margaret, and Helen Verrall, believes that she has the "uncanny, unaccountable" gift of telepathic healing. In her mind this power hinges on her being free from desires and remaining a "flawless crystal".[14] She exercises her power, "sacredly, incorruptibly", to calm Rodney Lanyon's strained nerves (*Uncanny* 85) whenever he can escape from his nerve-wracked wife, Bella. However, the arrival of mutual acquaintances, Molly and Harding Powell, at the farm next to her's throws her sacred relationship into a new light; she discovers desire lurking in Rodney, though "there were no lurking possibilities in her" (*Uncanny* 102).

Nevertheless, she submerges these misgivings, focussing her healing power on Harding, who is paranoid and nearly insane. Sinclair makes the contrast between his vision and Agatha's explicit through a moment of illumination that Agatha experiences at a height of land:

At that moment, in a flash that came like a shifting of the eyes, the world she looked at suffered a change.

And yet it did not change. All the appearances of things, their colours, the movement and the stillness remained as if constant in their rhythm and their scale; but they were heightened, intensified; they were carried to a pitch that would have been vehement, vibrant, but that the stillness as the movement was intense. She was not dazzled by it or confused in any way. Her senses were exalted, adjusted to the pitch.... In every leaf, in every blade of grass, this life was manifest as a strange, a divine translucence. She was about to point it out to the man [Harding] at her side when she remembered that he had eyes for the beauty of the earth, but no sense of its secret and supernatural light. (*Uncanny* 130–131)

Despite Agatha's supernormal insight, Harding's madness invades her after she breaks down "those innermost walls of personality that divide and protect, mercifully, one spirit from another" (*Uncanny* 176). Ironically, he now possesses her sanity (*Uncanny* 167).

To make matters worse, since she has been able to cure Rodney Lanyon's wife he no longer visits as frequently. Agatha increasingly desires him, expressed through the rhetoric of Herbart's threshold of consciousness: "Each time she beat it [desire] back, in an instant, to its burrow below the threshold, and hid it there, it ran underground" (*Uncanny* 142). As she becomes possessed, however, her desire emerges "naked and unashamed" (*Uncanny* 176–177). Love for Rodney prevents her from being completely engulfed by Harding, but eventually she views love as the impurity, the flaw in the crystal, which has sapped her psychic powers, and she decides to renounce this love. Through a limited first-person narration, Sinclair cleverly suspends the reader in a state of uncertainty, which Todorov theorizes is the very essence of the fantastic (25); this discrepancy between perspectives on alleged psychic phenomena was also characteristic of SPR psychical cases. Psychic experimenter Agatha Verrall might possess telepathic healing powers and ironically become the victim of them, or be a paranoid, sexually repressed spinster, or just possibly encompass both conditions.

In a response to a query about whether the story was based on actual experience, Sinclair confirmed her belief in psychic powers. She claimed in the *New York Times* that "the apparently 'supernatural' alone is true" in the story, and she detailed a number of cases of "extra-physical healing" by a variety of genuine healers who told her that "until the healer knows how to protect himself, this uncanny transference is a fact" (Letter to *NYT*).

In *The Combined Maze* (1913), Sinclair shifts her focus from the supernormal to a very physical world, dominated by athletics and sexual awakening. Nevertheless, several preoccupations of the short stories continue to resonate. One is the remarkable persistence of a personality trait, though not beyond death, as in "The Intercessor". The protagonist Ranny Ransome's optimism and decency become virtually indestructible, despite disastrous experiences. *The Combined Maze* also vividly illustrates the powerful effects of suggestion and repression. More importantly, as in *Audrey Craven*, Sinclair melds the influences of heredity with dynamic psychological explanations of behaviour, though she foregrounds the latter. The novel problematizes Sinclair's characteristic idealistic theme, the striving towards self-realization, by emphasizing Ranny's difficulty in surmounting certain kinds of obstacles in his personal and social life. One of the former, the overly close bond between mother and son, becomes a major theme. Sinclair treats it with just as great insight as D.H. Lawrence, whose *Sons and Lovers* was published later the same year. A glance at Ranny Ransome's relationship with his mother, its consequences for his relationships with Winnie Dymond and Violet Usher, and the sexual symbolism underlining these relationships will demonstrate advances in Sinclair's deployment of dynamic psychology.

Ranny Ransome, a lower-middle-class clerk, is an adherent of the Jamesian strenuous life, as promulgated by the Poly gym where he develops his physique (*Combined* 5); this is in reaction to his father's flabbiness and alcoholism. Thwarted in love because of her husband's addiction, Ranny's mother, who nearly died in childbirth with Ranny, has redirected her passions towards her son, Ranny, who

> had always been more like a lover to her than a son. Mr. Ransome's transports (if he could be said to have transports) of affection were violent, with long intermissions and most brief. Ranny had ways, soft words, cajoleries, caresses that charmed her in her secret desolation. Balancing himself on the arm of her chair, he had his face hidden in the nape of her neck, where he affected ecstasy and the sniffing in of fragrance, as if his mother were a flower. (*Combined* 47)

While kissing her, Ranny receives the suggestion to kiss Winny, a fellow athlete (*Combined* 15)[15]; however, he does not feel free to develop a relationship with this clever girl ostensibly because he lacks financial prospects, but also because he cannot bring her to his mother. Instead, he falls prey to the machinations of Winnie's friend, Violet Usher, whose violet perfume unconsciously evokes his mother (*Combined* 61, 70).

Ironically, a preacher, another of Sinclair's "surgeon[s] of the Soul" (*Combined* 92), inadvertently plants the subconscious suggestion in Ranny that passions are normal:

> In the mission church of St. Matthew's, Ranny underwent illumination. It was as if all that was dark and passionate in him had been interpreted by the preacher. Interpreted, it became in some perverse way justified. (*Combined* 92)

Just prior to Ranny's seduction by Violet, Sinclair draws more directly on Freudian imagery, suggesting that she had read something of the psychoanalyst's work, possibly *Three Contributions to the Sexual Theory* (1905, English trans., 1910)[16] during the course of writing the novel. Violet forgets her door key and assumes a passive, helpless role. Ranny consequently penetrates her house using his pocket knife to slip the sash (*Combined* 96).

More complex is the novel's central symbol, of the combined maze. An athletic spectacle in which women and men run together, weaving a pattern, the combined maze initially captures the innocence and potential of those who participate, including Winnie and Ranny (*Combined* 26). This sacred, dynamic activity, "the supreme symbol of the great wheel of Eight spokes, the Wheel of Life" (*Combined* 25), lifts these shop girls and clerks out of their regulated lives, and they experience a primitive joy. Eventually, however, the symbol expresses Ranny's entrapment through marriage to the unfaithful Violet, and the inevitability of their circumstances:

> They [Ranny and Violet] couldn't help themselves. They had been caught up and flung together and carried away in a maze; like the combined maze at the Poly., it was, when they had to run – to run, locked together. (*Combined* 190)

Sinclair's earlier idealistic championing of the potential for self-realization is thus tempered in this novel by her acknowledgement that instincts, particularly sexual ones, can play a large role in determining life's experiences.

The consequences of repressing the sexual instinct are revealed as pervasive and damaging in Sinclair's next novel, *The Three Sisters* (1914), one of her best.[17] As never before, almost all of the characters suffer from psychosomatic disturbances, which undermine their sense of self. These unconsciously motivated maladies provide the focus of the dramatic incident, drive the novel's plot, and yet generally arise naturally from circumstances. Sinclair makes one character, the by now recognizable soul doctor, sympathetic to the new dynamic psychological approach.

The father emerges as the major repressive force. Ostensibly an ascetic, Vicar Cartaret's secret sensuality torments him, and consequently he "stamp[s] on other people's passions" (*Sisters* 58), notably his three daughters'. After his youngest, Alice, decides to marry the socially inferior Jim Greatorex, who has impregnated her, the Vicar suffers a stroke. Sinclair underlines its psychosomatic genesis, since shock that his control has been undermined precipitates it, and a persistent symptom is loss of memory about the events leading up to it (*Sisters* 300, 331–332). Though in consequence the Vicar's tyrannical power is, at least outwardly, drastically reduced, by this time he has severely damaged his daughters.

All three are initially attracted to Dr Rowcliffe, virtually Garthdale's only eligible suitor. As a ploy to attract his attention, Alice develops hysterical symptoms (*Sisters* 80) and a death wish after she becomes aware of Rowcliffe's attraction to Gwendolyn (*Sisters* 175). Whereas the Vicar voices the nineteenth-century medical view that Alice should control herself, Rowcliffe, who has been reading Janet's *État Mental des Hysteriques*, understands and sympathizes with her restrictive situation (*Sisters* 180–181). He plants the suggestion in her to become acquainted with Jim Greatorex. That she has suffered permanent psychological damage from her environment is intimated when she develops a "morbid obsession" (in Rowcliffe's term) that she is responsible for her father's sickness, and that he is going to die (*Sisters* 294). Suzanne Raitt claims that Sinclair purveys "a fairly crude version of Freudian thought" (142) because she shows that for Alice "sex and then marriage and children with local farmer Jim Greatorex quickly put her right" (141), but in actuality Sinclair's portrayal is more subtle. In Alice's final scene, she is shown to be living in denial, making more psychological trouble probable. Alice has suppressed Gwendolyn's sacrifice for her: "She tended to forget it, as she tended to forget all dreadful things, such as her own terrors and her father's illness and the noises Greatorex made when he was eating" (367).

In contrast, Gwendolyn initially sublimates her stifled passion into love for Garthdale's natural beauty (*Sisters* 58). Nevertheless, she sacrifices herself for Alice's sake by leaving Garthdale (*Sisters* 185), a futile act because a third sister Mary steps in and claims Rowcliffe. This incident reflects Sinclair's interrogation of idealist self-sacrifice. Gwendolyn develops a psychic split between her passionate and submissive selves (*Sisters* 337) and unsuccessfully attempts to subdue the former through voracious reading of metaphysical books, including Bergson's *Évolution Créatrice*:

> She took to metaphysics as you take to dram-drinking. She must have strong, heavy stuff that drugged her brain. And when she found that she could trust her intellect she set it deliberately to fight her passion. (*Sisters* 347, 351–352)

Mary's response to repression is to develop the habit of posturing to such perfection that she loses all sense of self. However, slips of the tongue betray her guilt and unconscious hostility towards Gwendolyn (*Sisters* 313).

Though Dr Rowcliffe proves perceptive about several characters' unconscious motivation, Sinclair complicates his character by showing that he lacks insight about Gwendolyn's sacrifice (*Sisters* 201–202) and Mary's manipulation of him; an association he makes between a past love's red hair and Mary's finally ensnares him:

> Rowcliffe never knew that, though he had been made subject to a sequence of relentless inhibitions, and of suggestions overpowering in their nature and persistently sustained, it was ultimately by aid of that one unconscious and irresistible association that Mary had cast her spell. (*Sisters* 241–242)

Interestingly, Jim Greatorex demonstrates the most insight into Gwendolyn's mystical vision and its source in loneliness (Boll, *M.S.: Novelist* 227). Since he is the most instinctive character, and least subject to inhibition, Sinclair implies that his way is healthiest. In *The Three Sisters* Sinclair portrays more profoundly than in any earlier work the devastating consequences of repression, stunningly supported by poetic descriptions of the bleak natural environment of Yorkshire.

After publishing *Tasker Jevons* (1916), a relatively superficial portrayal of a writer, based on Arnold Bennett, who embodies Bergson's *élan vital*, Sinclair moved into new psychological terrain in *The Tree of Heaven* (1917). In part a study of group psychology, the novel imaginatively treats the implications of Wilfrid Trotter's *Instincts of the Herd in Peace and War*, published the previous year. Trotter had argued that herd behaviour is constantly at war with feeling and experience; it drives individuals into either resistance or mental instability, and in both cases into isolation (62–63). Sinclair elaborates on these individual responses to collective phenomena. She implies that only psychic experience transcends the pull of collectivism.

The novel primarily traces the extended Harrison family's responses to social change during the period from 1895 to 1916. Significantly, the older generation is depicted as suffering most from psychological ills, notably repression. Three maiden aunts can only vent their repressed emotion when they become involved in the suffragette movement (*Tree* 225). An uncle, Bartholomew, has succumbed to neurotic suggestibility, providing comic relief (*Tree* 74):

> he never would be better till chemists were forbidden to advertise and the *British Medical Journal* and *The Lancet* were suppressed. Bertie would read them; and they supplied him with all sorts of extraordinary diseases. (*Tree* 264)

The fate of two other misfit uncles is more serious and foreshadows best the event that will engulf the entire family. They are packed off to the Boer War, this act in miniature subtly suggesting society's eagerness to deal with its ills through war. One of them, Maurice, returns, wounded and depressed, his warning about war's reality unheeded (*Tree* 79–81).

The young, in revolt against the forces that have produced these victims (*Tree* 163), are nonetheless caught up in "vortices". Although Sinclair borrowed Ezra Pound and the Vorticists' term, for her it did not signify positive energy directed into new art forms, but rather the whirlpool of group behaviour that tends to draw in and destroy individuality.[18] The mass movement aspect of suffragism is the first major one interrogated. Dorothea, the neglected Harrison daughter, supports the cause of the Women's Franchise Union but repeatedly feels the "terror of the collective soul" (*Tree* 124, 225).

The mother, Frances, sees her children swept towards an "unclean moral vortex" (*Tree* 156), the second described by Sinclair. Frances's second son Nicky becomes a victim of the new sexual freedoms. He is sent down from Oxford for seducing a professor's wife when, in actuality, she had "made hysterical love to him" and he had lied to protect her (*Tree* 137). He then agrees to live with the woman he loves, Phyllis Desmond, who is pregnant by another man and becomes unfaithful to Nicky after the baby dies (*Tree* 200).

The eldest son, Michael, is, meanwhile, "being drawn into the Vortex of revolutionary Art" (*Tree* 233). However, his boyhood suspicion of collective activity resurfaces (*Tree* 18, 86) when he senses that the new doctrines are hardening. He feels "his old horror of the collective soul" and goes his own way (*Tree* 246).

The war is the most powerful vortex described, and it envelops all others (*Tree* 299). Trotter had argued that war stimulates the herd instinct mainly for positive ends, such as establishing homogeneity, the basis of morale (144), and that it makes isolation "intolerable" (143). Sinclair's view is, perhaps unconsciously, more ambivalent. She depicts the instinctive gathering of the herd in London after war is proclaimed using dynamic psychological discourse evoking the crowd's suggestibility: "all this movement, drunken, orgiastic, somnambulistic, mysteriously restless, streamed up and down..." (*Tree* 284). Everyone is eventually drawn into the war's vortex. The aunts knit socks, and Dorothea and the unfit men work for ambulance units. After Nicky takes Veronica as his second wife, with whom he has been psychically connected from childhood, he enlists and has an "exquisite" sense of being "up against reality" while in battle (*Tree* 369). Sinclair herself experienced this expansion of consciousness while at the front, as mentioned, and she viewed it positively because of her idealist philosophy ("From" 171). Once again, Sinclair suggests that at a vortex's centre is the sex instinct, through the voice of Michael, whose poem implying that Nicky's fight-feeling "is nothing but a form of sex madness" is rejected by Nicky (*Tree* 368). Even Michael, who revolted against the people gathered when war was declared, referring to them as "this demented herd of swine" (*Tree* 284), rationalizes that it is not the war itself but the "collective war-spirit, clamouring for his private soul" that has threatened him (*Tree* 376). Report of Nicky's death arrives and Michael decides to go out, deluding himself into believing that his own will and not the herd drives him. His reversal of attitude is somewhat unbelievable, despite Trotter.

Veronica's psychic gift is the one highly individualistic power transcending the war's vortex. While Nicky is fighting, she has a vision of him near the family's tree of heaven, symbol of unity and protection (*Tree* 370–371). This moment of being, with similarities to Lily's in Woolf's *To The Lighthouse*, brings her happiness, even though it turns out to be Nicky's farewell, since he is killed at about the time she experiences it (*Tree* 379). In psychical research discourse this is a crisis apparition, a hallucination generated by a telepathic message (Gauld 162). The SPR had documented an impressive number of cases, and Sinclair, as we have seen, was convinced of the phenomenon's verity. Veronica later psychically mediates between the dead sons' souls and their grieving mother (*Tree* 402). Her gift, tapping an inner reality more important than the outward strife, again illustrates how Sinclair viewed psychic resources as far more extensive than did Freud.

Though *The Tree of Heaven* can be overly sentimental and seems to advocate patriotic sacrifice, it is not simply "an unashamedly propagandistic novel", as claimed by Raitt (167). The psychological sub-text runs against the patriotism and betrays Sinclair's own ambivalence towards the war. Sinclair experienced a variety of emotions while at the front, from a kind of ecstasy to numbness to "a sorrow that transcends all sorrow that you have ever known" ("From" 178). Something of the latter is reflected in the Harrison family, whose mourning remains unresolved, as suggested by their preservation of their dead son's bedrooms (*Tree* 401). The novel closes with another separation, as the last potential victim, the youngest son, John, is driven off to battle "and was gone" (*Tree* 408). The presence of veteran Uncle Maurice, who offers "a crapulous salute", serves to remind readers of the war's horrors. The family's melancholy and lack of patriotism in the final scene offer no consolation or resolution (*Tree* 407–408).

4.4 Repressions and revolutions in form: Fiction 1919–1922

In May Sinclair's masterpiece, *Mary Olivier* (1919), the focus shifts back onto an individual's struggles, though in the context of family and friends. The main development is stylistic, for *Mary Olivier* is one of the earliest British stream of consciousness *bildungsromane*. However, similar to Virginia Woolf, Sinclair selectively records Mary's most striking sense impressions; she also employs other narrative viewpoints. In describing a long-past event, Mary may dissociate and begin with a distanced third-person perspective, then move to second and even first-person, thus conveying the event's persistent emotional power in her consciousness (cf. *Mary* 135–136). Sinclair also revealed incidents significant in Mary's consciousness by setting apart brief passages, marked off either by a series of dots or by section numbers within chapters, for example "She knows who I am now" (*Mary* 370, cf. 298, 363, 380). These imagistic set pieces do not necessarily correspond to outwardly significant life events. Sinclair's technical innovations advance her deployment of dynamic psychological themes.

The developmental perspective, expressed as the theme of struggling for selfhood and self-knowledge against forces of heredity and circumstance, features more prominently than in earlier novels. Sinclair traces Mary Olivier's life from infancy to middle age. Mary's first recorded childhood impressions depict her parents and have a sexual undertone. She awakes from a dream, and is terrified by her bearded, half-naked father moving towards her (*Mary* 4). She screams and is taken into her parents' bed where she caresses her mother's breast, this scene subtly suggesting a family romance fantasy (*Mary* 4). Freudian sexual symbolism and oedipal dynamics in particular infuse the entire novel, gradually becoming more complex as Mary's consciousness of her sexuality and family dynamics develop. In one early instance imbued with phallic symbolism, Mary builds a tower as an unsuccessful bid to draw her mother's attention away from her sons, who are building a snowman in the yard (*Mary* 9–10). As in

The Combined Maze, mother and son resemble lovers, making Mary feel a complete outsider:

> Mamma wanted him. Mamma had him. As long as they lived she would have him. Mamma and Mark were happy together; their happiness tingled, you could feel it tingling, like the happiness of lovers. They didn't want anybody but each other. You existed for them as an object in some unintelligible time and in a space outside their space. The only difference was that Mark knew you were there and Mamma didn't. (*Mary* 241)

This symbolism and these dynamics, however, provide the backdrop against which Mary's self develops. From her earliest years, moments of being enable her to transcend family conflict and bring insight and happiness:

> By the gate of the field her sudden, secret happiness came to her.
>
> She could never tell when it was coming, nor what it would come from. It had something to do with the trees standing up in the golden white light. It had come before with a certain sharp white light flooding the fields, flooding the room.
>
> It had happened so often that she received it now with a shock of recognition; and when it was over she wanted it to happen again. She would go back and back to the places where it had come, looking for it, thinking that any minute it might happen again. But it never came twice to the same place in the same way. (*Mary* 93–94)

Mary realizes that she possesses several selves, though Sinclair implies that Mary's "secret happiness" unifies her and makes her a distinct individual:

> Sometimes she had queer glimpses of the persons that were called Mary Olivier. There was Mrs. Olivier's only daughter, proud of her power over the sewing-machine. When she brought the pile of hemmed sheets to her mother her heart swelled with joy in her own goodness. There was Mark Olivier's sister, who rejoiced in the movements of her body.... And there was Mary Olivier, the little girl of thirteen whom her mother and Aunt Bella whispered about to each other with mysterious references to her age.
>
> Her secret happiness had nothing to do with any of these Mary Oliviers. It was not like any other happiness. It had nothing to do with Mamma or Dan or Roddy, or even Mark. (*Mary* 94)

Though her precocious reading also helps her to develop self-awareness (*Mary* 74–77, 82), several forces block that development. Mary fears that she has inherited a taint since her father is alcoholic and her spinster aunt an hysteric, who is locked away. Her reading of Darwin, Ribot, and Maudsley on heredity exacerbates her terror, and badly shakes her sense of self:

> There were no independent, separate entities, no sacred, inviolable selves. They [her family] were one immense organism and you were part of it; you were nothing that they had not been before you. It was no good struggling. You were caught in the net; you couldn't get out. (*Mary* 290)

However, the main force inhibiting Mary's growth comes from her manipulative "little holy Mamma" (*Mary* 69). Starved for affection by her husband, Mamma invests her love in her sons and perceives Mary as a rival. Mamma both withholds love from Mary (*Mary* 69–70, 145) and attempts to keep her dependent by controlling her. Notably, she tries to prevent Mary from educating herself and to force Mary to adopt her orthodox religious beliefs (*Mary* 114). At one point Mary recognizes that "to be happy with her mother you or she had to be broken, to be helpless and little like a child" (*Mary* 194). This passage must at least partially reflect Sinclair's reading of Jung on the mortal conflict with the great Mother in Mythology (Jung *Psychology of the Unconscious* 33), which she had drawn attention to in her review of his *Psychology of the Unconscious* ("Symbolism II" 145). Mary remains trapped in her mother's emotional net and ambivalent towards her, but she does preserve something of herself by becoming Richard Nicholson's mistress (*Mary* 353, 361) and by continuing to sublimate her thwarted passions through writing poetry (*Mary* 234).

The frequency of deaths in the family is a third force of circumstance which, Sinclair intimates, hampers Mary's attempts to develop a stable sense of self. Deaths punctuate the novel, including Mary's nursemaid, Jenny (*Mary* 74), her father (*Mary* 189), her brothers Roddy and Mark (*Mary* 268–269; 301–302), her mother (*Mary* 371), and her Uncle Victor, by suicide (*Mary* 327–328). As a child, Mary develops a phobia about funerals (*Mary* 71), and is later repulsed by funereal hypocrisy (*Mary* 198). Following her father's death, she wishes that she had died rather than him because she feels so oppressed (*Mary* 190). Each death also makes Mamma more dependent on Mary. Though her mother's death does release Mary, it comes too late since Mary's lover, Richard, marries another woman ten days after it. The death leaves Mary feeling guilty, implied in her comment that "It was horrible this living on other people's deaths" (*Mary* 372). This pervasive autobiographical theme of death forces the reader to acknowledge that if Mary has achieved clarity at the denouement, she has done so through considerable suffering.

In the Virago introduction to *Mary Olivier*, Jean Radford suggests that "the novel is too long; there are too many lovers lost, too much detail about her philosophical reading, too many scenes in which mother and daughter enact the same painful conflicts" (vii). Sinclair could be defended on the grounds that she was trying to capture the full reality of an individual's long-term suppression; emotional conflicts needed to be repeated again and again. Through the multiple deaths and departures of lovers, Sinclair perceptively suggests the origins of Mary's intellectual striving and developing artistry as a poet. Since human relationships prove inconsistent and even treacherous, and her passion is continually thwarted, Mary embraces the reliable, ordered world of philosophical texts and ideas. Unlike in Sinclair's earlier novels which focussed on creators in community with one another, in *Mary Olivier* she conveys the modern artist's isolation and alienation.

Sinclair's sophistication about the role of dreams, greater than in earlier novels, enables her to convey imaginatively her protagonist's half-realized fears and desires. Her earliest dream is provoked by a glimpse of her Aunt Charlotte's sexual nature, a taboo subject in her own family. In it she views her hysterical Aunt taking off all her clothes. Sinclair's understanding of repression and the Freudian distinction between manifest and latent content is suggested by Mary's response to the dream: "In the dream there was no break between the end and the beginning. But when she remembered it afterwards it split into two pieces with a dark gap in between" (*Mary* 38). Much later, dreams that her mother has died operate as wish fulfilment and underline Mary's intense animosity towards her (*Mary* 352).

Thus, Sinclair brought to her adaptation of the stream of consciousness technique the psychological sophistication and clarity necessary to plunge deeply into an individual's psyche. Most critics failed to recognize this subtlety and complexity. A critic in *The Little Review*, for example, hesitatingly grouped Sinclair with other moderns who employed Freud in the manner that a home dressmaker uses Butterick patterns (Heaps 30). This is unfair because Sinclair infused the novel not only with some Freudian elements, but also, characteristically, with discourses on heredity, idealism, mysticism, and the psychical. The latter she represented through moments of illumination, which at the denouement enable Mary to detach from her pain and to recognize the source of her happiness within (378). Not even E.M. Forster was able to fit Sinclair's *Mary Olivier* within his horizon of expectations about a novel's subject matter; he claimed that it "is a document rather than a work of art". At least he recognized that "there cannot be two opinions about [Sinclair's] book; it is a noble and a notable experiment, unattempted hitherto" (8).

Sinclair's 1920 novel, *The Romantic*, retreats from *Mary Olivier's* stylistic experimentation, but it contains thematic and structural innovations arising from Sinclair's engagement with dynamic psychology. It is the first Sinclair novel, and the third in British literature, in which a psychotherapist resolves the dramatic conflicts in a case study format.[19] Reviewers and, most recently, Zegger (129) have criticized that clinical dimension, with some justification; in her attempt to probe motivation, Sinclair took the analytic method to its logical conclusion. If *The Romantic* does not rank among her best novels, it is valuable in the present context since it clearly reveals Sinclair's attitude towards psychotherapy. Of additional interest, Sinclair cleverly makes a link between individual and group malaise in war time.

As in *Mr. and Mrs. Nevill Tyson* (1898), Sinclair employs a method of progressive revelation of character. In this case, the protagonist, Charlotte Redhead, along with the reader, gains insight into John Conway, whose viewpoint is never entered. Initially Charlotte is attracted to John sexually (*Romantic* 27) and, although she notices his "romantic apathy" (*Romantic* 29) and has several disturbing dreams about him, she joins an ambulance unit with him that is being sent to Belgium. As in *The Tree of Heaven*, Sinclair links the anticipation of battle with sexuality: "They were one in the almost palpable excitement that they shared; locked close, closer than their bodies could have joined them, in the strange and poignant ecstasy of danger" (*Romantic* 79). Gradually, however, Charlotte becomes disillusioned with the war (*Romantic* 112–113), but Conway continues to harbour romantic, heroic illusions about it. Despite his ecstasy, he leaves Charlotte stranded in dangerous situations until she is forced to admit that

> [John] funked and lied. The two things she couldn't stand. His funk and his lying were a real part of him. And it was as if she had always known it, as if all the movements of her mind had been an effort to escape her knowledge. (*Romantic* 131)

Worse still, John's cowardice turns to cruelty against Charlotte (*Romantic* 145). She never does untangle John's secret herself, since he is shot in the back and killed by a wounded Captain whom he is in the act of deserting (*Romantic* 187).

Instead, the psychotherapist, Dr McClane, leader of a rival ambulance unit, finally explains John's true nature. Initially Charlotte is suspicious of McClane, believing him jealous of John and biassed in predicting that John will "break down" at the front (*Romantic* 127). Only after her own commander, a medical doctor, advises her to consult McClane because "he's a psychotherapist. He knows more about people's souls than I know about their bodies. He probably knows all about Conway's soul" does she confide in him (*Romantic* 195).[20] Yet another of Sinclair's soul doctors, he interprets Charlotte's dreams as prophetic and telepathic and uses them to deepen her understanding of her repressed feelings of desire for, and anger at, John (*Romantic* 197). Drawing on Adler's theories about inferiority and power, Sinclair has McClane argue that John's aggression is really compensation for some physical inadequacy (*Romantic* 199). According to McClane,

> [John] jumped at everything that helped him to get compensation, to get power. He jumped at your feeling for him because it gave him power. He

jumped at the war because the thrill he got out of it gave him the sense of power. (*Romantic* 200)

By the time Charlotte finally admits the obvious sincerity of McClane's aims, the reader has already become sympathetic to his viewpoint.

Characteristic of Sinclair's doctors of the soul, McClane then offers the further profound insight which provokes a moment of illumination in Charlotte and sets John's dilemma into a much wider perspective. He implies that John has been driven by "something bigger than he was", "[s]omething that degeneracy is always trying to keep under.... Power. A power in retreat, fighting to get back its lost ground" (*Romantic* 202). In a visionary flash, Charlotte sees the romantically deluded John and then images "the long lines of beaten men, reeling slowly to the footway, passing slowly, endlessly, regiment by regiment, in retreat" (*Romantic* 203). The reader is left to make the connection, focussed in the word "retreat", that John's fantasy, with its underlying malaise, is a microcosm of the larger group phenomena which has resulted in such wide-scale destruction. In both instances retreat results in disillusionment and fear.

Following a comic, ironic novel, *Mr. Waddington of Wyck* (1921), treating a middle-aged egoist with fixed ideas, Sinclair returned to serious psychological study in *Life and Death of Harriet Frean* (January 1922). With great precision and economy, Sinclair evokes the pathos of Harriet's unfulfilled life, of meaningless sacrifices made to "do the right thing", to please her parents, which leave her bereft of any sense of self. Along with this implicit rejection of idealistic thought, Sinclair also shifts attention from heredity to focus primarily on environmental influences, a perspective more consonant with dynamic psychology. In this aspect, *Life and Death of Harriet Frean* is perhaps more forward-looking than *Mary Olivier*. It is also more innovative in its compressed, imagistic style and in its combination of stream of consciousness with omniscient narration. Harriet's is a much more restricted consciousness and therefore more difficult to convey vividly than Mary Olivier's; the technique gives needed perspective on her character.

Unlike Mary Olivier, Harriet's character is shaped by Victorian parents who are well-meaning and intelligent, if over-protective (*Harriet* 33, 48–49). Harriet does not inherit that intelligence, and does not question their assumptions; instead she decides to behave "beautifully; as beautifully as she could. They [her parents] wanted you to; they wanted it more than anything because they were so beautiful. So good. So wise" (*Harriet* 21). When Robin falls in love with her, Harriet insists that he not undo his engagement to her friend Priscilla. Harriet's parents reinforce this act of "goodness", her father claiming that "You've done the right thing" (*Harriet* 46), even though Harriet spends the next months crying herself to sleep.

From this point on, Sinclair convincingly depicts the psychological consequences of this climactic sacrifice. Priscilla eventually develops a "mysterious paralysis", a psychosomatic illness that forces her husband to keep his waning attention on her (*Harriet* 51). Harriet's world shrinks as her delusions grow. Although Robin's niece impresses on her the misery her sacrifice provoked, Harriet responds automatically that she would do the same tomorrow. However, she feels less certain about her adopted moral beauty (*Harriet* 108). Increasingly locked into emotional dependency on her mother, Harriet's sense of security slips away following her mother's death:

> The feeling of insecurity had grown on her...She had no clear illumination, only a mournful acquiescence in her own futility, an almost physical sense of shrinkage, the crumbling away, bit by bit, of her beautiful and honourable self, dying with the objects of its three profound affections: her father, her mother, Robin. (*Harriet* 109)

Reminiscent of Miss Quincey in Sinclair's *Two Sides of a Question*, Harriet, now in her fifties, becomes a victim of habit (*Harriet* 110, 119), prey to a lifetime of repressed feelings. During an illness, she relishes her doctor's attentions and malingers:

> She loved the doctor's visits at twelve o'clock, his air of brooding absorption in her case, his consultations with Maggie, the seriousness and sanctity he attached to the humblest details of her existence.... She didn't want to get well. (*Harriet* 119–120)

She dislikes leaving her house; Sinclair's demonstration of her obsessive affection for it draws on Freudian sexual symbolism:

> The house had become a part of herself, an extension of her body, a protective shell. She was uneasy when away from it. The thought of it drew her with passion.... (*Harriet* 124)

Gradually, Harriet surrenders "the grown-up self she had maintained with so much effort" (*Harriet* 124) and operates mainly on an instinctual level: "There was something voluptuous about the beginning of this state; she would give herself up to it with animal pleasure and content" (*Harriet* 126). Sinclair's depiction of instinctual behaviour underlying the self confirms her engagement with McDougall's and Freud's theories of instinct. Final release of repression occurs as Harriet awakens from being anaesthetized, but her disjointed statements about dead babies and keeping the doctor away also betray, in swift strokes, her mind's disintegration (*Harriet* 132–133). Her pathetic, regressed state is crystallized at the denouement when she mistakes her friend, Connie, for her "Mamma".

The Life and Death of Harriet Frean is Sinclair's most psychologically probing and yet moving study of a by now familiar character in Sinclair's canon: the weak person who fails to overcome circumstance in order to attain individuation. Typical of the misinformed criticism Sinclair received was T.S. Eliot's review, directed at Sinclair's use of psychoanalysis "because it is a scientific method, and rests upon a dubious and contentious branch of science". He also displayed ignorance of her work by claiming that Sinclair "will find herself forced to proceed from psychotherapy even to the supernatural" when in fact Sinclair had been exploring the meeting ground of psychological and supernatural in her short stories beginning in 1911 ("London" 330).

Although Sinclair continued to produce fiction bearing the imprint of her psychological knowledge, these subsequent works either tended to subordinate this knowledge to other aims, notably the comic, as in *A Cure of Souls* (1924) or, more frequently, to repeat, with slight variations, the psychological themes of the earlier books, as in *Arnold Waterlow* (1924). Also, these last novels were written quickly – seven between 1924 and 1927 – and consequently are not of the highest quality. Perhaps, as Zegger notes, this artistic decline contributed to her eclipse after her death (142).

However, as the preceding pages have attempted to illustrate, the depth, range, and versatility of Sinclair's writing warrant a revision of her literary fate. Though it would be a distortion to underestimate her genius, particularly her native intuition about character, it has become clear that the best features of Sinclair's fiction owe much to her thorough and committed engagement with dynamic psychology.

In summary, several characteristics and aims of her adaptation of the new psychology have clearly emerged. Her use of its discourses enabled her to present a more convincing vision of reality than had been conveyed by those previous and contemporary novelists who focussed on external realities. In her early fiction she provides glimpses, and in her later, more elaborate pictures of the unconscious desires shaping so much of our "rational" activity. Her dedication to expressing (and even exposing) these fundamental emotions, instincts, and yearnings is striking. She portrays sexual motivation, in particular, with effective candidness and vigour, and without moral disapprobation, as so many of her artistic forebears had done. Her commitment to showing the intricate relations of mind to body is also remarkable. With considerable insight, she depicts the consequence in psychosomatic illness of repressing instinctual behaviour, and yet her idealism prompts her to convey the possibility of release from confining psychological nets, and growth towards individuation. Through psychic doctors, she characteristically reveals sources of psychic conflict, as well as paths to recovery. In her eagerness to illustrate the possibilities offered by these new theories, of overcoming the determinism implicit in her religious background and much of her early reading on evolution, occasionally she errs in having these doctors reveal too much skeleton beneath the cloak of fiction. She is better off when she allows characters to unify disparate selves and achieve individuation through self-induced psychic experience, as in moments of illumination or dreams. For her this enmeshed spiritual-psychological reality is greater than any other. Finally, Sinclair never completely rejected the nineteenth-century discourses on heredity that impressed her in her youth, as her last novel *The Allinghams* (1927) well illustrates. Instead, prompted by her open-mindedness and her rapacious intellect, psychological discourses accumulate, blend, and provide an increasingly rich tapestry up to the period of her greatest insights into the psychology of the individual, in the novels between 1919 and 1922, notably *Mary Olivier* and *Harriet Frean*.

5

From Edwardian to Georgian Psychical Realism: Bennett, Lawrence, and Beresford

It may seem like a strange, almost uncanny act to link the most famous – and in some quarters notorious – Edwardian Arnold Bennett, the even more famous and thoroughly canonical modern novelist D.H. Lawrence, and J.D. Beresford, a Georgian novelist who worked with traditional novel structures and who has slipped into complete obscurity. Archaeological investigation, however, reveals grounds for comparing them. Prominent critic W.L. George (admired by Lawrence) saw Beresford as a successor to Edwardian realists including Bennett (*Novelist* 65). Furthermore, in 1924, the critic Abel Chevalley argued that, of the younger generation of Georgian novelists, including D.H. Lawrence, Frank Swinnerton, and Hugh Walpole, J.D. Beresford is "the one most equally endowed with that *intelligence* and that *imagination* of life which make good writers of fiction . . . ." (*Modern* 228). He added that "it is quite possible that [Beresford's] voice will be heard for a longer time" than the majority of his contemporaries (*Modern* 229).[1] Most importantly, all three novelists engaged with dynamic psychology in significant though disparate ways, and in all three cases Virginia Woolf contributed to the obscuring of that engagement by misreading these novelists, partially because of her anxiety of influence. This chapter begins by revisiting her pronouncements on her contemporaries before reconstructing Arnold Bennett as an Edwardian psychical novelist and elaborating on the varieties of psychical realism explored by Georgian non-modernists – or at least problematic modernists – Lawrence and Beresford.

5.1 Mr Bennett, Mrs Brown, and "a glimpse" at *The Ghost*

Of all the modernists, Virginia Woolf has been the most influential in perpetrating the myth of discontinuity between the modernists and their Edwardian predecessors. The number of times that Woolf elaborated on this polemic bears witness to her determination to promulgate her views. Subsequently, these essays, particularly "Modern Novels", "Mr. Bennett and Mrs. Brown", "Character in Fiction", and "Modern Fiction", have become fundamental to critics' arguments about radical innovations in the novel. Woolf's declaration that "on or about December 1910 human character changed", to account for Edwardian novelists' deficiencies and the necessity for Georgian novelists to discard Edwardian conventions and methods ("Character" 421, 430, 432), has, as Douglas Hewitt claims, become a *locus classicus* of modernist criticism.[2] In recent years, however, Woolf's claims have been interrogated for a variety of purposes (Daugherty; Kenney). I want to focus on Woolf's claims about the modernists' psychological innovations to show not only that Woolf seriously misrepresented her immediate predecessors, but that she deliberately ignored contemporary fiction developing along the lines she reserved for the moderns.

Admittedly, Woolf shows some awareness of her manoeuvre, claiming in "Mr. Bennett and Mrs. Brown" that she will "reduce Edwardian fiction to a view" ("Mr. Bennett" 385), but even so her view is striking for its restrictiveness. Her Edwardian camp comprises Arnold Bennett, along with John Galsworthy and H.G. Wells,[3] and they are ranged against the Georgians, limited to Forster, Lawrence, Strachey, Joyce, and T.S. Eliot ("Character" 421). She accuses the Edwardians of being materialists because, disappointingly, "they are concerned not with the spirit but with the body" and "spend immense skill and immense industry making the trivial and the transitory appear the true and the enduring" ("Modern Fiction" 210). These concerns cause them to fail in creating vivid, memorable characters as the Victorians had, and "Life escapes" their novels as a consequence ("Modern Fiction" 211). In contrast, the younger generation, of which Joyce is the most notable, "attempt to come closer to life", even if they must discard most conventions of the novel in order to do so ("Modern Fiction" 213). Joyce "is spiritual; he is concerned at all costs to reveal the flickerings of that innermost flame which flashes its messages through the brain" ("Modern Fiction" 214). Woolf also reserves "for the moderns" an interest in and appreciation of

> the dark places of psychology. At once therefore, the accent falls a little differently; the emphasis is upon something hitherto ignored; at once a different outline of forms becomes necessary, difficult for us to grasp, *incomprehensible to our predecessors*. ("Modern Fiction" 215, underlining mine)

Interestingly, Woolf attributes to the moderns both a spiritual approach and one probing the dark places of psychology, an association completely consonant with dynamic psychology.

Arnold Bennett is Woolf's "worst" materialist "culprit" since, as she admits in two versions of these essays, the label of "materialist" strikes wide of the mark for both Wells and Galsworthy ("Modern Novels" 32; "Modern Fiction" 209). Perhaps her target is not surprising when it is realized that Woolf wrote her polemics partly in reaction to Bennett's claim of her novel *Jacob's Room* that the characters do not vitally survive in the mind ("Mr. Bennett" 388). She drew her sole substantial example (in all versions) of Edwardian shortcomings from a single novel by Bennett, *Hilda Lessways*, to demonstrate that he spends more lines in describing his character's physical surroundings than in providing insight into Hilda's psyche ("Character" 429–431). Bennett, with his materialist concerns, is constructed as the antithesis of Mrs Brown, Woolf's fanciful archetypal character, symbol of "the spirit we live by, life itself" ("Character" 436), who has escaped Bennett's scrutiny. In imaging Mrs Brown as "a will-o'-the wisp, a dancing light", "a flying spirit" ("Mr. Bennett" 387, 388), and "that surprising apparition" ("Character" 436), Woolf imbued her not only with a psychical, supernatural quality, but also with a certain dynamism – attributes she clearly found lacking in Bennett's fictional characters.

However, Arnold Bennett wrote another kind of novel, one that drew on the discourses of dynamic psychology, particularly as expressed through psychical research, and he did so firmly within the Edwardian period. Both *The Ghost: A Fantasia on Modern Themes* (1907)[4] and *The Glimpse: An Adventure of the Soul* (1909)[5] attempt to capture something of the immaterial world, of his characters' inner spirit. In the former, Bennett's treatment of an apparition's higher nature and positive intervention in mortal lives aligns well with Myers's finding that as apparitions attain individuality they "rise" into love and joy (*Human* II 78). Singer Rosetta Rosa intercedes for the life of her new love, protagonist Carl Foster, by appealing to the apparition of her former fiancé, Lord Clarenceux, who loved her "with a passion so intense that it has survived the grave" (*Ghost* 270); she thus persuades him to leave off his jealous, vengeful behaviour.

Bennett's construction of the apparition reflects Myers's findings in two other ways. It does not physically resemble the traditional fictional conception of ghosts, criticized by Myers. When confronted by Lord Clarenceux's ghost, Carl claims

> To look at it, no one would have taken it for an apparition. Small wonder that till the previous evening I had never suspected it to be other than a man! It was dressed in black; it had the very aspect of life. I could follow the creases in the frock coat, the direction of the nap of the silk hat which it wore in my room. (*Ghost* 278)

As well, it does not perpetrate violence but acts upon the mind: "After all", Carl claims, "the ghost had no actual power over me; a ghost cannot stab, cannot throttle, cannot shoot. A ghost can only act upon the mind... Whatever the power might be, the fact that the ghost had indeed a power over me was indisputable" (*Ghost* 293).

Not only does *The Ghost* explore the psychological interaction between apparition and human, and illustrate survival of personality beyond death, but it also parallels a number of other attributes of the SPR psychical case study. Carl Foster is a young doctor who neither believes nor disbelieves in the supernatural at the outset (*Ghost* 63). In fact, he is rather sceptical of his cousin's wife's crystal gazing, until he himself sees a threatening vision in the crystal; even then, he feels his experience "might be the result of hypnotic suggestion, or of thought transference" (*Ghost* 70). When he becomes physician to Alresca, who also loves Rosetta and appears to be dying from sheer lack of will to live, Carl realizes the limitations of his empirical approach to medicine (*Ghost* 97). Nevertheless, as in a typical psychical case study, Carl emphasizes his normality: "Yet up to that period of my life my temperament and habit of mind had been calm, unimpressionable, and, if I may say so, not especially absurd" (*Ghost* 177). Once this condition, important for establishing veracity, has been met he, of course, becomes convinced that the ghost of Lord Clarenceux exists and that it is exerting power over him to prevent him from having relations with Rosetta. Carl disarms disbelief by stating that

> As for you who are disposed to smile at the idea of a live man crushed (figuratively) under the heel of a ghost, I beg you to look back at your own experience, and count up the happenings which have struck you as mysterious. You will be astonished at their number....I had strayed on the seashore of the unknown, and had picked up a pebble. I had a glimpse of that other world which exists side by side and permeates our own. (*Ghost* 267)

Bennett's slight mockery of credulous attitudes towards spiritualism, in this case crystal gazing, along with his light-hearted tone, replete with melodramatic flourishes, cleverly enables him to convey serious conviction about that other world, permeating our own, without seeming heavy-handed.

In *The Glimpse*, Bennett very deliberately contrasts the materialist world with the spiritual realm, which is much more fully and imaginatively realized than in *The Ghost* through a near-death, out-of-body experience.[6] Morrice Loring, wealthy and famous, initially appears to be suffering an existential crisis, to be depressed by the human spectacle he observes, that "sought happiness on the material plane instead of the spiritual" (*Glimpse* 20). Bennett seems to have based his character at least in part on famous psychical researcher Edmund Gurney. Like Gurney, Morrice has published a magnum opus on music, "The Development of European Music" (Gurney's 1880 treatise was called *The Power of Sound*), has been unsatisfied with his various successes, suffered recurrent melancholy, and now, at 42, contemplates suicide (in 1888 Gurney at 41 had overdosed on chloroform, a probable suicide).

However, there the similarities end. Loring to all appearances dies from a "paroxysm of the heart" (*Glimpse* 89) after his wife reveals her infidelity, but in actuality his spirit rises and floats above his inert body, and he experiences the auras or "thought-shapes" of those left behind.[7] Bennett may well have drawn on descriptions of near-death experiences in Myers's *Human Personality*. In one, a Dr Wiltse recounted his soul "floating up and down and laterally like a soap-bubble" (II 316); Bennett depicts Marion's floating thoughts as "not bubbles! Shapes more complex than spheres" (*Glimpse* 127). As well, he repeatedly employs the trope of envelope – whether chromatic, radiant or translucent – in order to describe these auras, claiming for example that "The casing of this 'me' in a coloured envelope which though fluid and not unresponsive was infinitely less so than myself" (*Glimpse* 170); it is tempting to suggest that Woolf borrowed this trope from the materialist culprit, in her famous description of life as "a luminous halo, a semi-transparent envelope surrounding us from the beginning of consciousness to the end" (*Modern Fiction* 212).[8]

During Loring's out-of-body experience, he comes to a number of realizations which demonstrate the depth of Bennett's engagement with depicting the non-material realm. Initially Loring has the revelation that just as "the living speak of the uncanniness of the dead", so "manifestations of human existence may be uncanny to the dead" (*Glimpse* 118), and then that mankind's devotion to the business of "moving matter from one place to another" is "ridiculous" (*Glimpse* 124). Witnessing his maid Marion's extensive inner life causes him to re-evaluate the human spectacle (by which he formerly meant his social inferiors) and to become convinced of the extensiveness of people's unconscious powers: "they were but awaking from unconsciousness into consciousness" (*Glimpse* 138). Invoking telepathy, Bennett claims that Marion "had fabricated volitional shapes and sent them, charged with her vital energy, infallibly to fixed destinations... she had physically and eternally influenced other beings at a distance" (*Glimpse* 139). Loring's new experience of the "reality of life" leads to an understanding of the "transcendent interpenetration of spirit by spirit.... The double bliss of realising my self and of simultaneously merging it in others!" (*Glimpse* 168). His discovery bears a striking affinity with Mrs Dalloway's transcendental theory in Woolf's novel (cf. Chapter 6). Ultimately, Loring gains the self-awareness that he "had masqueraded as a spiritual aristocrat" when he was in fact a self-absorbed egotist (*Glimpse* 177, 173). As is typical of the mystic's experience, Loring despairs of recounting it when he returns to life, and his indictment of the "gross medium of speech" has a Bergsonian flavour to it (*Glimpse* 174; cf. 82). As well, the novel has just the lightest touch of the psychical case study about it, since the narrator senses that the attending doctor attributes Loring's experience to the "deluding power of delirium and dream", although he is pleased by "the interestingness of [Loring's] case" (*Glimpse* 208).

Perhaps most significantly for present purposes, Bennett devotes seventy-seven pages to Loring's out of body, "timeless existence" (*Glimpse* 187), when only a short amount of clock time has passed, surely a substantial example, in Woolf's terms, of the accent falling a little differently, of a moment of being. Furthermore, Bennett employed the device of London clocks striking to bracket Morrice's out-of-body experience (*Glimpse* 118, 194), a technique Woolf used extensively in *Mrs. Dalloway* to punctuate characters' streams of thought. Although the resemblances between Bennett and Woolf seem uncanny, my point is not to establish a direct influence (or even a telepathic one), but to suggest that these resemblances may arise from their mutual interrogation of the discourses of dynamic psychology.

Woolf's injustice towards Arnold Bennett's work pales in comparison to her treatment of other writers of dynamic psychological fiction. She completely ignores May Sinclair's extensive canon although well aware of it, as will be discussed in Chapter 6. Woolf admits D.H. Lawrence into the Georgian camp only in a late version of her polemics, "Character in Fiction" (1924), as though reluctant to do so, and in fact she criticizes him for spoiling his early work by using Edwardian tools ("Character" 433). Her ambivalence towards him emerges more clearly in a 1920 review of his *The Lost Girl*, in which she almost writes him off for laboriously constructing a world of facts à la Bennett: "Mr. Lawrence indeed shows something of Mr. Bennett's power of displaying by means of immense industry and great ability a section of the hive beneath the glass" ("Postscript" 272). However, earlier in her review she had praised him for his "extraordinary sense of the physical world, of the colour and texture and shape of things" ("Postscript" 271). It would seem that her ambivalence has more to do with his probing of a particular dimension of dynamic psychology – sexuality – as intimated in her statement that "it was plain that sex had for him a meaning which it was disquieting to think that we, too, might have to explore" ("Postscript" 271).

J.D. Beresford was another of Woolf's contemporaries employing dynamic psychology in ways not approved by her, and thus not acknowledged in her polemical essays. In a review of his novel, *An Imperfect Mother* (1920), predating most versions of her polemical essays, she actually accused him of being too blatantly psychological because of his use of psychoanalysis as a key to unlock all doors ("Freudian" 196). Beresford had created "an interesting document" in "morbid psychology", and his "characters have become cases" ("Freudian" 197). Nevertheless, in her diary she admitted to being pleased to have been asked "to preside over" him (19 December 1920, *Diary* II 80). Although she criticized Beresford's subsequent novel *Revolution* for being over-deliberate, her review of it praised Beresford as a writer "who can make you interested in his characters" ("Revolution" 279). She also cited his psychological novels "*Jacob Stahl, The House in Demetrius Road* and *These Lynnekers*, to name three very memorable novels out of a total now amounting to fourteen", suggesting that she had read at least these three (*Essays* III 280).

Woolf's ambivalence towards Beresford may have been heightened by his response to "Mr. Bennett and Mrs. Brown", published in the *Nation and*

Athenaeum a few weeks after Woolf's appeared. Incensed by his disagreement with her, she referred to his article as "that stupid Mr. Beresford's" (*Letters* III 90). Though very rarely commented on, Beresford's "The Successors of Charles Dickens" (1923) actually presented a more accurate view of Edwardian writers than Woolf's, informed by his extensive knowledge of dynamic psychological discourses. He proposed "a valid psychological explanation" for the Edwardians' apparent weakness in characterization. Unlike the Victorians, who tended to highlight one feature of a character, the Edwardians present human beings that satisfy "our sense of probability; inasmuch as they are, like ourselves, composite, full of irresolutions, often self-conscious, and apt to change their minds" ("Successors" 487). This subtlety resulted from Edwardian writers' knowledge of heredity and their empirical approach. Beresford's own fiction had developed along these lines and illustrates the continuity between Edwardian and Georgian psychological realism. An examination of his and Lawrence's engagement with dynamic psychology will confirm the limitations of and distortions in Woolf's argument about the modernists' discovery of the dark places of psychology, as well as reveal the complexity of their interrogation of those dark places.

5.2   D.H. Lawrence: Dynamic consciousness and allotropic states

Daniel Schneider, in his detailed study of D.H. Lawrence as psychologist, claims that the key word in Lawrence's psychology is "balance", but it could just as well be "dynamic" since Lawrence's psychology is in essence exactly that (Schneider 73). "Dynamic" and a cluster of related tropes appear repeatedly in his psychological writings, most frequently in *Fantasia of the Unconscious* (1922). Although much has been written about Lawrence's appropriation of later dynamic psychologies, notably Freud's and Jung's, some of the earlier sources for his conception of dynamic psychology have been largely overlooked. An archaeological approach reveals that Lawrence assimilated some of the same discourses as Sinclair, including those of James, Herbart, idealism, and, most significantly, Myersian psychical research. The difficulty with unearthing these discourses is that, unlike Sinclair, Lawrence typically subsumed them covertly into his powerful mythologizing rhetoric about the psyche. Thus, in some cases it will only be possible to note affinities and correspondences, particularly in my necessarily brief analysis of *Women in Love*, the novel in which Lawrence most fully engaged his dynamic psychology.

Schneider argues that Lawrence early on interrogated Jamesian psychology. Most strikingly, Lawrence adapted James's theory of the emotions, that emotions arise out of visceral states rather than out of mental causes (Schneider 21). Lawrence greatly elaborated on this by suggesting that the body's great source of pre-mental or primal consciousness is the solar plexus and that this is always dynamic (*Fantasia* 29). Lawrence felt more ambivalently about the mysterious stream of consciousness. Immortal phrase of the immortal James! Oh stream of hell which undermined my adolescence! The stream of consciousness! I felt it streaming through my brain, in at one ear and out at the other. (*Psychoanalysis* 4–5)

While Schneider argues that Lawrence found it "horrid" because it negated the self (Schneider 22), it seems more likely that he disliked it because it emphasized the consciousness of *mental* activity rather than pre-mental, or what Lawrence termed "blood consciousness". Nevertheless, Lawrence found attractive James's attention to process and continuous flow. In *Fantasia of the Unconscious*, he wrote that

The supreme lesson of human consciousness is to learn how *not to know*. That is, how not to *interfere*. That is, how to live dynamically, from the great Source, and not statically like machines driven by ideas and principles from the head, or automatically, from one fixed desire. (*Fantasia* 67)

However, as important as James was to Lawrence's dynamic psychology, Lawrence drew just as much if not more so on Herbartian psychology. Schneider notes that Lawrence, during his study of education at Nottingham University College, read John Adams's *The Herbartian Psychology Applied to Education*, but Schneider considers it only to suggest further influences of James on Lawrence (Schneider 25–27). In Herbart, as conveyed through Adams's lively epigrammatic prose, Lawrence was presented with a psychology that maintained the soul's significance, though not in "its narrow theological meaning" (Adams 19), and that conveyed the dynamics of the psyche, including the concepts of ideas as active forces, of thresholds between conscious and unconscious ideas, of psychic equilibrium, and of inhibition. Adams stressed that "the mind is no doubt active, very active, but this activity can be regulated by what has gone before in the experience of the soul in question" (Adams 73). Ideas, or states of consciousness (Adams 49), compete to rise above the "threshold" of consciousness. Adams wrote that

in every soul there is a sort of order-of-merit arrangement of the ideas, – an order often disturbed, but to which there is a strong tendency to revert as soon as any unusual influence has been withdrawn. The ideas are, indeed, in a state of unstable equilibrium, which is easily disturbed and as easily recovered. (Adams 61)

Similar ideas in consciousness cluster and form apperceptive masses (Adams 55–57). In "some morbid states", an "*idée fixe*" takes permanent possession of consciousness and all other ideas must subordinate to it (Adams 61). When a new idea "claims admittance, there arises a struggle" (Adams 61) between similar ideas promoting it and contrary ones rejecting it, after which "a temporary equilibrium is gained" (Adams 61). If the idea occupies a position that it is really not entitled to, "the threshold in relation to it is called the *dynamical threshold*" (Adams 62). Ideas below the dynamical threshold do not perish but may influence those favoured above the threshold (Adams 63). Ideas not systematically associated with those favoured, that is gathered in apperceptive masses, will tend to be inhibited (Adams 76). Lawrence elaborated on this conception of unstable, temporary equilibrium, both within a psyche and in the interactions between male and female, as we shall see.

Herbartian psychology has a moral dimension that would have appealed to Lawrence as well, in that, as Adams put it, "if powerful, compact, well-organized masses of moral ideas are present in the mind, the isolated, though intrinsically powerful, ideas of evil are rapidly dismissed" (Adams 76). Herbartian psychology also has implications for education, in that it suggests that there is no point in "judiciously stuff[ing]" hard facts into a student's mind, since "each soul moulds its own facts" (Adams 67), a dynamic activity based on an individual's "self-development, development from within" (Adams 40). Years after reading Adams, in *Fantasia of the Unconscious*, Lawrence closely echoed this viewpoint, claiming that

> Education means leading out the individual nature in each man to its true fullness. You can't do that by stimulating the mind. To pump education into the mind is fatal. That which sublimates from the dynamic consciousness into the mental consciousness has alone any value.... Every extraneous idea, which has no inherent root in the dynamic consciousness is as dangerous as a nail driven into a young tree. (*Fantasia* 67–68)

In discussing approaches to education, Adams noted the influence of idealism, and took a critical attitude towards it, a position congruent with Lawrence's. In a letter, Lawrence asserted that he was "a passionately religious man, and my novels must be written from the depth of my religious experience" (*Letters* II 165). He violently rejected the dogmas of religion, but like many of his generation drew on idealism to express his religious experience although he disliked idealism's focus on abstractions, concepts, and the conscious mind (cf. *Psychoanalysis* 11; *Fantasia* 158). Similar to the idealist Sinclair, who argued that selfhood transcended divisions and seemed inviolable, Lawrence believed in the supremacy of individuality. In *Fantasia*, he stated that

> this quality of pure individuality is, however, only the one supreme quality. It consummates all other qualities, but does not consume them. All the others are there, all the time. And only at his maximum does an individual surpass all his derivative elements, and become purely himself. (*Fantasia* 25)[9]

Just as Sinclair believed that individuality holds it own precariously at times, so Lawrence acknowledged the forces, notably "the old mother–father connections", that oppose attainment of individuality, mankind's "highest goal" (*Fantasia* 25, 26). Lawrence also employed the concept of the Absolute in a variety of contexts: in one letter, for example, he claimed that "It is an Absolute we are all after" (*Letters* II 263) and in another that "the highest aim of the government is the highest good of the *soul* of the individual, the fulfilment in the Infinite, in the Absolute" *Letters* II 366). Most fundamentally, Lawrence believed that when a man and a woman attain union, a "star" equilibrium, they attain the Absolute.

As Schneider claims, Lawrence wanted to find a way and a vocabulary to fuse his moral, religious view with a naturalistic scientific view of human behaviour (Schneider 143, 145). What Schneider omits to mention is that Lawrence's discovery of the discourses of psychical research helped facilitate that fusion.[10] Lawrence's assimilation of these discourses has been overlooked partly because Lawrence was very cagey and ambivalent in admitting their impact. In his 1923 essay on Edgar Allan Poe, Lawrence acknowledged "For it is true, as William James and Conan Doyle and the rest allow, that a spirit can persist in the after-death. Persist by its own volition" (*Studies* 109). In *Fantasia*, Lawrence evoked a poetic image to convey his belief in the survival of personality beyond death: "How many dead souls, like swallows, twitter and breed thoughts under the thatch of my hair and the eaves of my forehead I don't know. But I believe a good many" (*Fantasia* 18). He added that

I am sorry to say I believe in the souls of the dead. I am almost ashamed to say that I believe the souls of the dead in some way enter and pervade the souls of the living; so that life is always the life of living creatures, and death is always our affair. This bit, I admit, is bordering on mysticism. I'm sorry, because I don't like mysticism. (*Fantasia* 18)

Lawrence's embarrassment, betraying anxiety,[11] may have a more personal root, attested to by a letter in which he wrote "I am afraid of the ghosts of the dead" (*Letters* II 342) and graphically illustrated by his character Paul's possession by his dead mother at the close of *Sons and Lovers* (456, 464).

Like James and Frederic Myers, Lawrence did not favour the Freudian unconscious, since it "is, by its very nature, unanalyzable" (*Psychoanalysis* 15). Lawrence's preferred term "dynamic consciousness" resembles Myers's subliminal in that it is an instinctive awareness that exists below the threshold of empirical consciousness and is superior because more profound than mental conception. Those who live from their dynamic consciousness have extended capacity for connection, and attain more individuality than those who operate from mental consciousness. Furthermore, dynamic consciousness has a telepathic dimension in the root sense identified by Myers as "feeling at a distance"; Lawrence believed this communication begins in the womb, between embryo and mother: "This consciousness, however, is utterly non-ideal, non-mental, purely dynamic, a matter of dynamic polarized intercourse of vital vibrations, as an exchange of wireless messages which are never translated from the pulse-rhythm into speech, because they have no need to be" (*Fantasia* 62).

Myers also claimed that, besides supernormal and degenerative material, the subliminal comprised "allotropic" states:

> modifications of the arrangements of nervous elements on which our conscious identity depends, but with no more conspicuous *superiority* of the one state over the other than (for instance) charcoal possesses over graphite or graphite over charcoal. But there may also be states in which the (metaphorical) carbon becomes *diamond*; – with so much at least of *advance* on previous states as is involved in the substitution of the crystalline for the amorphous structure. (Myers, *Human* II 85)

This impersonal, chemical metaphor, employed by Myers on several occasions (*Human* I 225; II 198), appears to have appealed to Lawrence, although he never attributed its source. Thomas Gibbons (339) first noted that Lawrence draws on it when he famously writes in 1914 of going beyond

> The old stable ego of the character. There is another ego, according to whose action the individual is unrecognisable, and passes through, as it were, allotropic states which it needs a deeper sense than any we've been used to exercise, to discover are states of the same single radically unchanged element. (Like as diamond and coal are the same pure single element of carbon. The ordinary novel would trace the history of the diamond – but I say "diamond what! This is carbon." And my diamond might be coal or soot, and my theme is carbon.) (*Letters* II 183)

Other scholars, such as Roger Luckhurst (259–260), cite Gibbons' claims without probing them further. In fact, Lawrence repeatedly conveyed these allotropic states, or subliminal variations that deepen our instinctive understanding of a character and link him to some larger force than himself, in *Women in Love*, as we shall see.

Given Lawrence's religious temperament, and his exposure to the expansionist, dynamic psychologies of James, Herbart, and Myers, it is not surprising that he adopted an eclectic attitude towards Freudian psychoanalysis, and had perceptions and misperceptions of Freud similar to Sinclair and Beresford, as well as many British psychologists and psychiatrists. In a 1914 letter, he claimed that "I am not a Freudian and never was – Freudianism is only a branch of medical science, interesting" (*Letters* II 218). Although he appreciated Freud's exploration of sexuality, he was also critical because "Freud is with the scientists" in saying "fie! to the religious impulse" (*Fantasia* 15). He perceived that "Psychoanalysis is out, under a therapeutic disguise, to do away entirely with the moral faculty in man" (*Psychoanalysis* 4), and also dismissed Freud's universal claims, stating "when Freud makes sex accountable for everything he as good as makes it accountable for nothing" (*Fantasia* 15).

Lawrence's attitude may also have been influenced by the eclecticism of the professionals who introduced him to later dynamic psychologies, Barbara Low and her brother-in-law David Eder. Low, for example, claimed that she and Eder "initiated" Lawrence to psychoanalysis in 1914 by lending him a book by Jung (Delavenay 313). Eder, who by 1914 favoured Jung and was translating his work, also recounted subsequently discussing psycho-analysis and corresponding with Lawrence about it (*Memoirs* 117, 119).[12] Although some of these letters have not survived, there is evidence, as Whelan notes, that Lawrence's discussions with Eder extended to the occult, as when Lawrence asked Eder whether he had read Madame Blavatsky's *Secret Doctrine* (Whelan 103). Lawrence's contact with Eder's friend, J.D. Beresford, whom he met with frequently over the winter of 1915–1916 and who lent Lawrence his Cornwall farmhouse (Beresford, "Memories" 241), may also have stimulated Lawrence's interest in eclectic dynamic psychologies, including psychical research.[13]

Although a detailed analysis of Lawrence's intricate assimilation of dynamic psychology in *Women in Love* lies beyond my scope, some indication of the direction Lawrence takes can be suggested by examining Lawrence's revelation of: Gerald's allotropic states, the unstable equilibrium both within Birkin and between Birkin and Ursula, and characters' dissolution through tropes evoking the uncanny. In the first half of the novel, Gerald is presented in widely differing environments and circumstances: presiding over a social function (a wedding reception); swimming in Willey Water; lusting after a woman among London decadents; reigning in his horse at a train crossing; and grasping for Gudrun's sketch-book. Gerald's actions may be viewed as allotropic states demonstrating the same radically unchanged element in Gerald: his will. Initially he is associated with the tropes of crystals (*Women* 14) and whiteness (*Women* 46), perhaps evoking Gudrun's initial superficial perception of him, but increasingly he comes to be associated with the dark (both literally and metaphorically) states of the diamond element: coal and coal-dust. When Gerald masters his horse, Gudrun is entranced by his "soft, white magnetic domination" (*Women* 113), but signs of "a hot world silted with coal-dust" surround them (*Women* 114), symbolic both of the industry controlled by Gerald and of his inner dissolution. Gerald may nearly attain a true diamond, or advanced state, in Myers's sense, when he drifts with Gudrun on Willey Water – at least she "wanted to see him like a crystal shadow, to feel his essential presence" (*Women* 178). Relaxing his will, he succumbs to his dynamic consciousness:

His mind was almost submerged, he was almost transfused, lapsed out for the first time in his life, into the things about him. For he had always kept such a keen attentiveness, concentrated and unyielding in himself. Now he had let go, imperceptibly he was melting into oneness with the whole. (*Women* 178)

Nevertheless, his sister Diana's drowning, which follows immediately, destroys any potential he might have had to live from this centre, since he "can't feel any grief" (*Women* 203). Lawrence reveals Gerald's denial and avoidance of feeling as a pattern modelled by his mother and developed from his earliest years, in the expository "Industrial Magnate" chapter, strategically placed after the drowning and after Gerald's allotropic states have been dramatically presented. There Lawrence underlines that Gerald's "mind was obedient to serve his will. Man's will was the absolute, the only absolute" (*Women* 223) and that he operates mechanically. From this point on, his self-destructive fate is sealed, and it is no surprise that Lawrence figures him as an unnatural, ghostly presence before dying, surrounded by black mountain slopes, in the snow (*Women* 470).

While Gerald has "no equilibrium", as he dimly recognizes, Birkin possesses an "odd mobility and changeableness" illustrative of unstable equilibrium (*Women* 232). At the novel's outset, struggling against the mechanical will of Hermione, he operates too much out of his head, strikingly conveyed in the "Classroom" chapter when he instructs Ursula to emphasize facts, not subjective impressions, in her teaching (*Women* 36), and even when he pontificates about blood consciousness (*Women* 43). Hermione's act of braining Birkin with her lapis lazuli paperweight precipitates Birkin's seeking out pure sensation among the primroses and lapsing into blood consciousness (*Women* 105–107), but he continues to oscillate between this mode of knowing and the mental. Without feeling it, he asserts to Ursula that he wants a "strange conjunction" with her, "an equilibrium, a pure balance of two single beings: – as the stars balance each other" (*Women* 148). In a manner similar to the way Herbart described the struggle of a new idea to gain admittance into the psyche, Birkin has trouble adjusting to the idea of Ursula before he comes to know her instinctively. After lapsing into physical passion for her, he recognizes that "I was becoming quite dead-alive, nothing but a word-bag", and although he scorns this other self it continues to "hover", perpetuating his instability (*Women* 188). Birkin begins before Ursula does to accept the need for his old self to die, and when he advances into this new state "he [is] the enemy, fine as a diamond" to Ursula, who has become dissolute (*Women* 198, 192). Birkin's and Ursula's relationship gradually develops into a "star-equilibrium" (*Women* 319), periodically destabilized by their succumbing to social convention and mechanical functioning. Ultimately, they do achieve blood communion, while still able to maintain their individual integrity.

Most characters do not, however, and Lawrence deploys uncanny, supernatural imagery primarily to convey un-individualized characters living unnaturally or descending into dissolution because they insist on operating from mental consciousness and dominating with their wills. Hermione is perhaps the supreme example of this, and Lawrence invokes her state with the most vivid, grotesque metaphors of the uncanny, such as the following:

> [Hermione] suffered the ghastliness of dissolution, broken and gone in a horrible corruption. . . . She strayed out, pallid and preyed-upon like a ghost, like one attacked by the tomb-influences which dog us. And she was gone like a corpse, that has no presence, no connection. (*Women* 89)

More than any other character, she is possessed by the ghosts of dead conventions and is condemned more harshly because she hypocritically affects a "sham spirituality" (*Women* 293, 307). In Herbartian terms, she is also possessed by the *idée fixe* that "the greatest thing in life [is] – to know" (*Women* 86), which keeps her static. Lawrence also imbues Gerald with supernatural imagery when in dissolute, degenerative states, as with Minette in the Pompadour, where he possesses "an uncanny smile" (*Women* 67). Ursula, too, before the birth of her new self, is "palpitating and formless within the flux of the ghost life" (*Women* 144). Even with Birkin, Lawrence deploys language invoking a ghostly self, as when he is divided between two modes of consciousness after tangling with Gerald: "He still heard as if it were his own disembodied spirit hearing, standing at some distance behind him" (*Women* 272).

Thus, in employing the uncanny to convey characters in unnatural states, Lawrence very much subsumed to his vision the science of spirituality he encountered through psychical research. More direct was his appropriation of Myers's allotropic states, which he used to try and probe a character's radically unchanged element lying beneath his behaviour in a variety of circumstances. Lawrence's transformation of Herbartian psychology was perhaps the most fundamental to his approach to characterization. In making his characters' development hinge on the degree to which they remained static or lived from their dynamic consciousness, and thus gained temporary equilibrium, Lawrence seems to have drawn on Herbartian terminology and descriptions of the activity of ideas that he encountered as a young man in teacher training.

5.3   J.D. Beresford: A case study in psychical realism

> I am not content to picture the doings and sayings of typical humanity; I want to know *why* they do and say these things, which is a mistake from the artist's point of view. That is work for the clinic. (*Writing Aloud* 143)

J.D. Beresford incorporated the discourses of dynamic psychology in a more overt and extensive way than Lawrence, and with different emphasis.

Though Beresford admired Lawrence, referring to him a "a man of genius" who was feverishly seeking truth and self-conviction rather than attempting to convert us to his own ideas" ("Experiment" 40–41), he claimed, for example, that Lawrence's

> obsession with sex bored me, as in this relation I have always been a normal man, regarding the animal expression of sexual love as one of the physical functions that, however important, is not of overwhelming interest. And to elevate sex, as such, into a subject of supreme importance, seems to me a dangerous distortion of human values. ("Memories" 244)

Beresford's fascination with dynamic psychology informs to a greater or lesser degree all of his forty-nine novels, as well as his short stories collected in five volumes. His innovations were, for the most part, in theme and characterization; he attempted on the one hand to go "deeper" than Edwardians like Bennett, by making "clinical dissections" in his novels (*Writing* 143), and on the other to bring various extensions of consciousness, including telepathic moments, into a plausible construct of realism. This section will highlight the stages of Beresford's development as a psychological novelist by focussing on: his early autobiographical *Jacob Stahl* trilogy that established his reputation; the contrasting early speculative classic *The Wonder* (1911); *Housemates* (1917); *God's Counterpoint* (1918), as an illustration of the consequences of adhering too closely to Freudian doctrine; *An Imperfect Mother* (1920) and *Love's Pilgrim* (1923), as the best examples of his integration of dynamic psychology; and *Writing Aloud* (1928), an experimental novel in process – or stream of consciousness manqué – that moves him closer to the modernist camp.

Beresford also contributed, in several autobiographical works, a most detailed account of the growth of his knowledge of matters psychological. In addition, he wrote critically about the impact of dynamic psychology on his literary contemporaries and on the novel as a genre. I want to begin by tracing the evolution of his engagement with psychology using these sources.

Above all else Beresford was a passionate truth-seeker who deliberately cultivated an eclectic attitude ("Memories" 355) and an "open mind", by which he meant "a mind emptied as far as it may be, of every preconception with regard to the meaning and purpose of life" (*What* 74). This discipline is clearly indicated by the number and variety of sources that Beresford assimilated. In the early years of his self-education (to about 1904), his thinking was shaped primarily by Samuel Laing (*What* 24), the evolutionist thinkers Darwin and Huxley, Nietzsche, and then Ernst Haeckel's *The Riddle of the Universe* (1900), F.W.H. Myers's *The Human Personality* (1903), T.J. Hudson's *Law of Psychic Phenomena* (1893), Henri Bergson (*Matter and Memory, Time and Free Will, Laughter*), William James, and Johann Herbart. During his first two decades as a writer (1910–1930), Beresford interrogated the discourses of: Freud, Jung, Adler, E. Coué, Sir Arthur Eddington, Gustave Le Bon, Maeterlinck, T. Troward, Louis Berman, E. Le Bec, and W.J. Dunne, among others.

Several circumstances of Beresford's early life help account for his determined quest to attain knowledge of matters psychological and spiritual. First, he suffered an attack of polio at age three-and-a-half, which caused permanent lameness. Whereas J.D. Beresford's ascetic, evangelical clergyman father viewed his second son's affliction as an embarrassment and refused to fund an expensive education for him, Beresford's mother, estranged from her husband, "proffered much maternal care" on Beresford; he explores this family dynamic repeatedly in his fiction. Even when Beresford did attend school, in Peterborough, he was bullied ("Memories" 38). In his autobiography he recollected that "My education was a very haphazard affair" ("Memories" 35). Beresford may well have taken up writing initially as an escape from the torments he experienced, as a way of imaginatively recreating a world in which he was not defective or his defect became an asset. His physical challenge appears to have widened his sympathy for individuals afflicted with either physical or psychosomatic difficulties, including inferiority complexes, since such characters frequently appear as heroes in his novels.

Secondly, Beresford viewed his evangelical upbringing as an impediment to his psychical growth that he became determined to overcome (*What* 15). He did, however, experience moments of inspiration, or "fugitive ecstasies" as he refers to them (*What* 16, 47), as a young man that he interpreted within a religious context. These experiences suggest that he did not merely adhere mechanically to his parents' creed but possessed "true religious feeling" (*What* 16). Nevertheless, Beresford does assert that "I never even began to think until I was 21" (*What* 53), at which age he threw off "those shackles of orthodoxy...in a single evening" ("Discovery" 133). The catalyst was a London doctor named G.F. Rogers, versed in Theosophy, who suggested that the "theories of Orthodox Christianity were neither logical nor probable" ("Discovery" 133).

For the next nine years, Beresford mainly read works which supported the materialist, positivist theory of evolution, including Laing's and Darwin's (*Jacob Stahl* 256). Probably during this period he also became interested in progressive education, including Herbart's, as did Sinclair and Lawrence (*Ford* 21). However, Beresford's entire way of thinking was transformed by F.W.H. Myers's *Human Personality and Its Survival of Bodily Death* (1903). Beresford recalled that

> in 1903, I came across a book of modern wonders that gave my mind a new twist. This book was F.W.H. Myers's *Human Personality*. It was in some sense my introduction to the new science of psychology, and I found in it a foreshadowing of the possibility that I might recover a prospect of

surviving death without incurring the awful penalties threatened by the creed in which I had been educated. For Myers made it appear inherently probable that there was a non-physical element in the human personality, even if it was only that contradictory, incomprehensible alter ego, the "Subliminal" self. (*What* 27–28)

Beresford initially attempted to "characterise and rationalise" Myers's subliminal self, but eventually realized that its amorphousness gave it an advantage over Janet's conception of subconscious or Freud's unconscious, the latter of which he described as "hopelessly misleading" (*What* 28). For Beresford, the subliminal was

at once wise and ignorant, immoral and beneficent, uncontrollable... and apt to manifest itself when violently opposed, particularly on moral grounds, by cunning subterfuges that might in extreme cases destroy the health, the sanity or even the life of its senior partner. (*What* 28)

Nevertheless, Beresford's "scientific habit of mind" (*What* 29) demanded evidence, which made the SPR's work particularly compelling. Beresford claimed that this line of enquiry

took me along a path that has never terminated in a dead end. I have on my shelves between sixty and seventy books dealing with Spiritualism and Psychic Phenomena, books by Richet, Geley, Schrenck-Notzing, Podmore, Carrington, Crawford, and a host of minor works, including a pile of the Proceedings issued by the S.P.R. The number of these authorities will testify to the eagerness of my examination of Spiritualism in search of evidence for the existence of the soul. But I have to confess that this particular evidence has so far failed to convince me that we can, in full possession of normal consciousness, step from this life to another in which, given the right conditions, we are able to communicate with those who are still in the flesh. So far I remain a sceptic in this condition. I am quite sure, nevertheless, that many strange phenomena, at present beyond the range of scientific enquiry, do occur, phenomena that illuminate some of the astonishing potentialities yet undeveloped in the great mystery that is man. (*What* 31)

Most importantly, psychical research led him, gradually, "to abandon the realist for the idealist position" (*What* 30). Beresford held that this is a spiritual, not a physical, universe (*What* 118) and that mankind was developing "an increased spirituality, a deeper, fuller consciousness" (*Writing* 118). His belief in the universe's non-material nature was strengthened by reading about the theory of relativity as well as Henri Bergson's *Time and Free Will* (trans. 1910) and *Matter and Memory* (trans. 1911).

The next major advance in Beresford's knowledge of dynamic psychology came with his introduction to psychoanalysis in 1912. In 1931 he recollected that

> I was first interested in P.-A. [psychoanalysis] somewhat before the war, through my friend Dr. M.D. Eder and his wife, and as you will infer my earlier reading was strictly Freudian. Later I reacted strongly in favour of Jung's psychology, which I found more inclusive and more probable, and it is still Jung's general position that I favour rather than that of Freud or even Adler. (as qtd in Hoops 104–105)

As did Sinclair, Beresford interpreted Freudian psychoanalysis in the light of psychical research and sought in it further information about the soul, "the ghostly family in occupation of the physical body" (*What* 34). Psychoanalysis also

> provided much rich material for the characterization of the strange partner whom I had first known as the subliminal self, a far more benevolent creature than the ravening, erotic "unconscious" portrayed by Freud. Not that I was ever convinced of its exclusively sexual preoccupation. Even before I read Jung, I could not make that theory work with what knowledge I already had of the working of the convention of body, mind and spirit we recognize as a human being. (*What* 36)

Aside from overemphasis on the sexual, psychoanalytic theory possessed several other flaws and limitations according to Beresford. First,

> The Freudians, like their master, have a particular dogma that leads them into all kinds of illogical absurdities. They can see only the theory they are looking for, and turn a blind eye to anything that may confute their own pet theory. ("Memories" 229)

Second, the Freudians' "uninspired terminology" (*What* 73), used to describe various levels of consciousness "as if they were strata in a geological formation", distorted these mental functions by making them appear as concrete entities when they were in essence neither spatial nor temporal (*What* 36–37, 73). Third, the findings of psychoanalysis

> gave no support to the theory of the survival of consciousness after the earthly partnership was dissolved. Indeed that which we commonly regard as our consciousness seemed the most ephemeral of the group, a kind of effluvium given off in our waking hours by the activities below. (*What* 37)

Finally, the psychoanalytic paradigm rendered no explanation of the moral sense (*What* 37).

What psychoanalysis did offer Beresford was confirmation of unconscious or subconscious powers and of the inadequacy of mechanistic theories (*What* 37). Along with psychical research, psychoanalysis helped Beresford develop a new, less rational, more symbolic technique of thinking, about the mind in particular (*What* 33). In addition, Beresford's reaction against psychoanalysis provoked further investigation into the source of man's religious tendency and the nature of soul and psyche. In the second decade of the twentieth century, he continued to find the most enlightened approach to these enigmas in SPR studies.[14] Several articles reflect Beresford's interest, including "A New Form of Matter" (1919), "The Crux of Psychical Research" (1920), and "More New Facts in Psychical Research" (1922). Beresford shared, and was encouraged in, this pursuit by his friend and collaborator, Kenneth Richmond, a psychotherapist and long-time member, along with his wife, of the SPR.[15]

Beresford's perception of psychoanalysis through the lens of psychical research conditioned his assessment of psychoanalysis's impact on the novel, conveyed in two of his most significant articles, "Psychoanalysis and the Novel" (1919) and *"Le Déclin de L'Influence de la Psycho-analyse Sur Le Roman Anglais"* (1926). In the first he considers why psychoanalysis has such an adverse effect on reviewers and the reading public when "of all theories of the nature of man ever put forward by a reputable scientist, that of Sigmund Freud is the most attractive and adaptable for fiction" ("Psychoanalysis" 426). Freud's theories deal with the novel's universal theme of sex, suggest the need for a freer morality, and provide unworked complications of motive for the novelist. Beresford's answer is that opportunist novelists – who grasp psychoanalysis intellectually and superficially and who apply it arbitrarily and mechanically – produce an effect of irritation and disbelief in the reader ("Psychoanalysis" 427). His subsequent discussion of psychoanalysis's status and limitations draws on the discourses of psychical research and about multiple personality (as developed by Morton Prince or Pierre Janet); overall he favours Jungian discourse as more balanced than Freud's, for example in "the assumption that the unconscious is the complement of the conscious" ("Psychoanalysis" 433). He concludes that

> the basis of the psycho-analytic theory was firmly established in literature before Freud applied it as a pathological method. But once such a theory as this is established – a probability one can hardly escape – how can any serious novelist afford to neglect the illumination it throws on the subtle problems of human impulse? ("Psychoanalysis" 434)

Beresford's optimism about psychoanalysis's potential impact on the novel had completely dissipated by 1926 when Beresford wrote *"Le Déclin de L'Influence...."* He argues that psychoanalysis had most significantly influenced the novel between 1918 and 1922 when three categories of psychological novels appeared: those that would have been written had Freud never existed; those in which the influence is subconscious rather than intellectual; and those

> based on the principle that the repression of thought and those infantile tendencies can reappear during the course of adult experience in the form of a perversion or of a "complex". (*"Déclin"* 257)

Beresford explores the third category, the most striking examples of which are Beresford's own *God's Counterpoint* (1918), Rebecca West's *The Return of the Soldier* (1918), and May Sinclair's *The Romantic* (1920).

According to Beresford, the rapid decline of psychoanalytic influence can be accounted for by three factors: British critics suspicious of the new and unhealthy themes; the censorious and hypocritical British public; and novelists' realization that Freudian theories, with their focus on abnormality, run counter to novelists' aim of presenting representative types ("Déclin" 261–264). Consequently, Beresford concludes "that there cannot be a future for the psychoanalytical novel" of the third type, and he admits this is based partly on his own experience when he focussed almost exclusively on applying Freudian theory to an abnormal individual in *God's Counterpoint* (1918).

What Beresford's essay reveals is the degree to which he has followed psychoanalytic propagandists in isolating Freudian discourse from other dynamic psychologies. His restrictive definition of psychoanalytic novels enables him to dismiss the theory as a lasting influence. The result is that, by omission, Beresford actually contributes to minimizing the larger impact on the novel of dynamic psychology.

Nevertheless, his fiction provides the best testimony to his extensive, multilayered assimilation of a variety of dynamic psychological discourses. From the outset of his career, Beresford's empirical, almost scientific approach to the minute details of human existence is moderated and balanced by his idealism, mysticism, and probing of the psyche, a broad tendency he shares with May Sinclair; he thus self-consciously presented a construct of reality (*Writing* 57). Drawing on nineteenth-century materialist psychology, Beresford reveals hereditary forces shaping his characters' behaviour, but he also portrays characters' inconsistency, gives access to their dream lives, and increasingly reveals the influence of subliminal processes on their actions. He consistently approaches characterization from a developmental perspective, assigning great importance both to crucial traumatic events and moments of illumination or uncanny, telepathic communication which may either block or facilitate growth into individuation. This growth is figured most frequently as a quest for truth about identity, vocation, and love.

Beresford's exposure to later dynamic psychologies, notably psychoanalysis, prompted him to focus on abnormal characters, although the normal and the abnormal become increasingly difficult to distinguish. As an influence, heredity slips into the background and is replaced by psychosomatic symptoms indicating repression. Moments of illumination are imaged more as the cathartic release of repressed impulses. He employs Freudian symbolism to reveal subconscious attraction and conflict. Finally, his engagement with psychoanalysis emerges in later works, as characters either undergo talking cures, initiate self-analysis, or employ literature as therapy.

Beresford's assimilation of both first wave and dynamic psychology within a construct of realism began in his first novel, *The Early History of Jacob Stahl* (1911), heralded by the *New York Times* (among others) as "one of the most brilliant psychological novels of recent years".[16] An autobiographical *bildungsroman*, the novel alludes to Jacob's inherited tendencies, but foregrounds traumatic incidents: notably Jacob's fall from a pram at seven months, causing him to become permanently lame (*Jacob* 13–14); and the death of his mother, with whom Jacob has an unusually close relationship. Beresford does deal with Jacob's sexual awareness, beginning in adolescence, but without supplying graphic details (*Jacob* 126–127). At several points, Beresford suggests that Jacob would interest an anonymous psychologist (*Jacob* 215, 256, 349) as "a pathological case", since Jacob "had come to believe in his own incapacity, and, mentally, wrote the story of his failure" (*Jacob Stahl* 358). In the sequel, *A Candidate For Truth* (1912), Beresford develops his protagonist's spiritual dimension, based on Jacob's attraction to the ideal of self-sacrifice.

The third volume, *The Invisible Event* (1915), expresses the "freer morality" that Beresford championed in psychoanalysis, in that Jacob lives together with his girlfriend Betty. Beresford astutely depicts the psychological stresses caused by this defiance of social convention. Jacob, for example, becomes aware of Betty's tendency to repress her qualms: "He had a queer picture in his mind of all those inhibited thoughts being thrust down and growing malignantly under the surface" (*Invisible* 188). Perhaps most significantly, Beresford under-lines Jacob's multiple, disjunctive selves, likely based on Myers's conception of multiplex, polypsychic personality, as revealed in Jacob's idea for a novel titled "The Creature of Circumstance". To Betty he confides that

> It's slightly fantastic...an allegory of sorts, I suppose – and yet the fundamental idea comes out of my own experience. The theory is of a man who reacts so tremendously to his circumstances that he is a different person altogether in different conditions. It's an enlargement of the Jekyll and Hyde business in one way, but treated realistically, you know. There would not be any romantic potions or spells. (*Invisible* 275)

He elaborates:

> The idea is that he goes on increasingly reacting to his circumstances until he can be, for all intents and purposes, a dozen different people in one day. (*Invisible* 276)

At the denouement, "my man discovers for the first time that he has a personality of his own that has been unconsciously growing out of all his reactions", a conception analogous to Myers's claim that individuality provided an underlying unity to personality (*Invisible* 276). Beresford's trilogy may not engage dynamic psychology in a particularly revolutionary way, but Beresford does enlist its discourses to help articulate the fluidity and complexity of the self's development.

Beresford's second 1911 novel, *The Hampdenshire Wonder* (published in America as *The Wonder*), more imaginatively plays with dynamic discourses, particularly Myers's conception of genius, Bergson's creative evolution, and the psychical case study. The novel traces the development and treatment by society of an abnormal child genius named Victor Stott. Although Beresford acknowledged a personal compensation fantasy at its root, as well as the influence of H.G. Wells's scientific romances, he took great pains to ensure that the story would be perceived as within the realm of probability. While an early reviewer recognized this, claiming that *The Wonder* "is told with all the verisimilitude of a scientific document, with an occasional footnote and a mention of actual men..." (Boynton 315), the novel was generally categorized as an outstanding scientific romance. One recent critic, Brian Stableford, has even claimed that "the book remains one of the best science fiction novels ever written" (Stableford 948). In fact, the main sources for the story were historical; Beresford claimed to have read Schoneich's account of a seventeenth-century child wonder, Christian Heinrich Heinecken in *Human Personality* ("Unchangeable" xvii), and he in all likelihood based the mysterious death of Stott, who is found drowned in a shallow pond, on the similarly mysterious death of psychical researcher Frank Podmore. Podmore, who had collaborated with Myers on *Phantasms of the Living* and was considered one of the most brilliant popularizers of psychical research, was found drowned in New Pool, near Malvern Wells, on 19 August 1910, the coroner commenting that the case remained "an unsolved mystery" (Hall, *Strange* 203).

Beresford certainly reflects Myers's discourse on genius, by having the narrator claim that "[t]he child was supernormal, a cause of fear to the normal man, as all truly supernormal things are to our primitive, animal instincts" (*Wonder* 55). As a child the Wonder initially arouses disgust and fear because of his massive, domed, bald head (*Wonder* 3). However, when his supernormal reasoning powers emerge he appears impeccably sane, whereas those around him, with their blindness, prejudice, and pride, come to seem abnormal and even insane. Beresford insinuates the limitations of various approaches to understanding the Wonder, including a first wave psychologist's and an evangelical minister's. The psychologist, Gregory Lewes (perhaps named after George Henry Lewes, and evoking Beresford's critical attitude towards physiological psychology), interviews the Wonder "with a mind predisposed to criticise, to destroy" (*Wonder* 171). His "inquiry into association in connection with memory" results in "a little brochure *Reflexive Associations*, which has hardly added to our knowledge of the subject" (*Wonder* 160–161). The dogmatic Rector, Crashaw, considers the child to be possessed and becomes his main persecutor, and possibly even his murderer.

As well, Victor is an embodiment of Bergson's creative evolutionary "skip".[17] Beresford suggests that Victor's father's phenomenal physical prowess and his mother's "open and mobile intelligence" (*Wonder* 60) were transformed into the Wonder's intellectual capacity; however, he cleverly adds that, ultimately, Victor's genius, "the genius of modernity" (*Wonder* 212), cannot be entirely explained. Beresford's assimilation of Bergson does explain why he dedicates all of Part One and a section of Part Two of the novel to the parents' histories, an emphasis misunderstood and criticized by Stableford as "appearing to have so little connection with the main theme as to be almost bizarre" (948).

The narrator's strategies, too, reflect some aspects of the psychical case study in that he early on establishes his credentials as a philosopher and the case's veracity, claiming that "what follows is literally true in all essentials" (*Wonder* 28). He unfolds the case in a rational manner and apologizes for his limitations in capturing the profundity of the phenomena, in this case the Wonder's mind (*Wonder* 115–117). Repeatedly, he claims that he is "sceptical – the habit of experience was towards disbelief – a boy of seven and a half could not possibly have the mental equipment to skim all that philosophy…" (*Wonder* 191). Nevertheless, his contact with the Wonder nearly overwhelms him, threatening his sanity (*Wonder* 116, 213). He is only saved from delirium and despair by another witness to the phenomenon, the idealist Challis, who recognizes that the Wonder's genius represents a paradox and is severely limited: "Sublimated material. Intellectual insight and absolute spiritual blindness.…The child has gone too far in one direction" (*Wonder* 151). Like Myers, Challis predicts an evolution of humanity's awareness, and privileges the mystic's power (*Wonder* 234–235).

Although Beresford's fascination with the psychology of individuals forced to confront mysterious psychical phenomena found expression in a number of his short stories of this period, including "The Criminal" (*English Review* 1912) and "A Case of Prevision" (*Forum* 1912), the main thrust of his work remained in realism. Beresford's *Housemates* (1917) traces, more boldly and intimately than in *Jacob Stahl*, its protagonist's mental odyssey, facilitated by a first-person viewpoint. The novel advances Beresford's exploration of psychological terrain by depicting the protagonist overcoming dividedness through a mystical moment of illumination, a construct consonant with William James's discourse on mysticism in *Varieties of Religious Experience*. Initially, boarding-house resident Wilfrid Hornby perceives his self to be fragile and insubstantial, referring to "the little glimmer of recording consciousness which seems at the last analysis to be the thing I recognize as my personality" (*Housemates* 3). With great insight, Beresford shows that Wilfrid's subliminal self became divided following his father's death, when Wilfrid suppressed his grief. He is not able to release his emotion until a cathartic event at the boarding house, when Rose Whiting, threatened with eviction for prostitution, strips off her clothes and screams that the landlord can turn her out naked. Wilfrid identifies with her vulnerability and internalizes the reckless passion which makes her "a single and powerful personality" (*Housemates* 133).

Much later, Rose is murdered at the boarding house. Wilfrid is in a "condition of nervous exhaustion which so often gives us the power to transcend our physical limitations" (*Housemates* 293). He thus becomes the medium to receive her cry. The cry may have reached his subconscious (*Housemates* 253), or his response may be attributable to "a supernatural agent" (*Housemates* 305). Though the incident is never conclusively determined, it is appropriate that Wilfrid should be linked psychically to Rose, since her earlier impassioned action opened his consciousness to his dividedness. Aside from nervous exhaustion, Wilfrid succumbs to other abnormal states, including paranoia and obsession.

Beresford's insightful suggestion that, through writing out his experiences, Wilfrid effected his own therapy is very much in keeping with dynamic psychological thought. At the denouement, Wilfrid confesses that

> when I began this book in January, I did it in order to forget. I was in danger of becoming insane then and I found relief by plunging myself back into the past. (*Housemates* 347)

In the novel's representation of the struggle to overcome dividedness and achieve individuation, acknowledgement of the role played by mystical illumination, and consideration of mental illness, *Housemates* contains many of the elements, some in embryo, which were to preoccupy Beresford in his future writing.

Beresford's next novel, *God's Counterpoint* (1918), deserves analysis as the first English novel thoroughly informed by Freudian psychoanalysis, according to Beresford,[18] and as the only one of his he *acknowledged* as thoroughly psychoanalytic ("*Déclin*" 259). Its main flaw, of clinical obtrusiveness, makes this pioneering work instructive. In contrast to Beresford's earlier novels, this one gives precedence to the impact of childhood emotional and sexual trauma on the protagonist's adult behaviour, over his intellectual development. Philip Maning's punitive father dominates his early years to the extent that Philip develops an inferiority complex, crystallized during an incident when Philip is fourteen. On the way to a railway station, a fantasy of feeling superior to workers vanishes while he is in a tunnel, and

> he became suddenly aware of himself as of something small and negligible, a creature of ignoble thoughts and ambitions. And the self that watched had no relief of conscious superiority. (*God's* 19–20)

Though in itself trivial, the event and the "beastly, mean feeling" that Philip associates with it develop into a complex through repetition. A second incident, when Philip happens on a couple making love in a forest, also seems "beastly" (*God's* 24) and causes Philip to "thrust his horror from him, deep down into the unknown spaces of his subconsciousness; whither it sometimes emerged at night.... What terrified him was not the note of fear but the undertone of repressed longing" (*God's* 24–25). Henceforth, he comes to associate beastliness and shame with sexuality (*God's* 33).

When he marries he treats his wife Evelyn as "an unattainable, intangible ideal" (*God's* 236) and suffers psychosomatic illness (*God's* 273) until Evelyn's French cousin Hélène visits. About this time, Philip finds a poetic correlative for his tunnel experience in Francis Thompson's "Hound of Heaven" (*God's* 312), the first subconscious change in him. He also prophetically dreams of embracing Hélène, before she transforms into Evelyn and then his mother.[19] After Evelyn leaves him, claiming his mind is "poisoned and unhealthy" (*God's* 304), Philip's long-felt fear of feeling abasement now becomes reality (*God's* 312), making him open to seduction by Hélène (*God's* 321).

As evidence of Beresford's idealism, he frames Philip's return to mental health as an integrating revelation. Following a break with Hélène, he experiences a moment of vision about humanity in which "all apparent discords and ugliness were, it seemed to him, but accentuations of the eternal rhythm; the necessary beat of an undertone, God's counterpoint" (*God's* 331).

Several flaws weaken this novel's effect. Philip's exposition of what he refers to as his childhood pathology perhaps resembles too closely a case study. Also, despite Beresford's cloaking of Philip's transfiguration as a moment of spiritual insight, the believability of this sudden change relies too heavily on knowledge of the Freudian cathartic release of repression. However, these flaws in themselves do not constitute novel's main problem. Nor does it arise, as Reinald Hoops claims, because the novel deals with an unusual individual of interest only to the psychologist (Hoops 99). Rather, in his enthusiasm for applying Freudian insights and scientific objectivity, Beresford does not permit the reader to become intimate with the protagonist, to feel either his agony or his joy. This problem is compounded by the fact that the priggish, fastidious Philip is not a particularly likeable character to begin with.

In *An Imperfect Mother* (1920), Beresford more nearly integrates his Freudian materials into an aesthetic whole, though the total effect is marred by a "Retrospect" that unnecessarily underlines the psychogenesis of the protagonist's "slight departure from the normal" (*Imperfect* 307).[20] The novel focusses on an overly close bond between mother and son, which presumably originated in an oedipal complex. Despite that bond, the son, Stephen, is not as fastidious as Philip Maning, and his sexual impulses receive more attention. Dreams and Freudian symbolism convey his conflicted desires regarding women. Not only has Beresford conscripted Freudian discourse, but similar to *God's Counterpoint* he also draws on Adler's inferiority complex in his portrayal of Stephen's father. Concepts and language of dynamic psychology reinforce the intensity of characters' moods. The novel's resolution hinges on misinterpretation of an hysteric response.

On the whole, Beresford convincingly traces the vicissitudes in Stephen's relationship with his mother Cecilia. Unfulfilled in her marriage, the selfish, passionate Cecilia unfairly leans on Stephen for intimacy until she finds a lover, a church organist, and deserts the family for an acting career in London. Stephen responds ambivalently, on the one hand having "lover's quarrels" (*Imperfect* 67) over her decision to leave, and on the other hand feeling freedom (*Imperfect* 68), especially since he has recently become infatuated with Margaret Weatherly, the schoolmaster's fourteen-year-old daughter (*Imperfect* 12). Stephen's unattainable desires for both mother and Margaret mingle in his dreams (*Imperfect* 132).

Several years later when Stephen seeks out his mother, he encounters Margaret again (*Imperfect* 198). He is afraid to pursue the latter, mainly because he would be unfaithful to his mother (*Imperfect* 198) and because his passion for her would drown his sanity "in one overwhelming lust for possession" (*Imperfect* 203).

The dynamics of the scene in which Margaret and Stephen, now a builder, are drawn together is reinforced with Freudian imagery. At the request of his six-year-old half-brother, Chris, Stephen self-consciously displays his building prowess by erecting a tower out of blocks. In a bid to capture her defiant little son, Chris, Cecilia inadvertently knocks over the tower. Cecilia takes the boy to bed while Stephen reconstructs the tower. Margaret admires his talent, claiming that "You really do it awfully well" (*Imperfect* 216), and expresses curiosity about visiting his "real building" (*Imperfect* 216). She eventually does so, and Stephen takes her up in the crane bucket, where she realizes that Stephen is different from the other men with whom she has been flirting (*Imperfect* 233). The symbolism of the mother, faced with a rival, attempting to castrate the son before he succeeds in captivating his lover through phallic prowess, would not likely be lost on, and might even seem obvious to, modern readers inured to Freud. Considering, however, that not one of the fifty to sixty reviewers of Beresford's previous novel, *God's Counterpoint*, even recognized that it was psychoanalytically influenced, it is probable that the imagery would have appeared fresh and might even have gone unnoticed by contemporary audiences ("*Déclin*" 261). Certainly two most perceptive critics, Katherine Mansfield and Virginia Woolf, did not mention this imagery in their critical reviews of *An Imperfect Mother* ("Two Modern" and "Freudian" respectively).

In spite of Stephen's initial success, Cecilia is not yet willing to surrender to her rival, until Stephen has a setback with Margaret and reveals that her cruel laugh reminds him of Cecilia's when he begged her not to desert him (*Imperfect* 280–281). His remark that at that time he felt like banging his head against the wall triggers Cecilia's memory of an incident from his childhood when she laughed at him and he actually did this. Stephen's comment, "I feel as if what you told me, about that first time, at home, explains everything", aligns well with psychoanalytic emphasis on childhood determinants of later complexes (*Imperfect* 282). This revelation would have been more convincing had incidents developing Stephen's childhood relation with his mother initially been portrayed by Beresford. Nevertheless, since Cecilia realizes that her hysterical laugh had been forced from her by her love for Stephen and that Margaret's must have been as well, she decides to explain this to Stephen (*Imperfect* 287) from the idealistic "motive of self-renunciation" (*Imperfect* 287). Stephen consequently pursues Margaret with renewed vigour and marries her, despite opposition from her father.

Apparently aiming at objectivity, Beresford claims that his "excrescent" retrospect "may be taken as a kind of appendix, or lengthy foot-note, designed to give a detached historical summary of certain subsequent events..." (*Imperfect* 307). Unfortunately, this academic retrospect in effect implies that the previous narrative should be viewed as a scientific case study. Virginia Woolf may very well have taken her cue from it when she claimed, in her review, that his characters had become cases ("Freudian" 154).

In *Love's Pilgrim* (1923), Beresford overcame his apparent enthusiasm for scientific objectivity and avoided the clinical retrospect. Though he treats psychological themes similar to those in his earlier psychoanalytic novels, his varied sources are less obtrusive and the net result is a far more convincing study of an individual. The protagonist, Foster Innes, is similar to Stephen Kirkwood in that his bond with his unfulfilled mother is overly close, to Philip Maning in that he is repressed and fastidious about sexuality, to Wilfrid Hornby in that he narrates his own story, and to Jacob Stahl in that he is a self-conscious cripple. Though Beresford continues to explore Freudian insights about the mother fixation, he considers more centrally the imaginative implications of the inferiority complex (as developed by Adler and Jung), and also brings his interest in psychical research, idealism, and mysticism more fully into play.

Having inherited a disability from his father, Foster Innes is drawn closer to his mother because she is overprotective and since he believes that "No woman, except my mother, could ever love me completely since I was incomplete" (*Love's* 26). His feelings of incompleteness, inferiority, and fragmentation are compounded by his sense of divided loyalties following his mother's "sinister" (*Love's* 36) response to his half-hearted attempts at love relationships (*Love's* 43, 58, 121). Efforts to hide his disability warp him in some respects because he moves into a fantasy world as compensation (*Love's* 58). This situation persists until he becomes angry at his mother after she tells him that his desire to have a relationship with a farmer's daughter, Claire, cannot be fulfilled. His anger prompts him to free himself from his mother's domination (*Love's* 158). Foster's burgeoning relationship with Claire receives a setback, however, when she confesses that her father, Mr Morton, has been tried for the murder of his wife (though she believes that her mother committed suicide).

Foster's loyalties remain split on a subconscious level until, during a drive, he views a panorama with Mr Morton and experiences a moment of heightened illumination. This experience gives them "a mystical knowledge of one another" and removes any doubt in Foster's mind that Mr Morton is indeed innocent (*Love's* 244). As William James had argued in *Varieties of Religious Experience*, this supernatural moment of certainty begins the process of healing dividedness. For Foster this process is completed upon his fulfilment of a selfless quest as "love's pilgrim" to find Claire's sister, who has hysterically confessed to the murder of her mother and then run off into a storm. Though Claire has acted as a confessor and carried out a natural analysis on Foster, thus helping him on the road to individuation, his love for her is essentially selfless. It is, therefore, fulfilling, unlike his love for his mother.

If *Love's Pilgrim* represents Beresford's most successful integration of varied dynamic psychological discourses into an accessible form of realism, certainly his most fascinating experiment in psychological, or more accurately psychical, realism is *Writing Aloud* (1928). This work is unique in its combination of: stream of consciousness novel in progress; critical commentary on the problems of using the stream of consciousness technique and of bringing psychological knowledge to bear on fiction; and autobiography, conveyed throughout "within the protective fence" of square brackets (*Writing* 4).[21] For its uniqueness, as well as for the quality and honesty of his insights into the impact on the creative process of psychological discourse and the reading public's expectations, this forward-looking, hybrid work deserves to be better known.

Beresford's description of the book's conception immediately reinforces the importance of psychical research on his consciousness as well as the conjunction of psychological and psychical (in this case automatic writing) in modernism. He began without purpose, and then

> it came to me that it would be delightful to write a formless book, allowing this impulse to manifest itself as it pleased, almost as if I were a medium engaged in writing automatic script. (*Writing* 1)

Initially he decides to let his protagonist, provisionally called "J.J.", tell the story in the first person, "through the medium of a single consciousness" (*Writing* 9), and in the body of his text he does generally allow his characters to guide him (*Writing* 53, 79); however, he also intersperses brief details of his external life and his opinions on diverse topics. Several attitudes emerge very clearly about psychoanalytic theory, its applications to characterization, and critics' and readers' response to it in fiction.

Once again, Beresford demonstrates that he approaches psychoanalysis from the idealist's viewpoint. He emphasizes that element which best aligns with what he refers to as his single theme of re-educating human beings (*Writing* 53), asserting that

The principle of it [psychoanalysis] is so admirable; it is the practice only, with its tendency to degenerate into dogma, that has smirched it in the popular estimation. It is so essential to keep the generating theory fluid. And the principle of P.A. [psychoanalysis] is that which I was considering a few minutes ago – the winning of self-knowledge and a free mind by the eradication of deep-seated habits of thought. (*Writing* 148)

Beresford avoids that dogmatic tendency by approaching psychoanalysis selectively. Though he recognizes that all good fiction must have a dream quality in it (*Writing* 147), and dreams play a significant role in his work, he discounts the Freudian interpretation of dreams when it does not fit the evidence and when he "can get no satisfaction from it, no sense of having gratifyingly solved the riddle" (*Writing* 85). Despite the flaws in its practical applications, psychoanalysis is contributing to the considerable change in human beings that Beresford observes. He claims that "I am willing to maintain that we do know much more about the hidden springs of conduct than our ancestors did" (*Writing* 118). For Beresford, the change in humanity also has a broadly religious element: "I do so sincerely believe in evolution, development; in the coming of an increased spirituality, a deeper, fuller consciousness" (*Writing* 118).

This idealistic attitude in turn shapes Beresford's conception of character. Although a reviewer of *Jacob Stahl* warned Beresford that character does not change, he has devoted his whole career to demonstrating otherwise (*Writing* 54). Beresford does not merely want to "present a slice of life, neatly dissected and displayed" (*Writing* 79), but desires to convey something of his "characters' inner life that could never be expressed either in action or speech" (*Writing* 117).

Several forces combine to thwart this desire and "to compel him to misrepresent humanity in fiction . . . [by] making it far too consistent" (*Writing* 144). Beresford repeatedly criticizes the tastes of the general reading public, who constrain his fascination with experimentation since he does not have economic independence (*Writing* 141). The general reading public, or "GRP", as he refers to them, want recognizable types that come from other books rather than from life (*Writing* 42, 142), do not care to know about the influence of heredity on behaviour (*Writing* 14–15), and in general lack interest "in learning anything new about themselves or the human mind in general" (*Writing* 174). Their response to psychoanalysis in fiction is particularly "shallow", some even arguing, for example, that because Dickens never wrote of anything approaching a passionate relationship between mother and son, the "mother-complex" either does not exist or is not a proper subject for a novel. (*Writing* 33, 34)

Critics share readers' aversion to psychoanalysis. Beresford muses that

If I am not careful I shall be told that I have written another "psycho-analytic" novel. The hint of a "suppression into the unconscious" will be quite enough to make some people sit up and write half a column about Freudianism being *vieux jeu* in fiction. (*Writing* 33)

Nevertheless, his "passion for discovery" of characters' unconscious motives necessitates bringing the insights of psychoanalysis to his work. In *Writing Aloud*, Beresford attempts to resolve the dilemma by proposing to disguise the psychoanalytic context. At one stage in his hypothetical novel, a mother, Emma, will come into contact, after nineteen years of separation, with his protagonist J.J., Emma's illegitimate daughter. Emma recognizes that the girl is confused about religion and will play the role of psychoanalyst without knowing it in order to help her achieve clarity about her feelings (*Writing* 133). Beresford claims that

I should love to do the interviews between these two if I could be sure of completely disguising the psycho-analytic technique and making the whole business appear as the outcome of a perfectly natural relation between mother and daughter in these very unusual circumstances, the mother alone knowing all the secrets of the daughter's conception and infant history. (*Writing* 134)

As he develops the idea, he supplies Emma with a motive for helping J.J., which "will distract, I hope, the reader's attention from all comparisons with the methods of the clinic" (*Writing* 135). He also gives a clear indication of what he is trying to achieve:

What I want is no more than a sound analogy between the two processes, and the typical Freudian complex in this case shall serve me only as a parallel that I propose to render into familiar everyday language. (*Writing* 135–136)

After struggling for some time to incorporate this conception, Beresford comes to the realization that, in the interests of making the action more natural and the characters more probable to the reading public and critics, he will have to discard any parallels with psychoanalysis (*Writing* 173–174). Furthermore, although all along he had intended to convey his heroine's stream of consciousness, "the psychical history" he has designed for her would make that direct method unacceptable, and perhaps impossible (*Writing* 178). Instead, Beresford decides to try and make it a "purely objective book", but he concludes that it will likely relate his own experience in a semi-autobiographical mode, as he has done in previous novels (*Writing* 202).

Thus, *Writing Aloud* records with considerable candour practical pressures on the novelist as he writes. Beresford reveals both his fascination with psychoanalysis, and with the obstacle it presents, his impulse to probe deeper mysteries of human conduct in his work, and checks to that impulse. In grappling with the issue of the general reading public's expectations, Beresford strikingly anticipates Hans Jauss's reception theory, based on the concept of readers' horizons of expectation.

Given Beresford's theorizing and experimenting in *Writing Aloud*, along with his earlier commentary on psychoanalytic experiments in the novel, it is not quite so bizarre as it might otherwise appear that he was asked to lecture on "Experiment in the Novel" the following year. Beresford highlighted what he called "ultra-realism", in works by Woolf, Sinclair, and Joyce; however, he privileged Dorothy Richardson's "new method" because of its unique "metaphysical value", its "mystical quality": "Dorothy Richardson has assumed the existence of a soul to which the consciousness has much the same relation that the intelligence has to the consciousness" ("Experiment" 46–47). Although Beresford only broached that new method in *Writing Aloud*, he shared her fascination with the soul and mysticism in relation to the dynamics of the psyche.

The foregoing analysis of nine Beresford novels confirms that he challenged novel conventions primarily through his fascination with this subject matter. In his early novels, Beresford interrogated the nature of selfhood, most fancifully in *The Wonder*, by drawing on Janet's, Myers's, and Bergson's discourses about subconscious motivation, genius, and creative evolution. He moved beyond his readers' and even his critics' horizons of expectations by treating unpleasant and pathological dimensions of his characters as his fiction progressed. Even reviewers generally favourable towards Beresford, such as Gerald Gould, called the psychological novelist in Beresford "wayward" and "truant" (29), and A. St John Adcock "deprecate[d] his excursions into eccentricities of psychology" (39). While Beresford's initial enthusiasm for the educative potential of psychoanalysis caused him to employ this discourse too blatantly and clinically, the first of his novels of this sort, *God's Counterpoint* and *An Imperfect Mother*, are, nonetheless, courageous. They probe frankly the neuroses and obsessions motivating individuals subconsciously, and thus frequently do not reveal these characters at their most impressive. Beresford's thematic treatment of the mother fixation and the inferiority complex were innovative for the time, though these themes may have worn thin since then. As Beresford's interest shifted (once again) towards the mystical and psychical, the psychoanalytic influence was absorbed into a larger metaphysical structuring of his novels. A glimpse of this change is provided in *Love's Pilgrim*, which depends less heavily on psychoanalytic thought and draws eclectically on idealistic and mystical ideas. On the whole, Beresford's profound engagement with dynamic psychological discourse was a positive one, widening his subject matter and deepening his insight into psychic functioning. He ought to be better remembered both for his pioneering fictional efforts and for his commentary on the psychologizing of the English novel, most originally revealed in his stream of consciousness manqué, *Writing Aloud*.

*　*　*　*　*

The literary critics W.L. George and Abel Chevalley, contemporary to Bennett, Lawrence, and Beresford, may have got wrong the literary fortunes of these novelists from the English Midlands, but ironically they were quite correct to group them together. All three drew on the discourses of dynamic psychology – Bennett most sensationally and perhaps most fleetingly, Lawrence most iconoclastically and covertly, and Beresford most extensively and overtly. Even more ironically, these novelists' reputations have been distorted by limited views of their engagement with this psychology: Bennett categorized as the quintessential Edwardian materialist culprit; Lawrence so frequently seen as interrogating later dynamic psychologies, as the mythologizer of Freud and priest of sexuality; and Beresford, originally critiqued for his excessive and eccentric excursions into psychology, then left behind because of ignorance about his particular form of experimentation. Their varieties of psychical realism deserve further investigation and serve to underline the pervasiveness of dynamic psychology's impact on modern fiction.

6

"The Spirit of the Age": Virginia Woolf's Response to Dynamic Psychology

> Let us always remember – influences are infinitely numerous; writers are infinitely sensitive.
>
> – Virginia Woolf, "The Leaning Tower" 163

Although Virginia Woolf argued that the moderns were "sharply cut off from [their] predecessors" (*Essays* III 357), she also believed in the continuity of culture, and in writers' role as "receptacles" of cultural currents (Meisel, *Absent* 160). S.P. Rosenbaum has examined some of the currents affecting Woolf herself, but his claim that Woolf's "writing was shaped by a series of intellectual assumptions about reality, perception, morality, government, and art" needs to be extended to include human psychology ("Virginia Woolf" 11). Through reading and discussions, Woolf directly encountered and interrogated psychologists' working hypotheses about all aspects of personality, and she responded to psychological discourse that had entered into contemporary culture. In her own ambivalent, idiosyncratic way, Woolf acknowledged both of these sources in a draft of "Character in Fiction" (1924), a paper given before the Cambridge Heretics Society. She claimed:

No generation since the world began has known quite so much about character as our generation.... [T]he average man or woman today thinks more about character than his or her grandparents; character interests them more; they get closer, they dive deeper in to the real emotions and motives of their fellow creatures. There are scientific reasons why this should be so. If you read Freud you know in ten minutes some facts – or at least some possibilities – which our parents could not have guessed for themselves. That is a very debatable point. But how much we can learn from science that is real...and make our own from science? And then there is a...vaguer force at work – a force which is sometimes called the Spirit of the Age or the Tendency of the Age. This mysterious power is taking us by the hand, I think, and making us look much more closely into the reasons why people do and say and think things.... ("Character" 504)

In a typical manouevre, after choosing Freud as representative of scientists of the mind, Woolf mystifies the process of assimilation, perhaps suggesting her ambivalence towards him and betraying anxiety of influence. Her choice of Freud is not surprising, however, because by 1924 he had the highest profile of psychologists whose ideas were discussed by the Bloomsbury group (L. Woolf, *Downhill* 164). Since the Bloomsbury connection with Freud has been documented (Meisel *Bloomsbury*), and Woolf's problematic relationship to psychoanalysis explored (Goldstein, Abel, Orr), I want to focus mainly on Woolf's and Bloomsbury's engagement with pre-Freudian dynamic psychological discourse. As with other British intellectuals, some Bloomsbury members, including James and Alix Strachey and Adrian and Karin Stephen, were first intrigued with early dynamic discourse, particularly as disseminated by the SPR, and this fascination prompted them to explore psychology further – several through careers in psychoanalysis. S.P. Rosenbaum's claim that Bloomsbury's attitude towards the SPR "was summarized by Forster's description of the S.P.R. as 'that dustbin of the spirit' " does not stand up to scrutiny (Rosenbaum, *Victorian* 110).

In the case of Virginia Woolf, a milieu in which questioning of formal psychological ideas occurred was established in her early youth through the influence of her father, Leslie Stephen. Through her brothers – Thoby and Adrian – and friends – Lytton and James Strachey – her connection with the psychological thought originating at Cambridge further advanced her psychological knowledge. By the period during which she wrote her first novel (1908–1913), these two sources had already helped shape Woolf's fundamental assumptions about personality and the individual's relation to the group.

Following a brief consideration of the possibility that May Sinclair, Woolf's immediate female forerunner in the psychological novel, directly influenced Woolf, Woolf's earliest sources of psychological knowledge will be evaluated. The similarities in basic psychological themes to the fiction discussed in earlier chapters will be illustrated in Woolf's two relatively traditional early works, *The Voyage Out* and *Night and Day*. Analysis of *Mrs. Dalloway* will show that these themes persist into her mature, modernist work.[1] My contention is that dynamic psychological discourse was interrogated by writers from the Edwardian period on; this common textual economy diminished the differences between advanced Edwardian writers and modernists like Woolf.

The evidence for Sinclair's direct influence on Woolf is not extensive. Woolf first mentions Sinclair in a letter to Violet Dickinson in November 1907. She defends Sinclair's *The Helpmate* (1907), although she claims not to have read it, against her friend Lady Robert Cecil's objection to it on moral grounds (*Letters* I 317). Less than two years later, Woolf writes in a letter to

Lady Cecil in which she mentions "these psychical people" that "yesterday I met your friend Miss Sinclair" (*Letters* I 390). Though critical of Sinclair's "medicinal morality", Woolf records that Sinclair "talked very seriously of her 'work'; and ecstatic moods in which she swings... halfway to Heaven, detached from earth" (*Letters* I 390). As has been discussed, Sinclair portrayed moments of ecstasy very similar to those of Woolf's from her earliest work on (Chapter 4). Woolf does not mention Sinclair again in her letters for over a decade, but, as Hrisey Zegger, among others, has pointed out, Woolf is indebted to Sinclair's ground-breaking 1918 essay on Dorothy Richardson's *Pilgrimage*, in which Sinclair applied William James's term "stream of consciousness" to Richardson's technique. Woolf drew on the same passage from James in "Modern Novels", published one year after Sinclair's article.[2] Woolf's more recently published reading notes confirm this. One notebook entitled *Modern Novels* contains both Woolf's notes on Sinclair's article and a sketch of her own essay. Woolf borrowed Sinclair's idea that the novelist must capture reality, described by Sinclair as "thick and deep", at first hand (Silver 18–19; 155–156). It is also tempting to suggest that in "Mr. Bennett and Mrs. Brown", Woolf borrowed Sinclair's strategy in *A Defence of Idealism* of creating fictional characters to make abstract critical points more concrete. Sinclair has a character, Brown, who tells stories to Mrs Robinson to illustrate the monist's approach to the Absolute; Sinclair states, for example, "If, in the infinite reverberations of the universe, there endure infinite echoes of Brown's story, they are echoes that only finite and incarnate spirits catch" (*Defence* 339). When Woolf does again directly refer to Sinclair, it is in response to Lytton Strachey's recommendation that Woolf read Sinclair's recently published poetic novel, *The Life and Death of Harriet Frean* (January 1922). On 8 or 9 February 1922, Woolf writes "And you read Miss Sinclair! So shall I perhaps. But I'd rather read Lytton Strachey" (*Letters* II 503). Woolf never confirms whether she took up Strachey's suggestion, and she makes no further reference to Sinclair.

While it is difficult to believe that Woolf did not read a single novel of the woman who was considered the leading psychological novelist prior to Woolf, especially since Woolf made a point of reading the works of other experimenters in the psychological novel, including James Joyce and Dorothy Richardson (Silver 155; Bishop 48–49), the fact remains that there is no evidence to suggest that she did. Nevertheless, striking similarities exist in their approach to human psychology and in the tropes they use to reflect psychic states. Both portray the self as fluid, insubstantial, and divided. They image consciousness as a web, net, or wave. Both draw analogies between female protagonists' rooms and their minds (Sinclair, *Audrey* 202; Woolf, *Voyage* 352). In *Audrey Craven*, Sinclair also expands the conception of artist to include social artist, an idea Woolf develops most fully in her portrait of Mrs Ramsay in *To The Lighthouse* (1927). Both use as focal points instances of telepathy, which suggest the existence of a supernatural, group, or collective, (sub)consciousness. The climax of Sinclair's *The Tree of Heaven* centres on Veronica's vision of Nicky near the tree of heaven in the garden. Correspondingly, Woolf's Mrs Dalloway is linked psychically to Septimus Smith near that novel's close; Lily Briscoe is connected to the group boating to the lighthouse, after she has had a vision of Mrs Ramsay, in *To the Lighthouse*. These resemblances point towards common sources in materialist and, more importantly, dynamic psychological discourses.

Woolf gained her earliest knowledge about philosophical psychology from her father, Leslie Stephen.[3] His literary theory included the tenet that "literature is the highest imaginative embodiment of a period's philosophy" (Hill 355). Stephen himself both was fully aware of philosophical tradition[4] and kept abreast of contemporary intellectual developments, including in psychology. In his work on ethics he was influenced by philosopher and psychical researcher Henry Sidgwick, whom he knew well.[5] In 1901, Stephen wrote a summary of Sidgwick's life in *Mind*, where even as an agnostic he acknowledged that Sidgwick

> brought to [psychical research] all the conscientious spirit of scientific investigation; and a desire to discover the truth of alleged facts led him to investigate them with the most rigid impartiality. ("Henry" 11–12)

Since Sidgwick's impact carries through to the Bloomsbury group, this article may well have had special significance; Leonard and Virginia retained two copies of it along with a selection of Leslie's books until their deaths (Steele 332).

Leslie Stephen's most important, though completely ignored, source of information about psychology was James Sully, a leading nineteenth-century luminary of psychology (Hearnshaw 132). Through his extensive connections and varied talents, Sully provided a link between psychological, philosophical, and literary thought for his and Leslie Stephen's generations, much as David Eder did for Woolf's generation.[6] Sully introduced himself to Stephen and became a close friend through writing a series of articles for *Cornhill* Magazine, under Stephen's editorship. These included "serious" ones on Self-esteem and Self-admiration and "The Laws of Dream-fancy".[7] The latter provoked Stephen to convey to Sully several of his dreams, and Sully claimed that Stephen generally

> brought his own experiences and his reading to bear upon what I was writing about. Among the subjects which drew him out in this way, I remember dreams, children's ways, and the precocity of genius. (*My Life* 299)[8]

According to Sully, his participation in the intimate Scratch Eight[9] walking excursions, organized by Stephen, provided "rich opportunities of increasing our mutual knowledge" (Sully, *My Life* 299). Since one of the Scratch Eight members, Edmund Gurney, was the Secretary of the SPR, this topic, along with philosophy, would likely have been discussed. After these excursions ended in 1891, Sully records that he took tramps with Stephen alone. Sully even visited the Stephens' summer house at St Ives about this time. That experience apparently had a similar effect on him to Virginia Woolf's experience there (fictionalized in *To the Lighthouse*), as he claimed "this visit to St. Ives was one of the memorable experiences of my life" (*My Life* 312).

While the extent of the two men's intimacy should now be clear, it is not as easy to summarize the impact of Sully's thought on Stephen. For purposes of brevity I will focus on Sully's knowledge of mental functioning. In his memoir Sully rhetorically and modestly asks, "Were we [Sully and Stephen] not, despite the differences in our years and status, scribblers who were supremely interested in the processes of thought?" (*My Life* 300). Sully believed that "psychology proper" was "the science which has to disentangle and reduce to simplicity the web of consciousness" (*Human Mind* vi). To this end he followed the tradition of dividing mental functions into three – thinking, feeling, and willing – and traced their separate development (*Human Mind* 71). In considering the role of feeling, Sully stressed the relationship between pain and pleasure, and quoted Leslie Stephen's claim that pleasure is a state of equilibrium (*Human Mind* 199). In his *Outlines of Psychology* (1884), Sully devoted considerable space to classifying different types of association and examining their effect on memory. He refers to trains of images and of movements in this connection (*Outlines* 242, 247, 618). He also showed that mind was active and acknowledged the importance of unconscious processes, claiming that

> at any time there is a whole aggregate or complex of mental phenomena, sensations, impressions, thoughts, etc., most of which are obscure, transitory, and not distinguished. With this wide obscure region of the subconscious, there stands contrasted the narrow luminous region of the clearly conscious. An impression or thought must be presumed to be already present in the first or subconscious region before the mind by an effort of attention can draw it into the second region. (*Outlines* 74)

Furthermore, Sully was particularly interested "in the borderland between the normal and abnormal, in the imaginative and the fanciful" (Hearnshaw 135), perhaps partly owing to his associations with psychical researchers Edmund Gurney and F.W.H. Myers.[10] He elaborated on his ideas about dreams, which so intrigued Stephen, in "The Laws of Dream Fancy" (1876), *Illusions* (1882), and "The Dream as Revelation" (1893). In the first mentioned, Sully argued that the dream consciousness exaggerates a persistent emotion: "through the blending of a number of images of a certain emotional colour composite images arise which greatly transcend in impressiveness those of our waking experience" (554). This is essentially what Freud would describe as condensation. He also recognized the symbolic function of dreams and suggested that dreams return us to the "mental condition of infancy" (555). Sully's ideas on dreams are cited with approval by Freud from the 1914 edition of *The Interpretation of Dreams* onwards, not surprisingly since they represent the earliest British example of the dynamic approach to dreams. They even pre-date Havelock Ellis's exploration.[11] First, in the words of Freud, Sully "was more firmly convinced, perhaps, than any other psychologist that dreams have a disguised meaning" and were not utter nonsense (*The Interpretation* 60). Sully was thus an early proponent of the unmasking trend in dynamic psychology. Second, Sully argued that these meanings often related to long-past experiences. He stated that

> our dreams are a means of conserving these successive [earlier] personalities. *When asleep* we go back to the old ways of looking at things and of feeling about them, to impulses and activities which long ago dominated us. (As cited in Freud, *The Interpretation* 60)

Third, Sully asserted that the interpretative function of dreams was similar to that by which sense is made of events in the waking state (as cited in Freud, *The Interpretation* 501–502). A fourth point, significantly not mentioned by Freud, was Sully's suggestion that dreams were not to be feared or dismissed because they not only revealed our grosser selves, but also our "worthier selves", an attitude consonant with the psychical researchers' approach. Finally, in *Illusions*, Sully made the then controversial point that "our normal mental life is thus intimately related to insanity, and graduates away into it by such fine transitions" (123), an attitude which anticipates a fundamental development of dynamic psychology. Thus, through Sully, Leslie Stephen certainly had the opportunity of acquainting himself with the latest developments in English psychology.

Though it is almost certain that at least the two books, *Sensation and Intuition* and *Studies of Childhood*, that Stephen is known to have read of Sully's would have been part of his library, to which Virginia gained access from 1897,[12] we have no record of whether the aspiring novelist ever read them, and cannot assume so. Nevertheless, we do know that Woolf knew Sully from references to him in her letters. In 1908 she wrote to Clive Bell that Professor Sully says "nice things" of her writing (*Letters* I 356). She apparently held his opinion in high regard, since in the following lines she enthusiastically speaks of how she will become a popular "lady biographist" and "shall re-form the novel and capture multitudes of things at present fugitive, enclose the whole, and shape infinite strange shapes" (*Letters* I 356). As late as 1912, she mentions to Madge Vaughan that she will write to Mr Sully "whom I well remember" (*Letters* I 501).

More important, however, are the correspondences in their basic approaches to human psychology. Like Sully, Woolf refers to consciousness as a web, and yet evokes the three functions of personality – thinking, feeling, and willing – in separate contexts in the characterization of her early works. She also uses the word "luminous" in referring to consciousness, as did Sully in the above quoted passage from *Outlines of Psychology* (74), and she attends very closely to her characters' states of consciousness. Her frequent references to variations on the train of thought metaphor demonstrate that she was aware of the importance of differing types of association in memory. Allusions to characters' unconscious feelings illustrate her familiarity with that concept. The information that she presents in the dreams contained within her narratives suggest that she held Sully's view that dreams were based on persistent emotions and carried hidden messages about conflict in the distant psychic past. Similar to Sully, Woolf dissolved the distinctions between sanity and insanity, expressing this through the theme of insanity versus visionary capabilities, which is particularly well developed in *Mrs. Dalloway*.

Leslie Stephen was also very much aware of William James's thought, and the latter is another psychologist whose discourse surfaces in Virginia Woolf's writing. Stephen wrote of James that "he is the one really lively philosopher, but I am afraid that he is trying the old dodge of twisting 'faith' out of moonshine" (Maitland 445). This comment neatly summarizes Stephen's attitude to James. Though Stephen admired him, as an agnostic he could not agree with the necessity to believe in a metaphysical system. Though he reviewed James's *The Will to Believe* (1897), which contains a chapter on psychical research, he later wrote to James of the rationality of his own position of holding neither a positive nor a negative religious creed, a position not considered in James's book (Annan 250). Leonard and Virginia Woolf possessed a copy of James's *Human Immortality* (1917 ed., Steele 307), which postulates the universe as spiritual and thought as "the sole reality into those millions of finite streams of consciousness known to us as our private selves" (15–16); it also suggests that Myers and the psychical researchers are rehabilitating exceptional phenomena which confirms this spiritual nature (24–25). As was already noted, Woolf probably drew on the same passage of James's on the stream of consciousness as May Sinclair likely did. J. Isaacs has pointed out that Woolf's imagery describing life as a "halo" and "semi-transparent envelope" closely echoes James's words in the section of *Principles of Psychology* on consciousness (88).[13]

Thus, at the very least, it should be clear that Virginia Woolf was raised in an environment permeated by current psychological as well as philosophical discourse. The impact of this earliest milieu was overlaid by Woolf's exposure to Cambridge thought, her second source of information about philosophical psychology. Michael Holroyd, among others, has asserted that Bloomsbury cannot be dissociated from Cambridge (*Lytton Strachey* 422);[14] the ideas of G.E. Moore are widely acknowledged as the central Cambridge influence on Bloomsbury.[15] However, Moore's status has obscured other

Cambridge thinkers significant to Bloomsbury. When it is realized that Moore's teachers included the most distinguished psychical researcher of his day, Henry Sidgwick; a classicist and psychical researcher, Arthur Verrall; an idealist, J. McTaggart; and two of the most eminent English psychologists, G.F. Stout and James Ward, one cannot help but wonder what impact the discourses they contributed to had at Cambridge.

Woolf certainly felt the impact to varying degrees of all of these thinkers, mainly second hand, through the friends and relations of hers who attended Cambridge and with whom she held numerous discussions as a Bloomsbury group member.[16] However, I want to focus on Woolf's knowledge of psychical research. Early on she may well have discussed psychical phenomena with Leonard Woolf. He recollected in 1967 that "I knew intimately Mrs Verrall [Arthur Verrall's wife] and her daughter Helen, who was secretary of the Psychical Research Society and have talked for hours with them about psychical research."[17] While Leonard remained unconvinced that mind existed independently of matter, Virginia kept an open mind, as will become apparent. Another significant source would likely have been James Strachey. Both his and brother Lytton's interest in the subject may have been stimulated by the influence at Cambridge of Henry Sidgwick, past President of the SPR.[18] The details of their engagement with Sidgwick cannot be treated here, but it will suffice to say that Lytton had met Sidgwick, who was revered by the Apostles and whose *Miscellaneous Essays* and work on ethics Strachey and the other Apostles had read in the fall of 1904 (Holroyd 95, 195–196). Lytton had also met Mrs Sidgwick, another intrepid psychical researcher, whom he claimed had "an infinitely remote mind, which, mysteriously, realizes all" (Holroyd 303). At any rate, James read, and discussed with Lytton, SPR reports as early as 1908. In July of that year James wrote to Lytton that he was spending his days "reading the extraordinary narrative just published in the S.P.R. Proceedings of Miss Holland and Miss V. They say that very soon the most remarkable of all – Miss V. and Mrs. Piper – will come out" (10 July Letters of James to Lytton Strachey, British Library). He became aware of both Frederic Myers' and Freud's ideas through this organization, which he joined in 1912 (Meisel *Bloomsbury* 27). In another letter to Lytton, James wrote:

> I feel that I *am* dead at last; and that I'm passionately trying, like the late F.W.H. Myers, to convince people that I'm not. Very often I can't even read, I sink into trances which leave me raving or in tears. (26 November 1908, British Library)

After he went down from Cambridge in 1909, James reviewed several books on psychical research for *The Spectator*, including a positive one of Frank Podmore's *The Newer Spiritualism* (*The Spectator* 15 October 1910: 608).[19] Virginia Woolf met James at about this time, and it is tempting to speculate that James passed on his new-found enthusiasm to Virginia at Bloomsbury psychological parties. In March 1911, for instance, Woolf invited James to a gathering at her cottage in Firle, at which, she claims, "There will only be the pleasures of the soul" (*Letters* I 452). Certainly by 1909 she demonstrated knowledge of psychical research in a letter, musing that

> there should be threads floating in the air, which would merely have to be taken hold of, in order to talk. You would walk about the world like a spider in the middle of a web. In 100 years time, I daresay these psychical people will have made all this apparent – now seen only by the eye of genius. (13 April 1909, *Letters* I 390)

Though slightly flippant, Woolf here shows some confidence that psychical research will provide the answer to a question about psychic connections which puzzles her.

Woolf subsequently reveals an interest in the psychical and super-natural in several of her essays. In a 1917 review of Elinor Mordaunt's supernatural tales, *Before Midnight*, she objects to the use of external super-natural phenomena such as ghosts[20] as a crude replacement for analysis of uncanny states of mind (*Essays* II 87–88). Woolf asserted:

> Nobody can deny that our life is largely at the mercy of dreams and visions which we cannot account for logically; on the contrary, if Mrs. Mordaunt had devoted every page of her book to the discovery of some of these uncharted territories of the mind we should have nothing but thanks for her. ("Before Midnight" *Essays* II 87)

A year later, Woolf reviewed Dorothy Scarborough's *The Supernatural in Modern Fiction* (1917) and approved of her inclusion of stories about "abnormal states of mind" along with ghost tales ("Across" 217). Woolf demonstrates a considerable understanding of the psychology of our attraction to these stories, and she draws on the concept of repression to illustrate the effect of this genre on an historical period:

> It is worth noticing that the craving for the supernatural in literature coincided in the eighteenth-century with a period of rationalism in thought, as if the effect of damming the human instincts at one point causes them to overflow at another. ("Across" 218)

Most importantly, Woolf acknowledges the function of psychical research as a source for the modern attraction to the supernatural in her claim that "a rational age is succeeded by one which seeks the supernatural in the soul of man, and the development of psychical research offers a basis of disputed fact for this desire to feed upon" ("Across" 219). In a third essay, "Henry

James's Ghost Stories", she praises those ghosts created by James which have their origins within us, as in "The Turn of the Screw" (*Essays* III 324). The insights Woolf expresses show that she had given some thought to the psychological processes involved in the supernatural. Woolf claims that these processes are to be found in much modern fiction ("Across" 220), and, it might be added, can be located in her own fiction.

Woolf's early engagement with pre-Freudian dynamic psychologies helped shape her attitude towards later dynamic psychologies, just as has been the case with Sinclair, Lawrence, and Beresford. However, Woolf's response to psychoanalysis was also influenced by a number of other factors, notably her response to the doctors who treated her, as Stephen Trombley has documented. Though they embraced nineteenth-century materialist conceptions of illness and believed in exerting control over patients, Woolf formed a distrust of the medical profession regardless of therapeutic technique. To Violet Dickinson she expresses this opinion forcefully: "all I can say is, why do you see doctors? They are a profoundly untrustworthy race; either they lie, or they mistake" (25 August 1907, *Letters* I 306), and she continued to hold it (*Letters* IV 227, 325–326, 342). Nevertheless, Woolf was intrigued by Freudian ideas and makes scattered references to them which vary in attitude throughout her life. I will restrict my discussion to her earliest opportunities for engaging with Freudian and other later dynamic psychological discourse.

The first "serious" document about Freud by a Bloomsbury member was Leonard Woolf's 13 June 1914 review of Freud's *The Psychopathology of Everyday Life* for the *New English Weekly*. Though Woolf refers to Freud's theories as "peculiar" ("Everyday Life" 36), he praises the subtlety of Freud's writing and his "broad and sweeping imagination more characteristic of the poet than the scientist or medical practitioner" ("Everyday Life" 36). His claim that "No one is really competent to give a final judgement upon even *The Psychopathology of Everyday Life* who has not studied *The Interpretation of Dreams*, and Freud's more distinctly pathological writings" ("Everyday Life" 36) suggests that Leonard had read these.[21] We do not know whether Virginia read any Freud at this time, but years later Leonard admitted that Virginia had read *The Psychopathology of Everyday Life* at some point before she wrote *Mrs. Dalloway*. He added that he did not think that Virginia had read *The Interpretation of Dreams* (Steinberg, "Note" 64). However, since the Woolfs owned a copy of David Eder's 1914 translation of *On Dreams* (Holleyman), Freud's popularization of his dream theory, it would have been more likely that she had read this lively account rather than the more technical *The Interpretation*.

In 1916 Leonard favourably reviewed another important work of dynamic psychology, Wilfrid Trotter's *Instincts of the Herd in Peace and War* (1916), a copy of which the Woolf's retained in their library (Holleyman). According to the critic Allen McLaurin, the book prompted Leonard "to see the crowd in terms of the non-rational or instinctive motivation" (37). Two weeks after the 8th July review, Virginia began thinking of a new novel, *Night and Day*. This sequence is significant because in the case of Trotter's book, we do know that Virginia was involved in discussions about it. Over a year later, in her 27 November 1917 diary entry, Woolf agrees with Roger Fry, whom she detects is influenced by "Trotter and the herd", about the future of the world (*Diary* I 80).

As well, Freud continued to be a topic of discussion, as a letter in which Virginia describes the ad hoc analysis that Leonard performed on her makes clear. She wrote to Saxon Sydney-Turner that after she had a nightmare and woke Leonard in the night to look for Zeppelins, "He then applied the Freud method to my mind, and analysed it down to Clytemnestra and the watch fires, which so pleased him that he forgave me" (*Letters* II, 3 February 1917: 141). By 1918, she was certainly aware of Freud's theories of sexuality, since in a 21st January diary entry she recounts having engaged in "hours of talk" with Lytton Strachey about his involvement in the British Society for the Study of Sex Psychology. Woolf wrote that

> Among other things [Lytton] gave us an amazing account of the British Sex Society which meets at Hampstead. The sound would suggest a third variety of human being, and it seems that the audience had that appearance. Notwithstanding, they were surprisingly frank; and 50 people of both sexes and various ages discussed without shame such questions as the deformity of Dean Swift's penis: whether cats use the w.c.; self-abuse; incest – Incest between parent and child when they are both unconscious of it, was their main theme, derived from Freud. I think of becoming a member. (*Diary* I 110)

Though Woolf initially mentions frivolous topics in her entry, suggesting a flippant attitude towards the Society, she moves on to the more serious issue of incest, which we now know from Louise DeSalvo's and others' work, would have had direct bearing on her own experience. The degree of fascination with these taboo subjects and with the Society is indicated by her intention of joining. Also in 1918, Woolf begins to make comments on fellow Bloomsbury members' involvement with psychoanalysis (*Diary* I 221). These pieces of evidence taken together suggest that Woolf had a fairly good working knowledge of Freudian thought by this time.

Out of the numerous references to Freud and the various opportunities that Woolf had to engage with dynamic psychology from this point on, I want to mention two books that might have had a particularly significant impact on Woolf. The Woolfs owned two 1921 issues from the International Psychoanalytic Press, both of which their Hogarth Press eventually took over publishing in 1924. One was British psychologist J.C. Flugel's *The Psychoanalytic Study of the Family*. Though this pioneering book makes passing reference to psychical researchers Myers, Gurney, and Hodgson, it mainly applies Freudian and Jungian tenets to family life, focussing particularly on emotions and conflicts. It contains an extensive discussion of various types of incestuous relationships, including how some cultures permitted incest between brothers and sisters (*Psychoanalytic* 90). Flugel suggests that since incest is a persistent universal occurrence, in spite of repression, it may have its source in natural selection, having allowed "rapid multiplication" and "greater consolidation" of the family unit (*Psychoanalytic* 198). He acknowledges its widespread occurrence in civilized societies, claiming that "A well known British psycho-analyst assures me that in the exercise of their profession he and his colleagues hear with astonishing frequency cases of incest, the report of which is otherwise suppressed. Particularly this is so as regards children" (*Psychoanalytic* 194). Leonard Woolf demonstrates knowledge of the book's contents in his autobiography, claiming that *The Psychoanalytic Study of the Family* "is an original book, an almost unknown classic in its own peculiar field, a publisher's dream" (*Downhill* 166). There is no way of knowing whether Virginia read it or discussed it with Leonard, but if she had, there is no doubt that she would have found it provocative and probably upsetting.

The other International Psychoanalytic Press book the Woolfs owned was *Psychoanalysis and the War Neuroses*, a collection of papers by Sandor Ferenczi and others, including an introduction by Freud. Freud makes the point that at the root of the war neuroses is an ego-conflict:

> The conflict takes place between the old ego of peace time and the new war-ego of the soldier, and it becomes acute as soon as the peace-ego is faced with the danger of being killed through the risky undertakings of his newly formed parasitical double. (Ferenczi 2–3)

Ferenczi emphasizes the symptoms of the war neuroses as "hypochondriachal depression, terror, anxiousness, and a high degree of irritability with a tendency to outbursts of anger" (Ferenczi 18). The source of this oversensitiveness, a consequence of shock, is the sufferer's withdrawal of interest and sexual hunger (libido) from the object into the ego (Ferenczi 18). If Virginia Woolf had read these essays she would have gained insight into the dynamics of the war-shocked soldier.[22] It is certainly possible to see Septimus Smith in *Mrs. Dalloway* as being in conflict between his peace-time and wartime ego, and as having the symptoms specified by Ferenczi, particularly as having withdrawn libido from Lucrezia.

While the probability is strong that Woolf knew more of psychoanalysis "than in the ordinary way of conversation", she continued to associate it with earlier dynamic psychologies, as a curious incident later in Woolf's life strikingly illustrates. Woolf avoided being psychoanalysed, despite being surrounded by friends and relatives, such as James and Alix Strachey and her brother Adrian, who were; however, in 1935 she consented to have a brief "analysis" with Charlotte Wolff, recommended by Aldous Huxley, an admirer of Frederic Myers' psychical research. Charlotte Wolff was a palm reader who had done "careful research in clinics and hospitals in an effort to make hand-reading a scientific discipline" (Orr 157). She read Woolf's palm, analysed her character and then, over tea, answered Woolf's questions about psychoanalytic therapy. Wolff had had a Jungian analysis and she described this experience to Virginia. Discussion of psychic phenomena along with psychotherapy would have seemed natural to Woolf because of her earlier exposure to psychical research in conjunction with psychoanalysis. Significantly, although Leonard Woolf called the palm-reading incident "disgusting humbug", Virginia kept an open mind and recorded that "I kept my distance [from Leonard's side of the argument], having the idea that after all some kind of communication is possible between beings, that cant [sic] be accounted for; or what about my dive into them in fiction?" (*Letters* V 452).

I now want to dive in to Woolf's two earliest novels in order to examine the degree to which dynamic psychological discourse helped her to "capture multitudes of things at present fugitive" (*Letters* I 356). On one level, both novels depict the consequences of the young protagonists' attempts to deal with the repressions forced on them by society, family, and their positions in that society as women. Whereas in *The Voyage Out* Rachel's bid is unsuccessful and leads to her death, in *Night and Day*, Katherine successfully overcomes restraining forces and develops her individuality, enabling her to marry a man outside the conventions established by her family's position. Since the Herbartian conception of repression had begun to circulate in Britain from the time of G.F. Stout's essays comparing Herbart with English psychologists (1888–1889), it is probably this general notion of repression that Woolf works with, rather than the Freudian. In both novels she shows that the repression bears on all aspects of the characters affected. Following an examination of this pervasive theme in *The Voyage Out*, it will become clear that her attitudes towards the consequences of repression, sublimation, dreams, intimacy, conscious states, moments of being, sexuality, the talking cure, and psychosomatic illness align well with dynamic psychological discourse on these topics.

In *The Voyage Out*, Rachel's perceived need to repress her feelings causes her to feel divided from others as well as within herself. Early in the novel, Rachel realizes that

> To feel anything strongly was to create an abyss between oneself and others who feel strongly perhaps but differently....It appeared that nobody ever said a thing they meant, or ever talked of a feeling they felt, but that was what music was for. Reality dwelling in what one saw and felt, but did not talk about, one could accept a system in which things went

round quite satisfactorily to other people, without often troubling to think about it, except as something superficially strange. Absorbed by her music she accepted her lot very complacently, blazing into indignation perhaps once a fortnight, and subsiding as she subsided now. (*Voyage* 32)

The quotation illustrates that Rachel copes with emotions which she feels she must deny by channelling them into her music. Woolf's concrete representation of the idea of sublimation resembles that which Sinclair depicts in *The Divine Fire* through the passionate piano playing of the stifled heroine, Lucia Harding (*Divine* 94–95, 155, 392–393); both writers drew on a concept that had been in circulation since Herbart and Nietzsche had described it. That Rachel has successfully channelled her rage is suggested by the fact that, immediately following her playing, she enters into a moment of union with her surroundings:

Inextricably mixed in dreamy confusion, her mind seemed to enter into communion, to be delightfully expanded and combined with the spirit of Beethoven Op. 112, even with the spirit of poor William Cowper there at Olney. (*Voyage* 33)

While this moment resembles a Paterian one in that it invokes a feeling of aesthetic harmony, the difference is that it is prompted by a psychological revelation. A second way in which Woolf suggests that Rachel's suppressed feelings are dealt with is through her protagonist's dream life. In a moment of passion on board ship, Richard Dalloway kisses Rachel. She forces down the emotion she experiences, though she realizes that "she and Richard had seen something together which is hidden in ordinary life" (*Voyage* 73). Nevertheless, the aroused feelings find expression in her dream that night:

She dreamt that she was walking down a long tunnel, which grew so narrow by degrees that she could touch the damp bricks on either side. At length the tunnel opened and became a vault; she found herself trapped in it, bricks meeting her wherever she turned, alone with a little deformed man who squatted on the floor gibbering, with long nails. His face was pitted and like the face of an animal. The wall behind him oozed with damp, which collected into drops and slid down. Still and cold as death she lay, not daring to move, until she broke the agony by tossing herself across the bed, and woke crying "Oh!" (*Voyage* 74)

The dream suggests, among other things, Rachel's terror at men's animal natures, as well as her feeling of being trapped and not able to move out of the situation she has been thrust into by Richard Dalloway. As a fearful tunnel dream which creates a feeling of abasement in the dreamer, it resembles Philip Maning's dream in Beresford's *God's Counterpoint*.

However painful the kissing incident is, it does awaken Rachel to her own sexuality, so long ignored. Her new sexual awareness in turn brings her into closer intimacy with Helen Ambrose (*Voyage* 81). Most importantly, it strangely enables Rachel, who has been described as "unformed" (*Voyage* 30), to discover herself as an individual:

> The vision of her own personality, of herself as a real everlasting thing, different from anything else, unmergeable, like the sea or the wind, flashed into Rachel's mind, and she became profoundly excited at the thought of living. "I can be m-m-myself," she stammered, "in spite of you [Helen], in spite of the Dalloways, and Mr. Pepper, and Father, and my Aunts. . . . (*Voyage* 81)

Rachel subsequently makes a valiant attempt at remaining true to her personality, but her self is eventually shown to be shifting. At the hotel dance, Rachel claims that "I've changed my view of life completely!" (*Voyage* 161). Helen comments that "That's typical of Rachel . . . she changes her view of life about every other day" (*Voyage* 161). After Rachel falls in love with Hewet, Helen justifiably finds the fluidity of Rachel's personality cause for alarm (*Voyage* 226). She compares Rachel's fluctuating moods "to the sliding of a river, quick, quicker, quicker still, as it races to a waterfall. Her instinct was to cry out Stop!" (*Voyage* 225).

Rachel and Helen initially become more intimate through their discussion of Rachel's experiences with Richard Dalloway, but the twenty years difference in their age blocks complete understanding of one another. Though characters typically fail to achieve intimacy in the novel, Woolf does suggest that human beings connect most significantly on a psychic level, beyond or below language. Onboard ship, Clarissa Dalloway experiences "fantastic dreams", and the narrator comments that

> The dreams were not confined to her indeed, but went from one brain to another. They all dreamt of each other that night, as was natural, considering how thin the partitions were between them, and how strangely they had been lifted off the earth to sit next each other in mid-ocean, and see every detail of each others' faces, and hear whatever they chanced to say. (*Voyage* 49)

Woolf's intimation of a group consciousness, or at least that characters can be in contact without using the five senses, may derive from McTaggart's idealism, as Fleishman claims (721, 725), or it could stem from Woolf's awareness of psychical research through James Strachey. During the expedition up the river into the jungle, Rachel and Hewet connect on this level. Once again Woolf uses the dream-state to invoke this deeper reality. In a trance-like state, "They [Rachel and Hewet] walked on in silence as people walking in their sleep, and were oddly conscious now and again of the mass of their bodies" (*Voyage* 277). On returning to the party, Hewet listens to the civilized talk and realizes

> that existence went on in two different layers. Here were the Flushings talking, talking somewhere high up in the air above him, and he and Rachel had dropped to the bottom of the world together. (*Voyage* 278)

At this level in which they have accessed subconscious, instinctual feelings, language hinders; hence, in the midst of conversation, they remain "perfectly silent at the bottom of the world" (*Voyage* 280). Hewet's recognition of two layers of existence, one in which language is effective and one which goes deeper than language, resembles Henri Bergson's two levels of consciousness, one of which is clear and precise, and the other "confused, ever changing, and inexpressible" (*Time* 129). These correspond with two selves, a superficial or social one and a deep-seated one (*Time* 125). Rachel's experience with Hewet in turn would seem to represent one of the few times when she is able to escape from her social self. Whether or not Woolf drew explicitly on Bergson in this passage, she certainly explored both the conscious and the subconscious states of her characters. Woolf uses the language of associationist psychology, probably as modified by a psychologist like Sully, in her many references to characters' trains of thought (*Voyage* 20, 182, 203) and in her illustration of characters' chance associations (*Voyage* 31, 47).

In her descriptions of her characters' conscious states, Woolf focusses alternately on thought, feeling, and will, a strategy which represents another parallel with Sully's threefold division of personality. For example, Woolf describes Rachel's will as an important element of her personality. The loss of "any will of her own" marks a critical stage in her illness (*Voyage* 351). Along with dreams, Woolf refers to other unconscious behaviours of her characters on numerous occasions (*Voyage* 174, 193, 205, 216, 270, 274). Throughout the novel, Woolf also works creatively with the discourse of dynamic medical psychology: Helen behaves "hysterically" (*Voyage* 26), Helen's and Rachel's moods and minds are described as fixed (*Voyage* 7, 31) and morbid (*Voyage* 290), and Rachel is "hypnotized" on at least two occasions (*Voyage* 174, 303).

Another psychological feature of the novel is that both moments out of time and memory have important roles. Rachel's moments of escape from "impersonal" (*Voyage* 123), objective time are not always positive experiences, as the one mentioned earlier was (*Voyage* 32). They can also involve feelings of loss of self. On one occasion after reading, Rachel succumbs to such a moment and

> Her dissolution became so complete that she could not raise her finger any more, and sat perfectly still, looking always at the same spot. It became

stranger and stranger. She was overcome with awe that things should exist at all.... She forgot that she had any fingers to raise.... The things that existed were so immense and so desolate.... (*Voyage* 123)

Similarly, memory has a dual function. It can make individuals feel more substantial by binding them together. Several hotel visitors share a common memory of Mrs Parry's drawing room and "they who had no solidity or anchorage before seemed to be attached to it somehow, and at once grown more substantial" (*Voyage* 145). However, memory can also be an oppressive force, as it is most often for Rachel. She recounts to Hewet that her aunts built up

the fine, closely woven substance of their life at home. They were less splendid but more natural than her father was. All her rages had been against them; it was their world with its four meals, its punctuality, and servants on the stairs at half-past ten, that she examined so closely and wanted so vehemently to smash to atoms. (*Voyage* 216)

Woolf also conveys that Rachel's failure to come to terms with her sexuality continues to cause her to suffer. Rachel's awakening to sexuality was forced, abrupt, and associated with pain. Though attracted to Hewet, Rachel's ambivalent feelings towards sexual passion persist. When the two interrupt Arthur Venning and Susan Warrington in their love-making, Rachel feels highly agitated (*Voyage* 138). In the aftermath of the experience

the impression of the lovers lost some of its force, though a certain intensity of vision, which was probably the result of the sight, remained with them. As a day upon which any emotion has been repressed is different from other days, so this day was now different, merely because they had seen other people at a crisis of their lives. (*Voyage* 139)

Rachel's emotions about the instinctual life remain "repressed" throughout the novel, though she is also attracted to this aspect of life, as Woolf reveals through a curious incident. In the midst of a futile conversation with Evelyn Murgatroyd about love, Rachel glances out the hotel window to the garden where, Evelyn informs her, they kill hens by cutting their heads off (*Voyage* 254). Rachel immediately decides to explore this "wrong side of hotel life, which was cut off from the right side by a maze of small bushes" (*Voyage* 255). In this garden she witnesses an old Spanish woman filled with "furious rage", triumphantly cutting off a chicken's head. The narrator informs us that "the blood and the ugly wriggling fascinated Rachel" (*Voyage* 255). The duality of hotel life appears to function as a metaphor for the split in Rachel between her controlled rational self and her hidden instinctual self. The elderly spinster Miss Allan also witnesses the scene and unwittingly provides appropriate commentary on it through her statement that it is "Not a pretty sight...although I daresay it's really more humane than our method" (*Voyage* 255). The old Spanish woman's direct expression of passion is more honest and, therefore, more humane than the repression of those feelings by civilized society. Miss Allan then invites Rachel to see her room, which is very ordered. On a symbolic level, Miss Allan presents the alternative to the free expression of passion, in her barren spinsterhood. Rachel finds the experience of being in Miss Allan's room to be intolerable and, upon finding the passage blocked as they walk down to tea, leaves Miss Allan abruptly (*Voyage* 260). Woolf reveals the accumulated effect of Rachel's denial of feeling throughout the day and her exposure to the instinctual level of life through her tears of frustration, her realization that "All day long she had been tantalized and put off" (*Voyage* 261), and her accompanying physical state:

> Meanwhile the steady beat of her own pulse represented the hot current of feeling that ran down beneath; beating, struggling, fretting. For the time, her own body was the source of all the life in the world, which tried to burst forth here – there – and was repressed now by Mr. Bax, now by Evelyn, now by the imposition of ponderous stupidity, the weight of the entire world. (*Voyage* 261)

Through imagery, Woolf implies that Rachel's repressions are linked to her fatal illness. At the onset of her illness, Rachel hallucinates about the movement of the blind in her room. It "seemed to her terrifying, as if it were the movement of an animal in the room" (*Voyage* 333). Later Woolf makes more explicit Rachel's fear of instinctual, sexual feeling. As Hewet kisses her, "she only saw an old woman slicing a man's head off with a knife" (*Voyage* 344). Rachel continues to associate the expression of passion with violence; it would appear that she has not dealt with the anger she must have felt after Richard Dalloway first forced a kiss on her.

Rachel's illness and the "therapy" intended to foster her health similarly reveal that Woolf's attitude is consonant with dynamic psychology. Helen Ambrose clearly resembles a doctor of the soul, sensitive to psychic conflict in her "patient". After Rachel confesses to Helen her feelings about the kissing incident, Helen realizes the extent of the younger woman's naivety, unnatural for her age. She decides to take Rachel under her wing and she relies primarily on talking for therapy:

> Talk was the medicine she trusted to, talk about everything, talk that was free, unguarded, and as candid as a habit of talking with men made natural in her own case. (*Voyage* 122)

Helen also acts as psychic confessor to Hirst and Evelyn M. (*Voyage* 160, 223). However, she achieves better results with these two because their feelings are less intense. With Rachel her "cure" fails because Helen understands neither the depth of Rachel's feeling nor the extremity of her mood changes (*Voyage* 225). Though Helen's instinct warns her to interfere (*Voyage* 225), she refrains from doing so and "a curious atmosphere of reserve [grows] up between them" (*Voyage* 224). Nevertheless, it is Helen who first recognizes that the doctor, Rodriguez, is incompetent, and who insists that a second opinion be sought (*Voyage* 342). The replacement, Dr Lesage, inspires more confidence because of his "sulky, masterful manner" (*Voyage* 347). Though their diagnoses are never directly revealed, both doctors would appear to possess limited understanding, since, in the tradition of nineteenth-century materialistic medicine, they only make pronouncements about Rachel's physical condition.

Woolf, however, clearly indicates that both the origins of Rachel's illness in repression and the symptoms are psychosomatic. Rachel experiences delirium (*Voyage* 338) and hallucinations (*Voyage* 346, 352), as well as a split between her body and mind:

> But for long spaces of time she would merely lie conscious of her body floating on the top of her bed and her mind driven to some remote corner of her body, or escaped and gone flitting around the room. (*Voyage* 352)

Also in accord with dynamic psychology, Woolf breaks down the distinctions between normal and abnormal. Hewet, supposedly sane, experiences hallucinations too. He believes that Rachel is better and talks to her, when in reality she is dead (*Voyage* 358). This moment quite possibly intimates a psychic union, which would be appropriate since, aside from Helen, Hewet shows the greatest awareness of psychic phenomena in the novel. To the rationalist, Hirst, he claims that people have invisible "bubbles" or auras around them and that "all we see of each other is a speck, like the wick in the middle of the flame" (*Voyage* 107). Following Rachel's death, Woolf invokes a more clearly supernatural element, which brings up the possibility of the survival of personality after death. At the hotel, Evelyn M. handles a photograph that Rachel had looked at:

> Suddenly the keen feeling of someone's personality, which things that they have owned or handled sometimes preserves, overcame her; she felt Rachel in the room with her; it was as if she were on a ship at sea, and the life of the day was as unreal as the land in the distance. But by degrees the feeling of Rachel's presence passed away, and she could no longer realize her, for she had scarcely known her. But this momentary sensation left her depressed and fatigued. (*Voyage* 369)

Thus, in her depiction of Rachel's illness and death, Woolf demonstrates an awareness both of the psychosomatic nature of illness, first given serious attention by dynamic psychology, and of the greater reality of psychic communication, studied exhaustively by the SPR.

Woolf's forays into these aspects of psychic life suggest that the philosophy Woolf presents in the book does not completely align with G.E. Moore's Realism. Though several critics have used Woolf's reference to *Principia Ethica* in *The Voyage Out* in order to substantiate their arguments about Moore's influence on the book, they have not pointed out that Woolf also appears to be critical of his approach (Johnstone 20, 126; Levy 2–3). On finishing *Principia Ethica*, Woolf wrote that "I believe I can disagree with him [Moore], over one matter" (*Letters* I 364). Given the evidence in *The Voyage Out*, I would speculate that the disagreement might have been about the truth-revealing capacity of language. Moore placed a great deal of emphasis on linguistic analysis in order to reveal ambiguities and to elucidate the truth (Collinson 138). However, Woolf reacts against this approach by pointing out the limitations of language in discovering the ultimate truth about individuals and relationships. For instance, Rachel and Hewet reach their most profound understanding of one another in the jungle, where they are silent. On this point Woolf would appear to come closer to Bergson's belief that language cannot capture the deepest feelings. Thus Woolf shows herself to be highly sensitive to the discoveries of dynamic psychology, and to draw eclectically on various philosophical and psychological sources in her first novel, *The Voyage Out*.

Woolf continued her inward, psychological voyage in *Night and Day* (1919), as an analysis of her treatment of repression, dividedness, dreams, and other psychic and spiritual states will demonstrate. In it, memory and the past are even more repressive forces than in *The Voyage Out*, and the psychological effects on the protagonist, Katherine Hilbery, are more intricately woven. Katherine belongs to a family which worships its illustrious ancestors, the most notable of whom was Katherine's grandfather, a famous nineteenth-century poet. Though she aids her mother in writing his biography, she has not inherited a poetic sensibility and would rather spend her time studying geometry (*Night* 36). Since she is forced to hide this original aspect of herself and feels constrained by the tradition of greatness into which she has been born, she feels depressed and divided:

> Katherine had her moments of despondency. The glorious past, in which men and women grew to unexampled size, intruded too much upon the present, and dwarfed it too consistently, to be altogether encouraging to one forced to make her experiment in living when the great age was dead. (*Night* 35)

Woolf reveals Katherine's dividedness by concentrating on her mental states. Very frequently we are told that Katherine engages only part of her mind on her present occupation or conversation. For instance, early in the novel Ralph Denham notices "that she [Katherine] attended only with the surface skin of her mind" (*Night* 7, cf. also pp. 123, 251, 271, 383, 392).

However, Katherine is not the only one divided between her inner reality and the external circumstance. Ralph Denham becomes divided in this way upon coming into contact with Katherine. He is an obscure young lawyer of a class lower than Katherine, who has become acquainted with her father through writing an article for his magazine (*Night* 24). Though he despises the supremely civilized atmosphere of the Hilbery's drawing room, his attraction to Katherine in that setting causes him to feel ambivalent about her way of life as well as his own democratic, working-class values (*Night* 29). In his behaviour towards Katherine, he manifests this sense of dividedness. On one occasion he muses about walking to her house and imagining her within,

> and then he rejected the plan almost with a blush as, with a curious division of consciousness, one plucks a flower sentimentally and throws it away, with a blush, when it is actually picked. (*Night* 117)

One of the ways Woolf deploys dreams in the novel is to make vivid Katherine's and Ralph's divided perceptions of themselves and each other. Ralph, for instance, concocts in his mind a "phantom Katherine" who is highly vital, imaginative, and sympathetic, and who does not correspond with the reality. He speculates that

> To walk with Katherine in the flesh would either feed that phantom with fresh food, which, as all who nourish dreams are aware, is a process that becomes necessary from time to time, or refine it to such a degree of thinness that it was scarcely serviceable any longer; and that, too, is sometimes a welcome change to a dreamer. And all the time Ralph was well aware that the bulk of Katherine was not represented in his dreams at all, so that when he met her he was bewildered by the fact that she had nothing to do with his dream of her. (*Night* 82)

Woolf also employs dreams in order to question the assumption that external reality is more substantial and significant than internal reality, and to show that two people's inner realities can coincide. Initially Ralph "pride[s] himself on a life rigidly divided into the hours of work and those of dreams" (*Night* 114), but as his feelings for Katherine grow, his dream life and waking life become less distinguishable. As Ralph waits for Katherine, the physical environment of Katherine's that he observes has the atmosphere of a dream. When she enters, "she overflowed the edges of the dream" (*Night* 131). Ralph is also described as looking as if he is walking in his sleep (*Night* 143), as are other characters on a few occasions (*Night* 163, 328). He comes to realize that he has "lived almost entirely among delusions" in the world that he formerly thought was substantial (*Night* 200). For Katherine, too, dreams initially function as an escape, but she has a stronger sense of their importance. On one occasion she wonders how she will avoid marrying William Rodney and then,

> putting the thought of marriage away, fell into a dream state, in which she
> became another person and the whole world seemed changed. Being a
> frequent visitor to that world, she could find her way there unhesitatingly.
> If she had tried to analyse her impressions, she would have said that
> there dwelt the realities of the appearances which figure in our world; so
> direct, powerful, and unimpeded were her sensations there, compared
> with those called forth in actual life.... It was a place where feelings were
> liberated from the constraint which the real world puts upon them; and
> the process of awakenment was always marked by resignation and a kind
> of stoical acceptance of facts. She met no acquaintance there, as Denham
> did, miraculously transfigured; she played no heroic part. But there
> certainly she loved some magnanimous hero, and as they swept together
> among the leaf-hung trees of an unknown world, they shared the feelings
> which come fresh and fast as the waves on the shore. (*Night* 127)

Katherine's dream world is thus less romantic and more therapeutic than Ralph's, since in this state her repressions are unloosed.

Eventually both Katherine and Ralph are able to exchange their actual conditions for something approaching the conditions of their dreams (*Night* 268, 393). Katherine disengages herself from the "unreal" William Rodney; in his relationship with Katherine, Ralph overcomes the external impediment of class. Through their intimacy, in which they express feelings honestly, they create an internal reality more powerful and immediate than all external forces, including the past, one of the most oppressive for Katherine. After her relationship with Ralph has developed, she continues to help her mother with the ancestral biography. However, her attitude towards this task, and her family's illustrious past in general, has changed. As she works, and waits for a telephone call from Ralph, we are told that, "She might hear another summons of greater interest to her than the whole of the nineteenth century" (*Night* 279). Her activities of the present moment have far greater significance than the past. Thus, through the voices of Ralph and Katherine, Woolf demonstrates an acute awareness of the function and importance of the dream life in transfiguring reality, an attitude completely consonant with dynamic psychology.

In addition, Woolf explores a variety of other psychological processes and states, both conscious and unconscious. Willing, thinking, and feeling states can often be distinguished. Ralph's will is an identifiable element of his personality, though interconnected with thinking and feeling states. Shortly after Ralph has first met Katherine, Woolf informs us that "his will-power was rigidly set upon a single objective – that Miss Hilbery should obey him"

(*Night* 55). With regard to thinking states, Woolf shows the process by which conflicting ideas compete for attention (*Night* 24), or press for utterance (*Night* 74). In describing the result of one thought dominating over another, she alludes to Pierre Janet's concept of *idée fixe*:

> These states of mind transmit themselves very often without the use of language, and it was evident to Katherine that this young man [Ralph] had fixed his mind on her. (*Night* 55)

Woolf images the succession of thoughts in the mind as streams (*Night* 141, 243), or more frequently as "trains" (*Night* 52, 153, 163, 167, 216, 245). Beneath these trains of thought lie feeling states. Woolf fully acknowledges the importance of the subconscious region in which these "wash". At one point Mary Datchet is besieged by "different trains of thought" until the lights of her building cheer her and

> all these different states of mind were submerged in the deep flood of desires, thoughts, perceptions, antagonisms, which washed perpetually at the base of her being, to rise into prominence in turn when the conditions of the upper world were favourable. (*Night* 154)

On several occasions Woolf shows that her characters' minds and behaviours are "unconsciously" motivated, affected, or occupied (*Night* 20, 58, 95, 101, 176, 200, 216, 425, 434).

Woolf also attends to her characters' spiritual nature and infuses major themes of memory, and reality versus unreality, with an ethereal element. In order to do so, she employs psychical discourse. Characters are "hypnotized" (*Night* 19, 241), fall into "trances" (*Night* 429), or write automatically (*Night* 149). Tropes of ghosts and apparitions appear in a variety of contexts, suggesting Woolf's belief in a realm beyond the five senses (*Night* 91, 275). In a description of Ralph's attitude towards the engaged couple, William and Katherine, Woolf links the supernatural world with the unconscious, as F.W.H. Myers had done. Ralph might feel anger at William Rodney

> [a]nd yet at the moment, Rodney and Katherine herself seemed disembodied ghosts. He could scarcely remember the look of them. His mind plunged lower and lower. Their marriage seemed of no importance to him. All things had turned to ghosts; the whole mass of the world was insubstantial vapour, surrounding the solitary spark in his mind, whose burning point he could remember, for it burnt no more. (*Night* 142)

Mary Datchet connects with the "ghosts of past moods" on a familiar walk (*Night* 167), and Ralph feels that his depression is "only a sentimental ghost" (*Night* 199). At the other extremity of mood, Ralph's feeling of communion with Katherine is framed as a moment of "almost supernatural exaltation" (*Night* 273). Finally, Woolf invokes the metaphor of survival of personality beyond death to capture Katherine's sense of the unreality of socializing and the reality of the dream life. Katherine isolates herself in the midst of a social gathering, looks out the window, and attempts

> to forget private misfortunes, to forget herself, to forget individual lives. With her eyes upon the dark sky, voices reached from the room in which she was standing. She heard them as if they came from people in another world, a world antecedent to her world, a world that was the prelude, the antechamber to reality; it was as if, lately dead, she heard the living talking. The dream nature of our life had never been more apparent to her, never had life been more certainly an affair of four walls, whose objects existed only within the range of lights and fires, beyond which lay nothing, or nothing more than darkness. (*Night* 319)

Thus, in the discourses that Woolf marshals in order to probe the psyche and spirit of her characters in *Night and Day*, she appears once again to draw on similar sources in dynamic psychology as Sinclair, Lawrence, and Beresford. We cannot be certain of the depth of her knowledge of Freud by this point, or whether she had read *The Interpretation of Dreams*. However, *Night and Day* can certainly be viewed as her interpretation of the importance of the dream life in overcoming repression.

Although in *Jacob's Room* Woolf began to experiment with a form approaching the stream of consciousness that would more nearly capture characters' fluidity and uncanny connections, she did not fully realize the integration of form and dynamic discourse until her subsequent novel *Mrs. Dalloway*. Woolf worried that reviewers would find it "disjointed because of the mad scenes not connecting with the Dalloway scenes" (*Diary* II 323), but the novel does achieve structural unity if the uncanny psychical connection between Mrs Dalloway and Septimus Smith is acknowledged and accepted.

During the novel's progress through a single day, we most often enter Clarissa Dalloway's consciousness as she prepares for her party. Similar to Sinclair's Audrey Craven, Mrs Dalloway has genius as a social artist (*Mrs. Dalloway* 69): she acts as a catalyst and draws people together. Her social self is thus highly developed and well defined, as she realizes upon looking at herself in the mirror:

> That was her self – pointed; dart-like; definite. That was her self when some effort, some call on her to be herself, drew the parts together, she alone knew how different, how incompatible and composed so for the world only into one centre, one diamond, one woman who sat in her drawing-room and made a meeting-point.... (*Mrs. Dalloway* 34–35)

However, beneath this social self she lacks a sense of being, reflected in her insubstantial physical presence. This structuring again corresponds with Bergson's two selves. We are informed that "She had the oddest sense of being herself invisible; unseen; unknown..." (*Mrs. Dalloway* 11). She later attempts to define this emptiness further:

> She could see what she lacked. It was not beauty; it was not mind. It was something central which permeated; something warm which broke up surfaces and rippled the cold contact of men and women, or of women together. (*Mrs. Dalloway* 30)

On revisiting Clarissa Dalloway after many years absence, Peter Walsh senses her insubstantiality. Woolf employs a dream in order to reveal the process by which Peter comes to articulate what he has realized about Clarissa subconsciously. Sitting on a park bench, Peter dreams, and Woolf, evoking dream condensation, states that "myriads of things merged in one thing" during it (*Mrs. Dalloway* 52). On awakening, Peter exclaims "The death of the soul", which clearly represents the dream's manifest content (*Mrs. Dalloway* 53). Through association, Peter gradually uncovers the latent content: "The words attached themselves to some scene, to some room, to some past he had been dreaming of" (*Mrs. Dalloway* 53). He recalls the moment at Bourton when Clarissa's soul died. She repudiated her close friend Sally Seton for making a remark about pre-marital sexuality; consequently Clarissa retreated into conventionality. Notice that Peter frames Clarissa's loss using spiritual discourse.

However, Clarissa's lack of a strong sense of identity has a positive aspect as well, in that it makes her particularly sensitive to others' identities. She believes that "Her only gift was knowing people almost by instinct..." (*Mrs. Dalloway* 10). Peter recollects that in her youth she had formed a theory in order to account for her experience. She felt herself "everywhere", rather than gathered into a unified, well-defined personality, and thus able to make contact with the most unlikely people and places:

> Odd affinities she had with people she had never spoken to, some woman in the street, some man behind a counter – even trees, or barns. It ended in a transcendental theory which, with her horror of death, allowed her to believe, or say that she believed (for all her scepticism), that since our apparitions, the part of us which appears, are so momentary compared with the other, the unseen part of us, which spreads wide, the unseen might survive, be recovered somehow attached to this person or that, or even haunting certain places, after death. Perhaps – perhaps.[23]

Clarissa's "transcendental theory", with its emphasis on survival of personality beyond death, clearly bears a striking affinity with that of the psychical researchers. They too believed that the world beyond the five senses was far more extensive than conventionally admitted. Clarissa's theory also provides the key to her uncanny connection with Septimus Smith, as will become apparent.

The novel's antagonist, Septimus Smith, who is shell-shocked and suicidal, superficially has no connection with Mrs Dalloway's set, since he is of a lower, self-educated class. And yet, through Septimus, Woolf breaks down the distinctions between madness and sanity and compares insane and psychically gifted visions. Septimus has been labelled insane, but several of his symptoms can be detected in those considered quite sane, including Peter Walsh, the doctors who treat Septimus, and Clarissa. Similar to Septimus, Peter's character is considered flawed (*Mrs. Dalloway* 96). Septimus shows signs of paranoia in believing that attention centres on him, when it is really focussed on the passing motor-car of a distinguished person (*Mrs. Dalloway* 15). Peter likewise manifests paranoia, as revealed in his recollection of a scene at Bourton: "he had a feeling that they were all gathered together in a conspiracy against him – laughing and talking – behind his back" (*Mrs. Dalloway* 56).

Furthermore, Woolf portrays Septimus's doctors as being far more "insane" than Septimus himself. Septimus has lost the ability to feel, and believes that he must seek "scientific" explanations above all things (*Mrs. Dalloway* 61). His doctors are shown to have similar characteristics in their inability to empathize with Septimus's suffering and in their "scientific" diagnoses of his case as "nerve symptoms and nothing more" (*Mrs. Dalloway* 82), or a lack of proportion. Whereas we feel sympathy for Septimus, they are reprehensible because there is no justification for their behaviour and because they are in positions of power, which they abuse. Both doctors are depicted as extremes. Dr Holmes takes a materialistic approach to medicine, which denies the spiritual, and the description of him as "the brute with the red nostrils" clearly associates him with animality (*Mrs. Dalloway* 83). Sir William Bradshaw, on the other hand, with his theory that health equals proportion, is associated with excessive rationality. In a fashion typical of the materialist treatment of mental illness, both doctors control their patients by restraining and secluding them in rest homes (*Mrs. Dalloway* 82, 87). Sir William Bradshaw is shown to be particularly "mad" in worshipping the Goddess Proportion. In making his cure of proportion a universal one, Bradshaw's approach to healing has become analogous to a dogmatic and rigid religion; ironically he lacks proportion himself.

On the deepest psychological level, aspects of Septimus are mirrored in Clarissa. Both have been profoundly changed through witnessing the death of someone very close to them. Septimus's mind became unhinged after her lost his close friend and officer, Evans, in the war (*Mrs. Dalloway* 78). Clarissa witnessed her sister being killed by a falling tree and evolved "an atheist's religion of doing good for the sake of goodness" (*Mrs. Dalloway* 70). Woolf suggests, obliquely in Clarissa's case, that both Septimus and Clarissa failed to mourn these losses properly and that this failure partly accounts for their difficulty in feeling.[24] Whereas Clarissa subsequently has a horror of death, Septimus has a fascination with it (*Mrs. Dalloway* 135, 60). However, death pervades both of their lives, which helps explain Clarissa's immediate understanding that Septimus's suicide was an act of defiance (*Mrs. Dalloway* 163). Most importantly, their streams of consciousness overlap, for instance both containing wave imagery and part of the line from *Cymbeline*, "Fear no more the heat o' the sun" (IV, ii, 258). In response to a feeling of rejection, Clarissa mentions the phrase (*Mrs. Dalloway* 28), and it later emerges in her stream of consciousness while she sews:

> So on a summer's day waves collect, overbalance, and fall, collect and fall, and the whole world seems to be saying "that is all" more and more ponderously, until even the heart in the body which lies in the sun on the beach says too, that is all. Fear no more says the heart. Fear no more says the heart, committing its burden to some sea, which sighs collectively for all sorrows, and renews, begins, collects, lets fall. And the body alone listens to the passing bee; the wave breaking, the dog barking, far away barking and barking. (*Mrs. Dalloway* 37)

Though Septimus's feeling of rejection by society is far greater than Clarissa's, he is similarly soothed by this current of thought. He lies on his sofa

> watching the watery gold glow and fade with the astonishing sensibility of some live creature on the roses, on the wall-paper. Outside the trees dragged their leaves like nets through the depths of the air; the sound of water was in the room, and through the waves came the voices of birds singing. Every power poured its treasures on his head, and his hand lay there on the back of the sofa, as he had seen his hand lie when he was bathing, floating, on the top of the waves, while far away on shore he heard dogs barking and barking far away. Fear no more, says the heart in the body; fear no more. (*Mrs. Dalloway* 124)

Clarissa never meets Septimus, but her sense of identification with him and the re-entry into her consciousness of the phrase "Fear no more the heat of the sun" when she hears of his death confirm their psychic connection (*Mrs. Dalloway* 165). Septimus's disjointed, hallucinatory visions do not seem so far removed from Clarissa's moments of vision. Thus, in yet another novel Woolf suggests that communication between individuals can transcend the limitations of the five senses. In implying that Clarissa and Septimus are linked in this way, and that other characters, including Septimus's doctors, manifest symptoms of madness similar to, or worse than, Septimus's, Woolf deliberately blurs traditional distinctions between insanity and sanity, madness and vision, a characteristic manouevre of dynamic psychology.

In a striking parallel with the significance attributed to memory in Bergson's metaphysical psychology, Woolf also demonstrates the pervasive influence and multiple significance of memory in the novel. Though Peter believes that "women live much more in the past than [men] do" (*Mrs. Dalloway* 51), both he and Septimus are as caught up in their memories as Clarissa is. Memory causes all three to suffer (*Mrs. Dalloway*: Peter 39; Septimus 60; Clarissa 156), but it also enriches them and provides a sense of connectedness with fellow human beings. Peter makes the association in musing that "The past enriched, and experience, and having cared for one or two people..." (*Mrs. Dalloway* 144). Both Clarissa and Septimus remember moments of intimacy in their past: for Clarissa, "the most exquisite moment of her whole life" was when her young friend, Sally, kissed her in the garden at Bourton (*Mrs. Dalloway* 33); for Septimus these moments occurred during the period of his close friendship with Evans (*Mrs. Dalloway* 77). With possibly a Freudian touch, Woolf alludes to the importance of childhood memory in one of Peter's speculations: "There was Regent's Park – Yes – as a child he had walked in Regent's Park – odd, he thought, how the thought of childhood keeps coming back to me ... (*Mrs. Dalloway* 51). Finally, it is Peter's memories of Clarissa, including one in which she descends the stairs in white (*Mrs. Dalloway* 46), which expand the moment and fill him with extraordinary excitement when he views her as the novel closes (*Mrs. Dalloway* 172).

As in *Night and Day*, Woolf once again privileges a non-material reality, which continuously rises up and subverts perception of the material world of objects. Although both Clarissa and Peter are "nominally" atheists (*Mrs. Dalloway* 70, 52), their experience of inner reality, and of moments of being in particular, causes them to embrace beliefs about a higher, spiritual reality. As we have seen, Clarissa has her transcendental theory. Peter, on the other hand, is an idealist, who believes in the existence of the soul, as his concern with whether Clarissa's soul has been stifled indicates (*Mrs. Dalloway* 65). During Peter's dream, Woolf expresses the idealist belief in mind over matter:

> By conviction an atheist perhaps, he is taken by surprise with moments of extraordinary exultation. Nothing exists outside us except a state of mind, he thinks...But if he can conceive of her, then in some sort she exists.... (*Mrs. Dalloway* 52)

Their transcendentalism and idealism, which emphasize the inner workings of the mind, envelope the novel as a whole and align well with the discourses of dynamic psychology.

Though *Mrs. Dalloway* is Woolf's first mature, modernist work, several of the psychological themes and ideas that Woolf introduced in her more derivative earlier novels persist here. Woolf shows that Clarissa Dalloway's personality is divided between a strong social self and an underlying insubstantial and fearful private self. Dreams and moments of being crystallize subconscious material. Woolf reacts against the materialist approach of doctors to illness and insists on the link between insanity and vision. Characters communicate on an intuitive, psychic level outside language. Memory is pervasive and creates both horror and richness of experience. The enduring presence of these ideas in Woolf's first four novels suggests that Woolf's engagement with currents of dynamic psychological thought during her apprenticeship years had considerable impact on her vision of humanity.

These currents of dynamic psychology continued to give shape to Woolf's individual thematic preoccupations in her subsequent mature modernist experiments as well. In *To The Lighthouse* (1927), which followed *Mrs. Dalloway*, Woolf entertains the possibility of the survival of personality through Lily's vision of Mrs Ramsay. In addition, as Erwin Steinburg has pointed out, Woolf fused Freudian symbolism with highly imaginative descriptions in that novel (Steinburg 4–5). In *Orlando* (1928), a biographical time-travel fantasy, Woolf extended the fluidity of self to include gender. The irrational and changeable protagonist, Orlando, begins life as a male Elizabethan before transforming into a female in the eighteenth century. In *The Waves* (1931), the work that Leonard Woolf referred to as her masterpiece, Virginia returns to an imaginative exploration of the idea of group consciousness, which had intrigued her two decades earlier following the publication of Trotter's book on the herd instinct. The selves of the six main characters merge and their voices become indistinguishable. Woolf's attraction to idealism resurfaces as well, since, as Jean Guiget points out, places have lost any reality outside the characters' perceiving consciousnesses (287). On one level the novel represents an attempt to capture a single act of perception, or moment of being (Guiget 287, 289). In her final work, *Between the Acts* (1941), Woolf articulates once again her idealist perception of the connection between science and spirit. Her protagonist muses that "It's odd that science, so they tell me, is making things (so to speak) more spiritual...The very latest notion, so I'm told, is, nothing's solid...." (138). In addition, she grapples more directly than ever before with the intense feelings of attraction and repulsion underscoring sexual relationships in this swan song. Her protagonist appears to lean towards the Freudian view, perhaps as a result of Woolf's reading Freud at this time: "Did she mean, so to speak, something hidden, the unconscious as they call it? But why always drag in sex....It's true, there's a sense in which we all, I admit, are savages still" (138–139).

Thus, Woolf both sought out knowledge of dynamic psychology and suppressed that knowledge throughout her career. In a similar manner, she expressed varying degrees of ambivalence towards her Edwardian predecessors Arnold Bennett and May Sinclair, as well as contemporaries J.D. Beresford and D.H. Lawrence, not acknowledging that they too had discovered the dark – in some cases for Woolf uncomfortably dark – places of psychology. Clearly, these five writers drew on similar psychological discourses; their interrogation of common sources helped them to avoid the limitations of the materialist's realism and to articulate a more profound and convincing psychic reality than some of their other contemporaries less familiar with these discourses.

7
Diving Deeper: Dynamic Psychology and British Literature

> Still more gratifying is the fact that we are now able to locate with something like certainty where the mind is. And it appears that it is away down – in fact is sinking into a bottomless abyss. What we took for the mind is only an insignificant part of it, a poor glimmer of intelligence, a rush light floating on the surface of an unknown depth. Underneath the mind lurks the *subconscious*, and away down under this again the *subliminal*, and under that is a *primitive complex*, and farther down, fifty feet in the mud, is the *cosmic intelligence*.
>
> – Stephen Leacock, "The Human Mind Up to Date" 1924, p. 36

By 1924, the year the first two volumes of Freud's *Collected Works* were published, satires and parodies of dynamic psychology, such as Leacock's, proliferated, reflecting not only that dynamic psychological discourses were widely disseminated in popular culture and provided good fodder for ridicule, but also, perhaps, that they aroused anxiety. That this cultural anxiety was deep-rooted is further intimated when one realizes that parodies and satires accompanied dynamic psychology throughout its evolution, from the time of Grant Allen's parodies of psychical research in "Our Scientific Observations on a Ghost" (1878) and "The Mysterious Occurrence in Picadilly" (1884) through Lytton Strachey's early Freudian parody, "According to Freud" (c.1914),[1] Rose Macaulay's satiric novel *Dangerous Ages* (1921), and Aldous Huxley's *Crome Yellow* (1921). Both parody and satire typically engage irony, a distancing technique, and yet they also incorporate and repeat the subject of the attack, thus in some sense demonstrating complicity with it. These satirists would well repay investigation since they point up most dramatically that ambivalence, betraying anxiety, towards dynamic psychology that has been expressed by the writers under study here. The most striking case is Aldous Huxley, who savaged believers in the self's extended powers, from automatic writing to mediumship to telepathy, in his first novel *Crome Yellow*. Mr Barbeque Smith, for instance, pontificates about "h-piritual truth" and practises automatic writing, enabling him to connect his "Subconscious with the Infinite" (*Crome* 50) – and to produce 3800 (presumably facile) words a day (*Crome* 46). Yet Huxley himself became convinced that telepathy, clairvoyance, and prevision existed (*Ends and Means* 259–260) and ultimately championed Myers's dynamic psychology.

The roots of writers' ambivalence and anxiety about dynamic discourse are no doubt numerous and tangled, but a few have emerged during the course of this study and might be provisionally summarized here. Most fundamentally, dynamic psychology, particularly those versions that investigated mankind's spiritual dimension, challenged the dominant scientific materialism, a culture becoming obsessed with material objects, the tenets of religious dogma, and, most pertinently, in the realm of aesthetics the conventions of traditional realism. It thus took courage for a writer to commit to the truths revealed by dynamic psychology.

Dynamic Psychology's sources in low culture nineteenth-century spiritualism and in the study of abnormal individuals, who had traditionally been kept apart, or "alienated" from society, also rendered dynamic psychology suspect. Similar to psychical researchers and mental scientists, novelists were faced with a mass of psychic material that was prey to fakery, charlatanism, and folly; they had to separate what they found to be truthful and worthy of attempting to capture in fiction from the rubbish. May Sinclair, for instance, felt that "the Society for Psychical Research may be trusted to deal with unorganized imposture", but she was wary of being suspected of "toleration for professors of the occult", by which she meant Theosophy and Christian Science (*Defence* 296). Other writers had less confidence in psychical-spiritual-mystical phenomena altogether, evidenced in Woolf's tentative attitude towards "these psychical people" and, through Mrs Dalloway, towards transcendental theories, and Lawrence's embarrassment at admitting survival and disparagement of mysticism.

Woolf and Lawrence in particular may have felt an anxiety of influence about dynamic psychological discourse, perceiving it as rival to their own imaginative exploration of "the dark places of psychology", to wit Lawrence's denigration of Freudian theory and his rewriting it in more mystical terms. Woolf's anxiety emerges strikingly in a 1925 incident. On 14 May James Strachey wrote to his wife, then in analysis, that he had dined with "the Wolves" and "Virginia made a more than usually ferocious onslaught upon psychoanalysis and psychoanalysts, more particularly the latter" (Meisel, *Bloomsbury* 264). He added that his book, the third volume of Freud's collected papers, had been published that day, along with Virginia's *Mrs. Dalloway* (Meisel, *Bloomsbury* 265). It seems likely that the simultaneous publication exacerbated her sense of rivalry and provoked the onslaught.

Writers' ambivalence about admitting engagement with dynamic discourse may also have been increased because the challenges posed by dynamic psychology as well as its suspect sources placed it beyond the horizon of novel readers' as well as critics' expectations, as J.D. Beresford most clearly and with most frustration articulated. R. Ellis Roberts makes this point in a 1923 review titled "Miss Sinclair among the Ghosts":

> while most people in Europe are more and more preoccupied with the supernatural, with the odd, with the inexplicable in life, there seems a conspiracy among the more cultured critics to treat any manifestation of interest in these subjects as a disgraceful lapse on the part of a novelist. (Roberts 32)[2]

Writers' ambivalence towards dynamic psychology along with early critics' hostility help to account for the erasures that this book has attempted to make visible again. However, larger forces have also been exposed. A certain symmetry has been revealed in the way that history has treated developments in the two disciplines brought together here. In histories of psychology, and particularly of psychoanalysis, the admittedly important findings of Sigmund Freud have been so magnified and divorced from their sources that they have overshadowed and in some cases obliterated earlier significant advances in psychological knowledge, especially those made in fields no longer considered reputable, such as psychical research. Similarly, brilliant innovations in literary form made by modernists such as Joyce and Woolf have so captivated the attention of literary critics that they have tended to ignore earlier, more modest enlargements of the novel's thematic territory made through engagement with all-but-forgotten dynamic psychologies. Both Freudian followers and exponents of high modernism helped ensure the triumph of their approaches by insisting on their novelty and by attacking or ignoring predecessors. In contrast to those claims, this book has attempted to rupture the mythologies, restore those predecessors and reconstruct continuity of thought and development in both fields during the early twentieth century.

The power and long entrenchment of these mythologies makes it likely that further excavation will bring to light even more extensive reciprocal engagement between writers and dynamic psychological discourse, and I want to suggest some terrain that might usefully be explored to that end. Dean Rapp, R.D. Hinshelwood and Sandra Ellesley have provided some fascinating glimpses into the popular reception of psychoanalysis in Britain, but a more inclusive study of the popular reception of dynamic psychology needs to be done. It would be instructive to analyse in detail the typical distortions that occurred, particularly in Freudian theory, when these discourses appeared in newspapers and magazines, since distortions would likely help explain some of the opposition to dynamic theories. In addition, since some writers gained most of their knowledge from these sources, this analysis could shed more light on their attitudes towards dynamic discourse. The engagement of popular genre writing with dynamic psychology would also be illuminating. In the mystery genre, Agatha Christie, who incidentally was a great admirer of

May Sinclair, frequently incorporated into her work a psychological and psychical dimension. Algernon Blackwood, the foremost supernatural writer of the twentieth century, moved the genre into new terrain by very quickly assimilating earlier dynamic psychologies of Myers and James and others, and then of Freud. His *The Wave: An Egyptian Aftermath* (1916), for instance, explores the oedipal complex in a supernatural context, and sets a precedent by being probably the first English novel to refer to Sigmund Freud by name.

Several other avenues of inquiry might also usefully be pursued, such as the impact of dynamic psychology on the other principle genres. In drama, George Bernard Shaw's early interrogation of psychical research comes to mind. Although tending to satirize it, he did continue to entertain the possibility of extended mental powers, as in his profound psychological study of the survival of personality beyond death, *Saint Joan* (1924), modelled after psychical researcher Andrew Lang's study of Joan of Arc. The short story genre as well proved a particularly fertile ground for explorations of dynamic psychological phenomena, as has been glimpsed through the analyses of a few of Sinclair's and Beresford's stories. Although isolated manifestations of the psychical case study have long been recognized, most famously Henry James's "Turn of the Screw", there is the possibility of an entire subgenre of psychical stories that has been unrecognized as such, by writers ranging from Arthur Conan Doyle and Agatha Christie to Kipling, Sinclair, Beresford and James.

The subversive nature of dynamic psychology might be further explored by unpacking various interconnections with early socialism, from Shaw to Eder and Wells. The profound emotional impact of dynamic psychology could be broached through a systematic examination of responses to traumatic losses by those most engaged with dynamic psychological discourse. The experience of early loss provides a fundamental common denominator between those most responsible for introducing dynamic psychology into Britain – the psychical researchers, notably Edmund Gurney and Frederic Myers – and the writers who most seriously explored the imaginative possibilities of this psychology in their fiction. Sinclair, Lawrence and Woolf responded profoundly to the tragic loss in their early years of family members, while J.D. Beresford lost his full physical capacity because of a childhood accident. To what degree did losses fuel the fascination with dynamic psychology, given that earlier dynamic psychologies in particular attempted to probe the possibility of unseen realities and, in some instances, to prove scientifically the survival of personality beyond death? These psychologies may thus have provided consolation and helped writers negotiate loss. On a much larger scale, dynamic psychology may at least temporarily have superseded first wave psychology because of the appeal it would have had for a society attempting to overcome loss of traditional religious belief, and, during First World War, to cope with the loss of loved ones in battle.

As these brief suggestions make clear, this psychological and literary terrain has great potential for further excavation, even though the yield thus far has been abundant. The present investigation has revealed that distortion and simplification have occurred in both psychological and literary history. Some years before the height of modernism was reached, writers of diverse backgrounds and aesthetic aims discovered the fictional possibilities of a new wave of psychology that articulated forces operating within the mind and explored extensions of mental powers, including telepathy, clairvoyance, psychic possession, and trance states. Their interrogation of this discourse aided these novelists in diving more deeply into hitherto hidden realities of existence, to capture, as Woolf put it, "multitudes of things at present fugitive" (*Letters* I 356).

Notes

Introduction

1. Frederic Myers asserted that "the highest wave of materialism" crested in about 1873 (*Human Personality* 7).
2. In so, doing dynamic psychologies often adapted concepts and metaphors from evolutionary biology. Frederic Myers, for example, incorporated into his dynamic psychology of the subliminal self concepts of fitness, evolution and force from Spencer's social Darwinism.
3. See, for example, Christie's "The Hound of Death" and "The Strange Case of Sir Arthur Carmichael", both of which conflate psychology and "the occult sciences" (Agatha Christie, *The Golden Ball and Other Stories*. 1924. New York: Berkeley, 1984: 136).
4. Brill, A.A. Translator's Preface. *Selected Papers on Hysteria and Other Psychoneuroses*. 1909. 2nd Edn. New York: Journal of Nervous and Mental Diseases Publishing Co., 1912.
5. According to the *Concordance* to Freud (Guttman, *et al.*), there are only nine references to "new psychological" and "new psychology", the earliest of which appears in a letter to Fliess, 6 December 1896.
6. *Journal of Society for Psychical Research* (April 1901): 57.
7. Several psychologists followed Woodworth's lead, including John Thomson Maccurdy (*Problems in Dynamic Psychology. A Critique of psychoanalysis and suggested formulations*. Cambridge: University Press, 1923), and Thomas Verner Moore (*Dynamic Psychology. An Introduction to Modern Psychological Theory and Practice*. Philadelphia: Lippincott, 1924).
8. Students of the Orthopsychics Society, a branch of the London Medico-Psychological Clinic, read Sinclair's *The Tree of Heaven* (1917) "as literature and as therapy" (Boll, *M.S.: Novelist* 234); in 1926 Beresford wrote "that numerous psychoanalysts frequently refer to this novel *God's Counterpoint* [Beresford's 1918 psychoanalytic novel]; of which they recommend the reading to their patients, in order that these could better understand the erring of their sexual penchants" ("Le Déclin" 260).
9. As early as 1916, Alfred Booth Kuttner wrote a "Freudian Appreciation" of *Sons and Lovers*. See also Daniel Weiss, *Oedipus in Nottingham: D.H. Lawrence* (1962), and Daniel Schneider, *D.H. Lawrence. The Artist as Psychologist* (1984).

1 Philosophy and psychology

1. Several other influential thinkers might have been included here but had to be omitted partly because of space limitations. Havelock Ellis, for example, made contributions to subjects bearing on dynamic psychology, including dreams and genius. Most importantly, he helped to establish sexuality as fundamental to shaping and revealing identity in his *magnum opus Studies in the Psychology of Sex* (1897–1928); however, his work was primarily descriptive and classificatory and he did not develop a dynamic theory of selfhood.
2. In *Stream of Consciousness in the Modern Novel* (Berkeley: University of California Press, 1965) 1. Isaacs 88.

3. *Scribner's Magazine* 7 (1890): 373, as qtd in Myers, *W.J.* 375.

4. Cf. Baillee 4; Le Roy 4; F.E. Hulme, as qtd in Kumar 12. Mary Ann Gillies claims that over 200 articles on Bergson appeared between 1909 and 1911 (28).

5. Nevertheless, several prominent students of McDougall's held similarly wide-ranging interests, notably psychical research, and adopted his eclectic approach, including Sir Cyril Burt and J.C. Flugel, the latter of whose work will be discussed in Chapters 3 and 6.

2   Medicine, mental science, and psychical research

1. Ellenberger 404. James, in turn, may have derived his ideas from G.F. Stout's.

2. According to Drinka, "Janet's attempt to locate in the brain the functions of the mind is really the heart of modern psychiatry. His thought seems solidly mainstream, quintessentially post-Freudian, and very modern" (Drinka 346).

3. S.A.K. Wilson, "Some Modern French Conceptions of Hysteria", *Brain* XXXIII (1910–1911): 294.

4. Hart, Bernard. "Freud's Conception of Hysteria", *Brain* Vol. XXXIII (1910–1911): 339–366.

5. Sigmund Freud. Letter to Ernest Jones, 10 March 1910. Sigmund Freud Papers. Library of Congress, Washington, DC.

6. Henceforth the Society for Psychical Research will be designated by the abbreviation SPR.

7. John Cerullo claims that, by the 1896 Munich Congress, psychical research "was on the verge of offering the psychological profession as comprehensive an interpretation of personal identity as had yet been had" (99).

8. Edmund Gurney and Frederic Myers, "Some Higher Aspects of Mesmerism", *National Review* 5 (July 1885): 703, as qtd in Oppenheim 249.

9. In a review of an article by Ernest Jones on Freud's psychology (*Psychological Bulletin* 15 April 1910), for example, T.W. Mitchell writes that,

> Freud's Unconscious is in truth not very different from Myers's Subliminal, but it seems to be more acceptable to the scientific world, in so far as it has been invoked to account for normal and abnormal phenomena only, and does not lay its supporters open to the implication of belief in supernormal happenings. (*Journal of the Society for Psychical Research* July 1910, 353)

10. Ironically, Freud's later metaphysical work narrowed the gap between Freud and Myers, as Mitchell noted in a Myers memorial lecture, entitled *Beneath the Threshold* (1931, 16).

3   "A piece of psycho-analysis": The British response to later dynamic psychology

1. Sociologist Roy Wallis developed the useful concept of sanitization in discussing the rejection of various bodies of knowledge, including psychical research ("Science" 598).

2. Edward Glover corroborates this. He wrote that, even by the 1920s, "there was still a numerical preponderance of non-Freudian over Freudian practitioners" in England, but "psychoanalysts were no longer on the defence" ("Eder" 101).

3. Wright, Obituary 204; The *Journal* of the SPR reported in 1915 that "Six members of the medical staff of the [Medico-Psychological] clinic belong to the SPR,

and the Chairman of the Board of Management is a member of our Council" (February 1915 25).

4. Roazen claims that Jones was "no friend of the independent Tavistock clinic" because of its eclecticism (350).

5. Freud's statement to Jones that "Your intention to purge the London Society of the jungish members is excellent", probably strikes closer to the truth of Jones's motivation than his later claims (Letter from Freud to Jones, 18 February 1919).

6. In another source, Jones adds the names of Morton Prince, Binet, Fere, and Pierre Janet ("Early History" 202).

7. Freud's work was less favourably reviewed in the *British Medical Journal* I (1907): 103–104.

8. 508, 792. Ernest Jones contributed to that myth by writing about commentators' assertions that "the three essays were shockingly wicked. Freud was a man with an evil and obscene mind" (*Freud* II 13).

9. J.A.H. *Nature*, 27 February 1913.

10. *Times Literary Supplement* (18 December 1913): 614.

11. In his biography of Freud, Jones similarly exaggerated the originality of the work, claiming that "The main conclusions in it were entirely novel and unexpected" (*Freud* I 384).

12. *The Nation* Vol. XCVI, No. 2498 (15 May 1913): 504.

13. Brown published over seventy articles and books on psychological topics.

14. "Obituary" *British Medical Journal*, 26 April 1941. Forsyth made contributions on psychoanalysis to the *Proceedings of the Royal Society of Medicine*, *British Journal of Psychology*, *Psychoanalytic Review*, and published *The Rudiments of Character* (1921) and *Technique of Psychoanalysis* (1922) in this field (*Who was Who* 1941–1950, 401). Freud wrote about the latter work that "Forsyth's little book is exceptionally good and full of sound judgement" (Letter to Jones, 23 March 1923).

15. *Daily Dispatch*, Manchester, 7 August 1913, as cited in Roberts "Social and Medical", *David Eder* 79–80.

16. This is confirmed by the British publisher, T. Fisher Unwin's, claim that " 'the Psychopathology of Everyday Life' has been well reviewed in the press of here and the sales are fairly satisfactory, though not as great as I had anticipated" (Letter from Unwin to A.A. Brill. 13 July 1914, Library of Congress, Washington, DC).

17. Nevertheless, when Freud came to write *Group Psychology and the Analysis of the Ego* (Eng. edn 1922), he referred to Trotter's work as "thoughtful", and wrote to Jones that "I am glad to have devoted a thorough study to Trotter's clever book..." (Letter to Jones, 8 March 1920).

18. I happen to own Bloomsbury associate Raymond Mortimer's copy.

19. Thus Eder, and not Rivers, as claimed by Rapp, first articlulated for the lay public an electic approach to shell shock (cf. Rapp 233).

20. Sinclair may have taken her cue from Eder's discussion of sublimation in "The Present Position of Psycho-analysis". He claimed that

> Psycho-analysis cannot be regarded as complete until this synthesis is achieved, although how far sublimation or re-education can be effected in any case depends, first, upon the completeness with which the resistances have been overcome; and secondly, upon the general level of the patient's intelligence and morale. (1214)

4   May Sinclair: The evolution of a psychological novelist

1. Not even accurate about her dates, Walter Allen wrote in *The English Novel* that, "May Sinclair (?1870–1946) stands rereading more successfully, yet she doesn't seem more now than a pioneer in a kind of psychological fiction later women novelists were to do better" (390–391). William Tindall dismisses her for being too scientific and lacking penetration (218–219).
2. For example, Suzanne Raitt and others have championed Sinclair as a feminist novelist, and Jane Miller has seen her as the more formally innovative feminine counterpart to H.G. Wells, particularly in the development of the sociological novel.
3. Letter to Charlotte Mew, 14 May 1914, New York Public Library.
4. Sinclair wrote that she had so little to do with her father in infancy that he was to all intents and purposes not known to her ("Way of Sublimation" 118).
5. Sinclair lost her brothers at disturbingly regular intervals, when she was twenty-four, twenty-six, twenty-eight, and thirty-three. Her last brother died in 1905, four years after her mother died (Boll, *M.S.: Novelist* 27).
6. Sinclair met James in 1905 (Raitt 96) and corresponded with him in 1908. In reference to an unknown query of Sinclair's, he responded: "How could you believe in a pack of psychologists? Of course I couldn't go to their meeting – the dismalist of pseudo-sciences!" (Letter, 12 May 1908).
7. There was a Psycho-Therapeutic Clinic for Suggestive Treatment in Liverpool prior to the Psycho-Medical Clinic (Boll, "Medico", 312, 316).
8. Letter from Laura Price to Theophilus Boll, 16 September 1962, Box 49, Sinclair Papers, University of Pennsylvania, Philadelphia.
9. According to Alan Gauld, cross-correspondences are "the series of parallel or interlinked communications obtained through different mediums and auto-matists" (274).
10. Letter from May Sinclair to Mrs Eveleen Myers, 7 July 1908, Myers Collection, Trinity College, Cambridge.
11. The novel certainly owes something to New Women novels, particularly Ella Hepworth Dixon's *My Flirtations* (1892), but Sinclair's attitude to the New Woman is critical, even ambivalent.
12. As early as 1876 Sully had described in a popular article the transformation of one person into the shape of another in our dreams as "a kind of metempsychosis" (Sully, "Laws" 545).
13. In 1908 Sinclair published a novella, *The Judgement of Eve*, drawing on James's idea of the strenuous life.
14. In describing the self, Henri Bergson, in a work translated in 1912, employs a similar trope: "There is, beneath these sharply cut crystals and this frozen surface, a continuous flux which is not comparable to any flux I have ever seen" (*Introduction* 11).
15. We are later told that, "as for making love, it was his mother who had put into his head that exquisitely agitating idea" (*Combined* 50).
16. As was mentioned earlier, we do know that Sinclair read this work, since several pages of her notes on it have survived (Sinclair, Notes).
17. Both the novel's setting, in the bleak Yorkshire dales, and her depiction of an oppressive Vicar's family, owe much to Sinclair's study of the Bronte family, *The Three Brontës* (1912). In its theme of the consequences of repression, the novel also owes much to Butler's *The Way of All Flesh* (1903).

18. As Raitt claims, "The image of the vortex expresses Sinclair's fear of a permeable subjectivity" (170). However, this fear was deep-rooted in Sinclair's personality, evidenced from her first novel on; it was not, as Raitt claims, "In part...her growing familiarity with psychoanalytic theory that stimulated her anxiety" (170).

19. Rebecca West's, *The Return of the Soldier* and J.D. Beresford's *God's Counterpoint*, both published in 1918, preceded it (Boll, *M.S.: Novelist* 245).

20. Notice that, for Sinclair, psychotherapy continues to be associated with spiritual healing of the soul.

5 From Edwardian to Georgian psychical realism: Bennett, Lawrence, and Beresford

1. Beresford lapsed into obscurity for a number of reasons, including, as Gerald Gould put it, that "he cannot be labelled" (Gould 17–18), that his later work became increasingly didactic, and that critics deplored his clinical treatment of unpleasant themes in fiction.

2. Though Hewitt recognizes that Woolf's statements have been used to construct "an ideology which ignores some of the evidence" (132), even he excuses Woolf on the grounds that she was "taking part in a local argument" (132).

3. Woolf does express gratitude to Hardy, Conrad, and W.H. Hudson, but does not explain why ("Modern Novels" 31).

4. Bennett completed the initial version of *The Ghost* on 23 January 1899. It was originally titled *For Love and Life* and was published in serial form (Hepburn 19, 53).

5. *The Glimpse* originated in a short story published in *The New Age*, 4 November 1909 (*Letters* 407; Drabble 161).

6. According to Bennett biographer, Margaret Drabble, Bennett had a particular affinity for *The Glimpse*, believing it among his best, and he claimed he was more like Loring than any of his other protagonists (Drabble 161–162).

7. Drabble claims that Bennett had been reading theosophist Annie Besant at the time (Drabble 161), and he may well have drawn on theosophical discourse for these conceptions, for example Annie Besant's *Theosophy and the New Psychology* (originally published in 1904 and reprinted in 1909), which engages extensively with Myersian dynamic psychology.

8. Other correspondences between Bennett's *The Glimpse* and Woolf's *Mrs. Dalloway* include Bennett's description of Bond Street where flags wave and "the wealth exceeds the space" (13).

9. This view would seem to echo Frederic Myers's claim that "the highest genius would thus be the completest *self-possession*, – the occupation and dominance of the whole organism by those profoundest elements of the self which act from the fullest knowledge, and in the wisest way" (*Human* II 193).

10. Myers's expansionist psychology, with its attempt to discover mankind's position in the Cosmos, "a moving system vaster than we know" (*Human* II 301), would certainly have held an appeal for Lawrence.

11. That anxiety surfaces in a 1915 letter Lawrence wrote to Lady Asquith: "You will be treating me as a sort of professional, directly, a mixture between a professor of psychology and a clairvoyant, a charlatan expert in psychiatry" (*Letters* II 335). Lawrence's association between the two "professions" completely aligns with the configuration of dynamic psychology.

12. According to P.T. Whelan, these discussions occurred at the Campbells' home where Lawrence and Frieda stayed between 24 June and 16 August 1914 and then when the Lawrences stayed at the Eders' home in January 1915 (Whelan 18).

13. Emile Delavenay dates Lawrence's "penchant for esoteric theories of consciousness" as early as 1908 (Emile Delavenay, *D.H. Lawrence and Edward Carpenter: A Study in Edwardian Transition*. London: Heinemann, 1971: 171).

14. Beresford also continued his associations with theosophy (Gerber, "Study" 35–36).

15. Richmond edited and introduced *Through a Stranger's Hands: New Evidence for Survival* (London: Hutchinson, 1935), as well as authoring other works. He collaborated with J.D. Beresford on *W.E. Ford* (1917), an experimental mock biography of a pioneering educationalist (Gerber, "Study" 29).

16. *New York Times*, 11 June 1911: 369.

17. Bergson's *Creative Evolution* and *Time and Free Will* are both directly cited in the novel (*Wonder* 236, 3).

18. *"Déclin"* 259. Given Beresford's strict definition of the psychoanalytic novel, this statement would appear to be accurate.

19. *God's* 296. The dream suggests, among other things, that Philip unconsciously realizes that both Evelyn and his mother have a sexual aspect and are not embodiments of the lofty ideals that he has made them out to be.

20. It may well have been inspired by Sinclair's diagnostic denouement in *The Romantic*, since Beresford admired Sinclair's courageous commitment to treating psychoanalytic themes (*"Déclin"* 263) and likely read her novel as the reader for Collins, who published it.

21. Beresford acknowledged the influence of Gide's notebooks (*Writing* 11–12), but these as well as others in this genre always lead up to the separate production of a novel, which Beresford's does not: his actual novel is contained within the pages of *Writing Aloud*.

6   "The Spirit of the Age": Virginia Woolf's response to dynamic psychology

1. Though excluded from the present discussion because of limitations of space, Woolf's early short stories, particularly "Kew Gardens" and "A Haunted House" also well illustrate Woolf's incorporation of dynamic psychology, particularly psychical discourse. See Johnson "Haunted".

2. *Times Literary Supplement*, 10 April 1919; Zegger 98.

3. Noel Annan, Stephen's biographer, claims that by the time his subject was twenty-eight, in 1860, "he had read Mill and Comte, Kant and his English adapter Sir William Hamilton, Hobbes and Locke, Berkeley and Hume and most of the main intellectual works of his day. . . ." (41).

4. This occurred through his work as historian of philosophy in *The History of English Thought in the Eighteenth Century* (1876, 1902) and *The English Utilitarians* (1900).

5. Annan 282. They had both resigned Cambridge fellowships because they could no longer adhere to orthodox religion, and together belonged to several select societies (Annan 277).

6. Sully's account of his friendships in his memoir, *My Life and Friends* (1918), reads like a list of Who's Who for the later Victorian Age. Not only did he know leading scientists, philosophers, psychologists, and psychical researchers such as Darwin, Huxley, Spencer, Sidgwick, G.H. Lewes, James Ward, William James, Edmund Gurney, and Frederic Myers, but he was also close to such literary figures as Robert Louis Stevenson, George Eliot, and George Meredith. In addition to his knowledge of evolution theory and psychology, he was gifted musically, was interested in aesthetics, had published short stories, and was an accomplished essayist.

7. Sully wrote these articles from 1875 to 1882, the year Stephen resigned as editor. Sully *My Life*, 298.

8. Stephen's interest in Sully's work also prompted him to go back and read Sully's first book, *Sensation and Intuition: Studies in Psychology and Aesthetics* (*My Life*, 299).

9. Maitland claims that this group, which included himself and the psychical researcher Edmund Gurney, "used to dine together and talk philosophy" (Maitland 363). Along with Sidgwick and Sully, Stephen also belonged to the Metaphysical Society, joining in 1877 (Maitland 362).

10. Sully shared with Myers the Secretaryship of the Second International Congress of Psychology, held in London in 1892.

11. Ellis claimed that he began writing on dreams in 1895 (Ellis, *World* vii).

12. In "Leslie Stephen, the Philosopher at Home: A Daughter's Memories", Woolf recalled with gratitude that her father allowed her "the free run of a large and quite unexpurgated library" when she was fifteen (*The Times*, Monday 28 November 1932: 16).

13. Woolf mentions the work of another American psychologist – John Dewey's *Psychology* (1886) – in her essay "Hours in a Library" (*Times Literary Supplement* 30 November 1916: 565–566; *Essays* II 55–61). Woolf may very well have read this work since she includes it in "a list of the books that someone read in a past January at the age of twenty" (*Essays* II 56), and we can speculate that this someone may well have been Woolf herself. Dewey's work contains sections on imagination and intuition, including intuition of God, and treats the Self as "a connecting, relating activity" (John Dewey, *Psychology* 1886. 3rd Edn. New York: Harper, 1891, 242).

14. Leonard Woolf wrote of "the historical psychology of an era" that helped condition personal relations at Cambridge, and he claimed that "the spiritual roots" of Bloomsbury were in Cambridge (L. Woolf *Sowing* 162).

15. Johnstone 20–45; Rosenbaum, *Victorian* 214–238. Leonard Woolf himself wrote that "The colour of our minds and thought had been given to us by the climate of Cambridge and Moore's philosophy" (as qtd in Levy 295).

16. These included her brothers Thoby and Adrian, her husband Leonard, Roger Fry, Lytton and James Strachey, and Saxon Sydney-Turner. We also know that Woolf read for herself Moore's *Principia Ethica* (*Letters* I 364), as well as McTaggart on mystical Hegelianism (*Letters* VI 6).

17. Leonard Woolf, *Letters of Leonard Woolf*, Ed. Frederic Spotts (London: Weidenfeld and Nicholson, 1990), 556.

18. Cambridge had become a centre for psychical research from the time of the founding of the SPR (1882), and psychical experiments had actually been carried out there in 1895 (Gauld, *Founders* 237).

19. Others include "Memory and the Individual" (16 April 1910: 618) and "The Meaning of Individuality" (3 November 1912: 710; Sanders 317–321).

20. She makes this clear in another essay (*Essays* III 324).

21. We do know that he read *The Interpretation of Dreams* in May, 1914, in preparation for the review (Bishop 29).

22. Neither Sue Thomas in "Virginia Woolf's Septimus Smith and Contemporary Perceptions of Shell Shock" nor Karen DeMeester in "Trauma and Recovery in Virginia Woolf's Mrs. Dalloway" mention this source.

23. *Mrs. Dalloway* 136. Clarissa also alludes to her theory of survival on page 10.

24. *Mrs. Dalloway* 70, 78. In Clarissa, this quality is manifested in her "virginity preserved through childbirth which clung to her like a sheet" and has caused her

to fail Richard, presumably sexually (*Mrs. Dalloway* 29). Peter Walsh refers to Clarissa's inability to feel as her woodenness and coldness (*Mrs. Dalloway* 55, 72).

7   Diving Deeper: Dynamic psychology and British literature

1. Grant Allen. *Strange Stories*. London: Chatto and Windus, 1884; Lytton Strachey. *The Really Interesting Question and Other Papers*. Ed. and Intro. Paul Levy. London: Weidenfeld and Nicolson, 1972: 111–120.
2. W.L. Myers also makes the point that what he calls extra-realism was not deemed proper subject matter for fiction. *The Later Realism*. Chicago: University of Chicago Press, 1927: 17.

Works Cited or Consulted

Abel, Elizabeth. *Virginia Woolf and the Fictions of Psychoanalysis*. Chicago: University of Chicago Press, 1989.

Adams, John. *The Herbartian Psychology Applied to Education*. Boston: Heath, 1898.

Adcock, A. St John. "John Davys Beresford", in *Gods of Modern Grub Street*. London: Sampson Low, Marston and Co., 1923.

Adler, Alfred. *The Neurotic Constitution; Outlines of a Comparative Individualistic Psychology and Psychotherapy*. Trans. B. Glueck and J. Lind. NY: Moffat, Yard, 1916–1917. London: Kegan Paul, 1918.

Alexander, Peter. "Introduction" to *Svengali. George Du Maurier's Trilby*. London: W.H. Allen, 1982.

Allen, Walter. *The English Novel*. 1954. New York: Dutton, 1958.

Annan, Noel. *Leslie Stephen. The Godless Victorian*. New York: Random House, 1984.

Arens, Katherine. *Structures of Knowing: Psychologies of the Nineteenth Century*. Boston Studies in the Philosophy of Science 113. Dordrecht: Kluwer, 1989.

Ashley, Mike. *Starlight Man. The Extraordinary Life of Algernon Blackwood*. London: Constable, 2001.

Banta, Martha. *Henry James and the Occult: The Great Extension*. Bloomington, Indiana University Press, 1972.

Barzun, Jacques. *A Stroll With William James*. New York: Harper and Row, 1983.

Beale, Dorothea. Preface. *The Application of Psychology to the Science of Education*. By Johann Friedrich Herbart. Trans. Beatrice C. Mulliner. New York: Scribner, 1891.

——. Letter to May Sinclair. 5 October 1897. Box 48, ms. May Sinclair Papers. University of Pennsylvania, Philadelphia.

Beer, Gillian. *Darwin's Plots. Evolutionary Narrative in Darwin, George Eliot and Nineteenth-Century Fiction*. 1983. Cambridge: Cambridge University Press, 2000.

Beharriell, Frederick J. "Freud and Literature", *Queen's Quarterly* 65 (1958): 118–125.

Bennett, Arnold. *The Ghost: A Fantasia on Modern Themes*. 1907. Toronto: Bell and Cockburn, n.d.

——. *The Glimpse. An Adventure of the Soul*. 1909. London: Chapman and Hall, 1912.

——. *Journals of Arnold Bennett*. 3 Vols Ed. Newman Flower. London: Cassell, 1932.

——. *Letters of Arnold Bennett. I Letters to J.B. Pinker*. Ed. James Hepburn. London: Oxford University Press, 1966.

Beresford, J.D. *The Early History of Jacob Stahl*. [Vol. I, *Jacob Stahl* trilogy]. London: Sidgwick and Jackson, 1911.

——. *A Candidate for Truth* [Vol. II, *Jacob Stahl* trilogy]. London: Sidgwick and Jackson, 1912.

——. "The Criminal", *English Review* XI (June 1912): 391–398.

——. "A Case of Prevision", *Forum* XLVIII (September 1912): 273–280.

——. "Introduction" to *Pointed Roofs* [Vol. I, *Pilgrimage*] by Dorothy Richardson. London: Duckworth, 1915, v–viii.

——. *The Invisible Event* [Vol. III, *Jacob Stahl* trilogy]. London: Sidgwick and Jackson, 1915.

——. *The Hampdenshire Wonder*. London: Sidgwick and Jackson, 1911; New York: G.H. Doran, 1917 [as *The Wonder*].

——. *Housemates*. London and New York: Cassell and Co., 1917.

——. *God's Counterpoint*. London: Collins, 1918.

——. "A New Form of Matter", *Harper's* CXXXVIII (May 1919): 803–810.

——. "Psychoanalysis and the Novel", *London Mercury* 2 (1919–1920): 426–434.

——. "The Crux of Psychical Research", Part I, *Westminster Gazette* (6 March 1920): 8; Part II, *ibid.* (13 March 1920): 8.

——. *An Imperfect Mother*. London: Collins, 1920.

——. *Revolution: A Story of the Near Future in England*. London: Collins, 1921.

——. "More New Facts in Psychical Research", *Harper's* CXLIV (March 1922): 475–482.

——. "The Psychical Researcher's Tale: The Sceptical Poltergeist", in *The New Decameron*, the 3rd Volume. Oxford: Basil Blackwell, 1922.

——. *Love's Pilgrim*. London: Collins, 1923.

——. "The Successors of Charles Dickens", *Nation and Athenaeum*, 34 (29 December 1923): 487–488.

——. "Unpleasant Fiction", *Bookman* (London), 68 (April 1925): 11.

——. "*Le déclin de l'influence de la psycho-analyses sur le roman anglais*", tr. par M. Vernon, *Mercure de France*, CXC (1 September 1926): 257–266.

——. "My Religion", *My Religion*, Essays by H. Walpole, R. West, J.D. Beresford, and others (Appleton and Co., NY, 1926): 55–61.

——. *Writing Aloud*. London: Collins, 1928.

——. "Experiment in the Novel", *Tradition and Experiment in Present-Day Literature, Addresses Delivered to the City Literary Institute by R.H. Mottram, J.D. Beresford, and others* (London: Oxford University Press, 1929): 25–53.

——. "The Discovery of the Self: An Essay in Religious Experience", *Aryan Path* (March 1931), 131–136; (April 1931), 237–243; (May 1931): 309–314.

——. *What I Believe*. I Believe, A Series of Personal Statements, No. 1, R. Ellis Roberts, ed. London: W. Heinemann, 1938.

——. *The Prisoner*. London: Hutchinson, 1946.

——. "Memories and Reflections", Unpublished ts. Collection of Jon Wynne-Tyson. Fontwell, Sussex.

Bergson, Henri. *Creative Evolution*. Trans. Arthur Mitchell. London: Macmillan, 1911.

——. *Laughter. An Essay on the Meaning of the Comic*. Trans. Cloudseley Brereton and Fred Rothwell. London: Macmillan, 1911.

——. *An Introduction to Metaphysics*. Trans. T.E. Hulme. New York: Putnam's, 1912.

——. *Matter and Memory*. Trans. Nancy Margaret Paul and W. Scott Palmer. London: George Allen and Co., 1913.

——. *Time and Free Will: An Essay on the Immediate Data of Consciousness*. 1889. Trans. F.L. Pogson. London: George Allen and Co., 1913.

Bernstein, Richard J. Introduction. *A Pluralistic Universe: Hibbert Lectures on the Present Situation in Philosophy*. 1909. By William James. Cambridge: Cambridge University Press, 1977.

Besant, Annie. *Theosophy and the New Psychology*. London and Benares: Theosophical Publishing Society, 1904.

Bird, Graham. *William James: The Arguments of the Philosophers*. London: Routledge and Kegan Paul, 1986.

Bishop, Edward. *A Virginia Woolf Chronology*. Boston: G.K. Hall, 1989.

Blackwood, Algernon. *The Centaur*. London: Macmillan, 1911.

——. *The Wave: An Egyptian Aftermath*. London: Macmillan, 1916.

——. *The Promise of Air*. London: Macmillan, 1918.

Blavatsky, H.P. *The Secret Doctorine: The Synthesis of Science, Religion and Philosophy.* 2 Vols. London: The Theosophical Pub. Co., 1888.

Boll, Theophilus. "On the May Sinclair Collection", *Library Chronicle*, XXVII (Winter 1961): 1–15.

———. "May Sinclair and the Medico-Psychological Clinic of London", *Proceedings of the American Philosophical Society*, CVI (August 1962): 310–326.

———. "May Sinclair: A Checklist", *Bulletin of the New York Public Library*, IXXIV (1970): 454–467.

———. *Miss May Sinclair: Novelist.* Rutherford, NJ: Fairleigh Dickinson U.P., 1973.

Boring, Edwin G. *A History of Experimental Psychology.* New York: D. Appleton-Century, 1929.

Boynton, H.W. "The Wonder", *Bookman* 45 (May 1917): 315.

Bramwell, J. Milne. "On the Evolution of Hypnotic Theory", *Brain* XIX (1896): 459–568.

Brewster, Dorothy and Angus Burrell. *Dead Reckonings in Fiction.* 1924. New York: Longmans, Green and Co., 1925.

Briggs, Julia. *Night Visitors: The Rise and Fall of the English Ghost Story.* London: Faber, 1977.

Brill, A.A. Introduction. *The Basic Writings of Sigmund Freud.* By Sigmund Freud. New York: The Modern Library, 1938.

Brivic, Sheldon. *Joyce Between Freud and Jung.* Port Washington: Kennikat, 1980.

Brome, Vincent. *Ernest Jones. Freud's Alter Ego.* New York, Norton, 1983.

———. *Havelock Ellis Philosopher of Sex. A Biography.* London: Routledge and Kegan Paul, 1979.

Brown, William. "Epistemological Difficulties in Psychology", *Proceedings of the Aristotelean Society* X (1909–1910): 63–76.

———. "Is Love a Disease?", *The Strand Magazine* (January 1912): 96–103.

———. "Dreams: The Latest Views of Science", *The Strand Magazine* (January 1913): 83–88.

———. "Psycho-analysis", *Report of the British Association for the Advancement of Science* 83 (1913): 688–689.

———. "Review of *Freud's Theory of Dreams*", *The Lancet* (19 April 1913): 1114–1118.

———. "Freud's Theory of the Unconscious", *British Journal of Psychology* VI Parts 3 and 4 (February 1914): 265–280.

———. "What is Psychoanalysis?", *Nature* 92 (5 February 1914): 643–644.

———. *Psychology and Psychotherapy.* London: Arnold, 1922.

———. "Psychology and Psychical Research", *Proceedings of the Society for Psychical Research* XLI (1932–1933) Part 127: 75–88.

Browning, Don S. *Pluralism and Personality. William James and Some Contemporary Cultures of Psychology.* Lewisburg: Bucknell University Press, 1980.

Butler, Samuel. *The Way of All Flesh.* 1903. London: Jonathan Cape, 1936.

Carr, H. Wildon. "The Philosophical Aspects of Freud's Dream Interpretation", *Mind* n.s. 91 (July 1914): 312–334.

Carus, Carl Gustav. *Psyche.* Pforzheim, 1846.

Cerullo, John J. *The Secularization of the Soul: Psychical Research in Modern Britain.* Philadelphia, 1982.

Chevalley, Abel. *The Modern English Novel.* 1924. New York: Haskell, 1973.

Clark, Michael J. "The Rejection of Psychological Approaches to Mental Disorder in Late Nineteenth-Century British Psychiatry", in *Madhouses, Mad-Doctors, and Madmen: The Social History of Psychiatry in the Victorian Era.* Ed. Andrew Scull. London and Philadelphia, 1981.

Clark, Ronald. *Freud: The Man and the Cause.* New York: Random House, 1980.

Clarke, J. Michell. "Hysteria and Neurasthenia", XVII *Brain* (1894): 119–136.

——. Review of Breuer and Freud's *Studien über Hysterie, Brain* XIX (1896): 401–414.

Colby, Robert A. *"The Mill on the Floss*: Maggie Tulliver and the Child of Nature", in *Fiction With a Purpose. Major and Minor Nineteenth-Century Novels*. Bloomington: Indiana University Press, 1967.

Collinson, Diane. *Fifty Major Philosophers. A Reference Guide*. London: Routledge, 1988.

Cooper, Frederic. *Some English Story Tellers: A Book of the Younger Novelists*. New York: Henry Holt, 1912.

Crabtree, Adam. *From Mesmer to Freud. Magnetic Sleep and the Roots of Psychological Healing*. New Haven: Yale, 1993.

Cunningham, Gustavus Watts. *A Study in the Philosophy of Bergson*. London: Longmans and Green, 1916.

Daugherty, Beth Rigel. "The Whole Contention Between Mr. Bennett and Mrs. Woolf, Revisited", in *Virginia Woolf: Centennial Essays*. Eds. Elaine K. Ginsberg and Laura Moss Gottlieb. Troy: Whitson, 1983.

Delavenay, Emile. "Early Approaches to D.H. Lawrence: Records of Meetings with Frieda Lawrence, Havelock Ellis, Barbara Low, Ada Lawrence-Clarke, and William Hopkin", *The D.H. Lawrence Review* 21 (3): 313–322.

DeMeester, Karen. "Trauma and Recovery in Virginia Woolf's Mrs. Dalloway", *Modern Fiction Studies* 44, 3 (Fall 1998): 649–673.

DeSalvo, Louise. *Virginia Woolf. The Impact of Childhood Sexual Abuse on Her Life and Work*. Boston: Beacon Press, 1989.

Dicks, Henry V. *Fifty Years of the Tavistock Clinic*. London: Routledge and Kegan Paul, 1970.

Drabble, Margaret. *Arnold Bennett. A Biography*. London: Weidenfeld and Nicolson, 1974.

Drinka, George. *The Birth of Neurosis. Myth, Malady, and the Victorians*. New York: Simon and Schuster, 1984.

Du Maurier, George. *Trilby* (3 vols) London: Osgood and McIlvaine, 1894.

Edel, Leon. *The Psychological Novel 1900–1950*. New York: Lippincott, 1955.

Eder, M.D. *The Endowment of Motherhood*. London: New Age Press, 1908.

——. "A Case of Obsession and Hysteria Treated by the Freud Psycho-Analytic Method", *British Medical Journal* (1911): 750.

——. "Freud's Theory of Dreams", *Transactions of the Psycho-Medical Society* 3 (1912): 1–20.

——. "Drs. And Dreams", *Daily Dispatch* (7 July 1913): 10.

——. "The Present Position of Psychoanalysis", *British Medical Journal* (8 November 1913): 1213–1215.

——. "Two Psychological Types", *Universal Medical Record* Vol. 5 (1914): 213–236.

——. "An Address on the Psycho-Pathology of the War Neuroses", *Lancet* 191 (1916): 264–268.

——. "Psychological Perspectives", *The New Age* XXIX 12 (20 July 1916): 284–285.

——. "The Psych-Pathology of the War Neuroses", *The Lancet* (12 August 1916): 264–268.

——. *War Shock: The Psycho-Neuroses in War: Psychology and Treatment*. London: Heinemann; Philadelphia: Blakiston, 1917.

——. *Memoirs of a Modern Pioneer*. Ed. J.B. Hobman. London: Victor Gollancz, 1945.

Edmund Gurney, *The Power of Sound*. 1880. New York: Basic Books, 1966.

Eliot, T.S. "London Letter: The Novel" [Review of Harriet Frean], *Dial* 73 (September 1922): 329–331.

Ellenberger, Henri. *The Discovery of the Unconscious. The History and Evolution of Dynamic Psychiatry*. New York: Basic Books, 1970.

Ellesley, Sandra. "Psychoanalysis in Early Twentieth-Century England: A Study in the Popularization of Ideas", Ph.D. Diss. University of Essex, 1995.

Ellis, Havelock. "Hysteria in Relation to Sexual Emotions", *Alienist and Neurologist* 19 (October, 1898): 599–615.

——. *The Evolution of Modesty, The Phenomena of Sexual Periodicity, Auto-Eroticism. Studies in the Psychology of Sex* (Vol. II). Leipzig: University Press, 1899.

——. *Studies in the Psychology of Sex*. 6 Vols. Philadelphia: F.A. Davis, 1899–1910.

——. "Review of Freud's *On Dreaming*", *Journal of Mental Science* 47 (1901): 370–371.

——. *A Study of British Genius*. London: Hurst and Blackett, 1904.

——. "Psychoanalysis in Relation to Sex", *Journal of Mental Science* 53 (1907): 351–352.

——. *The World of Dreams*. London: Constable, 1911.

Encyclopaedia Britannica. "Psychology", 9th Edn Vol. 20. Cambridge: Cambridge University Press, 1886.

Ferenczi, Sandor. *Further Contributions to the Theory and Technique of Psycho-Analysis*. 1926. London: Maresfield Reprints, 1980.

——. *Psycho-analysis and the War Neuroses*. London and Vienna: International Psycho Analytical Library, No. 2, 1921.

Fleishman, Avrom. "Virginia Woolf: Tradition and Modernity", in *Forms of Modern British Fiction*. Ed. Alan Warren Friedman. Austin: University of Texas Press, 1975.

Flugel, J.C. "Freudian Mechanisms as Factors in Moral Development", *British Journal of Psychology* 8 Part 4 (June 1917): 477–509.

——. "In Defence of Psycho-Analysis", *The Pall Mall Gazette* (7 January 1921).

——. *The Psychoanalytic Study of the Family*. London: International Psycho-Analytic Library, No. 3, 1921.

Forster, E.M. [Review of *Mary Olivier*] *Daily Herald* (30 July 1919): 8.

Forsyth, David. "On Psycho-Analysis", *British Medical Journal* No. 2740 (1913): 13–17.

——. "Functional Nerve Disease and the Shock of Battle", *The Lancet* (25 December 1915): 1399–1403.

Foucault, Michel. *The Archeology of Knowledge and the Discourse on Language*. New York: Pantheon Books, 1972.

Freud, Sigmund. *Selected Papers on Hysteria and Other Psychoneuroses*. Trans. A.A. Brill. New York: N.M.D.P., 1909.

——. *Three Contributions to the Sexual Theory*. Trans. A.A. Brill. Intro. J.J. Putnam. New York: N.M.D.P., 1910.

——. "A Note on the Unconscious in Psycho-analysis", *Proceedings of the Society for Psychical Research*. Part 66, 26 (1912): 312–318.

——. *On Dreams*. 1913. Trans. M.D. Eder. 2nd Edn. London: Rebman, 1914.

——. *The Psychopathology of Everyday Life*. New York: Macmillan; London: Fisher and Unwin, 1914.

——. *Wit and Its Relation to the Unconscious*. Trans. A.A. Brill. New York: Moffat and Yard, 1918; London: Routledge, 1919.

——. *The Interpretation of Dreams*. 1913. Trans. A.A. Brill. London: George Allen and Co.; New York: Macmillan, 1921.

——. *Collected Papers*. Vols I and II. London: Hogarth Press and the Institute of Psycho-Analysis, 1924.

——. "Dreams and the Occult", in *Psychoanalysis and the Occult*. Ed. George Devereux. New York: International Universities Press, 1953.

——. "The Uncanny", in *Art and Literature*. The Pelican Freud Library 14. Trans. James Strachey. Harmondsworth: Penguin, 1987.

——. Letters to Ernest Jones, Sigmund Freud Archive, Library of Congress. Washington, DC.

Frierson, William Coleman. *The English Novel in Transition 1885–1940*. Norman: University of Oklahoma Press, 1942.

"Future of the Novel", by various authors. *Pall Mall Gazette* (3 to 10 January 1921).

Galton, Francis. "Psychometric Experiments", *Brain* (July, 1879): 149–162.

Gauld, Alan. *The Founders of Psychical Research*. London: Routledge and Kegan Paul, 1968.

George, W.L. *A Novelist on Novels*. 1918. Port Washington, NY: Kennikat Press, 1970.

Gerber, Helmut E. "J.D. Beresford: A Study of His Works and Philosophy", Diss. University of Pennsylvania, 1952.

——. "J.D. Beresford: The Freudian Element", *Literature and Psychology* 6 (1956): 78–86.

Gibbons, Thomas. " 'Allotropic States' and 'Fiddle-bow': D.H. Lawrence's Occult Sources", *Notes and Queries* (September 1988): 338–341.

Gillies, Mary Ann. *Henri Bergson and British Modernism*. Montreal: McGill-Queen's, 1996.

Glicksberg, Charles I. "Literature and Freudianism", *Prairie Schooner* 23 (1949): 359–373.

Glover, Edward. "Eder as Psychoanalyst", in *David Eder. Memoirs of a Modern Pioneer*. Ed. J.B. Hobman. London: Victor Gollancz, 1945.

——. "Psychoanalysis in England", in *Psychoanalytic Pioneers*. Eds. Franz Alexander, Samuel Eisenstein, *et al*. New York: Basic Books, 1966.

Goldstein, Jan E. "The Woolfs' Response to Freud: Water Spiders, Singing Canaries and the Second Apple", *Psychoanalytic Quarterly* 43:3 (1974): 438–476.

Gould, Gerald. *The English Novel of To-Day*. 1924. New York: Books for Libraries Press, 1971.

Green, Thomas Hill. *Prolegomena to Ethics*. Ed. A.C. Bradley. Oxford: Clarendon Press, 1873.

——. *The Works of Thomas Hill Green*. Vol. III. London: Longmans, Green, 1888.

Grosskurth, Phyllis. *Havelock Ellis. A Biography*. Toronto: McClelland and Stewart, 1980.

Guiget, Jean. *Virginia Woolf and Her Works*. New York: Harcourt, Brace, Jovanovich, 1965.

Gurney, Edmund, Frederic W.H. Myers, and Frank Podmore, *Phantasms of the Living*. 1886. 2 Vols. Gainesville, Florida: Scholars' Facsimiles and Reprints, 1970.

Guttman, Samuel A., Jones, Randall L. and Parrish, Stephen M. *A Concordance to the Standard Edition of the Complete Psychological Works of Sigmund Freud*. 6 Vols. Boston: G.K. Hall, 1980.

Haanel, Charles F. *The New Psychology*. Saint Louis: MO, 1924.

Haeckel, Ernst Heinrich. *History of Creation*. New York: D. Appleton, 1876.

——. *The Riddle of the Universe at the Close of the Nineteenth Century*. [n.p.]: Rationalist Press Association, Watts Co., 1900.

Hall, Trevor. *The Strange Case of Edmund Gurney*. London: Duckworth, 1980.

Hart, Bernard. "A Philosophy of Psychiatry", *Journal of Mental Science* 54 (July 1908): 473–490.

——. "The Conception of the Subconscious", *Journal of Abnormal Psychology* 4 (February 1910): 351–371.

——. "The Psychology of Freud and his School", *The Journal of Mental Science* 56 (1910): 431–452.

——. "Freud's Conception of Hysteria", *Brain* XXXIII (1911): 338–366.

——. *The Psychology of Insanity*. Cambridge: Cambridge University Press, 1912.

Hartmann, Eduard von. *Philosophy of the Unconscious*. Berlin: Duncker, 1869.

Haynes, Renée. *The Society for Psychical Research 1882–1982: A History*. London: Macdonald, 1982.

Heaps, Jane. (1919). "Eat 'em Alive!", *Little Review* VI (December): 30–32.

Hearnshaw, L.S. *A Short History of British Psychology 1840–1940*. New York: Barnes and Noble, 1964.

———. *The Shaping of Modern Psychology*. London: Routledge and Kegan Paul, 1987.

Heilmann, Ann. "Narrating the Hysteric: *Fin-de-Siècle* Medical Discourse and Sarah Grand's *The Heavenly Twins*", in *The New Woman in Fiction and Fact: Fin-de-Siècle Feminisms*. New York: Palgrave, 2001, 122–135.

Herbart, Johann F. *A Text-book in Psychology*. 1816. New York: Appleton, 1896.

Hewitt, Douglas. *English Fiction of the Early Modern Period 1890–1940*. London: Longman, 1988.

Hill, Katherine C. "Virginia Woolf and Leslie Stephen: History and Literary Revolution", *PMLA* 96 (1981): 351–362.

Hinshelwood, R.D. "Psychoanalysis in Britain: Points of Cultural Access, 1893–1918", *International Journal of Psychoanalysis*, 76 (February 1995): 135–151.

Hoffman, Frederick J. *Freudianism and the Literary Mind*. 1945. Baton Rouge: Louisiana State University Press, 1957.

Holleyman, G.A., comp. *Catalogue of Books from the Library of Leonard and Virginia Woolf Taken From Monks House, Rodmell, Sussex and 24 Victoria Square, London and Now in the Possession of Washington State University, Pullman, U.S.A.* Brighton: Holleyman and Treacher, 1975.

Holroyd, Michael. *Lytton Strachey. A Critical Biography*. 2 Vols. New York: Holt, Rinehart and Winston, 1968.

Holt, E.B. "William James as a Psychologist", in *In Commemoration of William James 1842–1942*. Eds. Brand Blanshard and Herbert W. Schneider. New York, 1942. 34–47.

Holt, L.E. "Samuel Butler's Rise to Fame", *PMLA* 57 (1942): 867–878.

Hoops, Reinald. *Der Einfluss der Psychoanalyse auf die Englische Literatur*. Heidelberg: C. Winter, 1934.

Hudson, T.J. *The Law of Psychic Phenomena*. London: G.P. Putnam's Sons, 1893.

Huxley, Aldous. *Crome Yellow*. 1921. London: Penguin Books, 1936.

———. *Ends and Means*. London: Chatto and Windus, 1937.

———. Foreword. *Human Personality and Its Survival of Bodily Death*. By F.W.H. Myers. Ed. Susy Smith. New York: University Books, 1961.

Inglis, Brian. *Natural and Supernatural. A History of the Paranormal From Earliest Times to 1914*. London: Abacus, 1979.

Isaacs, J. *An Assessment of Twentieth-Century Literature*. London: Secker and Warburg, 1952.

James, Henry. *The Art of the Novel. Critical Prefaces*. New York: Charles Scribner's, 1934.

James, William. "Review of Janet, Breuer and Freud, and Whipple", *Psychological Review* 1 (1894): 195–200.

———. *The Varieties of Religious Experience: A Study in Human Nature*. New York: Longmans, Green and Co., 1902.

———. Letter to May Sinclair. Box 55, May Sinclair Papers. University of Pennsylvania: Philadelphia, 1908.

———. *A Pluralistic Universe: Hibbert Lectures on the Present Situation in Philosophy*. New York: Longmans, Green and Co., 1909.

———. *Pragmatism*. New York: Longmans Green, 1911.

——. *The Letters of William James*. Ed. Henry James. Boston: Atlantic Monthly Press, 1920.

——. *The Principles of Psychology*. 2 vols. 1890. New York: Dover, 1950.

——. *The Will to Believe and Other Essays in Popular Philosophy. Human Immortality*. New York: Dover, 1956.

——. "Frederic Myers's Service To Psychology", *Proceedings of the Society for Psychical Research* (London), Vol. XVII, Part XLII, May 1901. Reprinted in *William James on Psychical Research*. 1960. Eds. Gardner Murphy and Robert O. Ballou. Clifton: Augustus M. Kelley, 1973.

——. Review of "Human Personality and Its Survival of Bodily Death", *Proceedings of the Society for Psychical Research* (London), Vol. XVIII, Part XLVI, June 1903. Reprinted in *William James on Psychical Research*. 1960. Eds. Gardner Murphy and Robert O. Ballou. Clifton: Augustus M. Kelley, 1973.

Janet, Pierre. *L'Automatisme Psychologique*. 1889. Trans. Caroline R. Corson. New York and London: G.P. Putnam's, 1901.

——. "Psycho-analysis", *XVIIth International Congress of Medicine*, London, 1913. Section XII, 13–64.

——. *Psychological Healing: A Historical and Clinical Study*. 2 Vols. Trans. Eden and Cedar Paul. London: G. Allen and Unwin, 1925.

——. *Principles of Psychotherapy*. London: Allen and Unwin, 1925.

——. État Mental des Hysteriques [*The Mental State of Hystericals*]. 1892. Trans. Caroline R. Corson. New York: G.P. Putnam's, 1901. Rptd. and Ed. Daniel N. Robinson. Washington: University Publications of America, 1977.

Jauss, Hans R. "Literary History as a Challenge to Literary Theory", *Twentieth-Century Literary Theory: A Reader*, K.M. Newton, Ed. New York: St Martin's, 1997, 189–194.

Johnson, Ellwood. "William James and the Art of Fiction", *Journal of Aesthetics and Art Criticism* (1972) 30: 285–296.

Johnson, George M. " 'The Spirit of the Age': Virginia Woolf's Response to Second Wave Psychology", *Twentieth Century Literature* 40.2 (Fall 1994): 139–164.

——. "A Haunted House: Ghostly Presences in Virginia Woolf's Essays and Early Fiction", in *Virginia Woolf and the Essay*. Eds. Jeanne Dubino and Beth C. Rosenberg. New York: St Martin's Press, 1997.

——. *J.D. Beresford*. New York: Twayne/Simon and Schuster, 1998.

——. "May Sinclair: The Evolution of a Psychological Novelist", in *Literature and Psychoanalysis*. Ed. Frederico Pereira. Lisbon, Portugal: Instituto Superior de Psicologia Aplicada, 1998.

Johnson, R. Brimley. *Some Contemporary Novelists (Women)*. New York: Leonard Parsons, 1920.

——. "J.D. Beresford" in *Some Contemporary Novelists (Men)*. 1922. Freeport, New York: Books For Libraries Press, 1970.

Johnstone, J.K. *The Bloomsbury Group: A Study of E.M. Forster, Lytton Strachey, Virginia Woolf, and their Circle*. London: Secker and Warburg, 1954.

Jones, Ernest. "Review of Freud's *Studies on Hysteria*", *Review of Neurology and Psychiatry* 8: 2 (1910): 129–130.

——. *Collected Papers on Psychoanalysis*. London: Bailliere, Tindall and Cox, 1913.

——. "The Repression Theory in its Relation to Memory", *British Journal of Psychology* VIII Part I (October 1915): 33–47.

——, M. Nicoll, W.H.R. Rivers. "Why is the 'Unconscious' Unconscious?" (Contributions to a Symposium), *British Journal of Psychology* IX Part 2 (October 1918): 247–256.

——. "The Theory of Symbolism", *British Journal of Psychology* IX Part 2 (1918): 181–229.

——. Obituary of M.D. Eder. *International Journal of Psychoanalysis* XVII (April 1936): 143–146.

——. "Reminiscent Notes on the Early History of Psychoanalysis in English-Speaking Countries", *International Journal of Psychoanalysis* XXVI (1945): 8–10.

——. "The Early History of Psychoanalysis", *Journal of Mental Science* 100 (January 1954): 198–210.

——. Obituary of J.C. Flugel. *International Journal of Psychoanalysis* XXXVII (1956): 193–194.

——. *Sigmund Freud: Life and Work*. 3 Vols. London: Hogarth, 1955, 1956, 1957.

——. *Free Associations. Memories of a Psycho-analyst*. New York: Basic Books, 1959.

Joyce, James. *A Portrait of the Artist as a Young Man*. Ed. Chester G. Anderson. Harmondsworth: Penguin, 1968.

Jung, Carl G. "The Importance of the Unconscious in Psychopathology", *Lancet* II (5 September 1914).

——. "Psycho-analysis", A Paper Read Before the Psycho-Medical Society, London, 5 August 1913. *Transactions of the Psycho-Medical Society* 4, Part 2. Cockermouth: Brash Bros., 1913; *Psychoanalytic Review* 2 (1915): 241–259.

——. *Theory of Psychoanalysis*. New York: The Journal of Nervous and Mental Disease Pub. Co., 1915.

——. *Collected Papers on Analytical Psychology*. Trans. Constance E. Long. London: Bailliere, Tindall and Cox; New York: Moffat Yard and Co., 1916.

——. *The Psychology of the Unconscious*. Trans. Beatrice M. Hinkle. London: Kegan Paul, 1916.

——. "The Psychological Foundations of Beliefs in Spirits", *Proceedings of the Society for Psychical Research* 31 (1921): 75–93.

——. "On the Relation of Analytic Psychology to Poetic Art", *British Journal of Medical Psychology* 3 (1923): 213–231.

——. *Psychological Types*. Trans. H.G. Baynes. London: Kegan Paul; New York: Harcourt, Brace, 1923.

——. *The Psychology of Dementia Praecox*. 1909. Trans. R.F.C. Hull. Princeton: Princeton University Press, 1974.

Kantor, James. "Jamesian Psychology and the Stream of Psychological Thought", in *In Commemoration of William James 1842–1942*. Eds. Brand Blanshard and Herbert W. Schneider. New York, 1942, 143–156.

Keats, Gwendolyn "Zack". Letters to May Sinclair. February 1898–November 1903. Box 55, ms. May Sinclair Papers. University of Pennsylvania, Philadelphia.

Keeley, James P. "Subliminal Promptings: Psychoanalytical Theory and the Society for Psychical Research", *American Imago: Studies in Psychoanalysis and Culture* 58, 4 (2001): 767–791.

Kenney, Edwin J. "The Moment, 1910: Virginia Woolf, Arnold Bennett, and Turn of the Century Consciousness", *Colby Library Quarterly* 13 (January 1977): 42–66.

Kiell, Norman. *Freud Without Hindsight. Reviews of His Work (1893–1939)*. Madison, Connecticut: International Universities Press, 1988.

Kitchin, Darcy B. *Bergson For Beginners. A Summary of His Philosophy*. London: George Allen and Co., 1913.

Kolakowski, Leszek. *Bergson*. Oxford: Oxford University Press, 1985.

Kuhn, Thomas S. *The Structure of Scientific Revolutions*. 2nd Edn *International Encyclopedia of Unified Science* Vol. 2, No. 2. Chicago: University of Chicago Press, 1970.

Kumar, Shiv. *Bergson and the Stream of Consciousness Novel*. London: Blackie, 1962.

Kuttner, Alfred Booth. " 'Sons and Lovers': A Freudian Appreciation", *Psychoanalytic Review* III (1916): 295–317.

Lawrence, D.H. *The Lost Girl*. London: Martin Secker, 1920.

——. *Studies in Classic American Literature*. New York: Seltzer, 1923.

——. *Fantasia of the Unconscious*. 1922. London: Secker, 1930.

——. "Psychoanalysis and the Unconscious", in *Psychoanalysis and the Unconscious and Fantasia of the Unconscious*. Intro. Philip Rieff. New York: Viking, 1971.

——. *The Letters of D.H. Lawrence*. Eds. George J. Zytaruk and James T. Boulton. Vol. II 1913–1916. Cambridge: Cambridge University Press, 1981.

——. *Sons and Lovers*. Eds. and Intro. Helen and Carl Baron. London: Penguin, 1994.

——. *Women in Love*. Eds. David Farmer, Lindeth Vasey, and John Worthen. Penguin: London, 2000.

Leacock, Stephen. "The Human Mind Up to Date", in *The Garden of Folly*. Toronto: Gundy, 1924.

Le Roy, Edouard. *A New Philosophy. Henri Bergson*. Trans. Vincent Benson. London: Williams and Norgate, 1913.

Levy, Paul. *Moore. G.E. Moore and the Cambridge Apostles*. London: Weidenfeld and Nicolson, 1979.

Lewes, George Henry. *The Physiology of Common Life*. Vol. II. Edinburgh: William Blackwood, 1860.

Long, Constance. "Psycho-Analysis", *The Practitioner* 93, No. 1 (July 1914): 84–97.

Low, Barbara. *Psycho-analysis: A Brief Account of the Freudian Theory*. London: Allen and Unwin, 1920.

Luckhurst, Roger. *The Invention of Telepathy*. Oxford: Oxford University Press, 2002.

Macaulay, Rose. *Dangerous Ages*. London: Collins, 1921.

Mackenzie, W. Leslie. "Introduction" to *On Dreams* by Sigmund Freud. Trans. David Eder. London: William Heinemann, 1914.

Mahoney, Patrick J. *Freud as a Writer*. Missouri: International Universities Press, 1987.

Maitland, Frederic W. *The Life and Times of Leslie Stephen*. London: Duckworth and Co., 1906.

Mansfield, Katherine. "Two Modern Novels", in *Novels and Novelists*. 1930. Ed. J. Middleton Murry. Boston: Beacon Press, 1959, 170–173.

Marcus, Steven. *Freud and the Culture of Psychoanalysis. Studies in the Transition from Victorian Humanism to Modernity*. Boston: George Allen and Unwin, 1984.

Maudsley, Henry. *The Physiology and Pathology of Mind*. London: Macmillan, 1867.

——. *Body and Mind*. London: Macmillan, 1870.

May, Keith M. *Out of the Maelstrom: Psychology and the Novel in the Twentieth Century*. London: Paul Elek, 1977.

McDougall, William. "Critical Notices: *Human Personality and Its Survival of Bodily Death*", *Mind*, New Series, 12 (October 1903): 520, 524–526.

——. *An Introduction to Social Psychology*. 1908. Boston: John W. Luce and Co., 1910.

——. *Body and Mind. A History and Defence of Animism*. London: Methuen, 1911.

——. *Psychology: The Study of Behaviour*. London: Williams and Norgate [1912].

——. *An Outline of Psychology*. London: Methuen, 1923.

——. *The Energies of Men. A Study of the Fundamentals of Dynamic Psychology*. London: Methuen, 1932.

——. *Psycho-analysis and Social Psychology*. London: Methuen, 1936.

——. Autobiography. *A History of Psychology*. 1930. Vol. 1. Ed. Murchison. New York: Russell and Russell, 1961.

———. "In Memory of William James", *William McDougall: Explorer of the Mind. Studies in Psychical Research*. Comp. and Eds. Raymond Van Over and Laura Oteri. New York: Helix, 1967.

McLaurin, Allen. "Consciousness and Group Consciousness in Virginia Woolf", in *Virginia Woolf: A Centenary Perspective*. Ed. Eric Warner. London: Macmillan, 1984, 28–40.

Meisel, Perry. *The Absent Father: Virginia Woolf and Walter Pater*. London: Yale University Press, 1980.

Meisel, Perry and Walter Kendrick, eds. *Bloomsbury/Freud. The Letters of James and Alix Strachey 1924–25*. New York: Basic, 1985.

Miller, Jane Eldridge. "New Wine, New Bottles: H.G. Wells and May Sinclair", in *Rebel Women: Feminism, Modernism and the Edwardian Novel*. London: Virago, 1994, 163–202.

Miller, Jonathan, ed. *Freud. The Man, His World, His Influence*. London: Weidenfeld and Nicolson, 1972.

———. "Some Recent Developments in Psychotherapy", *Proceedings of the Society for Psychical Research* XXIV, Part LXI (1910): 665–686.

———. "Some Types of Multiple Personality", *Proceedings of the Society for Psychical Research* 26, Part 66 (1912): 257–285.

———. "A Study in Hysteria and Multiple Personality, with Report of a Case", *Proceedings of the Society for Psychical Research* 26, Part 66 (1912): 286–311.

———. Review of *Dream Psychology*, by Maurice Nicoll. *Journal of the Society for Psychical Research* XVII (October–November 1917): 103–104.

———. "Psychology of the Unconscious and Psychoanalysis", *Proceedings of the Society for Psychical Research* XXX, Part LXXV (1918): 134–173.

———. *Medical Psychology and Psychical Research*. London: Methuen, 1922.

Mitchell, T.W. *Beneath the Threshold*. London: Methuen, 1931.

———. "The Contributions of Psychical Research to Psychotherapeutics", *Proceedings of the Society for Psychical Research* Part 157 (1938–1939): 175–186.

———. Review of *Collected Papers on Analytic Psychology*, by Carl G. Jung. *Proceedings of the Society for Psychical Research* XXIX.

Mordaunt, Elinor. *Before Midnight*. London: Cassell, 1917.

Mordell, Albert. *The Erotic Motive in Literature*. New York: Boni and Liveright, 1919.

Morris, Lloyd. *William James The Message of a Modern Mind*. 1950. New York: Greenwood Press, 1969.

Myers, Frederic W.H. "Multiplex Personality", *Nineteenth Century* (20 November 1886): 648.

———. "The Principles of Psychology", Review of William James's *The Principles of Psychology*. *Proceedings of the Society for Psychical Research* VII (1891): 111–133.

———. "Subliminal Consciousness", *Proceedings of the Society for Psychical Research* VII (1892): 298–355.

———. "The Mechanism of Hysteria", *Proceedings of the Society for Psychical Research* 9 (June 1893): 3–25.

———. "Hysteria and Genius", *Journal of the Society for Psychical Research* (April 1897): 51–59.

———. *Human Personality and Its Survival of Bodily Death*. 2 Vols. New York: Longmans, Green, 1903.

Myers, Gerald E. *William James: His Life and Thought*. New Haven: Yale University Press, 1986.

Nicoll, Maurice. *Dream Psychology*. Oxford: Oxford Medical Publications, 1917.

Oppenheim, Janet. *The Other World: Spiritualism and Psychical Research in England, 1850–1914.* Cambridge: University Press, 1985.

Orr, Douglass W. "Virginia Woolf and Psychoanalysis", *International Review of Psycho-Analysis* 16 (1989): 151–161.

Pear, T.H. "The Analysis of Some Personal Dreams with Reference to Freud's Theory of Dream Interpretation", *British Journal of Psychology* Vol. VI Parts Three and Four (February 1914): 281–303.

Penzoldt, Peter. *The Supernatural in Fiction.* London: Peter Nevill, 1952.

Perry, Ralph Barton. *Present Philosophical Tendencies.* 1912. New York: Longmans, Green and Co., 1921.

Pykett, Lyn. "Writing Around Modernism: May Sinclair and Rebecca West", in L. Hapgood and N. Paxton (eds.), *Outside Modernism: In Pursuit of the English Novel, 1900–30.* London: Macmillan, 2000.

Raitt, Suzanne. *May Sinclair. A Modern Victorian.* Oxford: Clarendon, 2000.

Rao, Ayyagari Lakshmana. *Metaphysical Psychology of Henry Bergson A Critical Study.* Waltair: Andra University Press, 1971.

Rapp, Dean. "The Reception of Freud by the British Press: General Interest and Literary Magazines, 1920–1925", *Journal of the History of the Behavioural Sciences* 24 (April 1988), 191–201.

———. "The Early Discovery of Freud by the British General Educated Public, 1912–1919", *Journal of the Society for the Social History of Medicine* 3 (August 1990): 217–243.

Ribot, Theodule. *Heredity: A Psychological Study of its Phenomena, Laws, Causes and Consequences. [L'heredite Psychologique.* 1873]. London: H.S. King, 1875.

Rickman, John. Obituary of William Henry Butler Stoddart. *International Journal of Psychoanalysis* 30 (1950): 286–288.

Rivers, W.H.R. "Freud's Psychology of the Unconscious", *The Lancet* (16 June 1917): 912–914.

Roazen, Paul. *Freud and His Followers.* New York: New American Library, 1976.

Roback, A.A. and William James. *His Marginalia, Personality and Contribution.* Cambridge: Sci- Art Pub., 1942, 82–90.

Robb, Kenneth A. "May Sinclair: An Annotated Bibliography of Writings About Her", *English Literature in Transition,* Vol. 16, No. 3 (1973): 117–231.

Roberts, Harry. "Social and Medical Pioneer", in *David Eder. Memoirs of a Modern Pioneer.* Ed. J.B. Hobman. London: Victor Gollancz, 1945.

Roberts, R. Ellis. "Miss Sinclair Among the Ghosts", *The Bookman* (London, October 1923): 32–33.

Rose, Jonathan. *The Edwardian Temperament. 1895–1919.* Athens, Ohio: Ohio University Press, 1986.

Rosenbaum, S.P. "An Educated Man's Daughter: Leslie Stephen, Virginia Woolf and the Bloomsbury Group", in *Virginia Woolf: New Critical Essays.* Eds. Patricia Clements and Isobel Grundy. London: Vision Press, 1983.

———. "Virginia Woolf and the Intellectual Origins of Bloomsbury", in *Virginia Woolf: Centennial Essays.* Eds. Elaine K. Ginsburg and Laura Moss Gottlieb. Troy, NY: Whitson Pub. Co., 1983.

———. *Victorian Bloomsbury: The Early Literary History of the Bloomsbury Group.* New York: Methuen, 1987.

Routh, H.V. *English Literature and Ideas in the Twentieth Century.* 1946. New York: Russell and Russell, 1970.

Russell, Bertrand. Review of May Sinclair's *New Idealism. Nation and Athenaeum* 31 (5 August 1922): 625.

Ryan, Judith. *The Vanishing Subject: Early Psychology and Literary Modernism*. Chicago: University of Chicago Press, 1991.

Sand, Rosemarie. "Early Nineteenth Century Anticipation of Freudian Theory", *International Review of Psycho-analysis* 15 (1988): 465–479.

Sanders, Charles R. *The Strachey Family 1588–1932. Their Writings and Literary Associations*. 1953. New York: Greenwood, 1968.

Scarborough, Dorothy. *The Supernatural in Modern English Fiction*. 1917. New York: Octagon, 1967.

Schneider, Daniel J. *D.H. Lawrence. The Artist as Psychologist*. Kansas: University Press of Kansas, 1984.

Schwegler, Albert. *The History of Philosophy*. New York: D. Appleton and Co., 1889.

Scott-James. R.A. *Modernism and Romance*. London: John Lane, The Bodley Head, 1908.

Scripture, E.W. *The New Psychology*. In *The Contemporary Science Series*. Ed. Havelock Ellis. London: Walter Scott Pub., 1905.

Seventeenth International Congress of Medicine. Section 12, Parts 1 and 2. London: Henry Frowde, 1913.

Shaw, George Bernard. *Saint Joan: A Chronicle Play in Six Scenes and An Epilogue*. London: Constable, 1924.

Shepard, Leslie A. *Encyclopedia of Occultism and Para-psychology*. Vol. 1. 2nd Edn. Detroit: Gale, 1984.

Shuttle Worth, Sally. *George Eliot and Nineteenth Century Science: The Make-Believe of a Beginning*. Cambridge: Cambridge University Press, 1984.

——. *Charlotte Bronte and Victorian Psychology*. Cambridge: Cambridge University Press, 1996.

Sidgwick, Henry. "The Philosophy of T.H. Green", *Mind* New Series X (1901): 18–29.

——. *Miscellaneous Essays and Addresses*. London: Macmillan, 1904.

Silver, Brenda R. *Virginia Woolf's Reading Notebooks*. Princeton, New Jersey: Princeton University Press, 1983.

Sinclair, May. "Descartes", *Cheltenham Ladies College Magazine*. No. 5 (Spring 1882).

——. "The Ethical and Religious Import of Idealism", *The New World* 2 (December 1893): 694–708.

——. Review of Mary Pulling's *The Teacher's Textbook of Practical Psychology*. *Cheltenham Ladies College Magazine*. No. 33 (Spring 1896): 71–72.

——. Letters to Katherine Tynan. 1901–1926. Katherine Tynan Papers. John Rylands University Library, Manchester, England.

——. *Two Sides of a Question*. New York: J.F. Taylor, 1901.

——. Notes on Freud's *Drei Abhandlungen Zur Sexualtheorie* (1905). Box 37. Sinclair Papers. University of Pennsylvania, Philadelphia.

——. *Audrey Craven*. 1897. New York: Henry Holt, 1906.

——. *The Divine Fire*. 1904. New York: Burt, 1906.

——. *Mr. and Mrs. Nevill Tyson*. 1898. [Published in America as *The Tysons*.] New York: Grosset and Dunlop, 1906.

——. *The Helpmate*. London: Hutchinson, 1907.

——. *The Creators a Comedy*. New York: Century, 1910.

——. "The Flaw in the Crystal", *English Review* 11 (May 1912): 189–228; pub. as *The Flaw in the Crystal*. New York: Dutton, 1912; repr. in *Uncanny Stories*.

——. Letter to the Editor, *New York Times* (4 November 1912) [On "The Flaw in the Crystal"]. Sinclair Papers. University of Pennsylvania, Philadelphia.

——. *The Combined Maze*. London: Hutchinson, 1913.

——. *The Judgement of Eve and Other Stories*. London: Hutchinson, 1914.

——. "From a Journal", *English Review* 20 (May–July 1915): 168–183, 303–314, 468–476.

——. *A Journal of Impressions in Belgium*. London: Hutchinson, 1915.

——. *The Three Sisters*. 1914. New York: Macmillan, 1915.

——. "Symbolism and Sublimation I", *Medical Press and Circular* 153 (9 August 1916): 118–122.

——. "Symbolism and Sublimation II", *Medical Press and Circular* 153 (16 August 1916): 142–145.

——. *Tasker Jevons: The Real Story*. London: Hutchinson, 1916.

——. Letter, "To the Editor of the *Journal* of the S.P.R. April 26 1917", *Journal of the Society for Psychical Research* XVIII (May–June 1917): 67–68.

——. "The Spirits, Some Simpletons, and Dr. Charles Mercier", Review of Charles A. Mercier, Spiritualism and Sir Oliver Lodge. *Medical Press* (25 July 1917): 60–61.

——. *A Defence of Idealism: Some Questions and Conclusions*. London: Macmillan, 1917.

——. Letter, "To the Editor of the *Journal* of the S.P.R. Jan. 14 1918", *Journal of the Society for Psychical Research* (February–March 1918): 147–149.

——. "The Novels of Dorothy Richardson", *The Little Review* 5 (April 1918): 3–11.

——. *The Romantic*. New York: Macmillan, 1920.

——. "The Future of the Novel", *Pall Mall Gazette* (10 January 1921): 7.

——. *Mr. Waddington of Wyck*. London: Cassell, 1921.

——. *Anne Severn and the Fieldings*. New York: Macmillan, 1922.

——. *Life and Death of Harriet Frean*. New York: Macmillan, 1922.

——. *The New Idealism*. London: Macmillan, 1922.

——. "Primary and Secondary Consciousness", *Proceedings* of the Aristotealian Society, New Series, 23, No. 7 (1923): 111–120.

——. *Arnold Waterlow: A Life*. London: Hutchinson, 1924.

——. *A cure of Souls*. London: Hutchinson, 1924.

——. *The Allinghams*. London: Hutchinson, 1927.

——. *The Tree of Heaven*. 1917. New York: Macmillan, 1928.

——. "Between the Lines", *Harper's Magazine* 124 (December 1911) 28–41; repr. in *Tales Told By Simpson*. London: Hutchinson, 1930.

——. "The Intercessor", *English Review* 8 (July 1911): 569–601; repr. as "The Intercession: a Novel," *Two Worlds* (September 1926); repr. in *The Intercessor and Other Stories*. New York: Macmillan, 1932.

——. *Mary Olivier*. 1919. Toronto: Lester and Orpen Denys, 1982.

——. "The Way of Sublimation", Box 28, ts. Sinclair Papers. University of Pennsylvania.

——. Workbook, series three, No. 44, Box 37, ms. May Sinclair Papers. University of Pennsylvania, Philadelphia.

Slobodin, Richard. *W.H.R. Rivers*. New York: Columbia University Press, 1978.

Spencer, Herbert. *First Principles*. New York: Lovell, Coryell and Co., 1880.

——. *Principles of Biology*. New York: D. Appleton and Co., 1910.

——. *Principles of Psychology*. New York: D. Appleton and Co., 1910.

Spotts, Frederic, Ed. *The Letters of Leonard Woolf*. London: Bloomsbury, 1992.

Stableford, Brian. "*The Hampdenshire Wonder*", in *Survey of Science Fiction*. Ed. Frank W. Magill. Vol. 2. Salem: Englewood, 1979.

Stamirowska, K. "Virginia Woolf's Concept of Reality and Some Theories of Her Time", *Kwartalnik Neofilologiczny* 22 (1975): 207–217.

Steele, Elizabeth. *Virginia Woolf's Literary Sources and Allusions. A Guide to the Essays*. New York: Garland, 1983.

Steell, Willis. "May Sinclair Tells Why She Isn't a Poet", *Literary Digest International Book Review* II (June 1924): 513, 559.

Stephen, Adrian. "The Science of the Unconscious", *The Nation and the Athenaeum* Vol. 33, No. 21 (1923): 664–665.

Stephen, Karin. *The Misuse of Mind. A Study of Bergson's Attack on Intellectualism.* New York: Harcourt, Brace and Co., 1922.

Stephen, Leslie. "Henry Sidgwick", *Mind* New Series X (1901): 1–17.

Stoddart, W.H.B. "The Morrison Lectures on the New Psychiatry", *Lancet* I (1915): 583–590.

Stout, G.F. "The Herbartian Psychology (I)", *Mind* 13 (July 1888): 321–338.

——. "The Herbartian Psychology (II)", *Mind* 13 (October 1888): 473–498.

——. "Herbart Compared With English Psychologists and With Benecke", *Mind* 14 (January 1889): 1–26.

Strachey, James. Letters to Lytton Strachey. Strachey Papers. British Library. London, England.

Strachey, Lytton. Letters to James Strachey. Strachey Papers. British Library. London, England.

Sully, James. *Sensation and Intuition: Studies in Psychology and Aesthetics.* London: King, 1874.

——. "The Laws of Dream-fancy", *Cornhill Magazine* 34 (November 1876): 536–555.

——. *Illusions: A Psychological Study.* 2nd Edn. London: Kegan Paul, 1882.

——. *Outlines of Psychology with Special Reference to the Theory of Education.* London: Longmans, Green and Co., 1884.

——. *The Human Mind. A Textbook of Psychology.* 2 Vols. New York: D. Appleton, 1892.

——. "The Dream as Revelation", *Fortnightly Review* CCCXIII New Series (March 1893): 354–365.

——. *Studies of Childhood.* 1895. New York: Appleton and Co., 1901.

——. *My Life and Friends. A Psychologist's Memories.* London: T. Fisher Unwin, 1918.

Surette, Leon. *The Birth of Modernism. Ezra Pound, T.S. Eliot, W.B. Yeats, and the Occult.* Montreal: McGill-Queen's University Press, 1993.

Swinnerton, Frank. *The Georgian Literary Scene 1910–1935. A Panorama.* New York: Farrar, Straus and Co., [n.d.].

Sword, Helen. *Ghostwriting Modernism.* Ithaca: Cornell, 2002.

Tansley, A.G. *The New Psychology and Its Relation to Life.* London: Allen and Unwin, 1920.

Taylor, Eugene. "William James and C.G. Jung", *Spring: Annual of Archetypal Psychology and Jungian Thought* (1980): 157–168.

——. "William James on Psycho-Pathology: The 1896 Lowell Lectures on 'Exceptional Mental States' ", *Harvard Library Bulletin* (October 1982): 455–479.

——. *William James on Exceptional Mental States. The 1896 Lowell Lectures.* Amherst: University of Massachusetts Press, 1984.

Thomas, Sue. "Virginia Woolf's Septimus Smith and Contemporary Perceptions of Shell Shock", *English Language Notes* 25, 2 (December 1987): 49–57.

Thurschwell, Pamela. *Literature, Technology and Magical Thinking, 1880–1920.* Cambridge: University Press, 2001.

Tindall, William. *Forces in Modern British Literature.* New York: Vintage, 1956.

Todorov, Tzvetan. *The Fantastic: A Structural Approach to a Literary Genre.* Trans. Richard Howard. Cleveland: Case Western Reserve UP, 1973.

Trilling, Lionel. *Freud and the Crisis of Our Culture.* Boston: The Beacon Press, 1955.

Trotter, Wilfred. *Instincts of the Herd in Peace and War.* London: Fisher Unwin, 1916.

Van Over, Raymond and Oteri, Laura, comps and eds. *William McDougall: Explorer of the Mind. Studies in Psychical Research.* New York: Helix, 1967.

Wallace, Roy. "Science and Pseudo-Science", *Social Science Information* 24 (3): 585–601.

Ward, James. "Psychology", *Encyclopaedia Britannica*. 11th Edn Vol. XXII. Cambridge: Cambridge University Press, 1911.

——. "Herbart", 1902. *Encyclopaedia Britannica*. 14th Edn Vol. XI. London: Encyclopaedia Britannica Co., 1929.

Wehr, Gerhard. *Jung. A Biography*. Trans. David Weeks. Boston: Shambala, 1987.

Weiss, Daniel A. *Oedipus in Nottingham: D.H. Lawrence*. Seattle: University of Washington Press, 1962.

Wells, H.G. *The New Machiavelli*. London: Lane, 1911.

West, Rebecca. *The Return of the Soldier*. London: Nisbet, 1918.

Whelan, P.T. *D.H. Lawrence: Myth and Metaphysic in The Rainbow and Women in Love*. Ann Arbor: U.M.I. Research Press, 1988.

Whyte, Lancelot Law. *The Unconscious Before Freud*. New York: Basic Books, 1960.

Winnicott, D.W. "James Strachey 1887–1967", *International Journal of Psycho-analysis* 50 (1969): 129–131.

Winter, Alison. *Mesmerized: Powers of Mind in Victorian Britain*. Chicago: University of Chicago Press, 1998.

Woodworth, Robert Sessions. *Contemporary Schools of Psychology*. New York: Ronald Press, 1931.

Woodworth, Robert Sessions. *Dynamic Psychology. The Jessup Lectures, 1916–1917*. New York: Columbia University, 1918.

Woolf, Leonard. *Sowing: An Autobiography of the Years 1880–1904*. London: Hogarth Press, 1960.

——. *Downhill All the Way. An Autobiography of the Years 1919–1939*. New York: Harcourt, Brace, and World, 1967.

Woolf, Virginia. *The Common Reader*. New York: Harcourt Brace, 1925.

——. "Modern Fiction", *The Common Reader*. New York: Harcourt, Brace, 1925.

——. *Orlando*. New York: Harcourt, Brace, 1928.

——. *The Waves*. New York: Harcourt, Brace, 1931.

——. "Leslie Stephen. The Philosopher At Home. A Daughter's Memories", *The Times* (London) (Monday, 28 November 1932): 15–16.

——. *Jacob's Room*. 1922. Harmondsworth: Penguin, 1965.

——. "The Leaning Tower", *Collected Essays*. Vol. II. Ed. Leonard Woolf. London: Hogarth Press, 1966.

——. *Between the Acts*. Harmondsworth: Penguin, 1972.

——. *The Voyage Out*. 1915. Harmondsworth: Penguin, 1974.

——. *The Letters of Virginia Woolf*. 6 Vols. Ed. Nigel Nicolson, London: Hogarth Press, 1975–1980.

——. *The Diary of Virginia Woolf*. 5 Vols. Eds. Anne Olivier Bell and Andrew McNeillie. London: Hogarth Press, 1977–1984.

——. *Night and Day*. 1919. London: Granada, 1978.

——. *Mrs. Dalloway*. 1925. London: Granada, 1983.

——. *To the Lighthouse*. 1927. London: Granada, 1983.

——. "Kew Gardens", in *The Complete Shorter Fiction of Virginia Woolf*. Ed. Susan Dick. London: Hogarth, 1985.

——. *The Essays of Virginia Woolf*. Vols. I–III. Ed. Andrew McNeillie. London: Hogarth Press, 1986–1988.

——. "Across the Border", in *The Essays of Virginia Woolf 1912–1918*. Vol. II. Ed. Andrew McNeillie. London: Hogarth, 1987.

——. "Character in Fiction", in *The Essays of Virginia Woolf 1919–1924*. Vol. III. Ed. Andrew McNeillie. London: Hogarth, 1988, 420–438.

———. "Freudian Fiction", in *The Essays of Virginia Woolf 1919–1924*. Vol. III. Ed. Andrew McNeillie. London: Hogarth, 1988, 195–197.

———. "Modern Novels", in *The Essays of Virginia Woolf 1919–1924*. Vol. III. Ed. Andrew McNeillie. London: Hogarth, 1988, 30–37.

———. "Mr. Bennett and Mrs. Brown", in *The Essays of Virginia Woolf 1919–1924*. Vol. III. Ed. Andrew McNeillie. London: Hogarth, 1988, 384–389.

———. "Postscript or Prelude", in *The Essays of Virginia Woolf 1919–1924*. Vol. III. Ed. Andrew McNeillie. London: Hogarth, 1988, 271–273.

———. "Revolution", in *The Essays of Virginia Woolf 1919–1924*. Vol. III. Ed. Andrew McNeillie. London: Hogarth, 1988, 279–281.

Woolley, V.J. "Some Auto-Suggested Visions as Illustrating Dream-Formation", *Proceedings of the Society for Psychical Research* 27 (1914): 390.

Wright, Maurice B. Obituary of Thomas Walker Mitchell 1869–1944. *British Journal of Psychology*. Medical Section XX, Part 3 (1945): 203–206.

Zegger, Hrisey D. *May Sinclair*. Boston: Twayne, 1976.

Zusne, Leonard. *Biographical Dictionary of Psychology*. Westport: Greenwood, 1984.

Zytaruk, George J. and James T. Boulton, eds. *The Letters of D.H. Lawrence*. Vol. II. Cambridge, 1981.

Index